animation, ...esign and creation, and
digital painting ... s well as the next book in *The Lost Boys*
series.

THE
LOST
BOYS

LILIAN CARMINE

EBURY
PRESS

1 3 5 7 9 10 8 6 4 2

Published in the UK in 2013 by Ebury Press, an imprint of Ebury Publishing
A Random House Group Company

The Random House Group Limited Reg. No. 954009

Addresses for companies within the Random House Group can be found at:
www.randomhouse.co.uk

A CIP catalogue record for this book is
available from the British Library

The Random House Group Limited supports The Forest Stewardship
Council® (FSC®), the leading international forest-certification organisation.
Our books carrying the FSC label are printed on FSC®-certified paper.
FSC is the only forest-certification scheme supported by the leading
environmental organisations, including Greenpeace.
Our paper procurement policy can be found at:
www.randomhouse.co.uk/environment

Printed and bound by CPI Group (UK) Ltd, Croydon, CR0 4YY

ISBN 9780091953416

To buy books by your favourite authors and register for offers visit:
www.randomhouse.co.uk

I dedicate this book to Gillian Green, for believing in me and my story.

To my parents, Joao and Nise, for showing how important books are and for giving me all the support I ever needed and letting me be free to pursue my dreams.

To my second mother Selma and my second father Paulo, for always being there for me and for cheering me all the way.

I dedicate it to Eva Lau and everybody at Wattpad, for all their support; to Tamsin Jupp, my darling Dandelion girl, Robyn Williams and Hannah Rose, my first and most beloved Lost Girls.

I dedicate this book to the love of my life, my husband, my Tristan, for the encouragement, for showing me in example to always strive for excellence in whatever you choose to do; for being my unwavering arm in every storm; for being there for me and loving me no matter what, until the end and from the start.

To Tom, Doug, Danny and Harry, for teaching me what real friendship is all about, and to the amazing musicians with their beautiful songs which inspired me throughout each chapter of the book.

But most of all, I dedicate this book to the Lost Boys Army.

This book wouldn't be here if it wasn't for your immense love and support.

Keep on rocking,
Yours always,
Lily.

Chapter One

Flowers for the Dead

I really was lost.

I had been wandering in this old cemetery for about twenty minutes, trying to find my way out, but every time I thought I was getting near the exit I found myself even further in.

The deeper I went, the older everything seemed. The statues were more broken and the tombs were mossier and less cared for. Snow slumped over the graves, but the main path was surprisingly clear. I was seriously tempted to start shouting for help, like a pathetic child that had got lost from its mommy. I could already feel an embarrassed blush creeping up my cheeks at the mere thought.

And to think this whole misadventure had actually started with me and my good intentions.

It began when I suggested to my mother that I could go grocery shopping for her, since she was so busy at our new home, unpacking and getting a head start on her new job. She had been offered this new fancy position, with an astronomical salary and a bunch of amazing benefits, at a branch of a renowned law firm. It had resulted in a rushed move to this small town called Esperanza, just a couple of weeks before Christmas. It was all very sudden but the job offer had been so good that she'd had no choice but to accept.

We'd always struggled with our finances, but now finally we wouldn't have to. Mom was so happy with this surprising turn in her career; and if my mom was happy, I was happy.

Even if it had meant I'd had to quit my school and enroll somewhere new just so I could complete my final year and graduate.

As well as school, I'd had to leave all my friends, but somehow I hadn't been that upset. It had made me realise I wasn't that close to anyone anyway, and I supposed – hoped – that I would make new friends here.

Anyway, I'd left my mom in her new home office, buried under a huge pile of folders, but as soon as I headed out the door I bumped into this crazy-looking old lady with bright purple hair and big thick glasses, asking me to help her carry this humongous vase of flowers that she said she had to take to her husband. Of course, I had to help her. My mother had brought me up to always be respectful of my elders – and she was really old! What harm could it do if I gave her a hand?

I'd regretted my goodwill as soon as she handed me the vase of flowers. It was huge! And so, so heavy. I hadn't even walked half a block before my back was killing me. I also had dirt all over my face and at the top of my sweater.

The old lady, who was called Miss Violet, had kept up a constant stream of chatter all the way to wherever we were going to meet her husband, asking me all kinds of inappropriate questions, like where I was from, whether I had a boyfriend, what my name was…OK, fine, the name question had been appropriate enough, but the rest had been just plain nosy.

I mean, why had she needed to know about my relationship status? So what if I didn't have a boyfriend? That was none of her business! I hadn't been much into dating back in my old town anyway. I've never seen what was so great about it. Boys were so often annoying and bossy, trying to tell me what to do or that I should act more like a girl. I didn't need anyone telling me what to do or how to behave or that I should wear dresses instead of my baggy jeans. I was fine without a boyfriend, thank you very much.

The topic of boys had already put me in a sour mood, and then I had to try to be polite while I endured the conversation that always followed when I told a stranger my name. Miss Violet, for all her purple hair, was no different: she'd frowned at me from behind her big glasses. "Did you just say your name was Joe?" I could easily have bet my mom's swanky new salary on her next sentence. Come rain or shine, a certainty of life was always: "But Joe is a boy's name!"

Every freaking single time!

As usual, I had sighed loudly in response. It's not like I don't know that I'm a girl and Joe is a boy's name, people! You could at least try to be more creative with that clever observation!

Miss Violet, to her credit, had made an attempt to cover up her surprise. "I guess it's all right. Kids nowadays have all kinds of weird things going on: boys with earrings, girls with tattoos. A girl with a boy's name isn't all that bad," the old lady had said after a minute mulling over the weirdness of my name.

And then, finally, we had arrived at our destination, where Miss Violet's husband was apparently waiting for his flowers. I had been so shocked at the sight that I hadn't been able to make any witty comebacks. Because Miss Violet had led me straight into Esperanza's old cemetery, and then to her dead husband's grave, where she'd asked me to put the flowers down beside his gravestone. I'd felt so guilty for complaining about the heavy vase and the dirt that I'd quickly apologized and excused myself, to let the old lady chat with her "husband" in private.

It was one of those cold but crisp December days and I'd decided to go for a stroll around the cemetery. The pale sun had even peeked out from behind gray clouds, and the snow had stopped falling earlier that morning. It felt like winter was giving me a break today, letting me enjoy this little walk in almost pleasant weather, for a change.

At least, it *had* been enjoyable until the point when I'd got lost. And now here I was, aimlessly walking around an old graveyard, trying to find my way back to Miss Violet or, better still, the way out. A gentle breeze brushed over my face and the air suddenly smelled vaguely of carnations, even though I couldn't see any flowers around.

And that's when I saw him.

Chapter Two

Gray Eyes

A boy, just a few feet away. And he was beautiful.

He was sitting on a small mossy tomb and swinging his long legs up and down distractedly, his gaze fixed on some distant point on the horizon. He clearly didn't notice me standing there, watching him.

He looked about my age. And did I mention he was beautiful? He had smooth black hair, the same color as mine, but styled kind of funny – it was way too tidy for my taste. He had the neatest side parting I'd ever seen on a boy. I wondered what product he was using to keep it so slick and glossy.

He was wearing a white shirt tucked tidily into smart black trousers. I would have thought he was dressed for a funeral were it not for the well-worn black leather jacket that gave his more formal clothes a cooler edge. He looked sad, though. Maybe he'd lost someone too, like Miss Violet, and wanted to be alone.

In the end I decided to approach him. At the very least, he could show me the way out. I gathered some courage and closed the distance between us, stopping right by his side, thinking my proximity would cause him to notice me, but I still had to clear my throat to get his attention.

He jumped, startled, looking at me for the first time with wide eyes. Only now could I see his eyes clearly, and they took me completely by surprise. He had extraordinary gray eyes! But not the sort of gray we use to describe a pale tone of blue. His eyes were really, truly gray. As in the-absence-of-all-color gray.

He almost looked like an old photograph. And his monochrome clothes further enhanced the lack of color of his eyes. But his gaze wasn't dull; his eyes hinted at a sharp intelligence. They glinted with the wintry sun, flaring and piercing bright. And I swear to God that, for a split second, I saw them lighting up from the inside. Or perhaps it was just a trick of the light. The whole encounter was so eerie; it caused goosebumps to rise all over my skin.

At that moment, I was lost in his eyes. He seemed so surprised that he wasn't even blinking, his gaze locked upon mine, like he was in a trance of sorts. It took me a while to feel able to produce coherent conversation again.

"Hey. Hi, sorry, I was just…wondering if you could help me find my way back to the main gate? I'm a little lost," I said, still entranced by his gaze.

He blinked a couple of times now, like he was trying to snap himself out of his own stupor, and slowly looked around, as if to check I was really speaking to him. There was no one else around. Of course I was speaking to him!

"W-what?" he stuttered.

I frowned. What a strange boy! Maybe I had been wrong to think his beautiful looks were matched by a sharp mind. He seemed to be having a hard time understanding what I was saying.

"Can. You. Help. Me? Do you know a way out of here? I'm a little lost," I asked again, unable to keep the mocking tone out of my voice. I spoke loudly and slowly, like I was talking to a small child. Or a very stupid person.

It was his turn to frown. "You don't need to talk like that! I'm not an idiot, miss!" he said, offended. "I was just...surprised, is all...that you're talking to me."

Okay. That was definitely odd. And he wasn't making any sense. And he talked funny. Calling me "miss". Clearly Esperanza was more old-fashioned than I'd first feared. That or he was crazy. And there I was, all alone with a crazy boy, in an abandoned old cemetery. Commonsense dictated that I should get the hell out of there, and fast.

"Okay, sorry to bother you. You're obviously..." Mental, I thought. "...busy right now, so I'll just go, then. I'm sure I can find the way out myself, " I muttered, stepping away slowly so as to not startle the clearly deranged boy in front of me.

"No, wait!" he said, jumping off the tomb. He moved very softly and elegantly, I noticed, like an athlete. "I'm so sorry, miss! You must think I'm crazy, or something," he said, smiling the sexiest smile I have ever seen.

And I mean that; it was the most breathtaking, beautiful and honest smile I had ever seen in my whole life! It made my heart skip a beat. My resolve to get the hell away from him faltered and vanished in the brightness of his smile. "Or something," I muttered quietly, and glanced down in nervousness, but he heard me anyway and chuckled.

"That's all right. I assure you I'm not crazy, though. And I can help you find your way out. We're almost in the centre of the cemetery. It's a long walk from here to the front gates. You want the main entrance, I presume?" he asked, walking over to me.

I nodded. He was now standing a few inches from me and I could see his face in detail. He had a thin straight nose that defined his face, a strong, square jaw and, currently, a playful smile at the corners of his full lips. He had broad shoulders and a lean, athletic build. He was taller than me, but that isn't hard since I'm a shortie. He was staring down at me with those odd, piercing gray eyes.

"Who gets *'a little'* lost anyway?" he finally asked after a moment of silence. He looked properly amused now.

"What?" I asked, confused – and in truth, I'd got a little lost again, this time in his eyes.

"You said a while ago that you're *a little lost*," he said. "Either you are lost, or you aren't. Don't you agree?"

"Um…I don't know. I know where I am. I'm in the cemetery. I just don't know where exactly in the cemetery. That could be considered a 'little' lost. Because it's not completely lost," I said, crossing my arms over my chest defiantly, resting my case.

He let out a loud laugh. The breeze had picked up and some leaves twirled around us, and there was that carnation scent again, enveloping me.

"Maybe you do have a point," he conceded, turning to his left. "Come on. I'll show you the way out." He was already walking away.

I ran to keep up with him and those long legs of his. "Hey, you're not, by any chance, a murderer leading me to some secret spot where you kill and bury all your victims, are you?" I asked in a serious tone.

"A murderer?' He looked puzzled.

"You know...a crazy killer who's waiting for innocent lost girls to come ask for directions..."

Now he looked slightly bemused by my vivid description. "I'm not a criminal, miss. Or a murderer. Though if I were a crazy killer, well, I would probably lie to you about it. So you've got yourself in a pickle there," he said, laughing. "However, you're the one looking like you've been burying stuff here. You do know there's dirt all over your face, your clothes...and a bit in your hair, too?"

I dusted myself off, embarrassed as hell. "I-I just had an incident with a gigantic vase of flowers on the way here," I said, blushing beet-red. God! He must think I'm the crazy one now! Damn those stupid flowers! "So...what's your name?" I asked casually, trying to divert the subject from my grubby shabbiness.

He gave me a sideway glance, but continued walking, a little slower now. It took him some time to answer me. Which I thought was strange. *Once again.* He was definitely gaining points in the "odd" department.

"I'm Tristan," he stated and gave me a cautious look.

Tristan. It was a weird, old-fashioned name, which seemed to suit him. I didn't dare say anything, though. Not with my history; with my *curious* name. I would never throw stones at other people's glass roofs when I have a crystal-thin one of my own. "Nice to meet you, Tristan," I replied simply.

He side-glanced me again, a suspicious look in his eyes. "What? No funny jokes? No teasing? No smirking whatsoever?" he asked defensively.

"Why? It's a beautiful name," I said with a serious face. "It's from the Tristan and Isolde legend, right? He was a knight and there was something about a secret affair, or something like that, yes? I don't remember the whole thing right now. But it's a lovely story."

"Yeah. That's right. My mom had a thing for these sappy old romantic books," he mumbled darkly, and then raised an enquiring eyebrow at me.

"What?" I asked defensively. "I pay attention in English, that's all! And it so happens that the Tristan and Isolde tale is fabulous, not sappy at all, and I honestly enjoyed reading it very much. You know it's not pathetic to enjoy reading books!" I finished lamely. I caught him trying to stifle a laugh.

We walked for a while, me silently fuming in self-righteousness, him trying hard not to laugh at my silly fuming. I noticed he was slowing his pace.

"Well, I do think Tristan is a really nice name. Plus, who am I to make jokes? When I have a freaking glass roof," I mumbled, kicking a small pebble on the ground.

"I beg your pardon?" he asked, clearly confused. He really did talk funny, but maybe that was an Esperanza trait.

He stopped a few seconds later when he realized I had stopped walking, and turned to look at me with a half-curious, half-confused face.

"My name is Joe. Joe Gray," I said, and squinted my eyes, daring him to make fun of me.

We stared at each other for a few seconds, straight faces on.

"Joe, huh?" he said, squinting his eyes back at me. "It's a fine name."

"Right," I said.

"Right," he replied.

I eyed him suspiciously for a second and then we both

resumed walking, at an even slower pace. I wondered how much slower we could get.

"So, Joe..." he began. "Does your mom suspect by now that you're not actually a boy?"

"Does yours suspect you're not a real knight from the twelfth century?" I snapped back at him.

He gave another of those sharp laughs of his. My stomach fluttered a little at the sound.

"Ouch. Okay. Now that we've gotten *that* out of our systems, I'm calling a truce," he pleaded, and then he cleared his throat and invoked with a serious voice: "There will be no more name callings, my Lady Gray; that shall be my first commandment, true knight that I am."

"Well, you started it!" I laughed at him.

"Yes, yes. But now we can laugh about it and move on, without the two big elephants in the room to bother us," he said in an appeasing tone. "And also, you look nothing like a boy, so it shouldn't bother you that much."

"My father really wanted a boy, and my mom wasn't too much attached to gender conventions. And she also liked the name, so..." I mumbled, kicking another stone.

"Well, now that I know you, I can't imagine you having any other name, Joe," he said, flashing me his stunning bright smile. "Though I prefer Joey."

The nickname sounded strangely heartwarming coming from his mouth. "Thanks, Tristan," I said, blushing.

We had left the older part of the cemetery by now, and flowers in varying states of decay adorned some of the graves. Even the air seemed fresher and newer. A soft breeze brushed through my hair, making it flow like in the movies. I took a quick glance at Tristan and saw him looking at me with a strange expression on his face. He cleared his throat and looked away quickly, avoiding my searching gaze.

"So, Joey, if I may call you that, are you here visiting a...family member? Should I be offering you my condolences?" he asked uncomfortably.

"What? Oh. No, no! No one died," I answered, and he looked relieved. "I live just at the end of the block, and I was helping this old lady, my new neighbor actually, to bring some flowers to her husband's grave."

"Oh, you mean Miss Violet and Bobby?" he asked.

"Do you know her? She brought these flowers in this freakishly heavy vase. I swear to you, it weighed tons! I think it was made of iron. That's the reason I'm all covered in dirt, by the way," I said, eager to explain my current grubby state to him. "How about you? Are you...visiting?"

He looked around before answering me. "No. Not visiting. I'm here most days. I like to hang around here. It's quiet and nice...and no one bothers me."

"Oh. So you live nearby too?" I asked curiously.

"Yes. I live nearby. But I mostly just walk around in here. Killing time, you know how it is..." And he trailed off.

"You like to spend your time alone in a deserted cemetery?" I repeated incredulously.

He shrugged and looked away. "We're almost at the entrance. If you follow this path straight ahead, you'll end up at the front gates. You can already see it from here," he said, gesturing ahead of him.

"Oh. I see," I said, a little deflated and disappointed. I realized I'd had a romantic notion that he might walk me home. Apparently not. "So, thanks so much, Tristan. It was nice meeting you."

I extended my hand to him. He looked at it in silence, his hands shoved inside his pockets. He showed no intention of taking them out. Well. That was sort of rude, especially for someone as seemingly old-fashioned as him. While I retracted my hand with a puzzled look, he seemed seriously conflicted about something, but then he just shook his head sadly, dismissing whatever he was thinking.

"Yes," he said, finding his voice. "It was nice meeting you too, Joe Gray," he said ceremoniously, and there was this hint of sadness again in his eyes. "Maybe you can come back here tomorrow? I can show you the tourist parts of the cemetery. Did you know there's this sculpture of a famous artist in here? People come to take pictures of it all the time!"

I stared at him. He seemed like a decent guy. He dressed a bit too formal, but he was very good looking. As in the out-of-this-world-unbelievably-hot type of good looking. He wouldn't have problems finding friends. Or girlfriends, for that matter. Well, who I was kidding, he was good look-ing enough to have his own TV show! Or his own rock band, or whatever. Why on earth would he want to hang out with me, of all people, and in an old cemetery, of all places? There was something seriously strange going on with this boy!

I realized I had been staring at him in silence for a few minutes now, but I honestly didn't have a clue what to answer. That's when Miss Violet showed up out of nowhere, almost giving me a heart attack.

"Oh, hello, dear, still here? I thought you were going grocery shopping?" she inquired curiously, and glanced sideways at Tristan.

"Yes, hi, Miss Violet. I got *a little* lost," I said emphasizing the "little", which earned me a smile from Tristan. "Tristan here was helping me, showing me the way out."

She stared at Tristan, who just looked at the ground with his hands behind his back, shuffling his feet uncomfortably.

"Was he, now? How nice of him, such a kind soul," she said, looking intently at him. "I think it's time for you to go, dear," she said to me. "Your mom will be worried. And there's all the shopping to do yet," she added, grabbing my arm and yanking me away from Tristan, then pulling me to the gates with vigor.

I stumbled outside, rather puzzled by the crazy old lady's sudden insistence that I be on my way. I glanced back into the cemetery for a second. Tristan was still standing there, watching me go. I smiled awkwardly and waved him goodbye. He waved back with a soft sad smile and slowly walked away, disappearing from sight behind a big mausoleum.

And I didn't even have the chance to give him my answer.

Chapter Three

Extraordinary!

The next day, I woke up very early, in a very good mood.
I was going to track Tristan down at the cemetery after
lunch. I hoped he would be there, but since we hadn't
agreed plans to meet, I didn't know for sure. However, I had
nothing else to do, so I thought I should give it a try. After
all, the worst that could happen would be having a nice
afternoon walk alone in the cemetery. I had enjoyed walking there yesterday – before I got lost – and the weather
was still crisp and dry.

I wasn't fooling myself, though – mostly I wanted to see
Tristan again. I couldn't forget the sad look he had given
me before I walked away from the cemetery yesterday.
He'd looked so…lonely. What harm could it do to keep
him company today? I had really enjoyed talking to him;
he was clever, witty and charming, even if he was slightly
odd in his manner. The fact that he was drop-dead gorgeous
didn't hurt, either.

I passed the morning unpacking. After a quick lunch
with my mom, I put on my best jeans, my favorite orange
hoodie, my old Converse shoes, and re-styled my pony-tail

really high. I didn't like wearing my hair down much. It was always in a pony-tail and my mom was always complaining about it. She wanted me to let it hang loose since I had *"such beautiful hair"*.

But I was always on the side of comfort instead of beauty. Comfortable clothes, comfortable hairdo, comfortable shoes. Make-up was always a challenge for me, too. I've tried a few times, but I thought I always ended up looking like a hooker. You need to have skills to apply make-up, and I most certainly didn't have any. So I decided to stick with just my favorite tangerine lip-gloss today. After all, it wasn't like I was trying to impress a guy I'd just met yesterday. A pony-tail and lip-gloss were more than fine. I yelled to my mom to let her know I was going for a walk, grabbed a warm coat and left the house.

I got to the cemetery in less than ten minutes, much faster than the day before. I didn't have the gigantic vase of flowers to slow me down this time! I entered the front gates with light steps and walked around for a while. I didn't remember exactly where I'd met Tristan, since I had been lost at the time. I just remembered it was in the old part of the cemetery, somewhere at the centre.

I walked for about twenty minutes without finding a living soul. It was just me and the dead. After a while I started to recognize a few of the more elaborate decayed tombs and a beheaded angel with one broken wing that I'd seen right before I'd found Tristan sitting on a tomb. That tomb right over there! Hey! I had found it! I looked around for him, but there wasn't anyone in sight. What was I expecting? That he'd be here all day long waiting for me? Stupid, Joe.

I walked over to his tomb (it was *his* tomb now for me),

cleaned off the small mound of snow at the top and grasped the mossy edges, putting my feet on a crevice for support, and pulled myself up. I sat there surveying my surroundings. It was a nice view but the sun wasn't as warm as yesterday, and a chilly December breeze was biting sharply into my skin. I closed my eyes and inhaled the crisp fresh air happily. It was so peaceful up here. I was beginning to understand why Tristan liked it so much. Perhaps it wasn't so odd after all. I could stay here the whole day, just chilling.

"You know, you're in my spot there, Miss Gray," a voice said from down below. I scrambled up with a start at the sudden noise, almost falling in my haste.

"Jeez, Louise! You almost gave me a heart attack there!" I said, putting a hand over my chest, trying to slow down my pounding heart.

Tristan was leaning against the tomb, hands in his pockets, smirking. "I'm glad you decided to come. I thought Miss Violet would forbid you to see me," he said with a defiant glint in his eyes.

"Why would she do that?" I asked, stepping down carefully from the tomb.

"I don't think she likes me very much," he muttered darkly.

"Oh. So you're the local bad boy?" I teased. "Does she think you're a trouble-maker?"

He seemed offended. "No, I'm not! I don't know why she doesn't like me. Maybe it's because she doesn't like seeing me around here. But I've every right to be here too!" he said, a bit angrily. "She has no business telling me where I should be!"

"Calm down! I didn't mean to upset you," I said, approaching him cautiously.

He eyed me suspiciously and took a small step back, obviously uncomfortable with my sudden proximity. What was that about? He seemed almost...afraid. I stopped and watched him closely. He was wearing what appeared to be the same clothes he'd worn yesterday. Black trousers, white shirt and the same leather jacket. He must be freezing, I thought, as I took in his neat, slicked-back hair. So formal; so serious.

"Miss Violet didn't say anything to me. And even if she did, she's not the boss of me! I can do whatever I want," I said defiantly. "Well, everything that my mom lets me, that is." I shrugged and smiled weakly at him. He laughed at my lame rebel speech and seemed to relax a little. "So, what about that tour you promised, to see that famous sculpture?"

He beamed at me and made a fancy gesture with his hands, bowing slightly. "Follow me, milady."

We walked and talked all around the cemetery, back and forth through the shadowy lanes. He asked me a million questions, about my life, my old town, my friends, family and hobbies. I talked and talked endlessly and he listened with a contented smile. Sometimes he interrupted me to ask another question, but mostly he just let me ramble on. From time to time, he would point to a sculpture or a grave with someone supposedly famous in it. He always stopped and stayed quiet for a few minutes, like he was admiring the design – or listening intently to something – and then he would give me a lecture about the person buried there. It was so weird and funny at the same time! I tried to ask him questions too, but he kept deflecting the conversation back to me in such a natural way that it was a while before I noticed he was uncomfortable talking about himself.

A couple of times we passed this really old man, who looked like the caretaker of the place. He was clearing the smaller pathways and kept giving me odd glances whenever we passed him. I pointed it out to Tristan the second time we passed him by. "Hey, that old dude keeps giving me some weird looks. What's up with him?" I asked, annoyed. He was looking at me like I was a crazy person or something.

Tristan looked at the man, holding in a laugh. "Old Johnson, you say? He's harmless, don't worry about it, Joey. He probably thinks it's odd for a kid to wander around the cemetery alone, that's all."

"I'm not alone. You're with me," I pointed out.

"Yes, of course," Tristan said quickly, with an amused smirk. "I meant alone as in without adult supervision," he corrected himself.

"Oh, okay," I mumbled, feeling embarrassed now. The old man was probably thinking we were a couple of Goth kids, drinking and getting up to no good. That would explain the strange looks he kept giving us.

We carried on walking and I continued talking for a while, but then I glanced at my cell phone. It was past five o'clock. I was beginning to feel hungry.

"Hey, Tristan, how about we go grab a bite to eat? There's a coffee shop on the corner," I began, but he pulled a face that made me stop.

He stopped walking and shuffled his feet, a troubled expression on his face. "I...I'm sorry, Joe. I can't go," he said sadly.

I waited for him to elaborate and when he didn't I mumbled, "Oh, another time, maybe?"

"It's not that I don't want to but it's...uh, complicated.

But we can hang some more here, if you want to," he said, peeking at me hesitantly through long dark eyelashes.

I watched him, intrigued. His eyes were telling me he was trying to hide something, and that he was sorry about having to hide it. He looked trapped and guilty, but honest at the same time. "Okay. I guess we can hang out here a little more," I finally agreed. "But I'm tired, let's take a break from walking."

I sat on a stone bench nearby, below a tall tree. He sat by my side, a little way away. He really didn't want to get close to me at all, I was beginning to realize. He must have some kind of problem. I had read about this. People with germ phobia, wasn't it? Scared of touching anything, of getting contaminated. He must have freaked out big time yesterday at the sight of me all covered in dirt! That would've traumatized any germophobic for the rest of their life!

"So, Tristan, you haven't said much about yourself. I feel like I've been babbling about myself like a maniac, here!" I exclaimed, stretching my legs.

"There's not much to talk about, really," he said, looking at the view in front of him. "I haven't done anything interesting in ages. My life's pretty boring You have all these amazing things going on in yours."

"Really?" I asked, astonished. I wasn't aware my life was that cool or amazing.

"Yes, really," he said, laughing. "Are you kidding me? You've been lots of places, you play lots of instruments, you can do martial arts, you even worked briefly in a circus, for God's sake!"

"It was just a summer gig!" I said, laughing back at him, astonished at how much he had been paying attention when I'd told him about my life. "And I just helped set up the acts; it wasn't a big deal. My mom and I have this rule, you know: to be open to new things in life, good or bad. She's taught me that we have to always be ready to walk new paths, experience new things. She's always arranging some weird, different stuff for me to do. Now she has this new fancy job that she's really excited about. And here I am. New town. New life," I said, closing my eyes and enjoying the weak sunlight bathing my face. The wind was really sharp and cold now, reminding me that this was indeed the end of the year. I shivered and pulled my coat closer to my body.

"Aren't you cold, Tristan?" I asked, gesturing at his leather jacket.

"I don't feel the cold much," he replied simply. "You know, you are extraordinary," he said in a low voice, and his tone carried a deep longing and something else I couldn't quite discern.

I turned to look at him curiously. His eyes were fixed on me, sparkling silver in the fading sunlight, and filled with so much admiration and awe. I blushed fiercely as he looked away from me; clearly he was embarrassed that I had caught him staring.

"Well, um…it's getting late," I said, flustered. Then my cell phone rang with my mom's ringtone, the theme song from the TV show *Law and Order*, making us both jump. I fumbled in my jeans pocket and took the call. "Hey, Mom," I answered, noticing Tristan staring at me strangely, as if my phone were a two-headed monster. "Yeah, everything is fine. I know, I know, it's getting late. I was just coming home. Yeah, I am! I'm turning the corner of the block right this second. I should be home in, like, ten minutes! Okay? Bye!" I hung up quickly and stood up, patting my clothes awkwardly. "Sorry, Tris. I have to go. Last curfew." I shrugged apologetically and smiled at him.

He looked surprised when he heard me calling him "Tris". It had just come out of my mouth without a second thought. I smiled extra awkwardly then. He stood up and stuffed his hands back in his pockets with an amused expression. I guess he wasn't expecting a nickname from me so soon.

"Yeah. Okay. So . . . I guess I'll see you around, Miss . . . I mean, Joey," he said, nodding, "If you have some free time during the week and want to pass by, I'm usually around here."

"Okay. So, see you around," I replied, and before I could extend my hand for a goodbye shake, he turned fast and walked away. Oh my God! He was so weird! Then I remembered his germ phobia problem. Right. It had slipped my mind. No handshakes with him, Joey!

When I got home, my mom was in the kitchen, making dinner.

"Hey, Mom. This smells really good!" I said, rubbing my tummy. I was really hungry.

"Hey, munchkin, you're back!" she greeted me. "Dinner will be done in a minute. What have you been doing all afternoon?"

"I was just hanging with a friend," I told her casually.

"A new friend already?" she said, beaming happily. "That was fast! Is it a boyfriend, or a girlfriend?"

"It's a boy, but not a boyfriend. Just a boy who happens to be a friend," I corrected her. I knew how my mother's mind worked. I wasn't falling into that trap!

"Hey, who knows what the future holds! He might become more than just a friend, eh?"

Oh, good God! Here we go again. My mom was always trying to hook me up. Most moms tried their best to lock their daughters away from boys, up in high towers with guards and dragons at the front doors, but not my mom. I think she was trying to re-live her dating times through me ... and since I rarely dated at all, she was at a loss. She'd been ecstatic when I'd brought my first – and only – boyfriend over for a dinner, back in our old town. I only recalled that it had been one hell of an embarrassing evening.

"Is he the 'pretty kind' of boy that happens to be just a friend?" she asked teasingly while fumbling with the stove.

I thought about Tristan and his bright gray eyes, his eerily pale face, his big chest, athletic body and broad shoulders. And that smile ... my cheeks instantly turned red all over. Mom observed my reaction from the other side of the counter with amusement.

"That good looking, huh?" She smirked, raising an eyebrow.

I coughed and gave her a glare. "Let's just say he's easy on the eye. But we're *just* friends, Mom. So quit it!" I warned her.

"All right! All right! I give up. If you want to sulk and be alone for the rest of your days, it's your choice. No boy is ever good enough for you!" She scowled.

I grunted under my breath and she shook her head, giving up on the topic.

"So, Joey, I just received a welcome folder from Principal Smith at Sagan Boarding School!" she said, her face lighting up at the thought.

"Sagan?" I asked, at a loss.

"Yes! Your new school! Remember we talked about it as an option? You going to study there the rest of the year? It's a boarding school, actually, but it's not too far away. Only a couple of hours' drive. You'll get to sleep in dorm rooms with friends, just like in Hogwarts in *Harry Potter*!" she exclaimed, all excited now.

I rolled my eyes. "Mom, my Harry Potter phase is so over." *Was not. I still love you, Harry!* "I told you I wanted to study at a boarding school like that two years ago! That was a lifetime ago!"

She chuckled, shaking her head. "A lifetime! Don't be silly. Anyway, now that I have this important new job, thank you very much," she said, bowing, "I managed to get you in! It's the best school in the state, and now I can afford to send you there!"

"But... what about you? You'll be here all alone!" I cried out.

"Oh, I can handle being alone, Joey. I'm a big girl. You know I want the best for you, and this is the best. And it's not like you won't be able to visit every weekend," she remarked cheekily.

In truth, I was really excited by Sagan; the brochure was amazing. Mom and I talked about it over dinner and I went to bed happy. And then I thought about Tristan. Maybe tomorrow I could stop by the cemetery and tell him about my new school. It was exciting news! And I still really wanted to experience life at a boarding school. Although I felt a little sad because I wouldn't be able to see him any more after school started. That kind of sucked.

Before I drifted into sleep that night, I thought about how odd it was being sad at the idea of not seeing someone I'd just met two days ago, someone I barely knew. Tristan had made such a big impact on my life already.

Chapter Four

A Special Gift

The rest of the week passed really fast.

Christmas Eve was right around the corner, on Friday, to be precise. My mother spent most of her time during the week adjusting to her new job and making preparations for our first Christmas in our new home. I went to see Tristan at the cemetery almost every day that week. Some days, when it was snowing, I just stopped by to say a quick hello; some days, when the weather was good, I stayed the whole afternoon, hanging out with him. Our favorite place to hang was a lawn circle in the centre of the cemetery. Somehow we always ended our walks at that spot.

It seemed that Tristan was always in the cemetery, every day, at any hour. And he always had a knack of finding me, no matter where I was. I didn't know how he did it. I asked him about it one day.

"The ghosts around here always tell me if you have arrived and where you are!" he said jokingly, and then he laughed out loud at my slightly scared face. I glanced around worriedly and crossed my arms protectively over my chest. The wind suddenly seemed colder, somehow.

"You shouldn't make jokes about ghosts here, Tristan! It's not funny," I warned him.

He raised a suspicious eyebrow, smirking at me. "What, afraid of ghosts, are we?" he teased.

"No," I mumbled. "Just want to keep a healthy distance, that's all."

He laughed at my polite way of saying I was indeed very much afraid of ghosts. "Well, there's no reason to be afraid of ghosts, sweetheart," he said with another of his amazing smiles I was learning to cherish so much. "And I guarantee you, my lovely Joe, that I'll never let any ghost in here ever harm you! You have my word. So you needn't worry," he said, chuckling at my distressed face.

My nerves were so jittery as a consequence of this conversation that I got up from our lawn without looking where I was going and tripped over a cracked pavement stone. I ended up sprawled across the cold dusty ground. I patted my dirty jeans, embarrassed as hell.

Tristan sped over to me, looking really worried. "Joe, are you all right?"

"I'm fine. A little embarrassed, but fine," I said, slapping the palm of my hands against my pants. Once again, I was all dirty. What a klutz!

I glanced up, waiting for him to offer a hand to help me stand up, like any normal person would. Guilt and remorse crossed his eyes in a heartbeat. It passed in the blink of an eye, to be replaced by a smirking remark. "Come on, Gray! Are you going to stay there all day? Don't be so soft! Let's get going!" he said, walking away without waiting for a reply.

I frowned. It wasn't like I was expecting the damsel in distress treatment here; I knew how to take care of myself without any male assistance, thank you very much. But that was just . . . plain rude! I lay there, annoyed, for a bit before I finally stood up.

He was so bipolar, one day telling me I'm extraordinary, the next acting like this huge jerk! I felt so irritated by the incident that after a while I told him I had an important appointment and needed to go. I think he knew why I was leaving so soon. He knew it had something to do with that tripping incident and how rude he had been to me, because he looked profoundly sad and ashamed as he watched me leave. I was so upset that I didn't care how he looked. He was the one being rude. Not the other way round!

That had happened on Thursday. I mulled it over the rest of the day in my room, and by night I decided I had overreacted. So the next day, Christmas Eve, I went back to the cemetery to apologize for having left in a huff. I felt like I needed to do this, though I also knew I hadn't really done anything wrong.

I walked for half an hour and couldn't find Tristan. It was the first time I'd been there without finding him. The place didn't feel the same without him around. I couldn't help but think he was avoiding me now. After a while, I gave up looking for him and left. I walked back home in a gloomy mood and remained like that the whole day.

Saturday was Christmas Day. I stayed home during the day, helping my mom prepare our meal. We exchanged gifts after dinner, and that was about it for Christmas for the little Gray family party of two. I liked the holidays mostly because of the special meal deal, but my mom and I didn't care much about religious stuff. We could barely call ourselves Catholics. For years now we hadn't even celebrated at all, just stayed together and watched old movies, and that was usually that for the night's celebration.

This year, Mom had put extra effort into dinner, though, because she wanted to make it memorable: our first year in a new town, and I would be going off to school, too. Plus, she was happy about the fancy job and fat bank account (first time in many, many years). She had a lot to celebrate!

All the talk of celebrating made me think of Tristan, and I was really sad we'd ended our last meeting in such a bad way. I was watching my mom heading upstairs to get ready for her bath when I had this crazy idea of a good way to make up with Tristan. I glanced at the clock. It was still early, nine in the evening. I thought I could make it there and back again in twenty minutes. Mom takes these freakishly long baths. Twenty minutes was all I needed!

I ran upstairs to my room and fumbled through some boxes, trying to find the one with the Gray's memorabilia. And there it was! My box of old photograph albums. I grabbed the oldest one – it held my favorite photos – and flipped fast through the pages. I knew exactly what I was looking for. I found it, took it out of the album and ran back downstairs. In the living room I carefully wrote a note on the back of the photograph. Then I heard the bathroom door closing upstairs. Okay, time to run! I put on my sweater and sneaked out of the house as soon as I heard the bath water running.

I ran as fast as I could and in five minutes I was at the cemetery gates. Strangely, it stayed open until eleven, so I had plenty of time. I ran inside, counting my steps and retracing the path I had memorized during the week. I tried not to think about how creepy the cemetery looked at night, concentrating only on finding the path to Tristan's mossy tomb. He liked hanging out there, so he was bound to find my gift sooner or later.

I reached it in two minutes. I looked at the photograph in my hands. It was the photo taken of me while I was working at the circus, back in my old town three years ago. I was fourteen then, and was surrounded by a group of clowns, ballerinas and other circus people, holding my red balloons and beaming at the camera. I turned the photo over to check my note. On the back, in neat letters, I had written:

Tristan,
Remember,
Life is always full of possibilities.
Merry Xmas.
Joey.

I smiled, satisfied, and put the photo on top of the tomb, with a stone over it so the wind wouldn't take it away. And then I ran as fast as I could out of there! In another five minutes I was back home, a little breathless but safe and sound. And most importantly, not caught. My mom was still having her bath, unaware of my little nocturnal escapade.

I slouched on the couch, turned the TV on and flipped through the channels, happy with my late-night mischief. I hoped Tristan would like my gift. I fell asleep on the couch and dreamed about contortionists, ballerinas and clowns. And red balloons floating up to the sky.

Chapter Five

Promise

I passed Sunday finally unpacking the rest of my things. My mom had given me a deadline. It was to be done on Sunday, "Or else..." followed by The Look. You don't want to mess with The Look, I tell you. So I didn't dare go out and check on Tristan.

Monday I woke up in a cheerful mood. As I munched my breakfast, Mom bounced into the kitchen with good news: I had been officially accepted at Sagan Boarding School! I still had a week to spend with my mom until after New Year's, and then I would need to start packing (again).

I hoped the kids wouldn't be too snobby. I hated spoiled, rude, rich people! Mom was very excited, reminding me about all the activities they had there. I wasn't listening, though; my mind kept wandering back to Tristan's face. So I left for a morning "walk". My mom was happy that I was out of the house so much, having healthy walks and exercising. She wouldn't be so happy, though, if she knew where I was doing all the exercise.

I watched as the cemetery gates loomed before me, and

once again I darted inside as I'd been doing most days, taking the path to Tristan's mossy tomb. I didn't need to wait for him. He was already there, sitting at the top and swinging his long legs up and down as before. Before I could greet him, he turned his handsome face in my direction and smiled his amazing bright smile to me. It made my heart flutter.

"Hey, Gray!" he shouted at me.

"Hey, Tris! So, did you find my Christmas gift?" I asked in a rush, all excited. I was dying to hear what he thought of it. He jumped off the tomb with his usual ease.

"Yes, I did! Yesterday," he said happily. And then his face turned sad. "I feel really bad because I don't have any-thing to give you..."

I waved my hands at him. "That's okay, I don't mind. I just thought you'd like seeing that photo. It was kind of a lame present anyways," I mumbled, embarrassed.

He walked closer, his piercing silver gaze on me. I had missed his eyes. "It wasn't 'lame', whatever that means. It was the best present ever. Thank you, Joey," he said, smiling kindly. "It was very sweet of you to think of me."

"You're w-welcome," I stuttered, blushing.

"Come sit with me," he said, walking towards a stone bench a few meters away. "When did you come by to bring the photo? I didn't see you yesterday, or Saturday..."

"I came by Saturday night. It was Christmas Day so I had to come later, a little before closing time," I replied.

"You came at night? Weren't you afraid?" he asked, astonished.

I stared at him in confusion. Afraid of what? Dropping a picture by?

"Afraid of coming to a cemetery, alone, in the middle of

the night!" he said, completing his sentence as he saw my confused expression.

"Ah. Right," I mumbled. Then I remembered the ghosts. Well, now that I was thinking about it, I probably should have been afraid…"I don't know. I just wasn't. Or not much. I don't get scared easily. I guess I act a lot like a boy sometimes. It's the curse of *'The Name'*," I said, miming air quotes and making him laugh. We sat on the bench and I turned to look at him. "I came by Friday to talk to you, too. I didn't see you around."

He frowned, as if trying to remember what he'd been doing on Friday, and then a memory seemed to jolt him. "Ah, yeah, an old friend came to see me on Friday. I lost track of time talking to him. He has the most amazing stories…Sometimes I think he's half-mad. The things he says…" Tristan mused, chuckling. But then he turned thoughtful for a moment. "I wish some of the things really were true, though."

"Which things?" I asked curiously.

Tristan shook his head, dismissing the topic. "Nothing, really. A bunch of nonsense about magic and old spells; the crazy ramblings of an old man. But never mind him. He was probably making most of that stuff up, anyway. I'm glad we didn't miss each other today!" he said, happy now.

"Do you really come here every day, Tris?" I asked.

"Yes. I'm here every day," he answered plainly.

"I know why. I've thought about it these past few days and figured it out," I said, crossing my arms over my chest.

He looked startled and I watched as fear and apprehension shifted in his eyes.

"You work here!" I said. "You must work at the funeral home in the back of the graveyard! That explains why you have to be here all the time, and the somber clothes, and all." I stated my discovery proudly.

It actually explained a lot. It also explained his "touching" phobia: seeing dead people all the time must freak out any living person. I wouldn't want to go near anyone after seeing cadavers all day long! Just thinking about it made me shiver.

I glanced over at him. He looked relieved, and then embarrassed.

"I'm sorry, Joey. I-I thought you would freak out if you knew the truth. You must think I'm a total loser, having this weird job, and all," he muttered, avoiding looking at me.

"That's silly. I just wish you had told me. I don't care, it's just a job," I said sincerely.

The weather was really bad. The wind blew by us, making me shiver. I zipped up my heavy coat and hunched my shoulders.

"Joe, I need to ask you something," he said uncertainly.

"Ask away," I said.

"Do you ... do you really think that? What you wrote on the back of your photo? Do you honestly believe in that?"

I paused and thought about what I'd written. *Remember. Life is full of possibilities.* I smiled. "Yeah, of course, Tris. Don't you?"

"I'm starting to," he said quietly. But when he glanced at me, he looked trapped, as if stuck within a life without any possibilities at all.

"Come on, your life can't be *that* bad!" I said, trying to cheer him up.

He blinked at me, startled, and averted his eyes, clearing his throat uneasily. "So, are you excited about going to your new school?" he asked, changing the subject drastically. I guess he didn't want to talk about himself any more.

"Yeah. I just got the formal admittance letter. I've never been to a boarding school before. I think it's going to be fun," I said, trying to sound cheerful, but the thought of leaving actually wasn't so bright right now.

"When are you leaving?"

"A couple of days after New Year."

He seemed sad for an instant, but then he brightened up. "Really? So you'll still be here at New Year's?"

"Yes. I'll be here. Why?"

"Can you promise me something? There's this party that goes on around here at the cemetery on New Year's Eve. It's the only night the gates are open all night long! It's an old town tradition... and everybody comes to celebrate here and watch the fireworks. It's really fun! Do you think you can come? To see in the New Year with me? Before you leave?" he asked in a hopeful tone.

I watched him silently, trying to think of a good way to explain to my mother that I was going to be at a cemetery on New Year's Eve. Alone. With a boy. A very, very handsome, charming, utterly strange, mysterious boy. Did I mention handsome already? Yeah. Very handsome. There's no way in hell she'd let me come. Nope. No way. Mom had no objections to me dating boys in public places, or having dinner at home, but she'd have a big objection to me being completely alone with one, especially at a cemetery.

Tristan took my silence as rejection. "It's all right if you don't want to," he said quietly. He looked so crestfallen and sad.

"No, it's not that! I was just thinking that I'll have to come up with a good excuse so my mom will let me, but I'll come!" I said, cursing myself mentally. What was I doing? There's no way I could keep this promise.

"Really? You'll come?" he asked excitedly.

"Yeah. It should be fun!" *Crap. Crap. Crap.* Stop making promises you know you can't keep, Joey!

"Swell!" he cheered.

"What?"

"What, what?" he asked, confused.

"What did you just say?"

"I said, it'll be great! So you're really coming?"

"Yes, I'm coming," I said, smiling. I didn't have the heart to tell him that my mom would never let me. I never had anyone wanting me to be somewhere as badly as he did...

Wait! Was this like...a date? Was he asking me out on a date? Or was it just a goodbye-old-year party type of thing? A big send-off before I left for school? I was still pondering that when he turned around, like he'd just remembered something really important.

"So...I have to go now, Joey. But I'll see you around, right? We have all week until Friday night! I'll talk to you later, okay?" he said, standing up really fast and running away, waving me goodbye. "And thanks again for your amazing gift! I loved it!" he yelled from far away.

I felt warm inside my chest, despite the cold wind brushing past me. How could I say no to him? He was the most amazing boy I had ever met! New Year's Eve with him would be incredible. Maybe I could get a hug from him at midnight! Or even a quick kiss? It was a New Year's tradition after all, right?

I sighed heavily and felt really sad about going away to boarding school. That would mean leaving Tristan behind. Well, I could always visit him at weekends, when I came to see my mom. That was a plan of sorts. I walked back home with mixed feelings of excitement, sadness and worry. I needed to find a way to trick my mom into letting me go out on New Year's Eve. But what would I tell her?

The week went by like a hurricane. There was just so much to do, and so little time!

I had to go shopping with my mom, to buy new clothes for my new school. I got mostly sports clothes, baggy jeans, big sweats and Converse shoes, to my mother's utmost chagrin. I like being comfortable!

And after that came the best surprise news ever. I was having breakfast in the kitchen when my mom walked in asking me what I was doing tonight for New Year's Eve. Luckily, she had her back to me, or she would have seen me almost choking on my cereal. Before I could come up with a lie, she told me her office was throwing a big party, and asked me if I wanted to come.

I, of course, told her that I wasn't in the mood for office parties (just cemetery ones), but that she should definitely go (please, please, just go!), that I would be at home, chilling out (not!). I even told her she didn't need to call me at midnight because I'd probably be sleeping. She knew that I wasn't a big fan of New Year parties, never had been. Some years I'd spent the whole evening sleeping through it all. So she didn't think much of it. I, on the other hand, could NOT believe my luck! It was destiny giving me a thumbs-up to my New Year's cemetery celebration! I didn't even need to come up with a lie; Mom handed all of it to me on a silver platter!

Then I realized I hadn't been at the cemetery all week, because my mother always got me to do something as soon as she laid eyes on me. So I made up some lame excuse and darted out of the house before she could stop me, heading straight for the graveyard.

I was ambling through the cemetery, wondering if I would find Tristan today, when I noticed the place didn't look all that deserted any more. Pretty little lanterns were placed all over the place, hanging on the black naked branches of the trees; white flowers were placed on big vases at crossroad lanes, candle-holders were spread all around. The place looked dressed up, ready for a party. Tristan hadn't been lying about the big celebration happening here.

"Hey, stranger." Tristan's voice came from behind me. I merely flinched this time. Usually I just jumped out of my skin in fright, but now I was getting used to his silent surprise appearances.

I turned to look at him. He was still wearing his usual black and white uniform, and had a stern expression. "Hey, Tris! The place looks fantastic!" I cheered.

He gave me a small smile, which swiftly disappeared and his serious face returned. What was up with him today? "Yeah, it is a big town tradition, I told you. Things here have been crazy all week," he said.

"So, is everything set for tonight?"

"Huh... You mean you're really coming, then?" he asked, his mood lightening up.

"Of course! I told you I'd come!"

"You've been gone all week and... I thought you were here today to say you wouldn't be coming," he said, explaining his somber mood.

He was so cute! That was his way of pouting at me! I laughed out loud. "No, I'm definitely coming!"

"Your mom is okay with you being here?"

"She's fine," I lied. "She has her own party to go to.

She's been asking about you, though. When do you have time off of work? You could come by and have lunch or something…It wouldn't take long, my home is right at the end of the block!"

He squinted his eyes at me, suspiciously. "She's been asking about me?"

"Yeah, because I'm always talking about you and…"

"You're always talking about me?" he interrupted, giving me a playful, cocky smile.

"Hmm, you know, I'm always remembering something you said, or something we talked about," I said, rolling my eyes at him.

"Can't stop thinking about me, huh?" he teased, leaning sexily against an angel statue.

"You know what? If you're going to be impossible like this, I don't think I'll be in the mood for a party tonight!" I grunted, annoyed.

"No! No! I'm sorry!" he said, raising his arms apologetically and giving me his best bright smile. "I'll be good, I promise! I was just joking! You're still coming, right?"

I put my hands on my hips and cocked an eyebrow, doing my *let me think about it* straight face. He put his hands behind his back and rocked on his heels, giving me the best puppy dog eyes I had ever seen! They glinted and sparkled in the winter's light.

I couldn't hold it any longer, and burst out laughing loudly. "Okay! Stop with the pouting! I'll come!"

He beamed at me. "All right! We can meet at our spot on the lawn circle later, okay?"

"Okay," I said happily, and ran home all excited about the party.

I spent the rest of the day picking out my outfit. It was

going to be a very special night; I could feel it in my bones! And, oddly, I was suddenly in the mood for something more dressy than sports clothes now.

At long last, later that evening, I looked in the mirror, surveying my reflection. I had on my special-occasions-only black jeans and a silver tank-top under a fancy black coat that I had borrowed from my mother's closet. I'd even dared to put on some light silver eyeshadow. I'd decided lipstick was a little too much, though.

I thought I looked good. Didn't I? High self-esteem wasn't my strongest point. At the last minute, I decided to wipe off the eyeshadow. But I left my hair loose, for a change. Okay, that was better.

My mom had left hours ago and I was still at home, staring at myself in the mirror. I glanced at my clock and realized it was eleven already! I was so late! Tristan would be freaking out, thinking I'd stood him up. I ran downstairs fast, opened the front door, when someone called my name.

"Joey? Where are you going?"

Holy crap. It was my mom.

Chapter Six

New Year

"Hum…Hey, Mom! What are you doing here?" I asked, trying to disguise the panic in my voice. Oh no! This *cannot* be happening! What was I going to do now?

"I left the party early. I wanted to spend New Year's Eve with you. Where are you going all dressed up like that? Didn't you say you're staying home all night?" she asked suspiciously.

'I…well, funny you should ask…I was…" I mumbled, stalling for time. What was I supposed to say here? I was just leaving for this awesome party to be with this amazing guy, hoping with all my heart that he would kiss me tonight and, by the way, did I mention the party is at the local cemetery?

My mom was giving me *The Look*, waiting for me to answer.

"Is this something to do with this boy you're hanging out with all the time now?" she asked.

"His name is Tristan, Mom. I already told you that! And it was a last-minute thing. It's a party close by. I was going to call you, but it's almost midnight and…" I trailed off. "Please, Mom! Can I go now?"

"Okay, where's this party? I'll walk you there. Don't worry, I'm not going inside. I won't embarrass you in front of your friends!" she said after seeing the look of terror cross my face. "I just need to see where you'll be. In case something happens."

"Nothing's going to happen, Mom!" I whined.

"I know. It's just for precaution, honey. Come on," she said.

Oh. Crap. Now I was doomed, all right.

"Okay. Let's go, then," I said, speed-walking to the cemetery. It was really late. If Tristan was waiting for me at the front gates, maybe she'd let me go in. No one could resist his winning smile!

In eight short minutes we were at the cemetery. Lots of people were coming and going, chitchatting happily with drinks in their hands. The gates were fully open, candles decorating the iron sign above and yellow lanterns casting a warm light over the entrance. I couldn't see Tristan.

My mom stopped at my side, glancing at all the people mingling around us.

"Look at all these people! What's happening, here? Joey, is your party happening at the cemetery?" she asked in surprise.

"Well, yeah. It's no big deal, Mom," I said, knowing damn well that it was a huge deal. "It's a tradition in Esperanza. Isn't that cool? Everybody comes here to celebrate New Year's Eve!"

"And you didn't tell me because you knew I would never let you come alone to a party in a cemetery, Joe Gray!" she said, affronted, calling my bluff. Gosh. Maternal insights suck!

"Okay! Okay! But we're here now, and you can see

it's not dangerous *at all,* and it will suck very much if you won't let me go!" I pleaded. "Please, Mom!"

I could sense her resolve was faltering.

"And I promised Tristan I'd come. Are you really going to make me break my promise, Mom? It's almost midnight already!" I said, delivering the final blow. She was the one persistently trying to hook me up with a date. Now I officially had one.

And she was RUINING it!

She bit her lip, sighed and then threw her arms in the air in defeat.

"All right! But I need to meet this Tristan boy before I leave. No, Joe, I will not let you go there alone without having a word with this boy first! And that's final. After that, I'll leave and you two can... stay a little while longer. Just a little while, mind you!" she commanded.

I rolled my eyes, knowing damn well there was no use trying to argue with her now, and walked quickly to the spot where I'd agreed to meet Tristan.

The whole place was packed with people! What a strange little town, with strange traditions and strange people who went to a cemetery to celebrate New Year... It seemed, though, that most people were mingling by the main gates; the deeper we got into the old parts of the cemetery, the fewer townsfolk we met.

"Joey, where are you going? I don't think we're supposed to come this far," my mom whispered.

"It's all right, he's right over there," I said, and turned the corner.

And then I came to an abrupt halt. Sitting on a little folded wooden chair, at the edge of the circled lawn, was old Miss Violet. She had a little candle on the floor right next to her chair, and appeared to be staring at the centre of the lawn. When my mom stopped at my side, Miss Violet noticed us arriving and turned to face us. "Ah. Hello, dears. I was thinking we were going to pass midnight without anyone in here with us tonight... Silly me."

We? Was she talking about Tristan? Where was he?

Another voice came from the other side of the circle. An old lady's voice. "I don't like to boast, Violet, but I did tell you. It's going to happen tonight. Meg has seen it," the owner of the other voice bragged.

"Oh, shush, Margaret." Violet scowled. I squinted my eyes, trying to see better in the dark. On the other side there was a stern-looking old lady – Margaret, of course – sitting in another folded chair. Like Miss Violet, she had a candle by her feet. She was watching us with a hard stare. This was definitely getting weirder and weirder by the second!

"Okay, what's going on here?" my mom cut in.

As my eyes adjusted to the dark, I noticed a third old lady on the opposite side of the lawn. Exactly the same folded chair and candle. Even in the gloom, she seemed awfully old and pale and fragile. She sat in her chair in silence, watching us. She shouldn't be out in this cold, at this hour of the night, I thought to myself.

"So, when are you intending to show yourself, young man?" Miss Violet asked the shadows.

I peeked at the dark bushes in front of her, just in time to see Tristan emerge and walk to the edge of the lawn. He looked a little scared and avoided looking directly at me. What the hell was going on here?

"So, what did you intend to do this night, boy?" Margaret asked gravely.

Tristan didn't answer. He just lowered his head and stared at the ground.

"And when are you planning to tell the girl?" Miss Violet asked him.

Tristan lifted his head and there was a defiant look in his eyes.

"Tonight! I was going to tell her tonight," he snapped.

"Joey, who..." my mom began, but I cut her off.

"Tell me what? " I asked, looking directly at Tristan. I needed to find out what the hell was going on!

"I'm so sorry, Joey. I wanted to tell you the truth, I swear! I just...I thought you wouldn't believe me, and you'd leave. For good. I'm sorry," Tristan pleaded, taking a step forward inside the circle, in my direction.

"Tell me what? What truth, Tris?" I asked, scared. He looked so lost.

"Joe, who are you all talking to?" my mom snapped.

"I'm talking to Tristan, Mom!" I told her.

She looked around with a confused expression. Was she blind? He was right there, in front of us!

"Where is he?" she asked, sounding puzzled.

"What are you talking about, he's right over there!" I said impatiently.

"There's no one there, honey," my mom whispered, looking at me worriedly. "Just us and these ladies."

"Of course there is. He's right over there!" I said, pointing him out.

"She can't see him, dear. Or hear him," Miss Violet intervened.

"What?" I snapped.

"Only we – the occult-acquainted – can. Me, Margaret and Meg over there. And you, apparently," she stated.

"The what? Occult what?" I said. I was at a loss.

"Well, yes, you know, those familiar with the super-natural," she said, trying one more time.

I just stared at her. She was clearly a little crazy.

"She's saying only we witches can see him," Margaret elaborated. "Your boy over there, he's a ghost, dear."

"What? He certainly is not!" I shouted. Everybody could see him and talk to him, for God's sake! I walked towards Tristan, upset by all the nonsense going on. "Mom, come on, stop joking around, you can see him, right?"

I stopped right in front of him and turned to look at my mother. "Mom?"

She looked at me in alarm.

"Oh my God! What is wrong with you people?" I yelled, and turned to Tristan.

He looked back at me and his eyes were filled with desperation.

"Joey, please don't hate me. I'm so sorry..." he whispered softly to me. "I was going to tell you tonight. I lied so you wouldn't be scared of me. And...I was just happy...being with you. Even if it was only for a little while."

Fireworks started to explode in the sky. Hundreds of colorful fireworks dancing in the night.

The New Year had arrived.

"Are you freaking serious?" I screamed over the noise. I pushed angrily at his chest. My hand passed right through him! I stumbled forward and regained my balance, staring wildly at him.

He reached out for me, and, scared, I flinched away, staggering backwards. My foot got caught up in a tree root and I tripped, falling head first to the ground. I felt an intense, sharp pain in my head and in the palm of my hands. I heard my mom's voice, but I couldn't understand what she was saying. It was too distant, hundreds of miles away.

I opened my eyes and tried to focus. A chill wind was blowing and the candlelight flickered but didn't go out. I could make out a dark silhouette standing far away. It wore black heavy boots. I felt the earth beneath my fingertips. And somehow I didn't feel cold any more. Or scared.

Everything seemed to move in slow motion, like we were all submerged under water. No more loud noises, even though I could still see the fireworks dancing in the sky. Everything was silent and peaceful. It was so beautiful. Was it still midnight?

And then Tristan's face appeared next to mine. He was lying right by my side, smiling at me.

"Don't be afraid. You'll be fine," he whispered to me, wiping away tears that I didn't even know had begun to fall. He looked so calm and ethereal.

"I'm not afraid," I said softly. I felt calm and secure now, because he was with me. He reached out and held my hand lightly and I felt sharp pinpricks over my skin where his fingers touched mine. It felt weird, but in a good way.

"Do you hate me? For lying?" he whispered in a broken voice, so full of sadness.

"Of course not. I could never hate you, not in a thousand lifetimes," I said to him, and though this was a really weird thing for me to say, I also knew it to be true. But then he slowly vanished from sight, engulfed by darkness that seemed to be wrapping itself around everything.

Everything was dark. Everything was silent.

Was he really gone?

Dead and gone, something whispered ominously inside my head.

"Tristan?" I whispered. It was all so quiet, I couldn't hear his voice any more and I missed it. I missed the warmth it brought to my heart; I missed his silvery eyes and his mesmerizing smiles. I missed *him. "Tristan?"* My voice wavered in the dark.

"Don't be afraid," he whispered near me, his lips brushing my ears like feathers in the air. "Even if you cannot see me, I'm always be right here, by your side." Once again, his fingers intertwined with mine. My heart fluttered at his delicate touch. "I feel like I have always been by your side, and that I will always be. Does that make any sense?" he asked me, and his hand squeezed mine lightly. But I did know what he meant. Because I felt the same way. Like I'd known him for as long as I could remember, beyond time, even. "Wow. Joey. Can you see this?" he asked in awe.

"See what?" I asked, my voice still wavering a little. Everything was pitch black.

"You've...so much light coming from you, blindingly bright, covering me...so beautiful." He let go of my hand then and my heart whimpered at the loneliness and cold his absence brought to me.

"I-I can't see anything. I can't feel anything." I sensed him moving closer.

"Can you feel this?" he whispered, just a breath away from me now. Something brushed lightly against my lips, so soft I thought I was imagining it. Pinpricks of electricity spread through my whole body, making my heart beat furiously in overdrive, and then something jolted, like the earth itself was running back in time.

If I'd been drowning, I had now surfaced. Bright colorful

lights burst through my eyelids like fireworks lighting up from inside. The sound of their explosions filled my ears, deafening me. I felt so dizzy, like I could faint at any second. I heard my mom speaking, along with other voices, all talking at once. Time crashed in on me, running by rapidly, claiming back its lost moments in a fury. The wind rushed back on cue, thrashing and slashing, ice cold, cutting through everything in its path, freezing my bones and my soul. Pain pierced my head, stabbing hot needles in my hands. I grunted loudly.

"Joey? Honey? Are you all right?" I heard my mom's concerned voice and I felt her shaking me gently.

" S-stop, Mom!" I said, sitting up on the grass and holding my throbbing head. I breathed slowly, trying to control my beating heart. I looked at my hands and there were scratches on my palms from when I'd fallen.

My mom continued patting me, a relieved expression on her face now that she saw I was okay. "What's happening?" I asked, a little disoriented. I watched as the three old ladies hunched over someone on the middle of the lawn.

"You fell down and hit your head a second ago," my mom said, kneeling by my side, "and the next second this boy appeared right there on the lawn! He just popped up out of thin air, Joey! One second there was nothing there, the next there was a naked boy lying on the grass!" she whispered, completely freaked out.

I scrabbled to my feet, standing up too fast and feeling a little nauseous as I walked over to the three old ladies. As I got closer, I could see Miss Violet's hands resting on a boy's black smooth hair. He was turned away from me, so I couldn't see his face, but he was lying on the

ground, shaking spasmodically. He was totally naked. A
numb fear started to rise in my chest. I knew that smooth,
black hair.

It was Tristan.

Chapter Seven

Closeness

My mom took charge straight away, taking off her long black coat and handing it to Miss Violet. "Here, please, cover him up, it's freezing cold!" I couldn't see his face very well from where I stood but I could see that he was trembling. But how could he be here? He'd said he was a ghost and now...? Nothing made any sense!

I tried to steady myself and gather control over my churning thoughts. Now was not the time to panic.

The three old ladies were whispering intently to each other. "We need to get him out of the cold first," Miss Violet said at last.

"What *we* need is to take Megan back home! You know she's not well and this has taken it out of her," Margaret hissed.

"But we can't just leave him. Not now," Miss Violet replied.

"Bring the girl over. She can help him!" Megan said, speaking for the first time. Her voice was melodic and very low.

All three old ladies turned to look at me. I took a step back, scared.

"Joey, come over here! Don't be scared, dear. It's all right, everything will be all right!" Miss Violet said reassuringly.

I looked at my mom, and she nodded in consent. I walked over to Tristan and kneeled down on the grass, watching as his beautiful pale face contorted in pain. "What can I do?" I said in a small voice, feeling useless. I reached out and took hold of his hand, like he had held mine. Or had that just been a dream? Either way, this time my hand met solid flesh rather than going straight through.

When my hand touched his, sharp, hot pinpricks jolted through my fingertips once again. Tristan moaned but he appeared to relax, his convulsions easing. I looked at Miss Violet in surprise but she just nodded, looking relieved. What had just happened here?

"Can you take him to your house?" Miss Violet asked my mom. "Until we sort this whole mess out."

My mom nodded. "O-okay. Joey, dear, do you think you can manage to get him to walk?"

"I don't know. I can try," I muttered.

"Just keep him close to you, and you two should be fine!" Miss Violet advised as she turned away to help the eldest of the ladies, old Meg. She and Margaret were now supporting her, one on each side.

"What's *that* supposed to mean?" I asked as they started to walk away.

"Come on, honey. Let's get him home," my mom said, kneeling by my side.

I put the palm of my hand flat on Tristan's chest. My palm tingled at the contact with his skin.

"Tris, can you hear me? Do you think you can stand up? For me?" I pleaded.

He nodded, managing to half-open his heavy eyelids. My mom and I helped him up and wrapped the coat tightly around his body. I hoped no one would notice we had a naked boy inside it while we walked out of there. We managed to stumble through the cemetery lanes, Tristan leaning on both my Mom and me. As we reached the gates, people were still coming and going, but no one paid any attention to us. They were all too drunk or too distracted to notice anything anyway.

We left the cemetery as anonymously as we had entered.

A few minutes after everyone had left, a dark figure appeared on the grass circle.

He wore a heavy, dull, faded gray cloak, and it covered almost all of his pale face. He was tall, very thin and moved swiftly, his cloak billowing in the slashing wind. But he did not care about the cold. He did not feel cold. Or heat, or anything for that matter.

Those were mundane sensations, and he was far from being human and far from belonging to this world.

He looked around. He would have been intrigued, and slightly upset, if he were to have any emotion. But emotions, like sensations, were for humans. He only felt duty as his purpose. He sniffed the air. It smelled of magic.

And he was late. By only a few seconds, but late nevertheless.

He would fix it, though. He always fixed things. That was his job, the purpose of his existence: to fix things that were wrong and out of the natural order. He organized and corrected the many, many mistakes that happened all around. And there was always so much to do, so much chaos happening all the time...

He walked silently around the circle of grass. A group of young people appeared, shouting excitedly, carrying bottles in their hands. He did not worry about them; he knew they couldn't see him.

His kind was never witnessed. Never seen. Those were the rules.

The young, drunken party passed by, completely unaware of the cloaked figure standing only a few inches away from them, observing, analyzing. Something caught his attention, something almost invisible, but not to him: a tiny, minuscule, dark speck on the grass.

He kneeled down right next to it and touched it. Dark, wet, human blood.

No wonder the air smelled of ancient, powerful magic. All magic of that kind required an offering of blood.

He sniffed the tiny smear of blood on his fingertip. This was his trail, his lead. He could follow the blood to its source. Trace it to the mistake that he needed to fix. He always found them: the "mistakes". Found them and fixed them. It was only a matter of time.

He disappeared as silently and quickly as he had appeared, without a trace.

We finally got home. It had taken us about fifteen minutes to get there, but it felt much longer.

We half-walked, half-dragged Tristan to the couch and I slouched on to the armchair beside him. I felt like a truck had hit me.

"Well, that was a hell of a New Year's Eve," my mom murmured, sitting by Tristan's side and placing the back of her hand on his forehead to feel his temperature. "Jeez, he's burning up!"

She went to the hallway closet and brought back a towel, some sheets and a warm blanket. She was drying Tristan's face and hair with the towel when I felt a wave of nausea hit me like a brick wall, and my stomach finally gave up. I covered my mouth and ran quickly upstairs to the bathroom. My mom appeared at my side, and held my hair while I threw up.

This scene was repeated three times. The fourth time, my mom was bypassing concern city and heading straight to freaking-out town. I don't know how many times a person could throw up in one evening, but I'll bet I was going for the record! I didn't even have anything left to vomit any more; my stomach just kept contracting with empty spasms. And my head! Good God, my head felt like it was going to explode!

"Okay! That's it. There's something seriously wrong with the both of you. I'm taking you two to the hospital! Go downstairs and wait for me. Now, where did I leave the car keys?" Mom rambled in obvious panic.

I left her there and dragged myself downstairs, stopping at the front door. I felt horrible; I just wanted to curl up in a small ball and die already. I glanced at the living room and remembered I needed to check on Tristan. He was lying unconscious on the couch, eyes closed, his face pale like death. His hair was all drenched in sweat and he was trembling again. I walked towards him, and slowly slipped to the floor in front of the couch.

I leaned my head on the couch seat and extended my arm, resting my hand on Tristan's bare smooth chest. The tingling sensation came back, sharp and strong, and to my upmost surprise, I immediately felt better, like someone had just given me a shot with the most amazing, powerful drug ever!

I sighed in relief. The headache subsided unnaturally quickly and my stomach calmed down. I looked over to Tristan, then realization hit me! My mom was stepping down the stairs in a hurry, car keys dangling in one hand and her purse in the other, when I called out for her.

"Mom! We weren't listening properly!" I said, smiling weakly at her. "I'm fine now, we don't need to go to the hospital. I just need to be close to him! That's what Miss Violet said. Every time I'm far from him, I feel awful, but when I'm close I feel good. And look – Tristan was trembling and sweating a minute ago, but now he looks a lot better!"

"Yes, she did say that if you stayed close to him, you two would be fine," my mom said thoughtfully. "Nothing about tonight obeys any logic, so I might as well believe in that."

"I think I'll just hang here for a while," I said, laying my head on the couch and thinking I would rest my eyes just for a few seconds...

I vaguely remember my mom struggling to lift me up and put me on the couch next to Tristan, and then a blanket covering us up, turning everything soft and warm and safe.

I remember feeling his breath on me, the warmth radiating from his body and the lingering smell of his sweat mixed with his own natural scent. And the tingling sensation all over my body throughout that night...

I woke up and I was lying on the floor, but it felt odd because it was soft and grainy beneath me. When I stood up, I noticed I was actually lying on sand: warm, silvery, light sand. I couldn't see any ocean, only a beautiful desert as far the eye could see. I looked up at a moonless sky, full of infinite glittering stars and, although there wasn't any source of light, I could see everywhere perfectly.

There was a small black dot far away on the sand. Someone was there. I walked slowly in the person's direction, since there wasn't anything else to do in this alien place. As I got closer, I saw that it was in fact a girl, around my age, maybe a year or two younger. She was sitting on the sand, watching me approach. She had long black hair and big, round black eyes too, just like mine, but she was wearing heavy eyeshadow and eyeliner. She also wore lots of necklaces and bracelets, a tight ragged top, pants and boots, all as black as the sky above.

She eyed me curiously and, despite her heavy make-up, her face was almost angelical.

"Hi," I said.

"Hello," she greeted me in return.

"This is a weird dream," I mumbled to myself.

She frowned, like she couldn't disagree more.

"Why are you here, Joe?" the weird goth-looking girl asked.

"I don't know. I'm just . . . here. Isn't that how dreams are supposed to work?" I said with a shrug.

"But you shouldn't be. It's best that you go now," she said.

"Go where?"

"Anywhere but here. He'll find you here," she said, looking around uneasily.

"Who will?" I asked.

I looked to her left, and a blurred gray silhouette was starting to appear.

"Just wake up, Joe," she ordered. "It's for your own good."

I blinked, and when I opened my eyes again, bright sunlight invaded my sight. I blinked a couple more times, trying to adjust to the change of scenery. Dark moonless sky was now a bright sunny day.

I tried to make my brain start working, but my thoughts felt sluggish and murky. I glanced at my surroundings and realized I wasn't in my bed; I was lying on our living-room couch. Parts of the previous night started to drift back. New Year's Eve, cemetery, fireworks, pain...and ghosts. I shifted slightly and then realized a boy's arm was draped heavily around me. Tristan's arm. We had both slept on the couch! I smiled as I remembered hoping for a midnight kiss, and we had actually slept together last night. Literally speaking, that is, but still...

His hands loosely held mine. He had long, thin fingers; pianist hands...Mine looked so small beneath his. It was so intimate, the way he held me in his sleep. I could feel his face snuggled comfortably against the back of my neck, and the warmth of his breath on my skin.

I shifted slowly, trying not to wake him. He sighed heavily, but then he just rolled over and went back to sleep again.

I was free to move, so I turned over to look at him, resting my face on the couch. He slept so peacefully, his dark locks of black hair all messed up, falling over his calm face. His bare chest was uncovered, smooth and well shaped, moving up and down with the slow rhythm of his breathing. He didn't have a single hair on his chest, just a little trail below his belly button, heading ...south.

The soft blanket covered him to the waistline. Then I remembered he was actually kind of naked under there and

I felt my face turning red. I started climbing off the couch, to give him some privacy, when he blinked slowly, awakened by the movement.

I froze, not too sure what to do now. He looked confused for a second, but then he turned his face in my direction and his eyes registered me. And he smiled. His eyes crinkled a little and glinted in the sunlight that bathed the room. I was in awe of his eyes.

"Your eyes are still…really…gray," I muttered to myself.

He looked bemused; I guess it was a strange thing to say.

"Yours are still black as night," he replied softly.

"How are you feeling?" I asked in concern. It had been a rough night.

He raised his right arm, flexing his fingers, looking at his hand like it was the first time he'd been able to do this.

"It hurts all over," he said, wincing, and then grinned widely. "It's great!"

I frowned. "It's great hurting all over?" I asked, bewildered.

"It's better to feel pain but be alive than to feel nothing at all," he said quietly "It sucks being dead."

I thought about that for a minute in silence. "You should have told me. About your…condition," I said with a hint of sadness in my voice. "You didn't trust me."

He looked at me with a guilty expression. "I thought you'd be scared…"

"I don't scare easily. I told you that."

"I know. I'm so sorry, Joey," he said, and reached out towards me, brushing the side of my face gently with his fingers. It tingled lightly, but not like it had last night. Now the sensation was much more faint.

"You're the bravest person I know. And I trust you with my life," he added.

I looked into his eyes, and saw how much he meant it, the sincerity of his words. It made me smile.

"Do you remember what happened at the cemetery, when midnight struck? What you said to me?" he asked.

I paused, trying to gather up my memories. They felt like shifting sand, trickling through my fingers. It felt like a dream slipping away piece by piece after waking up.

"Not really…it's all hazy and jumbled," I confessed.

"Listen, I gotta tell you something about yesterday…" he started to say, tucking a lock of hair behind my ear. But then, as he realized something, he stopped.

"Hey, I can touch you now! How amazing is that?" he whispered, wonder lighting up his face.

He leaned his face slowly closer to mine. I could feel the warmth of his breath on my skin. One inch closer and his lips were going to touch mine…

Chapter Eight

Compromise

Apparently, the universe disagreed about that, because the front door burst open at that exact second. My mom's voice called out to us from the hall.

Tristan and I both jumped two feet off the couch, surprised as hell by her sudden arrival. I sat up straight, patting my hair, while Tristan pushed the covers up to his chest and leaned on his elbows for support.

I glanced at him and he looked a little flustered, his cheeks slightly pink. It was the first time I'd seen some color on his face: he was always so dead pale! I guess that was down to him being a ghost, but what was he now? Was he human?

My mom entered the living room, carrying a bunch of shopping bags. She must have found the only stores in town open on New Year's Day. "Hey, guys! You look like you were still sleeping!" she greeted us happily.

"Hum, yeah, we were. We were woken up by you slamming the door right now," I said, lying through my teeth. I glanced at Tristan and a tiny, almost imperceptible smile curled the side of his lips.

"I had to go out. I was worried about leaving you alone after last night...but you looked like you were fine sleeping, so I risked it," she said, smiling. "You two look a lot better, by the way."

"Yeah, I feel a lot better," I said realizing it for the first time, while Tristan nodded. "What time is it?"

"It's three in the afternoon already. Come on, Joey, help me prepare something for you two to eat in the kitchen. We have a lot to talk about," she said, pointing towards the kitchen.

" Okay. Just give me a sec, I'll go change and brush my teeth, I'll be right back," I said, patting my hair and realizing I must look like hell, wearing my old sleeping sweats and my hair like a bird's nest. I was so embarrassed!

"Alrighty. Tristan, I couldn't wait for you to wake up to ask what clothes you prefer, so I decided to go on my own. A girl at the store helped me pick them up for you; she guaranteed they were the latest fashion thing, very...tight!" Mom said, unsure about modern slang. "I didn't know your size, so I just guessed. I hope it all fits!" she said as she handed him the collection of bags.

He took them while trying to get up and cover himself with the blanket, all at the same time, resulting in a small avalanche of bags falling over him. Typical of my mother: whenever she needed to cope with stressful situations, she went shopping! By the amount of bags on Tristan's lap, she must be pretty stress-free now...

"T-thanks so much, Mrs. Gray. I don't know how I'll repay you..." he began, but Mom cut him off.

"Nonsense. It's just a couple of things, you can't go around wrapped in blankets!" she said, dismissing his gratitude. "Joey! You're still there? Come on, chop, chop!

Tristan, the bathroom is upstairs and right off the hallway, first door to your right. Take your time. We'll be in the kitchen all right? Call me if you need anything. But when you're both dressed and we've had something to eat, we will have a serious talk."

She turned and walked to the kitchen. She was like a special kind of a hurricane, my mom. I shrugged and smiled at Tristan's surprised face, and then darted upstairs to get myself cleaned up and presentable.

Soon enough, I was ready and stepped downstairs all perky in my new jeans, my favorite sweater and my hair tied back in my usual pony-tail. I peeked at the living room. Tristan wasn't there, but I heard water running in the hallway bathroom. I went on in to the kitchen where my mom was at the stove, frying some eggs.

"Hey, Mom, I'm here. What can I do to help?"

"You can set the table, get some glasses, orange juice, milk. I think I'll do a big brunch for you two, how's that sound?"

"Sounds great," I said uneasily.

"Is Tristan all right in there?" she asked with her back to me.

"I think so ... He's in the bathroom now."

"You know, if I hadn't witnessed the whole thing, I would have never believed it," my mom said thoughtfully.

"I'm trying not to think about it. It's too surreal," I mumbled.

"Joey, honey. You know we do need to talk about it, don't you? I mean, this is too crazy! Do you really believe in what those old ladies were saying? Do you think Tristan was really a ... a ghost?" she asked, turning to look me straight in the eyes.

I shifted uncomfortably. "I don't know what to think, Mom, honestly. I punched him in the chest last night, and it went right through him! And you couldn't see him, but I've been talking to him and meeting him for days!" I said in a shaky voice.

"And this is where you were hanging out? The cemetery?"

I nodded, staring at my lap. "I know I should have told you. I'm sorry, Mom. But you would have made it into a big deal, and said it's dangerous, but I knew I was safe with Tristan!"

"How could you possibly know that, Joey? You just met him!" she said, upset.

"I just know, all right! I mean, look at him! Do you think he could hurt anyone? He's so polite and kind and sweet!" I exclaimed.

"You're letting your judgment be clouded by his good looks, honey," she said with a knowing smile.

My cheeks flamed in embarrassment and I snapped, "It's not like that, Mom! He's my friend! Fine, he was lying to me about the 'ghost' thing, but he explained everything! He was scared of my reaction. And, I mean, can you blame him? I wanted to run away the second I discovered he was a ghost! This is not exactly easy news to share with some-one," I grumbled, fumbling with the hem of my shirt.

"Yeah, but honey, what the heck happened last night?" my mom wailed, her eyes wide as she remembered Tristan's materialization out of thin air.

"I'm not sure...I think it's something to do with the time, and the place...Miss Violet might know something; she was there with her two old friends. She seemed to know Tristan was a ghost all along," I muttered, trying to put the pieces of the puzzle together. Had one of the old ladies also mentioned they were witches?

My mother nodded. "Yes, I think so too. That's why I have invited her to come talk to us today. Maybe she can shed some light on this mystery for us," she said thoughtfully. "And maybe the boy could have some answers as well," she added and paused, deep in thought. Then she shook her head, snapping out of her wonderings. "Anyway, as I said, we can all talk about it later, after we've put something in our stomachs, all right?" And she resumed her egg frying.

I stared at her back, scrunching up my lips in guilt. "Mom?"

"Yes, honey?"

"I'm really sorry, for all this mess. I feel like this is all my fault. I should have known something was wrong, I mean, the signs were all there! He never left the cemetery; he was always there. And he never ever touched me, not even for a quick handshake. And he looked so lonely and so sad," I said, looking down at my feet.

"Joey, please," she interrupted, taking the pan off the heat for a second, turning to look at me. "This is nobody's fault. Not yours. Not his. He must be feeling pretty scared right now, can you imagine? And he's your friend, you obviously care a lot about him, so we'll do our best to help him through this and support him, okay? Don't worry about it. We'll sort this out."

I sighed in relief. "Thanks, Mom." I knew I could always count on my mom. She was the best!

She gave me a comforting smile and a nod, and then turned back to her cooking.

"So," she said, without looking at me, "this is the boy

who's been keeping you so busy since we've arrived, huh?"

"Huh. Yeah. This is him."

"He's really cute," she said and I knew for sure she was sniggering, even though she had her back to me.

"Okay, Mom. I know where this is going," I said, rolling my eyes.

"What? I didn't say anything! I was just telling you my perception of his appearance, that's all. He seems a lovely young man. Very handsome," she said in a stern voice.

We heard someone clearing their throat close by and turned to see Tristan leaning against the doorframe. He was watching us, and something flashed across his eyes for a second. I thought of asking if he had overheard what my mom and I were talking about, but as soon as my wide-eyed gaze landed on him, I couldn't think of anything to say. I was absolutely speechless.

"Oh, my God! Look at you!" my mom exclaimed. "You look adorable!"

Adorable was definitely NOT the description that came to my mind. Smoking hot was more like it.

He was wearing baggy jeans – I guess my mom had chosen them to be sure they would fit – a bright blue T-shirt that hung perfectly on his body, and some sneakers. He looked very, very good. *Very!* His hair was a little messed up from pulling the shirt on, giving him – unintentionally – the look most boys favoured: the methodically messed-up hairstyle. His new look was so modern, so utterly different from his tidy hair and formal clothes from before. From monochrome to vibrant, vivid, ocean-blue colors. It was like an old photo coming alive, in a breathtaking image. He looked at us expectantly, waiting for a response.

"Is this all right?" he asked uncertainly. "It looks sort

of strange to me. Not many kids visited the cemetery, so I don't have much basis for comparison," he mumbled, putting his hands inside his jeans pockets. "And they're not like the jeans I wore when I was...um...alive."

"Oh. It's all right," I answered slowly, trying to steady my voice. "It's...good."

"Come and sit, Tristan, your eggs and bacon are almost ready!" my mom said, beckoning him to the table and turning to me, mouthing a silent *"Oh My God"*. I shook my head in despair. I would never hear the end of this!

"Joey, dear, sit here, next to Tristan. I'll get your plate ready! There's bread and fruit as well. Help him out, honey!" she ordered, bustling round the kitchen.

We sat at the table and stared at each other. I looked into his strangely blue eyes.

"That's odd. Your eyes are blue now," I said curiously.

He looked down at his new shirt and smiled timidly. "Actually, they're still gray. I've checked in the bathroom mirror. It's color reflection, I think. The shirt," he said, pointing to his blue shirt.

"So, if you were wearing a green T-shirt, you'd have green eyes, then?"

"I suppose so," he said shrugging.

"That is *so cool*. You can change eye color." I was a little jealous of that.

"They're not actually 'changing' colors, they're always gray, but I get your point," he said, growing a little impatient at my obsession with his eyes. Then his stomach made a loud rumble. He blushed, embarrassed. "Sorry. I'm...really hungry," he said staring at his plate "I forgot about that."

"Forgot about what?"

"You know, being hungry," he said quietly, putting his hand on his belly.

"It's one of the many fabulous perks of being alive. Still happy about it?" I said, smirking.

"Yeah. I'm still happy," he said, smiling softly, with indeed so much happiness in his eyes.

That knocked me a little sideways, and it was my time to stare at my plate in an awkward silence, but not for long. My mom appeared with two plates heaped with eggs and bacon. "Here we go! Eat up, you two!" she commanded.

Tristan ate in silence, focusing on his food, while my mom and I chatted non-stop about all the things that happened yesterday, retelling the incident from our points of view. We tried not to ask him questions, to give him time to adjust and feel more at ease, more comfortable so he could start trusting us. Even though my head was buzzing with a thousand questions. When did he die? And how? Was he now fully human? Would he age? Did he know what happened at the cemetery and why he was alive now? He would glance at us occasionally, sometimes looking mystified, sometimes looking like he was avoiding something, but he didn't say a word. When we were done eating, he stood up and grabbed our plates.

"Don't worry, Mrs. Gray, I'll do the dishes. Thank you for a wonderful meal, everything was great!"

My mom raised her eyebrows at me, clearly impressed. I guess you could say that whatever time Tristan was from, it was one where people had far better manners!

The doorbell rang and my mom jumped. "Oh, dear. Look at the time! She's here already. Miss Violet's come for a visit," Mom said, rising from her seat. "She'll want to talk to us all. Tristan, you can leave those dishes there. Don't worry, they'll still be here when you get back."

Tristan frowned and reluctantly left the dishes at the side of the sink. He clearly did not want to have this conversation; I could tell by his sudden sour mood.

We walked into the living room while Mom answered the door. We greeted Miss Violet as she entered, and we all sat down: Tristan on the couch next to me; my mom and Miss Violet in the armchairs either side of us.

"How's your friend doing, Miss Violet?" I asked, remembering how frail the old lady had looked yesterday evening.

"She's doing all right now, dear. It's very nice of you to ask," Miss Violet said. "She actually helped me last night to unravel part of the mystery you've got yourself into."

"I-I've got myself into?"

"With the help of your friendly ghost over there, evidently," she retorted.

Something dark flashed in Tristan's eyes as he glared pointedly at Miss Violet.

"Now, about your little predicament here," she said, looking at me and not caring at all about Tristan's glares. "We did some research into the Gray family tree – as much as we were able, at such short notice. The internet is a wonderful thing, my dears," she said as an aside, surprising both Mom and me. "Apparently, there's witch blood in your bloodline, which is why you were able to see Tristan when he was a ghost, Joe. And probably why you were able to perform that spell even without realizing. The magic in you is untamed, but it's really strong. You seem to have developed quite a lot on your own already."

"Are you seriously saying I'm a witch?" I shrieked, freaked out.

"I'm always serious, dear," she said a little sharply. "But no, that's not what I said." Then she added quickly, "Well, you're not a witch yet. You have potential, but it requires work, training, commitment, lots of practice and a lot of study to become a real witch."

"That's nonsense!" I shook my head in denial. "I have nothing magical going on here. I'm just plain Joey. And witches don't exist."

"Oh, you have no trouble accepting ghosts that come back to life, but you have difficulty accepting witches, now? That's funny," Miss Violet scoffed, mildly offended.

"I-I . . . that's not what I meant. I'm just saying I have no witch blood in me whatsoever," I corrected myself, looking at Tristan.

Suspicion passed across his eyes. Did he think I was lying?

"I'm not lying!" I snapped at him. "How can you think that?"

"How did you know what he was thinking?" Miss Violet asked squinting her eyes at the both of us.

"I just . . . saw it. In his eyes," I mumbled, feeling confused.

"She always does that," Tristan said quietly. "Even when I was a ghost. She always knows exactly what I'm feeling when she looks at me. It's been bothering me for some time now. I didn't know how she was doing it. But it is always very . . . accurate."

"It's not quite telepathy, more empathic insight. You need visual contact to do it, right? You can read what the other person is feeling. Quite handy," Miss Violet said to me.

"Everybody can do that. It's normal, right, Mom? Did you not see suspicion in his eyes just now?" I asked, bewildered.

"No, dear," said Miss Violet, "We just saw him looking at you. Nothing more. He had a pretty blank expression. I don't know what he was thinking or feeling, and I'm a pretty good observer of human behavior. I have been around in this world for some time now. I know how to read people. And he was letting nothing out."

I shot my mom a pleading look, silently asking for her help.

"You have always been spot on about people's feelings, honey," she said thoughtfully. "I just thought you were very perceptive, but you're scarily accurate. I've got used to it over the years, but strangers sometimes notice, don't they? Remember your friends at your old school used to say it kinda creeped them out. After a while you stopped vocalizing your reads, but you could still see, right?" she asked me.

I bit my lip and shifted uneasily on my seat.

"What about this spell you talked about, Miss Violet? What actually happened last night? Do you have any theory that could help us figure this out?" My mom finally decided to ask the million-dollar question. She didn't seem upset at all by the revelations happening in her own living room. Perhaps she too had suspected there was some "witch blood" in our family, and was only now verifying this.

"Well, we're still trying to figure that out, but it seems that Joey here managed to set a very powerful spell in motion. We knew something was going to happen; my friends and I had seen some signs alerting us. That's why I'd been going there a few days each week lately, to see if

I'd catch something. I suspected it was something to do with the girl – you, Joe – when I saw her first speaking to a ghost boy without realizing it. After that, I asked my husband to keep an eye on her...on you,." she said, looking at me. "We never thought this could happen, though. To bring back the dead...it's tricky and dangerous. Not to mention extremely difficult. It takes many powerful elements to be combined at the same time and requires a lot of power to perform such an act. We never knew what those elements could be, but from what we observed last night, we now have a vague idea."

"Elements? Spell? Bringing back the dead?" I asked, stunned. It was just too much information and nonsense for my head. And I'd done this?

"Apparently we had seven people present there last night. Seven is a powerful number for magic. Five elements were combined – fire, air, earth, water and the most important one, the one that made the connection between the boy and the girl. Also, there was the importance of place and time. Everything combined at that place, in the exact centre of the graveyard, as the old year ended and a new one began. The result you get is right there, sitting on your couch, living and breathing for the first time in what...sixty years?" she said, looking now at Tristan.

Tristan died sixty years ago? That meant he was last alive in the 1950s. No wonder his manners and vocabulary were so strange. But what had Miss Violet also said? "Seven people? There's a mistake right there," I said, counting on my fingers. "You and your friends, that's three. Me and Mom. That's five."

"Forgetting about Ghost Boy over there, are we?" she asked, raising an eyebrow.

"Oh, yes. I didn't know a ghost could be counted as 'people'. Sorry, Tris. But that's still only six."

"Yes, there was also another one. A very important one. You missed it because you were in transition during the spell, but it was there all right," she said, avoiding my eyes.

"It?" Miss Violet ignored my question and, under her withering gaze, I let it go for now. "Okay, seven people." I counted again. "And five elements...fire, air, earth, water and something else."

I mentally identified what each could have been. Fire. From the candles. I remembered their flames vividly after I had bumped my head. Air was the wind. I remembered how fierce it had been, how it swept through my whole body. Earth beneath my fingers from when I was lying down on the grass.

"What was water? And the something else?" I asked.

"You were crying. That's the water part," Miss Violet told me.

"I-I was?" I didn't remember crying. It all felt like a distant foggy memory. "So what about the something else?"

"Did you cut yourself yesterday?" she asked.

I turned the palms of my hands upwards. There were scratches and tiny cuts all over both hands from when I had fallen.

She smiled, seeing me stare at my scratched hands. "Blood is a powerful thing for spells. It created the bond between you and him for the spell to work, and it sealed the deal."

I remembered that everything had gone dark and I hadn't been able to see Tristan any more, but that I could feel him close to me. I had felt something on my lips. And pinpricks of energy...I think. The memory was blurred now, like I was seeing it through distorted glass. But I think that was when the spell was bound. The final touch. The second his lips had touched mine, I'd been jolted back and Tristan had appeared out of thin air.

"And this spell has its price. All magic does," Miss Violet continued. "It'll be collected, heavily taxed, mind you. The boy should've thought about that before going through with it," she snapped at him.

I turned to Tristan. He crossed his arms defensively over his chest. "You knew this was going to happen?" I asked him in surprise.

"I-I– No! That's what I wanted to talk to you about before, when we...woke up. I heard this wild tale, from that friend I told you about, you know, the one with crazy stories about old magic? He told me that it could be possible, you know, to have a second chance to live. There was a song, or a poem, or something. I don't quite remember it how it went. It said it could happen, a true second chance in life, if there's a living soul able to truly see you. And when you did, Joey, when you saw me, and talked to me, I thought it could be possible...to live again. I was only seventeen when I...I died. And I've been trapped in the cemetery every since. The song talked about that special place in the cemetery. That's all. I didn't know about the binding spell, or any tax! I swear! If I'd thought it could harm you in any way, I would never..." He trailed off, unable to continue.

"And now that you have your wish, boy, what are you going to do with it?" Miss Violet inquired firmly.

Be careful what you wish for...My mom used to say that when I was little. Tristan had wished to live. Now he had to deal with his wish becoming true.

"I...I don't know. I'll figure something out!" he snapped, fear crossing his eyes.

"The sickness you two experienced last night, it's not going to stop, you know that, boy? It's a side-effect from the spell she cast; a price you have to pay for the magic bond you've created. I spent the whole night researching this. It's a cycle sort of thing. It'll happen again and again. And you two will need to stay together when it happens. What are you going to do about it? Is living again worth compromising the girl's wellbeing? Or is it worth having her shackled to you?" she asked him again, her voice firm and unwavering.

"No! I didn't know this would happen! I don't know what I'm going to do, okay? I just...don't know. I never meant to harm her! Joey, you have to believe me!" he said, looking desperately at me and then turning angrily to Miss Violet. "Why do you hate me so much, old woman?"

"I don't, but your place isn't here, son. You know that," she answered plainly.

"No, I don't know that! Who's to say my place is in that cemetery for all eternity and not here? Why have I been trapped there for all these years if not for this? I don't want to disappear or just cease to exist! Everybody else has a second chance, why can't I? Who are you to say I don't deserve it?" he shouted, his eyes filling with tears and uncertainty.

"Okay. Calm down now." My mom stood up from her seat. "I have heard enough. Tristan, you have done nothing wrong, and I'm sure you meant no harm when you asked Joey to the cemetery yesterday. I've always thought everybody deserves a second chance, in life or in death. So we have to make the best of your second chance now.

Since I'm going to presume for the moment that you have no family left who can take care of you, you're staying with us, and that's settled. We'll go through this together and I'll make sure you and Joey are safe and sound," she said, smiling kindly at him. "We'll figure something out about your history. We can say you're Joey's cousin, or something like that. And that you're staying with us from now on. Now, you two leave Miss Violet and me alone for a minute. I need to talk in private with her."

I glanced at Tristan. He was hunching down by my side, angrily wiping at the corner of his eyes. He nodded politely to my mom, his lips pursed and a deep frown etched on his face as he stood up and walked towards the front door without so much as a glance at Miss Violet.

"I-I...I'll just go talk to him, calm him down," I said, standing up too. "Thank you, Miss Violet, for coming here and explaining all these things to us. We'd be pretty lost if it weren't for you. He...he didn't mean to shout at you. He's just really, really scared. But I can see in his eyes that he truly cares about me. He never meant to harm me. He has a good heart. I'll go check on him now." And I ran outside after him.

Tristan was leaning on the small brick wall in front of the house, arms crossed over his chest, staring at the ground with a clouded expression. I stood next to him, my hands behind my back. I had never seen him so upset before. Apparently, being alive brought out a whole set of strong emotions from him.

I also noticed he was avoiding looking at me now. That was just great! He was never going to look at me again, now that he knew what I could really see.

"Joey..." he began. "If it's really true, about what you

can do...with your eye-reading there...do you believe in me when I say I never meant you any harm? That you're really important to me, and I'd never do anything bad to you? You can see that I'm not lying, right?" He lifted his head and looked me in the eyes.

I didn't need to look at his eyes to know the answer, though.

"It's not like I can do it all the time," I mumbled, shuffling my feet. I needed him to believe this lie now, or he would never be with me without his guard up again. I could never say to him that seeing his emotions through his eyes came as naturally to me as breathing. And I couldn't make it stop. It was like asking me to stop seeing with my eyes open.

"I have to concentrate really hard, and sometimes I can't even read anything at all. Maybe if I practice a lot, like Miss Violet said, but it's not that easy. It's like a short-circuit; it comes and goes," I said, lying some more.

"Can you try it now? I need you to see that I really mean what I said. That I'd never hurt you," he pleaded.

"Tristan. I know that. I believe you," I said, holding his face between my hands. "Everything will be all right, okay? We can do this together!"

The front door opened and Miss Violet walked in. I let go of Tristan quickly and stood by his side. He went back to sulking with his arms crossed again when he saw Miss Violet approaching us. She stopped right in front of him.

"Tristan, dear, I'm sorry if I was too hard on you in there. I needed to know what your true intentions were, and people tend to slip up when they are angry. So I tried poking you a couple of times to get your true feelings out. Not everybody has Joey's keen eyesight, right?" she said softly. "I had to use my own ways to see it, and reassure myself that the girl wasn't in any harm. Now I know that, I'm going to do my best to help both of you. If you ever need me, my door will be always open," she said, extending her hand to him.

He softened his scowl and uncrossed his arms, eyeing her with caution. Then he held her hand and shook it softly. "I'm sorry for my bad manners, ma'am. I didn't mean to shout. I hope you'll forgive me, it was disrespectful of me," he apologized.

She beamed at him, happy that peace was restored. "Oh, by the way, Rose asked me to tell you there's some dishes with your name on it in her sink!" She chuckled lightly.

"Oh, gosh! I completely forgot about that! Excuse me, please, I have to go!" he said darting into the house.

Miss Violet turned to me. "Joe, dear. I talked to Rose, to your mom, and she'll keep me posted on any developments in your situation. If you need me, you know where to find me – next door," she said, hugging me.

"Thanks, Miss Violet. Will do."

"And remember to stick together, then you two will be fine," she said, and paused before adding, apprehensively, "But not too much together, you know. Just the necessary togetherness, to guarantee that the spell cycle won't break. With the way that boy's looking at you, you'll have to beware of too much closeness."

I blushed all shades of pink then. "That's all right, Miss Violet. I can take care of myself," I said, waving her good-bye as she shuffled down the steps and back to her house. I was glad she hadn't caught the way *I* was looking at that boy, or I would be the one in trouble right now!

I shook my head in amusement and went back into the

house. There was so much to discuss and resolve. And I was due to go to school on Monday. What was I going to do now?

Chapter Nine

Tales from the Past

Thank God for my mom! She was The Man! *A Man with a Plan*. Well, a Mom with a Plan. But you know what I mean.

By the time we woke up next morning, she already had a whole scheme figured out. She was going to ask her boss at her new law firm for help. He had helped with my application to Sagan Boarding School and he was really influential in the town. He could easily arrange another spot for Tristan at Sagan too! Since money was no longer such an issue for us, all we needed to worry about was the paperwork and how to justify Tristan's sudden presence in our lives. She was going to tell her boss some bogus story about Tristan being her step-son and my half-brother, abandoned by his natural mother, and appeal to his good heart to see if he could pull some strings to help us now.

I hoped the plan would work. Especially as it involved Tristan going to school. With me. Because of our special magic bond, wherever I was going to be from now on, Tristan needed to be close nearby. WITH ME! Wasn't that absolutely amazing?

I couldn't believe my luck! It was the best news ever!

I wished I could pack him up in my suitcase and just go already! As a consequence of my mom's brilliant scheming, I also got let off my first week at school. She said I could stay home and help with the arrangements for Tristan's admission. There was a lot of paperwork to fill in, since Tristan, legally speaking, was dead. That was a hard one to explain.

I also needed to help Tris adjust to his new life. It was a brave new world for him. Lots of new modern things happening all around. I laughed so much when he saw the microwave working for the first time! That was so hilarious! His eyes looked like two big saucers. It was like having my own private *Back to the Future* boy. Only backwards because he was from the past and was now stuck in the future.

Tristan slept on the couch again on his first night at his now official home, but this time he slept alone. We weren't feeling sick so we decided (and by we, I mean Mom decided) that I should go back to my room, where I belonged, and he should stay down there, on the living-room couch. Suddenly her matchmaking skills were no longer apparent. What a coincidence they went away when I needed them most!

On Monday after work, Mom started to move her stuff out of the home office so it could be used as Tristan's new bedroom, where he could have a door and more privacy. He tried to protest, but my mother didn't pay him any attention, replying simply that he was being officially adopted and should have his own room in the house. His bed would be arranged soon.

She'd also started researching Tristan's past during her lunch hour, and had found the archive of the local paper at the library – and Tristan's obituary from 1950. It said he was survived by his mother, but her obituary appeared in a later column, my mom discovered. Tristan was really sad when he saw the second newspaper clipping, and from then on my mom tried to be more subtle when she told us the information she was gathering.

One day I went to check on Tristan after mom had gone to work, and I caught him sneaking out the front door. "Going out?" I asked from the top of the stairs.

He flinched in surprise. "Oh, hey, Joey. I was just going out for...for a little walk," he said, looking down, avoiding direct eye contact. Which meant he was lying; he always averted his eyes when he was lying, for fear I might catch him out.

"Really. Just for a 'little' walk, you say?" I asked sarcastically, knowing full well he was doing something else he didn't want to tell.

He hunched his shoulders and sighed in defeat. "All right, you caught me. Would you walk with me? I need to take care of something really important," he said, extending his arm politely for me to take it. I joined him and we walked in silence along the sidewalk, while he pointedly avoided elaborating on his plans or even saying where we were headed.

"Just so you know, I'm not a fan of mysteries. I'm starting to notice you have quite a lot of those going on with you all the time," I muttered quietly at his side.

He looked sharply at me, but continued walking down the block. "I wasn't lying! I AM going for a walk," he said, annoyed. "I just thought it wasn't necessary for you to know what I was going to do, and it will only take a minute. Plus, I knew you'd make fun of me!"

"Tristan, when have I ever made fun of you?" I said in a hurt voice.

"Well, let's see, just today about two times already, when you were trying to explain about computers. And the other day when you showed me the machine that heats food with waves of...stuff," he said, upset.

Okay. Maybe he was a little touchy about my laughing at his modern ignorance. I should be more tactful from now on. "Fair enough. I'm really sorry I made fun of you. I promise I won't do it again. What's going on? Where are we going?"

"We're going to the graveyard," he said crossing the street. The front gates already loomed a few feet away from us.

"Are you serious? I thought it'd be the last place you'd want to go now."

"There's something I need to get from there."

"What do you need to get from a graveyard?" I asked, genuinely curious now. This oughta be good.

"Your gift. I left your Christmas gift in there. I need to get it back," he said, still upset. "I know you'll think it's silly, but it's mine and I want it back!"

Oh. My photograph. He wanted to get my photo back. That was...the sweetest thing. I was really sorry I'd laughed at him now. I was such an idiot! "It's not...silly, Tris," I mumbled. "It means a lot to me that you don't want to leave my gift behind."

He seemed to relax after realizing I wasn't making fun of him, and led me back to the tomb were we usually met in the cemetery.

"There's something I need to show you too, Joey," he said as we approached the mossy tomb. He wiped some snow off the stone front so I could finally see the inscription.

I widened my eyes and approached cautiously, a smidgen of fear lacing my steps. This was sort of scary, but I was too curious not to look at it.

"I know you have a lot of questions," he murmured, watching me intently. "Maybe this answers some of them . . ."

I peeked at the inscription, carved in the cold gray stone of his tomb. It read:

TRISTAN HALLOWAY 1938–1950
BELOVED SON AND TRUE VALIANT FRIEND.
TAKEN FROM US TOO SOON.
YOU WILL NOT BE FORGOTTEN.

A broken rosebud was engraved at each side of his name. Tristan passed his thin long fingers across them, a secret smile on his lips.

"Broken rosebuds symbolize lives cut short, I was told," he said, staring at the inscription, his gaze hooded with a strange emotion. Then he turned to look at me, his eyes searching for something in mine. I'd always thought of this as Tristan's tomb – never realising that was literally the truth.

He climbed on his tomb, moving as gracefully as always, and extended a hand to help me climb up after him. When I was safely sitting by his side, he clasped both hands on his knees and stared at the distance as he asked me, "What do you wish to know?"

"I-I don't know if it's all right... I mean, I know it must be hard talking about your life... before," I began tentatively.

"Don't worry about it. It's not hard. It was a long time ago, you won't upset me. Ask me anything you want," he reassured me, turning to look at me with a soft smile.

"O-okay. Well, I was wondering how...how you died?"

"I died in a car crash. The last thing I remember before I died was a car hitting me. It didn't hurt; I didn't feel anything, actually. Just the impact, then darkness, then nothing."

He turned to stare at the horizon.

"The memory is very hazy, like something out of a dream," he continued. "I do remember I was confused and very scared. I didn't understand what was happening at the time. My vision was all blurry and everything was so dark, but I saw someone standing far away, like they were waiting for me to get there, and I had this nagging feeling, gripping me on the spot, keeping me from moving. I knew there was something really important I needed to do, that I needed to stay where I was. That's what I did. And then I woke up here, in this cemetery. And I've been here ever since," he finished calmly.

"Do you think you have something unfinished to resolve? That's why you didn't, erm...pass over?" I asked curiously, grasping for the right words..

"Maybe. Yeah, I think so. Maybe this is it, what happened to us now. It feels like this could be it. Maybe I was supposed to have a second chance?" he said, looking at me for answers.

"Maybe you weren't supposed to die the way you did, or when you did," I suggested, grappling for some reason behind all this.

"Maybe," he agreed, looking down, deep in thought.

"Are there any others like you here? I mean, other

ghosts?" His face was all the answer I needed. "You said the ghosts always told you where you could find me in here. You weren't kidding, were you?" I asked with sudden realization.

He chuckled at my startled face. "Yeah, it was the truth. There are a few others around who couldn't move on, like me. Everybody has a different reason for staying, though. I'm so glad I can walk past those iron gates now. You have no idea how amazing is to be able to leave this place," he said, exhaling in relief.

"You really couldn't leave? What happened when you tried?"

"My feet got rooted to the floor. I couldn't move or take a step forward at the edges of the entrance. I tried for many years before I finally gave up."

"Oh, that's horrible. So you've been trapped here for, what, sixty years or so?"

"Yeah, give or take. It doesn't feel like it, though. Time passes...differently for ghosts, you see. It's more like blurs of moments through the years. But I won't lie to you, most of the time it was boring as heck, pardon my language!" He barked out a laugh. "Being dead is awful. You can't feel anything – cold, heat, hunger, pain, nothing. But you sure can feel angry, and sad, and bored, though.

"I did make a few friends along the years, you don't need to look at me like that!" he added in haste after seeing the pitiful look plastered all over my face. "There's old Mr. Wakefield, he's the one who told me about the spell and that old song. And little Joanne, such a sweet kid, she passed when she was only ten years old but she's very smart and creative. I wasn't completely alone," he mused, taking a quick peek at me. "But the days I've spent with you here have been the best of my life. Or death. I don't know. This is all very confusing." He scratched the back of his head, a faint pink covering his cheeks as he averted his eyes.

"What about your family? Have you seen any of them here?" I asked, trying to change the topic a little and cover up my blushing face, but I instantly regretted it when I saw his eyes brimming with so much sadness.

"My mom came for a while, always bringing fresh lilies for my grave," he murmured quietly. "It was just me and her, we had no other family left back then. My grandparents died when I was little. She cried a lot. I hated seeing her so sad because of me. And then she stopped. I guess it was probably around the time she died. I never got the chance to say goodbye, she just stopped coming. I think maybe I would've got to see her again, if I had walked to that person that was waiting for me when I died. But I can never be sure now. How can I know for sure?" he asked in anguish.

"I don't know either, Tris. I'm so sorry," I told him, putting my hand over his and trying to pretend the little jolt of electricity did not happen as we made contact. I also tried to pretend I wasn't noticing the flurry of tiny butterfly wings inside my stomach as I held on to his hand. "I guess that's enough of questions for today, eh?" I proposed, trying to lighten the mood a little.

He nodded and squeezed my hand ever so softly, before raising his sterling-silver eyes to meet mine. "Thank you for helping me through this, Joe. I will never forget it," he vowed.

"Come on, let's get your present and get out of here!" I urged him with a smile. "There's a whole world outside for you to see now."

The grin that spread across his face then was worth a thousand smiles. It made my heart beat so loud, I swear he could hear it.

"All right. I'll be right back, miss." He jumped off the tomb and disappeared behind it in a blink of an eye.

"That night...How did you manage to hold the photo anyway?" I asked loudly, thinking about it for the first time. Could a ghost move stuff around?

He chuckled from somewhere behind the headstone. "It wasn't an easy feat, I tell you! It took me all night and part of the morning to do it. The stone you put it on was a grievance. But ghosts have a sort of wind trick. Huff and puff long enough, you'll get things moving," he said as he returned with the photo in his hand, beaming happily.

"Here it is. We can go now." He put the photo in his back pocket and extended his hand to help me down from the tomb, like the true gentleman he was.

"I knew you weren't that rude, that time you didn't even try to help me get up after I fell down!" I chuckled, accepting his aid.

He blushed vividly, coughing in embarrassment. "Sorry about that, by the way. I was truly mortified about it, but I couldn't let you know I was...well, dead. Sorry."

"That's water under the bridge now. Come on!" I said, pulling at his hand.

We walked briskly to the front gates, but as we were about to cross the boundary I felt this eerie feeling creeping over me, like I should be hurrying to get out of there right away. Something deep in my guts told me to stay away from that cemetery from now on, but for what reason, I had no idea.

I suddenly remembered the strange dream I'd had that

night, about the goth-looking girl, warning me about some-one. Someone who was looking for me. Someone that shouldn't find me.

When we got back home, I still felt apprehensive, though I didn't feel able to confide in Tristan. I drew all the curtains and locked all the windows. After that day, I could never totally shake that feeling of unease.

Chapter Ten

Fade to Gray

The rest of the week passed in a blur.

Mom was at work first thing in the mornings, and left us by ourselves all day long. Sometimes she called to check up on things. She had Tristan's admission and paperwork situation almost resolved now but there were still a few tricky things to work on, so she ended up arriving back pretty late most nights.

For Tristan, the week was kind of a massive, super-fast, twenty-first-century training program. For a kid from the fifties, he had a lot to learn to get up to date.

I spent every day trying to explain how stuff worked in the modern world. He picked up on things pretty fast. Amazingly fast. He was incredibly smart.

He thought everything was very modern and "swell". On that point, I had to advise him to never, ever, say that word again. I remembered he had used it before and it definitely had to go. I presented him the current "awesome", "cool" and "wicked". He'd pick up on more teen slang later.

I thoroughly instructed him about computers and let him play for a while on my laptop. He was flabbergasted by

Google Earth! He could not believe mankind was able to come up with an invention that made it possible to travel anywhere on the planet without leaving the house. That and the internet kept him distracted for days.

And then I introduced him to my iPod. He fell instantly and completely in love with modern music. I could see it in his eyes, all the awe, reverence and excitement. So I downloaded a bunch of songs from different periods of time, and let Tristan keep it for the time being. From that day on, whenever Tristan was too quiet, you could look for him and he'd be sitting with music blasting on high though his earphones, happiness flashing inside his eyes like battery charges.

Then I taught him about cell phones, texting, ringtones, GPS, the cell gadgets. I knew it was a lot to take in, and that he was only absorbing a little of all the information I was giving him, but as I said, he was a fast learner. He'd have plenty of time to fill in the gaps later.

One day I took him to the nearby mall.

He still tried to comb his hair way too formal for my taste, so I messed it all up before we stepped foot outside the house, despite his frowning, disapproving scowl. We walked aimlessly round the mall for a while, so he could get a feel for the place and the people around. His eyes showed a mix of excitement, caution and flickering attention. The first thing he noticed was some girls sauntering past us, wearing jeans and loose sweaters, same look as mine.

"Now I understand why you're always dressed like a boy, Joey," he said. "Look, there's some girls here dressed just like you! Is it a modern uniform for girls these days?" he asked curiously.

I looked at him in surprise. "Uh, no. It's not a uniform. But not all girls dress this way," I mumbled, embarrassed.

He thought I dressed like a boy?

But in his defense, I guess I did. A very sloppy, untidy, unattractive one. It served me right for being such a tom-boy! Me and my *I have to wear comfortable clothes all the time* rule. My mood went a little sour after that, but I don't think he even noticed.

He soon realized some girls of today also wear really short skirts, really high heels and really tight tank-tops. I had to punch him in the arm every time a short skirt passed by and I could see his eyes wide open and his mouth twitch-ing slightly in a playful smirk. That was a modern thing he was learning to enjoy quite a lot.

My mood also dipped a few more degrees when I saw the reaction Tristan was getting from his female audience. Girls were twisting their necks and turning around to have a second look at him. There were giggles, whisperings, admiring looks and flashing smiles.

What did I expect? I'd always thought he was... well, very handsome, but the girls at the mall were acting like he was a younger, hotter Brad freaking Pitt! I don't think he realized, though. There was just too much to absorb; he was overdosing on information and missing a lot of the subtleties. Although some of those girls were hardly subtle!

I tried to pretend it didn't bother me. It *shouldn't* bother me! He was just my friend. I needed to stop feeling jealous and focus on helping him adjust to his new life. This whole situation with him being back in the land of the living was so insane, and everything was happening so fast, it was kind of scary for me. It was best we remain just friends anyway. That way we could both adjust better to this new reality filled with magic, spells and resurrections.

At one point, Tristan asked me about the other boys. He had noticed a lot of tattoos, piercings and guys with strange-colored hair – and messed up hairstyles like the one I'd given him. I guess it was all quite shocking for a guy from the 1950s. I tried to explain that it was just the latest fashion trend. It was considered a "good look" now. He seemed mystified about the modern concept of *good looks*.

After that he just walked by my side with his hands behind his back, fiercely observing everything around him. When we got home he was in a silent, thoughtful mood.

Then came entertainment instruction day!

I browsed through some channels, talking briefly about current TV shows. Then I had to turn the TV off fast to explain special effects to him because he had seen some alien show while I was channel-hopping, and he looked shocked and scared. So that took a while for me to explain. I only turned the TV back on again when I was certain he wasn't going to freak out at the special effects any more.

After the initial scare, he seemed to enjoy modern TV. He exclaimed a lot, glued to the couch as he watched things blow up, aliens get shot and people flying. As my special treat of the day, I made him watch my favorite movie of all time: *Jurassic Park*! That was a blast! He kept asking me if I was absolutely sure that "those things" weren't real. We got popcorn and sodas, and laid out a bunch of junk food. We watched old movies all day long and part of the night too. Well, old movies for me; they were all brand new for Tristan!

I had a great time that day – and I laughed a lot. It almost felt like a date. But it wasn't, and I kept telling myself we were just good friends hanging out.

And then the week was over, and on Saturday my mom announced I was going to school the next day to get my things settled in my dorm room, with no more delays. And Tristan would stay back for a while to sort out his papers. He still needed to get his ID certified. My mother had made some underground contacts through her job as a lawyer, and managed to get him a fake birth certificate and other documents he needed. She wasn't happy breaking the law like that, but in her defense, it wasn't like she could tell everyone she had a ghost boy back from the dead living with her now. They would think she was nuts!

She gave me *The Look* after informing me of my departure for school the next day, and I knew it was no use trying to dissuade her. I sighed heavily and went to my room to start packing. After a while, I heard Tristan calling out my name downstairs. I left my suitcase open on my bed and went to find him. He wasn't in the living room, so I headed for my mom's ex-office, now Tristan's bedroom, and stopped by the door.

At first glance I couldn't see him anywhere, but then I caught sight of him sitting on his bed, his legs crossed in a relaxed position, looking directly at me. There was something different about him, though. It was hard to explain. He seemed faded, engulfed by his surroundings, like he was a part of the background. My eyes registered his presence and sending that message to my brain, but I could hardly see him. And my brain was starting to poke me, to certify which data was correct. Was he there? Was he not? Which one? Make up your mind already!

I frowned and squinted my eyes, looking straight at him. "Tris? What's going on? What are you doing?"

He looked a little surprised by my reaction. "You know I'm here? That's...odd." He scratched his head. "I'm a little confused now. Maybe...maybe it's only you."

"Only me what?" I asked, waiting for him to make any sense.

"Okay. Watch this. I'm going to call your mom here, but when you understand, don't let her know, okay?" he said.

"Let her know what?" I asked, but he cut me off, calling out for Mom just like he had done to me a few minutes ago. Mom walked by and stopped by the door, looking around the room. Tristan was right in front of her, but she didn't seem to notice him there.

"Oh, hi, honey." she greeted me "Do you know where Tristan is? I heard him calling me..."

I turned to look at Tristan, and then back at her. And then back at him again. She couldn't see him! That's what was going on! To me he seemed faded, but for her he had faded away. How was that possible?

"Joey, hello! Space to planet Earth! Have you seen Tristan?" my mother asked loudly.

"Uh. No. Yes. Hum...yeah, I already took care of it. He needed help with...the...um..." I looked around in a panic, trying to come up with some lame excuse, but I couldn't find any. I was still in shock from my discovery. Then I turned to Tristan and watched him pointing to the alarm clock on the desk.

"Alarm clock? Yes! The alarm clock. That's what it was. The alarm went off! Yeah, and he didn't know how to turn it off. But it's all good now, Mom. You can go, don't worry!" I said, smiling at her in relief.

She looked at me suspiciously, but then just shrugged her shoulders and walked back to her room upstairs.

"Tristan, what the hell?" I whispered to him, worried that my mom might still hear us.

He smiled and relaxed, and I felt him coming back to normal, standing out from the background again.

"See? Weird, right?" he said, gesturing for me to come and sit next to him on the bed.

"What the hell was that?" I asked, sitting down by his side.

"I don't know. I was getting dressed in here earlier, and I forgot to close the door. Then your mom bustled in. I guess it took me by surprise, I was embarrassed and I reacted by doing...that. She took some papers off her desk, and didn't even acknowledge me naked inside the room. I thought...well, that it was odd. So I tested it again a couple more times and it worked every time. She never sees me when I'm in this...state. I don't know what to call it. I don't even know what it is that I'm doing!" he said excitedly.

"And then you guinea-pigged me too."

"Well...yeah. But it didn't work on you, though, so...I don't get it."

"Yeah, but it kind of feels weird, when you were doing it. I can see you but you're kind of faded. Is it an ex-ghost special ability thing?"

"I really don't know, Joey. I have never been an ex-ghost before, so this is all new territory for me." He paused and looking thoughtfully at the ceiling.

"Maybe Miss Violet will know," I pondered.

"Hmm, yeah, about that. I knew you'd say this. But, maybe she doesn't have to know. Well, at least not right away. We'll tell her later, okay?"

"Huh. All right, I suppose," I said, standing up and walking to the door.

That boy sure liked having secrets!

"I'll go finish packing, then. I still gotta go to school tomorrow, with or without your fading skill there. Let me know if you develop any more 'special' abilities any time soon."

I was really glad his "thing" didn't work on me. Otherwise I would be constantly on my guard, thinking he was playing tricks on me too!

Sunday started as gloomy and clouded as my mood. I knew I should feel excited about going to my new school, and that Tristan would be joining me soon, on the next weekend, but somehow I couldn't manage to feel happy about it.

And the crappy day wasn't helping either. There was a soft annoying rain falling on and off all day, which left everything damp, humid and freezing cold. The sky was filled with gray, ugly clouds and the streets with murky puddles of water.

I stood there at the bus platform, watching the driver stuff my luggage into the bag compartment.

"Are you sure you don't mind going to your new school by bus all alone, honey?" my mom asked, all worried and guilty. The mechanic was holding her car hostage, apparently, and he would only release it on Tuesday. For a heavy ransom. The solution to my problem: bus transportation.

"It's fine, Mom. I already told you that like a million times. Don't worry, I know how to take a bus. It's not rocket science, you know."

"I know, I know, honey, but it's your first day! At your new school! I wanted so much to be there with you!" she said, teary-eyed. Oh, dear. There went the water works.

"Mom, come on! Please, please, don't start crying here!" I whispered, looking frantically around me. Tristan was chuckling behind her back.

"You laugh all you want now, pal, she'll do the same with you too, you know?" I warned him. He stopped in mid-chuckle and kept a straight face then.

"Okay, Mom! I gotta go now, the bus is leaving. I'll see you guys next weekend, right?" I said, hugging my mom.

"Yeah, that damn mechanic better have my car fixed by then, or I'll give him hell! We'll be there at the weekend and you can show me your new school, your new room, your room-mates!" She squealed in excitement.

"All right, all right, settle down," I said, patting her shoulder and turning to Tristan.

He had both hands inside his pockets, his usual stance when he was nervous, as I'd learned to recognize by now. He glanced sideways at my mom. I guess he was embarrassed to say or do something in front of her. The fact that she was looking at us with googly eyes wasn't helping either.

"Uh...well, have a safe trip to your school, Joe. I'll see you soon," he said, extending his hand to me formally.

I took his hand, a little embarrassed myself. "Thanks, Tristan. I'll see you soon."

We shared a brief handshake and I blushed at my mom watching us like a hawk. She was grinning like a mad woman, too. Well, that was...awkward. I got on the bus after that and watched through the window while my mom wiped tears from her eyes. She was leaning on Tristan's arm for support, and he stood still by her side, smiling shyly as I waved goodbye.

I leaned back in my seat, regretting my awkward handshake with Tristan. I wished I had hugged him. Now it was too late for that.

I stared at the road ahead of me. Sagan Boarding School, here I come.

Chapter Eleven

A Light at the End of the Tunnel

I watched the murky road and heavy clouds in the sky for the whole two-hour trip to school. It wasn't raining any more, but everything still seemed damp and soaking wet. I felt a little queasy inside, my anxiety holding my stomach in a tight grip.

What would this new school be like?

I knew it was a highly regarded school for wealthy people, and I was kind of worried I wouldn't fit in there, wouldn't find any friends, either. That was worrying me. A lot.

I hated dealing with high-maintenance, spoiled rich brats! I hoped the school wouldn't be filled with them. What was I thinking, of course it would! And now it was too late to go back. I'd have to suck it up and endure a whole year of spoiled brats!

I was so engrossed by my grim thoughts that I didn't notice the bus had stopped. Before I could glance outside, the driver called out my name.

I lifted my hand in confusion as he made a sign for me to follow him. I grabbed my backpack and stepped off the bus with a puzzled face.

There was a huge pothole in the road, with soft red mud gushing out. A big limo had tried to pass through it and got stuck in the mud. The wheels screeched and rolled, but the car remained in the same spot, blocking the road. I turned to look at the bus driver by my side.

"Hey there, miss, " he said, taking another look at the road. "Seems we have ourselves a problem here. I've been telling people about this hole in the road for weeks and nobody did anything. Now look at it!" He pointed at the mess of mud ahead of us.

I looked at the limo and then at the bus. "The bus won't be able to pass," I stated.

"Sorry, miss." He nodded an affirmative. "But your school's just there." He pointed beyond the limo to the horizon, where I could see the big gray stone walls of Sagan Boarding School looming. It would take only a few minutes to walk there.

"Okay, then. I'll walk. Can you get my luggage, please, sir?" I asked politely, and the man nodded, relieved that I wasn't going to hold up the rest of his passengers, and went to fetch my things.

While I was waiting, a tall, blonde, Barbie-looking girl stepped out from the limo. She approached me slowly, head raised high like she owned the damn road. I eyed her suspiciously. She was well groomed with bouncy curls, high heels and perfect posture, dressed to kill in an impeccably tailored haute couture dress and coat.

Definitely a spoiled brat. Definitely filthy rich.

She was carrying an expensive-looking purse over her slim shoulder.

"Are you heading for Sagan as well?" she asked in an imperative tone. No, she didn't ask. She demanded to know.

"Yes," I answered plainly. I wondered idly why she wasn't at school already. Maybe she'd had important shopping to do!

The bus driver returned with my suitcase. I grabbed it and thanked him for his assistance. He walked quickly back to the bus and was soon on his way.

"Are you walking to school?" Barbie Girl asked, surprised.

"Do you see another way of getting there?" I replied, getting a little annoyed. She was momentarily taken aback by my sharpness. I wasn't always that rude to people I didn't know, but something about the girl's tone bugged me.

"Do you know who I am?" she asked again, interest glinting in her eyes.

"No."

"I am Tiffany Worthington the Third," she intoned, as if giving her academic credentials.

"Good for you," I said, grabbing the handle of my suitcase. It was on wheels so I could easily pull it to the school. "Now, if you'll excuse me, I gotta go do this amazing thing called *walking*," I said in a mocking tone.

Barbie Girl – sorry, Tiffany-the-freaking-Third – was definitely surprised now by my sarcastic response. She looked mystified for a second, but then quickly regained her composure. "I suppose I can walk up there too," she said, mostly to herself. "Here, take this." She pushed her heavy, expensive purse into my arms.

I held the bag in wonderment. "Wait! What?" I barked at her.

"I'll let you carry that for me. How long do you think it'll take for us to walk up there?" she asked, turning her frowny face to the school, calculating the long miles of torture she was about to endure.

That was it! I was now officially pissed off. Who the hell did this girl think she was?

"For me, only a few minutes. For you, with those high heels of yours, maybe half an hour. Good luck with that," I said through clenched teeth and shoved the bag back into her hands – hard. "And thanks for the offer, but you can carry the bag your damn self."

And with that I stormed off. The nerve of that girl! Let ME carry HER bag. Pft! Yeah, like that was going to happen. When hell freezes over!

I dragged my case without looking back, taking extra care not to slip on the muddy patches of the road. After a few minutes, I started to feel less angry; a few minutes more and I almost forgot about annoying Barbie Girl. The school buildings were getting closer, and the walk in the cold air was invigorating.

I was starting to enjoy the view when I heard the crunching sound of wheels on asphalt. I looked back and saw that the limo had managed to get unstuck and was now driving up the road, in my direction. Just great! She was going to rub it in my face now. If I had just sucked it up and carried her purse, I'd have a ride to the school now. I shook my head. I have my pride. I would rather walk a million miles on foot than suck up to Barbie-the-Third!

The limo accelerated and passed right through a puddle in front of me, splashing me all over with murky mud. What the hell? I stood still, frozen, shocked and disgusted, red mud dripping from all my clothes. Did she get her driver to do that on purpose? The little bitc—

Okay. Calm down, Joey. Breathe. That's it. In and out.

Continue walking. You cannot start your first day at school with a spot of cold-blooded murder.

I clenched my jaw tight and kept walking, a dark cloud of evil thoughts thundering over my head.

After about five minutes, I reached the school's entrance. A large bronze sign half-covered the huge oak front doors. SAGAN BOARDING SCHOOL. And parked right in front was the limo with Barbie Girl standing next to it, surrounded by an entourage of other Barbie-looking girls. I guessed this was the bitch-welcoming-squad from hell.

I walked up to the front doors, shooting daggers from my eyes, but Barbie-Girl-the-Third stepped in my way, blocking my passage.

I looked sharply at her. For a split second I saw surprise and pity flashing in her eyes, but it passed as fast as I saw it, to be replaced by something else. I was too pissed off to try to decipher anything. There was nothing inside that girl's mind that interested me anyway.

"Oh, my. Look at you. I guess you should've been nicer to me back there on the road, dontcha think?" she said, voice dripping with sarcasm. Her squad sneered along with her, glaring at me with contempt. "I guess I can let you try it one more time. Here's my purse. Why don't you carry that to my room upstairs? It's on the third floor, honey," she said, pushing her purse into my arms for the second time.

I looked down at her purse, and then up to her face. A warm smile spread across my lips, and joy glinted in my eyes. She seemed pleased with my change in attitude. So I grabbed her purse carefully with both hands, and dropped right in the middle of a big, stinky, deep puddle of mud at my feet, grinning like the devil all the time.

I heard gasps of indignation and outrage from her loyal

crew, and a little squeal from herself. Boy, that was so worth it. I clapped my hands at a job well done, grabbed my case again and climbed the steps to the front doors, without looking back and with no regret in my heart.

I walked through the hall with people staring and whispering behind my back, but I didn't care any more. I must've been quite a sight! Dripping wet with mud, and too angry to care. This was turning out to be the worst first day at school ever! I grabbed a poor kid and growled at him, asking for directions to the secretary's office. After a while, I managed to find it. A small, fat, grumpy old lady was sitting behind her desk, scribbling on something. She didn't even bother to stop or to look at me. What was it with this school and rude people?

"Yes, dear?" she said in a bored tone.

"I need my room number," I growled at her. "I'm a late enrollment for the second semester."

"Name, dear?" she asked, still not looking at me.

"Joe Gray."

She typed fast on her keyboard, squinting at the computer screen, then grabbed a Post-it note and scribbled a number on it.

"There you go, dear, Room 101, Block B."

I yanked the paper out of her hand and stormed out. I didn't care if I was being rude any more. No one in this school deserved my niceness! I grabbed a few more kids on the way, and directions were promptly handed to me. Nobody wanted to mess with the crazy mud-all-over girl. Soon I was standing in front of the door to my room. Now I had to deal with my obnoxious roommates. They would probably be another bunch of spoiled Barbie girls. I was so doomed in this place! I pushed open the door to see a blond boy reclining lazily on a bed right in front of the door. He was reading a book but looked up, startled by my sudden entrance into the room.

"Hey, what are you doing here?" I grunted.

He looked me up and down, knitting his eyebrows at the ghastly view displayed in front of him.

"I'm reading," he said, flapping the book in his hand for showy effect.

I pursed my lips in frustration. "I mean, what are you doing here in this room? You do know this is the girls' dormitory, right?" I asked, losing my patience now.

"I'm sorry, but this is the boys' dormitory. Block B. B is for Boys. And this is MY room," he declared, resting his book on the bed and giving me another inquisitive look.

"This is Room 101, Block B?" I said, hesitating a little now.

"Yep."

"B is for b-boy?"

"Yep."

Crap. Boys' dormitory. Of course. The curse of the name. They thought I was a boy! Joe Gray. A boy. *Crap. Crap. Crap!*

"Crap," I said, stepping into the room and slamming the door behind me.

He looked a little shocked as I dragged my suitcase to what I assumed to be the bathroom door, muttering, *"That's just freaking great"* on the way in. And then I slammed the bathroom door with a loud thud and locked it with a loud click.

I would deal with this situation later. Now what I needed was to get clean and change my muddy clothes. After twenty minutes under a hot shower, I was feeling loads better and ready to deal with Blond Dude outside. I got dressed in baggy jeans and a black sweater, and unlocked the door, stepping outside cautiously.

The boy was still leaning back on his bed, legs and arms crossed casually, the book abandoned. Now that I was calmer, I could take a better look at him. He was wearing faded blue jeans, white T-shirt and white socks. His sneakers were scattered on the floor. There were a lot of scrambled pieces of papers strewn across his bed that I hadn't noticed when I entered the room. His bright blond hair was meticulously messed up in a spiked, pointy hairstyle. It was hard to describe it, but it looked good on him. He was eyeing me again, with curious hazel eyes. I decided it was a good time to apologize for my earlier angry stampede.

"Hey, I'm sorry about that entrance. I'm having a really crappy day, as you might have noticed. I guess they gave me this room by mistake, and I'm going to try and fix it now," I said apologetically.

A little smile showed at the corner of his mouth. "Don't bother. All the rooms are taken. School's already started; nobody will want to change rooms now. You can leave a note with the secretary; maybe there's still an open spot somewhere in the girls' dorms. But I guess you're stuck here for now until they solve this problem. I'll be your roomie, then. I'm Seth. Nice to meet you," he said, extending his hand to me.

"Joe. Joe Gray," I said, shaking his hand and preparing myself for the script line.

"But...Joe is..."

"A boy's name. Yeah." I flopped onto the bed next to him. "Hence the room mix-up. They must have muddled up my birth certificate and registration papers."

He scratched his head, messing up his blond hair. He looked so cute doing it. "I guess you must get that a lot, right?" he said, embarrassed.

"Just...always. Never failed me. Not once in my life," I muttered, looking around the room. There were two other beds. One looked kind of broken. I guessed the other would be mine, then.

"So, Joe, would you mind telling me the tale of your muddy clothes? That was quite a sight!" he said, chuckling. I thought he was making fun of me, but I saw only genuine curiosity in his eyes. And now that I was closer, I could also see how handsome he was. Thin lips matching a thin nose, and hazel eyes that sparkled with honesty. The total effect made you instantly trust him.

Maybe I shouldn't try to switch rooms after all, I thought. He seemed like a pretty decent guy; rooming with him might not be so bad. It was a large room and there was a decent-sized bathroom I could change in, for modesty's sake. And if I did switch rooms, I could easily end up with one of those horrible Barbie girls from the Tiffany Squad. That idea gave me shivers.

I sat cross-legged on my bed and told Seth all about my first encounter with Tiffany the Third, the walk up to the school, the big mud splash, the dropping of her purse in the puddle of stinky mud. That earned me a round of loud laughter from him. His laughter was so free and fun that I started giggling myself.

"Come on! Did you seriously do that? To Tiffany? Man, you have some balls, I tell you that!" he exclaimed.

"How come?"

"Well, you do know she's like the richest person in this entire school, and that is not an easy feat cos there's some seriously loaded people here. She owns like half the state in properties and business enterprises. Well, her parents do. Nobody here dares to contradict her, for fear she might retaliate. And when a Worthington retaliates, you better not be around!" he said, passing his hand over his blond head. "She's like our own private Paris Hilton. She's used to people groveling before her all the time."

"Oh. I see," I said, a little wide-eyed.

He looked curiously at me. "You didn't know, did you?" he asked, understanding my nervous stance.

"Nope. But it doesn't matter. I wouldn't change a thing of what I did back there. If she wants to retaliate, it's up to her. I don't grovel to anyone," I said firmly.

"Well, you have my support. If you need backup from the Vengeance of the Thirds, you give me a shout out," he said, reclining on his bed.

"So what about you? Aren't you afraid of her retaliation?"

"No. And I don't grovel either. That's not how I roll," he said, adopting a cool position on the bed for show. He was funny. I liked him.

After that we chatted for a while, exchanging life stories. Seth was a real sweetheart. I was really glad I'd ended up his room-mate. He told me he'd been going to this school since he was little, and he pretty much knew everybody and everywhere around the place. He also told me about his parents and that they lived in another state, that he had no siblings and that basically he was pretty much loaded too. Not like Tiffany, but enough. Even though I was still a little skeptical and apprehensive about him, Seth was nothing but open and kind towards me, not one ounce of "bratty" about him. He offered me his friendship without judging me, or asking for anything in return.

I wasn't used to trusting people easily, but Seth broke through my protective barriers within half an hour of conversation. His smile was warm and confident. The future at Sagan didn't seem so gloomy any more: Seth was like a light at the end of a very dark tunnel.

After a few hours, he went out to meet some of his friends, and I spent the rest of the day unpacking and talking to my mom on the phone. I skipped the whole mud incident, and my current living arrangements – she didn't need to know about those – and just told her everything was fine my first day at school. Tomorrow, Monday, would be my first official day with classes and teachers; I would have a lot more things to talk about after that. I went to bed early, and didn't even hear Seth return to the room.

I woke up the next day with the sound of his alarm clock pounding in my ears, and his heavy hand crashing over the snooze button. I could only discern a mess of blond hair from beneath a pile of soft blankets on the bed next to mine. I smiled under my covers.

Monday had started!

Chapter Twelve

The Vengeance of the Thirds

It was early, so it was still dark outside the window, but I was so excited that I couldn't stay still in bed for one more second. Even though this day wasn't that special for everybody else here, since it was week two of their second semester and they'd known their routine, classes and teachers already for half a year, for me it was my first day of school.

Seth got up from his bed and went to the bathroom, shirtless but with sweat pants on. He didn't seem to mind having a girl sharing the room with him.

He soon emerged all dressed up and with his hair fully styled. How he could manage that amazing hair in so short a time, I would never know. He noticed me gawking and smiled.

"So, looking good?" he teased lightly, smoothing the side of his hair.

"Yeah. Not many people can pull that hair off, but you totally manage," I mused. He really did. Waves of blond locks pushed tightly upwards in a small mohawk. He looked really good.

Seth beamed, satisfied with my answer. "Better hurry up and get ready quickly, Joe, otherwise I won't be able to give you the tour!" he said, winking and putting his sneakers on.

I jumped out of bed and darted to the bathroom. I was showered and dressed in ten minutes, with my baggy blue jeans and gray sweater on, hair high up in my usual pony-tail. That earned me raised eyebrows from Seth.

"Whoa, that was wicked fast! I have never witnessed a girl get ready so quickly. You're something else, Joe Gray."

I shrugged my shoulders and grabbed my backpack, deciding to take that as a compliment.

Seth walked with me to his locker first, and helped me find mine afterwards. Then he showed me the school venues, pointing me first to the west wing, where the girl's dormitories were. The boy's dormitories were in the east wing. The classrooms were in the middle of the stone building, and at the back were located the basketball court, pool area, music auditorium and theater. The building in its entirety was three storeys high, and apparently the third floor was designated as the teachers' private quarters along with some exclusive students' bedrooms. Third-floor students didn't have to share rooms. No wonder obnoxious Tiffany was up on the third floor.

The school looked like a gigantic old monastery. Everything was built with gray, dull blocks of heavy stone. The hallways were freezing cold, and constantly swept by a chilling wind.

Then the bell rang, indicating the start of classes, ending my tour around the school. I wasn't sharing any classes with Seth today, but after we hastily exchanged our time-tables I saw that we were in many classes together over the week. That cheered me up a bit. Seth walked me to the door of my first classroom and waved me goodbye, disappearing to find his own.

I glanced inside the room and rolled my eyes, mentally cursing the Gods of Destiny. Of course, my very first class, on my very first day at school, would have to be the same one as Tiffany-the-freaking-Third's and her cheerleading squad from hell. Why was I even surprised? I looked at them and they all sneered at me in unison, like they'd rehearsed it!

So typical. So damn predictable.

I huffed, annoyed, and walked in, sitting on a chair at the back of the room, a few chairs behind Tiffany's place. Then began a series of whisperings and backward glances in my direction. I took the time to study my situation. I decided I wasn't going to follow the old, done-to-death script of high school teen movies. I wasn't going to stand for any bullying from bleached pompom squads.

I watched them huddle in front of me, yapping and sneering. They were like a bunch of hyenas. And I was the new blood entering their prairie. They were testing the ground, checking to see what kind of animal I was. Was I a lion? Or a feeble baby deer?

If I started walking round with my head low and sagging shoulders, I was doomed. They would tear me apart and eat me alive. I could not show any sign of weakness. This was trial time. So they thought they owned the place. I'd show them. I wasn't going to fall into Bambi category, if I had any say in it!

And I should definitely stop watching the Animal Planet channel so much...

I rearranged my stance to a more assertive, imposing position. I didn't care what anyone thought of me. I was beyond those petty blonde things in front of me. The teacher entered the classroom and glanced at a piece of paper in his hands.

"Good morning, class. Settle down now, please," he greeted, looking at the paper. "So, it seems we have ourselves a new student attending Sagan this year. Joe Gray, raise your hand, please?"

I held up my hand, and the teacher nodded in my direction. I heard one of the blondes from Tiffany Squad whispering (a little too loudly) in front of me.

"Oh my God! She has a boy's name, and apparently dresses like one too!" She giggled evilly.

I rolled my eyes. The teacher bellowed from the front of the class. "Miss Gray, why don't you come up here and present yourself to the class?" he commanded.

Okay. That was my cue. I would set my future by these next few minutes. I mastered my nonchalant face and cool facade. It was now or never.

"I don't mean to disrespect you, sir, but everybody knows I'm the new kid at this school, and you just told them my name. So how about we consider my presentation done? I'm sure you have a busy schedule today; we don't have to waste any more time," I said, casually crossing my legs and flipping my book open, faking interest in the pages in front of me.

The teacher looked baffled for a moment, but then nodded and stuttered the pages we needed to be reading. Alrighty, that was easy! I smiled, satisfied with my Oscar-winning performance. A few students were glancing at me curiously, some even looking impressed. I was now officially a lion on the prairie!

I was focusing hard on my book, but risked a quick

glance up. Tiffany had turned around on her seat a couple of chairs ahead of me, and was looking intently in my direction. There was definitely a strange look passing over her face...Before I could figure it out, she turned quickly away. Good as I was at reading people, I was having a hard time deciphering that girl; she was really good at covering up her emotions!

The rest of the class passed uneventfully. I thought I was in the clear from then on. Everything was sorted and my time at that school would be peaceful and undisturbed. Apparently, I was very naive.

It turned out Tiffany was in almost every class with me that Monday. And she did her absolute best to make my life a living hell! It was a constant stream of bullying, teasing, smirking, sneering, laughing in my face, making snarky remarks at my name, at my clothes, my bag, my shoes, the way I walked, the way I sat, the way I breathed. I felt like I was being hazed as part of a military training session.

I guessed that was the beginning of The Vengeance of the Thirds. Seth had warned me about it and I hadn't quite believed him. I tried my best to hold my ground and deflect all her attacks, but by the end of the day I was feeling down after all the emotional abuse. I walked into our dorm room feeling like Rocky Balboa after a beating...Which reminded me, I should definitely watch those movies with Tristan some time. The thought made me smile, despite the hellish day I'd had.

Seth was hunched on his bed flipping through papers spread all around him. He glanced at me and winced. "Wow. Bad first day, huh?" he asked sympathetically.

"Bad doesn't even begin to describe it," I mumbled, throwing my bag on the floor and flopping heavily on to my bed. Then I told him about The Revenge of the Thirds. He was instantly pissed off.

"She can't do this to you!" he shouted from his bed. "Do you want me to talk to her?"

I leaned on my elbows, smiling weakly. I hardly knew him and he was acting so over-protective. That was sweet of him. "Seth. I'm a big girl. And NO, you will not talk to her! I can handle this, please!" I said, trying to calm him down.

He looked upset. "You think I can't help you. That I'm intimidated by Tiffany?" he huffed.

I stood up and moved to sit next to him on his bed. "No, I don't think that at all, Seth. I just need to fight my own battles, otherwise it's you who will think I'm some poor, weak, whiney girl that needs a man to defend herself from the mean girls. I can't have that." I nudged him in the ribs. He chuckled at me, somewhat appeased. "But I know that you've got my back, if I ever need you. It means a lot to me, thank you."

"All right, then. As long you know that," he said, blushing a little and turning back to his papers.

"What is all this mess anyway?" I asked, peeking over his shoulder at all the scrumpled sheets spread over his bed.

He looked embarrassed, but then grabbed a piece paper and showed it to me. "It's kind of a song I'm working on…It's all drafts and roughs for now, but maybe I can turn it into something presentable," he said, scratching his blond locks. "It's been a little tricky, though. The words won't come together anywhere. But the basic idea is here…somewhere."

"You're a songwriter?" I asked, surprised.

"Oh, well, yeah, I guess you could call it that. I'm in a band. It's mostly me and Sam writing the songs for now.

The other two just stand at the side and criticize everything we write. We haven't managed to come up with a good catchy song yet. Maybe this could be it." He stared at the paper like he was daring it to contradict him.

I looked at the scrawled lyrics. It was a mess. I was glad Mom had paid for my music lessons. I could hear the tune strumming in my head as I read the music sheet.

I grabbed a blank piece of paper and started jotting down a few notes, taking bits and pieces from here and there, and asking about things that weren't clear to me at first glance. Seth answered promptly, clearly a little surprised. Then he got really excited by my suggestions, so I kept going. When I looked at the clock, I realised we'd been working on his song for hours!

He kept staring at my sheet and then back at his messy pile of notepads, muttering "brilliant" to himself. I was happy that he liked my rearrangement of his lyrics. All I had done was put things in their right places, fixed some notes, balanced the rhythm and rhymes, and the song was there, right in front of us! He thanked me like a dozen times, holding the new lyrics on his hand reverently.

"I can't wait for the guys to see this! It's so good, they won't believe it!" He beamed happily.

"I'm glad I could help. If you need a hand with other songs, let me know. Your drafts were really good, Seth. You just have to work on assembling your ideas, that's all."

My phone vibrated and I jumped, startled, off the bed. I picked it up and saw "Mom" flashing on the screen. "Hey, Mom. What's up?" I greeted half-heartedly. Tiffany's bullying had taken all the cheer out of my voice, and Mom noticed. I walked back to my bed, leaving Seth absorbed in his papers.

"Hey, munchkin, what's wrong? You sound sad," she asked, worried.

"Nah, I'm just really tired. First day is always hard," I half-lied. I still didn't want her to know about my run-ins with Tiffany. I could handle this problem myself. "So what's new with you?" I asked.

"Well, today I got all of Tristan's paperwork finally settled! As soon as I have my car back, I'll be able to take him to school!" she said happily. "So if people ask, he's your half-brother, all right, honey? I already called the school explaining the whole situation. How are you feeling, by the way? Any sickness?"

"No, I'm fine, don't worry, Mom," I said, relieved. "Huh...how's Tristan doing?"

"He's fine! He's in his room now, listening to music. I took him shopping today! He needed a whole lot of new clothes for school. I didn't know buying clothes for boys could be so much fun!" she exclaimed excitedly.

"You think buying clothes for anybody is fun, Mom," I muttered.

"Oh, but he's so much better than you at shopping. He doesn't fight with me every step of the way, and actually accepts my suggestions."

"That's because he doesn't have a clue what to wear," I retorted.

"And you should've seen the look on the faces of the girls at the store! They were practically asking to go inside the changing room with him! I had to mount a guard outside, so he wouldn't be bothered! I think you're going to like his new look!" she said happily.

I bet I will, I thought to myself. Anything looked good on him.

"So, that's all news for now. I gotta go, honey! I'll call you tomorrow, bye!" Mom said, hanging up.

I turned my phone off and spent the rest of the day picturing Tristan in his new clothes. And then I remembered that he was supposed to be my half-brother now. That was...kind of weird. I sighed, wishing I were there with him. I went to bed early again and had a restless sleep. I suspected that tomorrow was going to be another hellish day with Tiffany on my case.

And it turned out I was right. I left really early to have my breakfast in peace, thinking that maybe Tiffany and her squad would still be in bed, but there she was. My own private nemesis, standing in the middle of the corridor waiting for me, with her bitchy squad at her flanks. Oh boy. It was really, really, early. I wasn't even fully awake yet! Couldn't she give me a freaking break? I sighed heavily and lifted my head up, walking towards her in a very bad mood.

"Gray. I need to have a little word with you before classes start," she commanded, signaling to an empty classroom on her left.

I shrugged and entered the room. I could easily beat the crap out of her if I needed to. Maybe even take a few of her cheerleaders too. I was brown belt in Aikido and yellow belt in karate. I had been very into extracurricular activities back in my old town.

"So, Gray," she began, leaning against the teacher's desk. "After the try-out we gave you yesterday, I think you must have learned your lesson by now. I'm going to give you one more chance to apologize to me. And an opportunity to redeem yourself. You apologize now and carry my books all day long, and all is forgotten. What do you say? It's your last chance, remember that. If you thought yesterday was bad, I was only warming up. I can have you expelled, if I want to."

I stared hard, focusing all my energy into trying to fish all I could out of her. She was right. She could have me expelled in a snap of her pretty rich fingers. But she would never do it. I could see it in her eyes. She was lying. She was lying bad. About everything.

"You know what? You go ahead, do what you think is right," I said. "I'm not going to apologize, because I don't have anything to apologize for. You're the one with the attitude problem. You should be the one apologizing! You think treating people like crap earns you respect? They don't respect you!" I said, pointing to her cheerleaders. "They fear you and they idolize you, but they do it only because of your money. Lose your dollar bills, and you might see there's not one single ounce of real friendship in any one of them."

I turned to leave, but then remembered one last thing to say. "Just leave me alone, Miss Worthington the Third, and go back to being a horrible, shallow and cruel human being. At some point in your life, you'll need a true friend, and you'll realize then how truly poor you really are," I said, walking out and closing the door behind me.

I headed for the cafeteria and finally had breakfast alone and in peace. The rest of the day was a blissful reprieve. Tiffany wasn't in any of my classes that day. One or other of her cheerleaders were, but they didn't dare to say or do anything to me without their leader. They didn't even dare look at me. That felt good.

I shared a couple of classes with Seth, too. That was a breath of fresh air. He always sat next to me, making jokes and goofing around, earning me a few jealous glances from the girls. I had so much fun with him that it almost made me forget about the whole incident with Tiffany in the morning. I wasn't worried about it, though. I knew Tiffany didn't really hate me. I had seen it. Even after all I said to her. I wondered if maybe I had been too hard on her back there. Nah. Probably not.

So I put the incident to the back of my mind, and didn't even tell Seth.

Morning classes ended and I had lunch alone with no sign of trouble ahead. I headed back to my room and bumped into Seth on the way. We were walking together, talking about our first lessons and assignments, when I noticed Tiffany leaning on the wall right outside our dorm room.

She was waiting for me. I instantly tensed in anticipation of another showdown. I really wasn't in the mood for any more fights with her. God! Could she just leave me alone already? Seth sensed my irritation and tensed nervously at my side. Tiffany spoke before I could scream or do anything drastic to her.

"Hi, Gray. Huh…can we talk for just a minute? I won't take too much of your time, I promise," she asked politely. That was a first one. Who would guess she could actually be civilized?

"Okay, I guess," I agreed reluctantly, gesturing for her to follow me inside the room. Seth followed right behind me. He had a serious, pissed-off expression. He was still mad about what she'd done to me the day before.

I sat on my bed and Seth was right beside me. Tiffany glanced around the room and took a seat on Seth's bed, right in front of me.

"Hum...can I talk to you in private, maybe?" she asked, glancing at Seth, looking kind of embarrassed.

"Anything you have to say to me, you can say in front of Seth, here. He's my friend. You know, one of the true ones I mentioned to you earlier today," I said sharply. She winced at my harsh words.

Seth was looking between us, trying to fill in the blanks.

"Ouch. I guess I deserved that one." She smiled warmly at me.

Wait. What? That was weird. Why was she acting so nice all of a sudden?

"Listen, Joe. You were right, I think I own you an apology. I'm really sorry," she said, crossing her long legs.

It was my turn to reel back in surprise. Seth leaned in closely and whispered loudly in my ear. "Joe, what the hell did you do to make a Worthington apologize to you?"

Tiffany looked at him, obviously annoyed, and waved a hand in his direction, dismissing his silliness. "Listen, you really made a big impression on me today, Joe. You've got attitude, very much like me, and I like that. Well, I have to admit I wasn't paying much attention to you when we first met on that muddy road on Sunday. I thought you'd be just another student, faking liking me only to get on my good side, groveling for favors all the time, like my dear cheer squad. Yes, yes, I do know they aren't my real friends, Joe Gray. I'm a smart girl," she said, twirling a lock of curly hair between her fingers.

"So I was very surprised when you shoved my purse back at me and stormed off on the road like that," she continued. "It was very unusual. That got me paying attention. So I tested you once again, when I had my cheer squad by my side to put on some pressure. I wanted to see how you'd react then. I was damn sure you'd cave in. And when you dropped my Gucci bag on the mud! That was priceless! The dropping, not the bag. The bag was quite expensive, though, I can tell you." She chuckled.

I listened with my jaw hanging open. She continued her monologue.

"So I tried one last time today, to see if you'd buckle. Brought out the big guns, so to speak. You know, no one has ever called me on my expell-threat-bluff before. You didn't even hesitate. That was a hell of a speech you gave me back there. You have some balls, I'll tell you that," she said, winking at me.

I glanced at Seth, who was still at my side. That was the exact same line he had used on me before. He still had a serious face on, but his eyes twinkled with a smile. How could he smile only with his eyes? That was a neat trick!

"So I'm here to say I'm officially dropping the bitchy fake attitude. You passed all tests with high honors. As you said before, it's really hard for me to meet true friends. If you'd let me, I'd like very much to be yours. I'll understand if you don't want to, after what I've put you through, but at least say you forgive me and accept my apologies?" she said, looking at me.

I was shocked when I saw respect and admiration flashing back at me in her eyes. "I-I-I..." I was at a loss for words. Definitely did NOT see that one coming. "Okay," I said, when nothing more came to me.

"Really?" she asked, excited. "Gosh, I'm so relieved! I'm not used to bullying people. I was feeling so guilty for doing it with you! I'm really sorry, Joe," she blurted out, sincerity obvious in her voice.

"That's okay. You splashed me on the road; I dropped

your Gucci in the mud. You pestered me for a whole day; I gave you a brutal speech. We're totally even. How about we have a fresh start? Hi, nice to meet you, I'm Joe Gray," I said, extending my hand to her.

"Hi, Joe! Nice meeting you too! I'm Tiffany, but you can call me Tiff." She beamed happily and shook my hand vigorously.

Seth grinned, relaxing as he watched us shake hands. "Okay, then," he said, standing up and jumping on to his own bed, making Tiffany wobble and lose her balance at the impact on his mattress. "Now that I don't need to intervene in any fights, I can get back to chilling out here. Oops, sorry about that, your highness," he said, joking around with Tiffany and crossing his legs on the bed. That was Seth for you. He was just too sweet to hold a grudge for long.

Tiffany uncrossed her legs to regain her balance and glanced at Seth with a scowl. But then she turned to me, shaking her head and smiling again. "Boys. No manners whatsoever." She tutted at Seth, then remembered something. "I was about to ask you, what are you doing registered in the boys' block, Joe? It was very hard tracking you down here!"

"Oh. It was the school administration. I guess they did it by mistake, because of my name...Yeah, I know, I know, I have a boy's name," I mumbled. "I was a little bugged at first, but now I kind of like it in here. I don't think I would fit in well in the girls' block...I've seen how girls are at this school! One day locked in a room with any of them and I'd have to kill myself!" I said, flapping my arms at the air, making Seth and Tiffany laugh out loud.

"I don't think you have a choice, Joe. They are bound to

find out sooner or later. Co-ed rooms aren't allowed here at Sagan," Seth pointed out.

"Oh. Really?" I said, feeling sad. That was a bummer. I really liked Seth being my roomie.

"I'll see that they do allow it now!" Tiffany said, seeing my mournful face. "I'll have a word with the school secretary, so you don't have to worry about it any more. Then you'll really forgive me for yesterday!"

"Tiffany, you don't need to do this for me to forgive you. I told you, we're even," I said, waving my hand at her.

"I insist. I'll go over there right now! I'll see you around tomorrow, then. Bye Joe!" she said, darting out of the room before I could reply.

I looked at Seth and he shrugged, kicking off his shoes.

"I guess we're officially room-mates now!" he said, reclining lazily on the bed. "They won't dare to contradict her. She owns this school. You'll probably need to get your mom to verbally agree to it, so they won't get sued. Other than that, you're pretty much in the clear now."

I smiled happily. The day sure ended a whole lot differently than yesterday! From hell to heaven. Very different indeed.

Chapter Thirteen

Conversations, Phone Calls and Best Friends

Next day, Tiffany found me early at the breakfast table. She greeted me cheerfully and grabbed a seat in front of me. I was still finding her drastic change of attitude very unsettling. What can I say? I'm a suspicious person.

"Hey, Joey! Is that all right if I call you Joey? I have great news for you!" she said, putting her tray of food down on the table. I shrugged at her, a sort of acceptance to her news and to her nicknaming me so soon. "So, about your illegal co-ed living situation. All is taken care of! The school administration was a little baffled at first, but they agreed after I vehemently 'insisted' on it. Plus, they were stuck in a tight corner, since there aren't any rooms left in the girls' dormitories for you, so they had to agree. They said your mom needs to be told, sign some stuff, though. Is your mom a prude?" she asked, casually munching an apple.

I looked at Tiffany shyly, a little uncomfortable about owing her a favor like this already. "I don't think so ... but I have never had a boy-sleeping-in-the-same-room situation before." My thoughts immediately flashed to Tristan. "So I'm not sure what she's going to say about it."

"Never had a boy wanting to sleep in your room before? That's a hard one to believe, Joey Gray! A feisty girl like you, you must have had dozens of boys lining up at your door, begging for a chance!" She winked at me.

"Yeah, very funny, Tiffany," I mumbled, feeling even more uncomfortable. I kept having this nagging feeling she was somehow still making fun of me, but when I looked at her I saw only playful teasing on her face.

"Please, Joey, call me Tiff. Anyway, you're now officially authorized to stay in the boys' dorm wing. Speaking of which, where's your room-mate? I thought he'd be here with you," she said, looking around.

Oh, so she was expecting to see Seth here, huh? It was my time to mess a little with her, see how she'd react to some playful teasing. "Seth? Last time I saw him he was fighting with the snooze button of his alarm clock. Did *not* want to get out of bed today! Why? Did you want to see him? Does someone have a little crush on a certain blond room-mate of mine?" I wiggled my eyebrows.

She looked at me while trying to sip nonchalantly at her juice-box straw. "No, I don't. Okay, he's sort of cute, but there are plenty of cute guys around here. Look, there goes one passing by right over there. And other one over there. See? Plenty of fish in the seas around here," she said, pointing to some random guys walking near us with bored expressions. None of them looked as good as Seth, though.

"Yeah. Right," I said, getting back to eating my breakfast but not buying her lack of interest for a moment.

"I actually prefer to stay away from relationships here,

you know? I have the same problem with boys as girls; they're all just fake liking me because of my money." She looked down at her tray and tried not to sound upset.

"Well, not only because of your money, give yourself some credit, Tiffany!" I said, teasing again. "They also fake-like you because of your body, your long perfect legs and spectacular blonde hair! Not to mention the boobs! That must've got you some extra fake-likings too, I'll bet."

She stared at me with wide eyes and then cracked up laughing, really loud. "Oh, good God! That was awesome," she said, wiping tears from her eyes. "You're damn right, Joey! Boys can so easily forget about money when there are boobs involved in the scenario! Points to you on that one!"

We chatted more freely after this. Tiffany was actually a lot fun to be around. I felt bad for having stereotyped her before, thinking she was only a stupid blonde bimbo with nothing but air inside her head. I couldn't have been more wrong. Tiffany was witty, funny and very smart. It seemed she had everything in life: money, beauty and brains. And somehow there she was, trying to do her best to please me. That got me puzzled like you wouldn't believe! What was it she had seen in me?

We had a couple of classes together that morning, and whenever she bumped into me in the halls, or at some class-room, she would greet me excitedly, hug me, and chat away like we were old buddies. She was really putting an effort into trying to charm me to be her friend.

The girls in her cheer squad were just lost. They didn't understand why they had to give me hell one day, and then were forbidden to any more. Whenever one girl tried a snarky remark or a mean glance at my way, Tiffany retaliated fiercely. They soon learned that I had immunity now, granted by a Worthington the Third. That got them to back the hell off, fast.

Tiff and I also had lunch together that day. I had never been much good at having girlfriends before, but Tiffany seemed to be my first promising one. Nevertheless, I still acted a little cautious around her. We were finishing our dessert when my phone rang with the *Law and Order* theme song. "Hey, Mom! What's up?" I answered.

"Hi, Joey. It's me, Tristan," he said nervously down the line. "Is it a bad time to call?"

I tensed and tried with all my will not to blush, because Tiffany was right in front of me, finishing her chocolate mousse. I didn't realize how much I'd missed his deep voice until that moment. "Hey! No, it's not a bad time, I can talk!" I squeaked, and mentally cursed myself. "How are things going?" I tried again in a more serious voice.

"Oh, everything's fine here. Your mom taught me how to use her cell phone and gave me your number! And it worked!" he said, obviously thrilled.

"That's great! It's really easy, and you're a fast learner!" I said, trying to stifle a laugh with my hand over my mouth. He was so cute trying to learn modernity!

"Thanks," he said, his voice filled with pride. "How's school going?"

"Well, I had kind of a bumpy start, but now everything is really good!" I glanced at Tiffany sitting the other side of the table. She smiled a little weakly and fumbled nervously with her hands. She knew the bumpy start had been caused by her.

"Bumpy start, huh? That sounds like a story," he said in an amused tone.

"It is. I'll tell you all about it when you get here. When are you coming anyway?"

"Your mom is trying to get everything set so we can come up this Saturday, for your birthday. I didn't know you'd be turning eighteen this Saturday! Why didn't you tell me?"

"Yeah, It's no big deal," I said sincerely. In fact, I kind of hated celebrating my birthdays. I was hoping Mom had forgotten all about it and I'd have some peace and quiet this year. Apparently not.

"Well, your mom doesn't seem to think that way. We went out today to get your birthday present!" he said happily.

"Oh dear. She's making you do a whole lot of shopping this week, isn't she? I'm really sorry about that. Just hang in there and it'll be over soon!" I said over-dramatically. I did hate shopping. It was such a huge waste of time!

I heard his sexy chuckle. Boy, did I miss that laugh.

"It's no problem. I've been talking a lot with your mom these days. She's really swel- hum, a-awesome?" he said, correcting himself in time.

"Yes, she is awesome. You two have been talking a lot, huh? About what, may I ask?" I was instantly filled with curiosity. What could they possibly be talking about so much? God, please don't let it be about tales of my awkward childhood! I'd die of embarrassment! I felt my cheeks burning bright red at the thought.

"You know, things . . . life, the past, the future," he mumbled. Jeez. Vague, much?

There was an awkward pause. Tristan coughed uncomfortably down the line.

"So . . . I guess I'll see you on Saturday?" he said, breaking the silence.

"Yeah, see you then," I said, feeling heat rising up my neck at the thought of seeing him again.

"Okay, then. Bye, Joey."

"Bye, Tris," I said, and hung up.

I was about to sigh loudly when I remembered Tiffany was right there, watching me intently, so I just cleared my throat awkwardly and picked up my tray to clear the table. She cocked an eyebrow at me, following my moves.

"So, boyfriend calling?" she asked with curiosity.

I tried to regain control of my emotions. Tristan always had the power to completely push me out of my tracks. "No, it's just my . . . half-brother," I said, testing the brother lie out loud for the first time. It sounded weird. And wrong. Then I shook the thought away. It's not like he was really my brother! But I could already foresee this lie was going to bring me a lot of headaches in the future . . .

I said goodbye to Tiffany shortly after that and headed off to my next lesson. Once afternoon classes were finished, I decided to go to my room and try to get started on some of my heavy load of homework.

As I walked into the room, Seth was sitting on his bed, a guitar case resting by his side on and yet another pile of papers scattered around him. That boy could not live without scattering piles of paper! I greeted him while walking to my bed and dumping my backpack on the floor.

"It looks like you've had a better day today," he greeted in return.

"Yes. I'm as surprised as you are!" I laughed, reaching into my backpack to haul out my books. "Can you believe Tiffany was serious about being friends with me? I actually had a great time with her at lunch! Maybe I should give her a chance . . . what do you think?"

"Well, I don't know, maybe she was really being honest yesterday. It's up to you, Joe." Seth began throwing his papers inside his backpack. He seemed in a hurry. "I don't know if it counts for anything, but I have never seen her bullying people here before. She does walk around like she owns the place, but I guess she does in fact own the place, so it's an honest attitude on her part."

I was about to reply when a boy barged into the room without knocking. He looked calmly at Seth, a guitar case looped over his shoulder. He had a skater/surfer look about him, but his most noticeable feature was the wildest, deepest, darkest crimson hair I have ever seen. The contrast with his pale skin made his eyes really stand out with their vibrant green color. He was a little shorter and thinner than Seth, and had a small silver lip ring. And he was incredibly beautiful. No one should be allowed to be that beautiful.

Seth turned towards the door and greeted Skater Boy excitedly. "Hey! It's about damn time, Harry! I've been waiting for you guys for ever in here. Wait. Where's Josh? Why isn't he with you?"

"I dunno, man. You know Josh, always disappearing, doing 'Joshy things'. Sammy is already at the rehearsal room waiting for us," Harry answered quietly. Then he noticed me for the first time and immediately tensed, averting his eyes. "Hey, Seth, man, there's a chick in your room," he mumbled shyly.

Seth continued to stuff the last remains of his papers into his bag. "Yeah, that would be Joe Gray. I've told you about her, remember? She'll be my room-mate for the rest of the year, so please do try to knock before entering our room from now on, dude. Joe Gray, this is Harry Ledger. Bass player and most awesome friend," he introduced, grabbing a quick cool handshake with Harry.

Harry looked at me shyly and nodded a short greeting. "Hey, Joe."

"Hello, Harry," I replied, leaning back against my headboard and waiting for him to stick to the expected script about my name...It never came. Harry just stuffed his hands inside his baggy shorts pockets and waited patiently for Seth to be ready to leave.

I was stunned. That was a first. No, really, that was *the first time* someone had been introduced to me without the *"But Joe's a boy's name"* line coming up. The. First. Time. Ever.

I guess Tristan hadn't *exactly* mentioned it the first time we'd met, but I knew he'd been thinking it and restraining himself from asking because I was daring him to say anything about it. Harry seemed like he didn't care at all; that he wasn't even masking the thought.

Harry must have noticed me gawking at him, because he started to shuffle his feet uncomfortably, anxious to get out of the room. He looked incredibly shy. Which was really strange. Beautiful boys like him were usually full of themselves, all smirks, winks and cocky replies. Harry, apparently, was nothing like that.

Seth finally finished his packing and grabbed his guitar case, throwing it over his shoulder, and headed for the door with a relieved Harry tagging behind. "So, Joe, we'll be at rehearsals! See ya later, okay? Come on, Harry, we'll wait for Josh there. I have a surprise song to show you guys. You won't believe how good it is!" He winked at me before closing the door.

I smiled to the room, enjoying how excited Seth was

about his new song. I hoped he'd let me hear him playing it some time. I decided now was a good time to take a bath, since I had the whole room to myself.

I took out my special tangerine shampoo for "happy occasions" only, and hurried to the bathroom. When I was done with my bath I walked out all cleaned up, properly perfumed, fully groomed, hair all nicely combed, and dressed in my black sweat pants and black tank-top.

I came to a sudden halt when I saw that another boy was sitting on Seth's bed, with his back to me. He had really large shoulders and was thumping on his legs with two drumsticks. He turned to look at me when he heard me coming out of the bathroom.

"Hey, Seth, man, I've been waiting here for ev— Oh. Hi. Hello. You're not Seth," he said abruptly, a puzzled look on his face.

The lightest, bluest eyes stared back at me from a handsome, thin face complemented by thin lips. His hair was really short and as black as mine, almost shaved at the sides but a little longer at the top, where he was sporting a small mohawk.

"Hey, you must be Josh. I'm Joe, Seth's new roommate," I said, offering my hand to him.

He shook it, smiling kindly. "You have the name of a boy, but you sure don't look like one!"

I smiled back at him. There it was. A variation of the traditional script, right on cue. It really was only Harry, then.

"They left for rehearsal a while ago. I heard Seth asking about you. He has a new song to show you guys. You should probably hurry, he must be anxious waiting for you." I threw myself on to my bed and grabbed a book.

"Yeah, right," he said, standing up.

Whoa! He was tall. And had really broad shoulders and a strong chest, but a lean build. Seth didn't need to worry about playing good songs – not with everyone in the band looking like they did. He could try opening a modeling agency, in fact.

"Nice meeting you, Joe! If Seth starts annoying you too much, just let me know and I'll take care of him for you!" Josh gave me a warm smile and a tiny wink, then he left the room in a hurry.

I spent the rest of the afternoon doing my homework as planned. After dinner I tried to wait up for Seth, reading a book in bed. I was really curious to hear the band's comments on the new song, but sleep overwhelmed me and I didn't even hear Seth sneak back into the room late that night.

Chapter Fourteen

Birthday Present

Thursday started pretty uneventfully.

I got up early and went to grab some breakfast on my own, leaving Seth still sleeping. Tiffany arrived fifteen minutes later, chatted with some friends and again headed to my table with her tray of food, to join me for breakfast. I noticed that this got me some weird looks from people around us. It was two days in a row that Tiffany had joined me for meals. People were starting to notice me, the weird-looking tomboy girl that captured Tiffany's attention.

I felt a little awkward about the spotlight being on me, but I kept on munching my breakfast and trying to hide from all those prying eyes. We talked a little – well, Tiffany did most of the talking; I wasn't much of a talker in the mornings – and then we parted ways to head for our classrooms.

I remembered that I needed some books from my locker, so I made a small detour to grab them first. On the way to the lockers, I started to pick up a few threads of conversation passing by me. At first I didn't connect the dots, but soon I began to understand that all the whispers, hushed murmurs and side glances were directed at me.

"I heard she stood up to Professor…"

"…a boy's name, that's her over there…"

"The cheerleader squad are scared of her, nobody knows why…"

"She even stood up to Tiffany! She must be crazy…"

"…and they are best friends now? What's the catch?"

"Who is she anyway?"

That last comment was made by a group of jocks to their captain, Bradley Finn. Seth had pointed Bradley out to me the other day, warning me to stay clear of him. Apparently, there had been a fight between them last year and Seth had left the basketball team. It was the first time I'd seen Seth so disgruntled about something. Bradley was a living, breathing jock stereotype: the school basketball team captain, big, dumb, massively loud, rude, pretentious and very conceited. Every quality I despised in a person. I had seen him walking round the halls before, but now Bradley had turned his face in my direction and was studying me with deep interest. I tilted my head down and continued walking to my locker, trying to draw the minimal amount of attention to myself, but people kept pointing and whispering at me all the time. I realized I was getting quite a name for myself. Fantastic. Not even one full week at school and I was already the crazy, deranged new girl. Just great!

I hurried to my locker and grabbed my books as fast as I could. The buzzing around me was starting to make me feel really uncomfortable. As I closed the locker door with a bang and turned to leave, a big heavy chest stopped me mid-turn. I stumbled backwards, startled, slamming loudly into my locker. When I looked up, I saw the smug, square-jawed face of Bradley staring down at me.

"So, you're the new girl everybody is talking about! I

don't see what all the fuss is about. What's your name, new girl?" He dragged his big hands through his short, sandy hair and smirked unpleasantly.

I regained my balance and puffed out my chest, trying to impose myself a little. Bradley didn't seem impressed. "I'm Joe. Joe Gray," I said quietly. I should keep it cool now. I didn't need any more fights in this school.

"Hah. That's fucking hilarious! What's your mom's problem, giving you a boy's name like that!" he barked in a mocking tone.

I squinted my eyes at him, starting to feel my blood boiling. "Your mom's half responsible for your pea-sized brain, but you don't see me asking what's her problem, do you?" I snapped. So much for keeping it cool.

His brow creased with the effort of thinking. "Are ya calling me stupid?" he barked again. He looked angry now, rather than amused.

"You know, the fact that you even need to ask that really answers your own question, dontcha think?" I said, crossing my arms defiantly with my books against my chest.

Bradley leaned really close to me, forcing me to step back and bump against the locker door again. I mentally cursed myself: stepping back would give him the impression I was scared. Definitely not a good move in a fight-for-power-position. He extended both arms either side of me, blocking my escape.

"This pea-brain here is going to give you a lesson, though. It's not very smart to piss off the most popular guy at this school!" he said menacingly.

I stared at him with my jaw clenched tight. He did not know who he was messing with. I had my martial arts belts to prove him wrong! "You back the hell off, or I'll make you regret it," I warned with a growl. I shifted my legs, giving myself enough balance to stand on one foot, while preparing a *kick in the nuts* routine. It wasn't an approved manoeuver, technically speaking, but with a guy his size I needed to fight dirty to have some starting advantage.

But before I could do anything, a hand grabbed Bradley's shoulders and pushed him away from me, hard, making him stumble backwards, almost falling on his ass. I was as surprised as he was.

Bradley regained his balance at the last second and stood up straight, turning to look at a furious Harry in front of him. Harry had his arms firmly at his sides, fists clenched tight. He looked really angry, but when he spoke his voice was low and calm. His hands betrayed the cracks in his calm façade, though. "I think it's time for you to leave, Bradley," Harry said.

Bradley wasn't happy about being pushed around roughly like that. "Yeah? Who's gonna make me? You, little rocker boy?" he barked. Bradley barked a lot. He reminded me of a pit-bull.

"Yes, the little rocker boy and I," said Josh stepping up to Harry's side.

Josh wasn't as *little* as Harry. He had an impressive height, although Bradley was broader and bigger in the muscles department. But apparently Josh's threat was enough for Bradley to reconsider his next move. Bradley glanced quickly around and noticed the absence of his buddies, the basketball team he always had by his side for backup. Now he was alone. And outnumbered. So he did what was expected of conceited cowards. He backed off.

"Fine. She's all yours! Have fun with the tomboy there!

She's not even worth the aggravation!" he said, walking away with a sneer on his face.

Harry approached me and kneeled down to pick up a book I'd dropped, handing it cautiously to me. "Are you okay?" he asked in the same calm voice of minutes before, but now all the anger was gone there was a hint of softness to it.

"Yeah. I'm fine. Thanks, Harry," I said, taking my book back. "I'm sorry to get you guys into trouble. He's going to want to get his own back on you two later."

Harry smiled softly and shrugged his shoulders, with an expression that said he couldn't care less about Bradley's retaliation.

"Don't worry about it," Josh added. "We'll walk you to your class. Where are you headed?".

"It's…this way. It's not really necessary, guys! I can take care of myself," I insisted as they walked by my side through the hallway.

They weren't buying it, though. Why would they? All they had seen was a scared little girl being hustled by a huge bully. One minute later they would have seen a little girl kicking the bully hard in the nuts, though. I was a little annoyed at them thinking I was that helpless. But they meant well and were just trying to protect me, so I let them tag along.

"So, Joe, Seth showed us his new song," Josh commented casually.

I was happy with the change of conversation. "Yeah? What did you guys think of it?"

"It was pretty good." Josh smiled.

"Very, *very* good," Harry added from the other side of me.

"Good! Seth was very excited about it. He must be happy that you guys approved. He said you two are a bit picky in the lyrics department."

"We're not picky! We just like songs that don't suck, that's all!" Harry laughed. "And that one definitely did not suck. Thanks, Joe."

Crap. They knew I'd had my hands on the song? But I tried to play dumb anyway. "Thanks for what? It's Seth's song."

They both laughed at the same time.

"Yeah, yeah, right. We know there's a little Seth in it, but we suspect you must have helped quite a lot!" Harry said, glancing sideways at me.

"Well, I just pointed out some little things. It is Seth's song!" I repeated firmly.

"Okay. Whatever you say, Joe." Josh smirked.

We arrived at my classroom door then.

"Here you are, safe and sound. Thanks for pointing out those 'little things' for the song! We appreciated it," Josh said, patting me lightly on my shoulder.

"Sure, no problem. Thanks again for escorting me here. You really didn't have to. I'll see you guys around." I smiled and stepped into my classroom.

Josh waved me goodbye and Harry nodded slightly, with his face a little down, avoiding direct eye contact. He had a little smile at the corner of his mouth. He was so adorably shy! I entered the classroom, smiling happily. I was really glad they liked the song.

The rest of the day passed by fairly fast. I shared some classes with Tiffany, a few with Seth and Josh together, and one with Harry. They always greeted me happily and arranged to sit in a chair next to mine. Which attracted a few more envious stares from other girls. It turned out I was gathering quite an awesome group of friends in this school! The only thing that could possibly top that would be Tristan's arrival on Saturday.

And with that thought in mind, I drifted into a haze throughout all my classes on Friday. I was so anxious about Saturday that I didn't pay attention to anything else. In the afternoon, some guy from school maintenance went to our room to fix the broken bed next to the wall, and at night Mom called to let me know she was coming at midday tomorrow. Then Saturday finally arrived! (Oh joy!) I was so anxious I woke up really early, even though I didn't have to. I stared at the ceiling for like a hundred hours, until I gave up and got out of bed, deciding it was best to get ready and wait outside the school.

It was a pleasant day, a bit windy, but not too cold. The school had a huge campus with landscaped gardens, small fountains, big lawns and lots of beautiful trees everywhere.

At some point, I'd found this really private place on campus, with an amazing, impressive oak tree set alone in the middle of it. It seemed like a lovely spot to spend some time. I explored more of the grounds the whole morning, and just before lunch I bumped into Tiffany right outside the cafeteria.

We had lunch together and I told her my mom and half-brother would be arriving shortly. She clapped her hands, excited by the news. Tiffany was always in a cheerful, over-excited mood. It was hard to feel gloomy around her; she radiated joy and positive vibrations like the surface of the sun.

She waited with me by the front doors, the same place I'd dropped her Gucci bag on my first day at school. She was sitting on the small brick wall by the side of the steps, legs crossed sexily, and I was standing at her side, staring fixedly at the road, waiting for any signs of my mom's car on the horizon. I tried to act relaxed, but inside I was squirming with anxiety. In fact, I was more than squirming; I was raging with nervousness.

Tiffany chatted excitedly, her hair bouncing wildly in the strong wind, oblivious to my jittery nerves and shaky mood. "So, tell me, Joey, is your brother as feisty as you are? Should I be putting my Gucci bags away? I can't have mud on any of my babies again, you know!" she teased.

"Well, you'll see for yourself soon enough, Tiff," I said, giving her a vague answer. But before Tiffany could come up with another question, my mom's car appeared at the bend of the road. "Here they are!" I said, beaming happily and pointing at the approaching car.

My mother's car stopped a few feet away from us, and I walked slowly towards it. Suddenly the level of anxiety multiplied a hundred times over, making my palms sweaty and my heart pound fast. I saw Tristan looking up at the school from inside the car. The thought of talking to him again made me feel so nervous, I was almost sick to my stomach. I didn't have time to think about anything else, because Tristan opened the passenger door and stepped slowly outside, carrying a small backpack over his shoulders.

He was wearing black jeans, not too tight, not too loose, and a dark green T-shirt that made his eye color turn into a deep shade of green too. I thought nothing could ever top that ocean blue shirt I'd seen him in over a week ago, but boy was I wrong! Deep green definitely suited him. He had a black beaded wristband on his forearm. His black hair was all untidy because of the wind, which worked nicely in his favor. I knew he didn't like messy hair, but it looked so good on him that I had to mentally thank the Gods of Wind around us.

Tristan turned in my direction and gave me that bright, open, warm smile of his. It made my legs a little wobbly. Without even realizing what I was doing, I closed the few steps between us, running to hug him so tightly that I even heard a light "Oof!" from him. I wasn't thinking straight. I just wanted him close to me. It was such an overwhelming urge; it took over my entire body and mind. Never in my life had I had acted like this before! Never had I allowed myself to feel such uncontrollable emotions. Was it the bonds of the spell forcing me to act this way? Making my brain go all crazy, fuzzy and inadequate?

I felt Tristan tense in surprise under my hug, and the moment we touched this vibrant jolt of electricity passed through my entire body. It was like a heavy discharge of accumulated energy residue. So it really was the spell affecting my actions, I thought. It was forcing the need for close contact, to unload whatever it was we had been charging up all week long when we'd been apart.

I let go of him quickly, startled by that weird reaction. I think he also felt it because his eyes were wide and he was clearly in some sort of shock. Before we could gather our wits and say anything, we heard Mom yelling from the other side of the car. "How about me? Don't I get a hug too?" she asked happily.

I ran round to my mom, overflowing with joy, and gave her a crushing embrace as well. I had really missed her! I glanced sideways at Tristan, waiting at the other side of the car while I wrapped my arms around her. He was watching us with a slightly puzzled expression.

Tristan remained a little distant from me while we unpacked the car. I think he was a little freaked out with what had just happened a few seconds ago. Once we'd finished unloading, we walked to the school steps, where Tiffany was waiting for us.

"Hey, Mom, Tristan, this is my friend Tiffany," I introduced.

"So nice to meet you, Mama Gray! And...Tristan." Tiffany looked at Tristan with raised eyebrows, clearly very impressed with what she was seeing. Who wouldn't be? He looked amazing. Damn him!

He nodded his head politely, taking one of Tiffany's hands in his and kissing it lightly. "It's a pleasure to meet you, miss."

Tiffany froze with her hand in his, staring at him in surprise. She thought he was making fun of her, but he had such a serious straight face on. I decided to intervene before Tiffany became suspicious.

"Don't mind him, Tiff. Tristan, stop it! Always goofing around, that brother of mine!" I said, waving his hand away from hers and nudging him in the side.

Mom gave a nervous little laugh, and tried dispersing the awkwardness by changing the subject. "So, let's get these bags inside, shall we? I called the secretary yesterday and they gave me his dorm room number, so we need to get him settled in now. We'll see you later, Tiffany," Mom said in one rushed breath.

Tiffany smiled, a little confused, and nodded. "Of course. I'll catch up with you guys later, then!" She waved us goodbye and jogged up the steps ahead of us.

We all entered the school through the massive front doors, and only when I saw Tiffany disappearing round the corner was I able to breathe properly in relief. "Tristan, try not to do *that* again, will you? That's not how kids greet each other nowadays!" I said, walking by his side.

He frowned, not understanding what he'd done wrong back there. "How do people greet each other now?" he asked, bewildered.

"You know…just say 'Hi'. Some people don't even do that," I muttered.

"Well, that's just rude," he stated, frowning, and then he stopped at an intersection, looking around in bewilderment. "This place is huge! What did you say my dorm number was, Mrs. Gray?"

"Oh, I wrote it on this note," my mother said, fumbling with the piece of paper as she added in an urgent whisper, "But Tristan, you should call me Mom here, remember? Ah, here it is," she said more loudly. "It's Room 101, Block B, on the second floor. The secretary told me I needed to sign some consent papers first…and she said they were sorry for the mix-up. I didn't quite get what she meant, but I'll sort out whatever it is now that I'm here."

I glanced at her nervously. Gosh. Room 101-B.

"Yeah, about that, Mom. Room 101 B is my room too," I said, watching her reaction.

"Oh, goodie, they have co-ed dorms here! What luck, huh? Now you can share a room together and look after each other! So, show us the way, Joey! Come on! These bags are really heavy!" she said, huffing and looking ahead at the hallways.

"Huh…So, okay, follow me. This way," I said, gesturing ahead. I decided to tell her later that it wasn't a co-ed dorm room. If she wasn't making a big deal about it, I sure as hell wasn't going to, either!

We walked straight to the east wing, and up the staircase to the second floor. I knocked softly on the door before entering our room, Tristan and my mom following behind.

Seth was on his bed, leaning against the headboard as usual, legs casually crossed, reading a book. I walked in and introduced my mom, and then Tristan as my brother and our third room-mate for the year.

Seth stood up and greeted my mom, and then held out a hand to Tristan, who looked smugly at me, silently saying, "See? People do still shake hands, at least." He shook Seth's hand firmly.

Seth watched Tristan stow his bags in the room with a cautious side-glance. I noticed Seth was feeling intimidated by Tristan's confident stance. Tristan did have an impressive presence. My mom was busy inspecting the room, the wardrobes, window views and bathroom, so I just sat on my bed and let her roam around. Then I thought it would be a good thing to leave the boys alone for a while, and asked my mom if she'd like a tour of the school grounds. She agreed happily and was ready to leave in a heartbeat.

"You get settled, Tristan. Unpack your things and I'll give you a tour tomorrow, all right? We'll be right back," I said, waving him goodbye. He nodded calmly, sitting on his bed at the other side of the room.

As I closed the door I saw him looking at Seth with a strange expression.

While I showed my mom around, I tried to explain the co-ed dorm situation. At first she looked deeply disgruntled, but then I pointed out that she'd been quite okay with it just a few minutes ago, and that she had no reason to be upset about it now. And then I reassured her that Seth was a really cool, decent, respectful guy, and so was Tristan, so she had nothing to worry about. After a few minutes of intense persuasion, she agreed to sign the consent form in the admin office. I was mentally jumping up and down with joy. I couldn't let her see how thrilled I actually was that she'd let me stay with the boys! It was too good to be true!

When we got back to the room, we found Tristan and Seth getting along just great. They were laughing happily about something, but as soon we stepped inside, they turned it down, and changed the subject fast. Seth's initial distrust and intimidation were completely gone from his eyes now.

My mom soon started asking a bunch of "casual" questions to Seth, then, which could have been interpreted as mild curiosity, but I knew damn well that she was in fact giving him a light interrogation because of the room-mate deal. He didn't seem to notice it, though, thank the gods! After a while Mom seemed satisfied with Seth's "debriefing" and quit with all the weird questions. Then she jumped up, smacking her forehead loudly.

"Tristan, I was almost forgetting! Please, get Joey's birthday present! I want to see if she likes it!" she said in excitement.

Tristan smiled and grabbed a white box from inside his suitcase, handing it swiftly to my mother.

She thrust the box into my hands, bursting with good cheer. "Happy birthday, munchkin!" she said with a wide grin.

Seth raised his eyebrows, and gave a yell of complaint. "Hey! I didn't know today was your birthday!"

I took the box from my mom, thanking her with an eye roll. "Yeah, sorry about that, Seth. I just don't like celebrating my birthday, is all. It's no big deal."

"She never lets me buy a cake, or call her friends, or

throw a party!" Mom whined at my side. "I have to put my foot down on the presents, though. If it was up to her she'd let the day pass by like it was any other normal day!"

"It is a normal day, Mother! What's so special about birthdays anyway? So I was born this day, eighteen years ago. Do we have to keep remembering this for the rest of our lives? And the celebration? What is that for? Congratulations, you've managed to live for yet another year. That's just ridiculous!" I said, exasperated. They all laughed at my pouting face.

"All right, dear. We understand you don't celebrate birthdays. But this one is special! It's your eighteenth birthday! Would you open your present already?" Mom said, patting me condescendingly on the shoulder.

I huffed, annoyed, and put the box onto my bed, lifting the top lid off. I took this beautiful dark-red dress out. It was such an amazing dress! I stroked my hands over the soft silky fabric. It looked expensive. I couldn't picture myself in that dress. It was too much for me. The dress was just so elegant, and extraordinary. And I was just so...plain me.

"Gosh, thanks, Mom. It's beautiful!" I said sincerely. She didn't need to know that I would never have the courage to wear it.

"Isn't it? When I saw it, I just had to buy it for you!" she said, radiating happiness.

I nodded and folded the dress carefully back into the box, then put it in my closet.

My mom left at sundown, asking me to call her whenever I could, and to promise that I'd visit at weekends.

Tristan, Seth and I had dinner together that night, and Tiffany joined us at the table in the middle of the meal. She kept looking from Seth to Tristan with curious glances. I tried to take a peek in her eyes, but as I'd already noticed, she was really good at hiding her emotions. I couldn't decipher what she was feeling. I was so used to getting instant feedback just by looking into people's eyes, that when I couldn't with Tiffany I felt a little annoyed.

We talked for a long time at the dinner table, and Seth insisted on buying me a chocolate cupcake to celebrate the day while Tiffany had a fit over me not telling her today was my birthday. I forbade them to sing any birthday songs, and glared at them quite evilly so that they saw I was dead serious about it. It was really late when we all called it a night.

Our room felt warm and cozy as we snuggled inside, the wind rattling outside the window. My heart was still beating erratically because Tristan was now here, and in the same room, with me. He was going to be my room-mate! How awesome was that?

I was getting ready to go to bed when Tristan stood up from his bed, like he had just remembered something. He fumbled quickly in his suitcase and came over to sit next to me, holding something in his hand. A few butterflies rose softly inside me when his arm brushed past mine.

"I meant to give you this for your birthday. It's just a small token, but I hope you like it. Happy birthday, Joey," he said, handing me a strip of paper.

I looked at it in surprise. It was one of those instant-photography-booth strips of snapshots, with Tristan making all sorts of faces to the camera. There were sexy ones, funny ones, weird-looking ones, one with his profile (I guess he was looking at something outside), one with him pointing smugly at the lens . . . And my favorite of them all, one of him simply looking intently at the camera, a tiny, practically imperceptible smile at the right corner of his perfect lips, and his eyes slightly crinkled with the smile that threatened to break through. He looked so happy! So full of life. So...perfect.

I was speechless. It was the most perfect gift. The best I have ever received. I turned it over and was further surprised to see a note on the back of the strip, in neat handwriting:

Life is indeed full of possibilities.
Thank you for showing that to me.
You're the most amazing possibility that has ever happened to me.
Happy Birthday!
T.

"I thought you might like it, since you have this tradition of giving presents in the form of photographs of happy moments," he said, smiling as he stood at my side.

I turned my face to him, trying to stop my watery eyes from spilling over. He was looking at me intently, watching my reaction to his gift. I tried to speak, and my voice came out quivering. "Thank you, Tris. It's...perfect." And I gave him another hug. This time he didn't tense up but hugged me back. I felt the tingling again, but a little fainter than last time.

Seth came out of the bathroom at that moment, and we ended our hug quickly, before we could draw too much attention to ourselves. Tristan stood up and went to his bed. "Good night, Joey. Sleep tight," he said quietly.

Before I went to bed, I put Tristan's gift safely inside my closet, hidden neatly under my new red dress. Then I snuggled beneath my soft covers and turned the light off my night-stand lamp.

This had turned out to be the best birthday I had ever had.

Chapter Fifteen

Charming Ways

That first night after Tristan's arrival at the school, I had the strangest dream.

I was at this circle-shaped plaza filled with people. But there was a kind of grayish, foggy look about everything and everybody, like we were all in a ghost town.

I looked down at myself and saw that I stood out from everything else. I was sharply defined, with vibrant, vivid colors emanating from my skin and my clothes. I felt like an intruder in this place, like I didn't belong there. I glanced up and saw this eerie, cloaked figure standing a little away from me. It looked like a man, because of his posture and size, but I couldn't tell for sure. He also looked different from everybody else. Although he didn't have vibrant colors, like me, and had only this long, light gray cloak covering himself, he was similarly defined, even more sharp-edged than I. He looked intensely solid, a massive presence in that hazy place.

And he was looking straight at me. He started moving slowly towards me, but his movements seemed strange, alien, like someone not used to walking. He kind of floated in my direction.

His cloak hood was down, so when he got close enough, I was able to see his face. I wish I hadn't, though. It was the scariest thing I have ever seen. A blank, expressionless, dead face stared back at me, with black holes instead of eyes. It didn't look human. I didn't know what the hell that thing was, but I was sure I didn't want to stick around to find out. I was so terrified, I couldn't move or scream or do anything, only watch that scary, horrible creature getting closer and closer to me. He stopped a few feet from me, those black holes in his face boring into my eyes.

When he spoke, his voice was low and soft, like a whisper. I was expecting something hoarse and gritty, something really scary, but his voice was nothing but cool and calm, almost soothing.

"I found you," he stated.

It wasn't a question, merely an observation. And I realized he wasn't opening his mouth to speak, either. His voice simply sounded inside my head, without the need for vocalization. I was so freaked out, I could barely stand still without trembling. He tilted his head to the side, slowly, making me think of a bird of prey.

"But I cannot find it," he whispered, again just stating his facts. "Where is it? Where is the anomaly?" He straightened upright, waiting for me to answer.

"I-I-I don't know," I managed to mumble after a few moments of uncomfortable silence.

"It is hidden, guarded from me. I must find it and fix it. Where is it?" He repeated his question.

He wasn't making any sense. "I don't know what you are talking about," I blurted out in sheer panic.

He tilted his head the other way and frowned. It was the first time I saw some sort of expression on his face. "It is no use hiding it from me. I'll find it, no matter what. It is only a matter of time," he said, taking a step closer to me. "You also have a way to guard yourself from me," he continued. "At least in the physical world. That is an inconvenience. At the moment I can only summon you when you are in a sub-conscious state," he said, still taking another step. He was really close now. Scarily close. "And I know you two are linked, bonded. But I have found *you*. You must tell me its location. It is my job to fix it. This cannot go any further."

He held out his hand to me. I tried to run, but my feet were stuck, like an old tree rooted to the ground. Why couldn't I move?

This was only a nightmare. A horrible nightmare. I just needed to wake up!

His hands were almost upon me and I recoiled, terrified. The last thing I saw was his long, sharp fingers reaching out to me, his pale face coming in my direction, black hol-lowed eyes narrowing in eagerness. I shut my eyes hard and I heard his whispered, surprised voice inside my head. "No!" And then I woke up in my room, panting heavily and terrified out of my mind.

It took me several minutes to get my breathing back to normal. Another several minutes to gather my wits. I ago-nized for a long time in bed, debating whether to wake up Tristan, but after a while I realized I was just being stupid. I wasn't going to disturb him because of a silly nightmare! What was I? Five years old? He would think I was a stupid little girl! After some time trying to settle down, I managed to drift back into a restless sleep.

The next day I woke up really tired. Seth had left early to meet Sam. They were going to work on some new lyrics.

I was curious about Sam; he was the only member of the band I hadn't yet met. But I was so tired and in such a sour mood that I thought it best to meet him some other time. I got myself washed and dressed, but without much energy.

Tristan, who was already dressed, noticed my weariness and asked what was wrong. I sat on my bed and told him about my weird silly nightmare. He listened in silence, fumbling with his black beaded wristband. When I finished my dream tale, he remained silent for a long time in a thoughtful mood.

"This cloaked thing in your dream, did he really say *'It is guarded from me'*?" Tristan asked at last, seated on his bed across from mine, finally risking a comment.

"Yeah, I think it was something like that. Why? It was just a weird dream. A stupid nightmare," I said, trying to look at his eyes, but he kept his face down, staring at his wristband.

"Yes. It could be. But analyzing your dream, it seems this person might be looking only for me. You were dragged into the middle of all this because of me, because of bringing me back, and our bond. I put you in this situation," Tristan said in a really worried voice.

"Tris, come on. Stop blaming yourself. You didn't plan for any of this to happen. You didn't know. And for all we know, maybe this is just a dream, a nightmare, nothing more!" I said, trying to reassure him everything was going to be all right.

"Miss Violet came by your house every day last week to check on me. Before I left, on my last day, she gave me this." He showed me his beaded wristband. "She said to keep it on me at all times. It's some sort of amulet. She said it would 'keep me guarded'. Strange choice of words, huh? The same as in your dream...Maybe I should give it to you – to ward off your bad dreams..." He made a move to remove the band but I stopped him.

"No, she meant for you to have it, but maybe we can ask Miss Violet for another one, then we'll be both guarded from whatever the hell that thing was, and it won't be able to find us. Problem solved. Plus, it looks really cool on you! You should definitely keep it on, it's very trendy!" I said, smiling at him.

"Yeah. I suppose so." He smiled weakly.

"Come on, let's not worry about things we can do nothing about. And I promised you a tour of the school today, so let's shake a leg!" I said, standing up and getting ready to leave the room.

He followed me, still in a thoughtful mood, but after a while we completely forgot about the dream and ended up having a pleasant day, talking and walking lazily around the school grounds on a warm Sunday afternoon.

At first, I thought Tristan would have difficulties fitting in at a new school. After all, it had been decades since he'd spent time with kids his own age. I also thought that it would be hard to disguise his antiquated manners and speech. I thought people would think he was some sort of weirdo, or just plain crazy.

At least my mom had taken care of his clothes; that was a relief. She'd always had amazing fashion sense, so his clothes were quite modern. That was one thing that I didn't need to worry about.

But what about the handshaking and old-fashioned courtesy – the pulling out chairs for girls, the over-polite manners and general weird ways? How could I explain all those things? I thought it would be only a matter of time before someone discovered his secret.

By secret I meant Tristan being from the Fifties. The other secret, about him not really being my half-brother, was another thing that was constantly in the back of my mind, worrying me.

I was really anxious about Monday, his first day of classes. It was going to be a disaster, I thought. But on Sunday, during our afternoon walk around the school grounds, I started noticing that Tristan seemed to have changed. He was *different*.

That first week when I'd met him as a ghost, he'd been constantly on his guard, trying to cover up his "condition". He'd had this armor around himself that he used to control his emotions, and keep me from getting too close. He'd been evasive and mysterious. A puzzle wrapped in an enigma.

The second week, as a living boy, he'd been engulfed in a tidal wave of emotions. He'd ranged between surprise and insecurity, wonder and excitement, worry, fear and happiness. He had been thrown into a whole new world full of alien, modern things he didn't understand, drowning in new information. He'd tried to absorb all he could master in one single gulp, but I could see how overwhelmed by everything he really was.

And then there was the Tristan after a week of adjustment. The Tristan I was seeing now, walking by my side on his first day at school. And he *looked* adjusted, believe you me! He looked different, yet at the same time, it was like he was showing his true self for the first time – as if he hadn't really changed, but was just really himself now. This was who he was supposed to have been all along.

The Tristan I saw now was assertive, relaxed, calm and filled with confidence. He wasn't looking for approval from anyone; he wasn't worried what people might think of him. He'd had many years to reflect and ponder about the important things in life, and what truly mattered, and that insight showed in his stance. This self-assurance and maturity radiated from him, showing itself in the way he acted, talked, even looked at other people.

All of these things could have been quite intimidating, if it weren't for the fact that he was also amazingly charismatic. It was like he had a unique magic. Maybe it was another special talent, like his ability to fade into the background. He had this unbelievable charm pulsing like a radioactive wave out of him, and people could not help but be affected by it.

I noticed the full effect of this during our first complete day together on Monday. People milled around him like moths to a very bright, charming, flame. He was just really, really, likeable. People even thought his polite manners were endearing and oddly cool, can you believe that? And I'd been so worried about covering that up! Then, after a couple more days, people started to want to be near him, to talk to him; they wanted his approval, they wanted so badly to impress him by being the best they could around him. Normally it was only for a few minutes, and when he was gone they returned to their usual flawed ways. But for those brief minutes near Tristan, they actually acted like decent, admirable human beings. It was the most amazing thing to watch!

Even Bradley had fallen for Tristan's charm. He had arrived, huffing and puffing, trying to intimidate him and show who was the cock in the hen house, ready for a showdown. Just like he had done with me. But Tristan just smiled his bright smile, clapped his arms around Bradley shoulders, and walked with him down the hallway in such a carefree way, chatting away like they were two long-lost friends catching up on old times. It was only a matter of a few seconds before Bradley was completely conquered.

At Tristan's very first class, he actually had the audacity to arrive in the room talking with the teacher like they were good buddies! And it had been the same teacher for whom I'd refused to stand up in class and introduce myself. Tristan, on the other hand, had no such worries. He entered the room deeply engaged in conversation with the teacher, and the two remained like that for a while, Tristan leaning on the teacher's desk with his legs crossed. As though they were old colleagues, they chatted on about the town history, current events, the weather, all sorts of conversation, unaware of the students staring at them in silent amazement.

Tiffany turned to me, whispering quietly, "So I guess all Grays have notable first days at school, huh?" She stifled a laugh.

I realized there and then that even teachers weren't immune to Tristan's charm!

After fifteen minutes of this nonsense, Professor Martin remembered he actually had a class to teach, so he cleared his throat, presented Tristan to the room and told him to sit down so he could start teaching stuff. Tristan nodded to the class, getting some giggles from the female populace, and then headed to a seat next to me, giving me a quick wink as he sat down. I realized then that he could get away with pretty much anything he wanted to. He could rule this school with his grace and charm, and people would gladly obey without resistance. I wondered if he'd been like this when he'd been alive before. Or was this another side-effect of the binding spell that had brought him back to life?

The whole first week went on like this. It turned out I needn't have worried about Tristan at all. He was doing just fine. In fact, he was doing way better than me.

Wednesday was Extra Curricular Day.

Tristan, Seth, Tiffany and I were standing in front of the list board in the locker-room hallway. I knew I had to pick at least two extra activities if I were to graduate in July. But Tristan and I had arrived late, and all the cool activities were full by then. That was a bummer.

"Hey, Joey, I'm team captain of the cheerleader squad. I can get you in, if you like," Tiffany suggested, poking me in the ribs.

I looked at her with a *"Really, me?"* expression on my face. "Tiffany, don't take this personally, but I rather die a horrible death than get caught in one of those cheerleader outfits. And I'm not much of a cheerful person, as you might have noticed. Plus I suck at anything that vaguely resembles dancing. So, I don't think so. But thanks!" I said, smiling at her.

She crossed her arms, pouting at me. I pretended not to notice and kept on skimming through the lists on the board.

Then Seth pointed to a list with just a few names on it. "You can sign up for the music class! I'm in it. Well, kinda. I'm enrolled, but I don't actually take the classes. We have a special deal with Professor Rubick," he said, leaning on the board.

"We?" I asked.

"Yeah. Me, Harry, Josh and Sam. You know. The band," he said, all smug.

"Really? Music class...it sounds good," I muttered to myself. I'd had a great time with Seth rearranging his song. And I'd had quite a few piano classes in the past, and some guitar too. It should be fairly easy to follow those up here. I wondered, though, why the music list had so few names enrolled. Well, I guess music wasn't for everybody...

Tristan was all over the board, scanning up and down the lists with a frantic expression. He was having a hard time picking just two things out of all the options. He thought everything was great, and interesting, and exciting, and couldn't decide which one was the best. This was another thing he mentioned all the time to me: how great it was to be able to go back to school again, to actually finish his studies, since he hadn't been able to back then. He was thrilled to have this second chance and he showed it every way he could! I think there wasn't a single student out there more excited about school than Tristan. He sure was taking his second chance in life very seriously.

He peeked over my shoulder to see what list I was looking at now. "Ooooh, man! Music class? That would be swell...I mean great!" he corrected in a heartbeat. "I definitely want to do that one!" he said, grabbing a pen and scribbling his name on the list.

I shrugged my shoulders and wrote my name on it too. I still had one activity left to choose, though. "What are yours, Tiff?" I asked. Maybe I'd like the ones she'd picked.

"Oh, I have my cheerleader squad, that you clearly hate so much," she said, sticking out her tongue at me, "and acting class. It's loads of fun!"

Before I could consider that option, my eyes passed swiftly over another quite empty list on the board. My eyes widened in wonderment. Martial Arts! I'd loved my aikido and kung fu classes back at my old town, and I'd been really good at them both!

The grayish cloaked figure drifted back into my mind and it made me think that maybe this would be a good time to pick up my martial arts training. Maybe it'd be good to be able to defend myself with more efficiency.

I remembered how scared I'd felt with those black empty eyes and sharp fingers stretching out to me in my dream. I hate feeling scared and defenseless. Maybe it was time to be prepared to fight back. Martial Arts class it was, then! I scribbled my name on the list. Seth leaned on my shoulders, peeking to see what I'd chosen as my second activity.

"M.A., really?" he asked, amused.

"Yeah, it should be fun," I said, trying to sound casual. I didn't want him to know about my inner fears and private nightmares.

"Fun is not a word to describe Sensei Kingsley's classes," he said. "But you'll have to run if you're serious about attending. The first M.A. class starts in...fifteen minutes. And let me tell you, Kingsley does not like late attendees. Seriously. Go. Now!"

Seeing Seth's dead-serious face, I bolted to my room, leaving a dumbstruck Tiffany behind and a laughing Seth at her side. Tristan was still darting back and forth in front of the board, trying to pick his second activity. I needed to change into my sweats and T-shirt, and my room was so freaking far away! I'd have to run like the wind to get there in less than fifteen minutes!

Sixteen minutes later, I arrived, panting heavily, in the M.A. practice room. I glanced around, relieved to see that Sensei Kingsley hadn't arrived yet. A few students were already there, properly dressed, stretching and chatting, waiting for the class to start.

And then I noticed Bradley amongst them, his bulk standing out from the small group of boys around him. I grunted quietly, right about the same time he glanced at my way and saw me standing there at the front of the room. He smirked evilly and headed towards me. Apparently, the truce with charming Tristan wasn't extended to family members. Bummer.

"So, are you lost, Gray? Shouldn't you be looking for the cheerleader try-outs? I'll bet Tiffany can sneak you in without anyone noticing. Who says you need to have skills, or good looks to get in, if your BFF is captain of the squad?" he jeered, sneering at me.

Ouch. I was glad I hadn't accepted Tiff's offer, or I would be feeling like crap right now. And he'd just called me ugly and uncoordinated. That kind of stung. I knew I wasn't model material, but hearing all that out loud was kind of hurtful. Bradley was a real jerk!

"Well, Bradley, I guess that means you're not far from having your special dream come true, then! Even with your ugly mutt and monkey gait, I think Tiffany can get you in the cheer squad if you really want!" I retorted right back at him. A few students sniggered behind his back.

His expression changed again from amused to pissed off. I seemed to have a knack for making that happen to him. He walked with a menacing stride towards me. "You're very good with the talking, Gray. But why don't we start training a little early today? Care to join me for a practice on the mat? Or are you too afraid, without your little rocker boys at your side?" he mocked, with an evil glint in his eyes.

I looked around the room. I was the only girl, and all the boys were looking eagerly between Bradley and me, waiting for the show to start. I could see he wanted to teach me a lesson and scare the little girl away from this class. I wasn't sure if this was the right thing to do, but Bradley-Jerk-Face left me no choice in the matter. If I backed down now, it would look like I was chickening out. I gave him a quick glance to check on his belt color. It was white. Come on! Was he kidding me? He was totally underestimating me, just because I was a girl! And because he was two times, make that three times bigger than me! But size didn't matter on the mat. Anyone with a brain knew that. Well, brains sure weren't at the top of Jerk-Face's list of qualities.

So I shrugged and walked on to the mat, accepting his invitation. He was momentarily taken aback, but quickly regained his composure. I stopped at the middle and turned to look at him. He followed reluctantly; he'd thought I was never going to accept it, just crawl back the way I came, in fear and shame. Guess again, pal!

I put one foot in front of the other, gaining balance and preparing to make my moves. White Belt wasn't going to know what hit him! I reached out my arm and made the famous *Matrix* hand invitation. It was kind of cocky, and showy, and totally unnecessary, but I couldn't help myself. The look on his face was just priceless!

Then he charged in my direction, like a bull seeing the reddest flag of his life!

Chapter Sixteen

Vigil

The whole thing was over quite fast. It was easy to swerve out of the way of Bradley's first charge. I didn't even know what he was trying to do; there was no coordinated plan of attack, no training whatsoever, he just ran at me like a stunned cockroach. So I let him pass by me with ease. He stumbled forward and turned around, surprised at my quick side-step.

I shrugged at him with a *"What was that?"* look on my face and a tiny smirk. It made him even more pissed. That was good. You can tell if your opponent is good or not by how quickly you can make him lose his temper. You lose your temper, you're bound to make a mistake. A really bad mistake.

He charged again, even more carelessly than before, but faster this time. I was a little impressed at his speed, given he was such a burly guy. But I guessed he was captain of the basketball team, and you couldn't play that well if you were a slow mover.

I decided I wasn't going to kick his ass today, then. He was a white belt, after all; it wasn't allowed. You have to honor the high color of your belt, otherwise it isn't truly earned. I only needed to deflect and defend for now.

I switched my feet, giving another step to the side. I was just shuffling around, doing aikido evading moves. I let him pass by me again, giving a small push on his back, which added to his momentum and made him stumble forward even harder. He fell face first on to the mat. I heard a lot of muffled laughs around us. An audience was gathering for the show. I needed to finish this quickly and with as little fuss as possible.

Bradley stood up fast, facing me. Time to make him a tiny, wee bit more angry.

"What? How are you supposed to fight me if you can't even catch me?" I teased, relaxing my fight stance on purpose so he would think I had my guard down. He took the bait and lunged forward, trying to grab my arms. That was a bad, bad mistake. You never try to grab an arm from an aikidoka. Had he never seen a Steven Seagal movie? It was such a classic move!

His hands brushed my wrists for a fraction of a second. The secret was all in the timing: you had to let him make the first part of the move, but not complete the action entirely, so you could use his own movement against himself. I twisted my wrists in a fluid twirl, making his fingers lose his grasp completely, and took another half-circle side-step, ending up by his side. While I was shifting my position, I swiftly grabbed his arm, twisting it backwards.

So within a few seconds, I had him hostage. If he tried to make a move, I'd twist his wrist just a fraction, which would force him to stop or he'd break his own arm. It was all about twists and pressure applied in the right places.

You didn't need muscles; you just needed to be fast and use your opponent's own moves.

He soon realized he was immobilized. And under my power. The more he struggled, the more I tightened my grip on his wrist and the more it hurt. If he pushed or pulled too hard, he would cause his own wrist fracture. Our training session was officially over! Ta-da!

I heard clapping from someone in the group. I raised my eyes and saw that it was Josh. So he'd signed up for Martial Arts class too! And he seemed to be enjoying the scene immensely. I gave him a tiny, quick smile. It wasn't right to gloat over your rival's misfortune, especially someone with just a white belt. Bradley tried to pull away from me again, but I didn't let him. I twisted my grip just a little, making him wince in pain. I leaned forward a fraction so that only he, and not our audience, would be able to hear me.

"So, before I release you, let's make a deal, shall we? After I let you go, don't try any payback, Bradley. It would only make things worse. And you have to remember how important a wrist is for a basketball player, isn't that right? I'd hate to see you hurt, I really would. But if you attack me again, I WILL defend myself. And believe me, I know a lot of different ways to break a lot of bones in your body. That's not a threat, it's a promise," I said quietly. "Do we have a deal?"

He nodded, his face a mix of white fear and red anger.

"I'm sorry, didn't quite get that. Speak up, please." I twisted a little more.

"Yes! Yes! We have a deal!" he said through gritted teeth.

I let him go and took two steps away from him, just to be on the safe side. A few guys stepped in, coming to Bradley's aid, and Josh came over to my side, clapping my shoulder in greeting.

"That was impressive. It wasn't very fair, though; you should be wearing your brown belt as a warning to the cocky ones in here!" he said, laughing.

"How did you know my belt color?" I asked, bewildered.

"Oh, us brown belts know how to recognize one another," he said, winking at me.

Oooh, so he was an advance student too! That was so cool! "I didn't know you were in this class! Hey! That was why Bradley backed off so fast that other day at the locker room when you showed up with Harry! He knew you'd kick his ass so bad!" I said with a chuckle.

"Well, yeah. But I see now it was totally unnecessary for me to intervene." He shrugged.

"I told you I could take care of myself!" I said, still laughing.

Bradley was huddling with his buddies, giving me quite the evil glare from far away.

I was glad he was only glaring, but keeping our deal.

I actually enjoyed my first M.A. class. I had the opportunity to observe Sensei's teaching techniques with close attention, and I got to study all the other students as well, see their flaws and best moves. Bradley kept his distance during the entire class, and I had Josh as my practice partner for the day.

Class ended and I said goodbye to Josh, hurrying to my room to tell Tristan and Seth about what happened in M.A. class today.

But I couldn't find them. I guessed they were busy at activity classes of their own. I finally bumped into Tristan and Seth at dinner, and found out Tristan had chosen Music class and Basketball for the afternoon period. Tristan and

Bradley bonding and being buddies at basketball practice
gave me the shivers.

That night I had another strange dream.

I was in this wide, beautiful garden. There were huge,
opulent trees and a lot of exotic flowers and vines curling and crawling up cast-iron frames. There were flowers I
had never seen before; they looked alien and extraordinary,
with vibrant colors. The light was soft and ethereal, that
timeless light we have in dreams – not quite morning, afternoon, dusk or dawn. Everything was so lovely, quiet and
peaceful. The place was deserted; there was only me sitting
on an iron garden bench.

I was surveying the outstanding view when I noticed
a boy about my age sitting on another iron bench very
near me. He was so close, how could I not have seen him
before? He was looking at me with a blank expression on
his face. He had long locks of soft black hair falling over
his face, and the whitest, palest face I have ever seen. His
eyes were as black as mine and he had a thin face and nose,
his features so pretty and delicate that he almost looked like
a girl. Come to think of it, he did have this androgynous
way about him.

And I couldn't make out what he was wearing, only that
it was something gray, a shirt, maybe some pants. He stood
up and walked in my direction. Well, tried walking. Instead,
he kind of half-lurched, half-staggered in my direction. It
was like he was trying to imitate walking, but wasn't getting it right, as if he wasn't familiar with the mechanics of
locomotion. So weird.

Then he sat on my bench, but not too close. He was trying to give me some space. When he spoke, his voice was
soothing and soft, like a whisper.

"I did not mean to scare you," he said, looking intently at me with those black eyes.

Something about him made me very uneasy.

"You didn't," I said suspiciously. *Not right up until now.*

"I thought maybe you would feel more comfortable in this kind of place, with this relatable appearance of me. Is this young male avatar more acceptable to you?" he queried in genuine concern.

"You mean this is not what you really look like?" I asked, getting more suspicious by the second. I was sure I had never seen him before. But he sounded very, very familiar. "You were saying that you didn't mean to scare me, but you weren't talking about now, were you? You're the cloaked figure of my dream. You sound like him."

He tilted his head slightly to the left, just like he had done before. His eyes were always focusing, never blinking; it made him look even more like a bird of prey.

"Yep. That's you, all right. Same head tilt there. You might try not to do that, it's kind of creepy. Humans don't do that. Well, normal ones, at least. And you might consider blinking once in a while too," I said, shifting on my seat, moving an inch away from him.

He frowned just a fraction, absorbing my crazy speech, and then tried blinking. It was a train wreck. He sucked at mimicking human actions.

"Okay. That's ... good. But now you should try to blink a little less than that. Right. You're getting the hang of it. So, what the hell do you want with me? It would be fantastic if you could stop gate-crashing my dreams, you know? It's upsetting. And it's making me grumpy during the day," I said, moving another inch away from him. Soon the bench would end and then what would I do?

He wasn't budging from his spot, though. Maybe he wasn't thinking about attacking me again.

"I mean you no harm. I only want to do my job. I need to fix this. You must tell me where it is," he said, sounding more anxious now.

"Right. What is your name?" I asked.

He flinched in surprise, not expecting that question. It was like I had slapped him in the face. He was a weird boy. Man. Being. Thingy. Ugh.

"What?" he asked, looking frightened.

"Your *name*. What is your name?"

"I don't have a name. It is not necessary," he said, annoyed now.

"Well, that is a bummer. I can't call you 'Psst, hey, you!' Let's see... you have quite the stare going on, don't you? It's like you're always watching, silently observing, always vigilant. I shall call you Vigil," I stated.

"*What?* No! I do not have a name!" he said, quite panicky now.

"Now you do. I just gave you one," I said, satisfied with a job well done. "It suits you, don't you think? Vigil."

"I-I..." he mumbled. He looked confused and aggravated. I was glad I'd managed to take that blank stare off his face. "You just gave me one..." he repeated, astonished, and trailed off.

"So, Vigil, why do you need to find Tristan so badly? What do you want with him?" I asked. That was the big question. I tried to sound breezy, but I was all tensed up inside.

Vigil was staring at the ground, still shocked by the naming thing. He frowned and looked up as he realized I had just asked him a question. He stared at me in silence for the longest time, the blank expression back on his face. He had stopped blinking again. It was all so very creepy.

"Names have power. Great power. Why have you willingly handed that to me? I am now stronger than I ever was before. Now you have a name to fear. Fear is another powerful thing to yield," he said slowly, like he was trying to put pieces of a puzzle together.

"I do not fear '*you*', Vigil. I fear what you might do to someone really close to me. I fear your actions. What do you want with Tristan?" I repeated my question harshly.

"*Tristan*," he said, selecting another piece of the puzzle in his head. "*Tristan* is a mistake. I fix mistakes; that is what I do. That is what I am. I watch. I observe. I put things back in their right places, in their right order. I need to fix *this*."

So Tristan wasn't supposed to be alive. That was what Vigil was talking about. Our spell had disturbed the natural order of things by bringing a ghost back to life. And Vigil was supposed to "fix it". I was getting angry now. "So, when you do find Tristan, what are you going to do? Are you going to kill him?" I finally gathered the courage to ask the horrible question thundering in my mind.

"I am going to restore order. I'll put him in his rightful place."

"You're going to kill him."

"I will do what I am meant to do."

"You will *kill him*."

"If you prefer to put it in those terms."

"But you need me in order to find him. You need my help. Without me, you won't find him, you won't ever touch him." I stood up, really mad.

He stood up too, with a puzzled expression; he didn't

understand what I was so angry about, why I was trying to fight the natural order of things.

"So, listen up, Vigil. If fear is what makes you stronger, you won't have any of it from me, you hear? I don't fear you! I won't ever fear you!" I said, walking towards him, seething with fury. Just the thought that he could take Tris away from me made me lose my mind. I didn't know where all this anger was coming from; all I knew was that I had this instant gut-wrenching reflex reaction when Tristan's life was threatened, and I just acted on it without thinking straight. Vigil simply stood there, watching me with those dead black eyes, no emotion showing on his pale cold face. He was a dead thing. A horrible cold thing.

"You will have to get past me first to get to him! And I won't let you! I won't EVER let you! Do you understand that? You might as well give up. Go fix something else!" I shouted at him.

"You are just a human girl. What makes you think you can stop me? I have lived for millions of years. You can do nothing to prevent this from happening, girl," he said in a cold, detached voice.

I remembered what he had said in my last dream.

He would find him, no matter what.

It was only a matter of time.

"I HATE YOU!" I screamed at his face. I was beyond mad now.

He gave me a tiny smile. "Hate is a powerful thing," he said, leaning closer, his eyes piercing with a blackness that engulfed all light. There was no hope. His eyes told me this. Nothing could escape him. Nothing ever could.

"NO!" I said, punching him in the chest.

A sharp, bright, painful light shone in the place where

my fist connected with him. My whole body hurt badly with the impact, and a thundering noise filled my ears, deafening me. I was only a few inches from his face, so I could see the surprise flashing inside his eyes, the pain that he felt too, the shocking realization that I was capable of hurting him. I could read him well enough to know that no one had ever done that before. I saw fear taking him over, for the tiniest moment, and then he was gone.

And I woke up.

Chapter Seventeen

Lost Boys

My heart was pounding in my chest and my arm hurt like hell. It felt like it was dislocated or something, but gradually the pain subsided and after a few minutes the ache was completely gone. Yet another restless night for me. I was beginning to suspect it wasn't going to be my last. I knew that sooner or later Vigil would return to haunt my dreams again. It was only a matter of time, as he had said himself . . .

I tried to get back to sleep but, wary of my dreams, I was unable to do more than cat-nap. In the morning, I was weary, but I tried to disguise it as best I could. I decided I wasn't going to tell Tristan about Vigil. I needed to talk to Miss Violet first, to see if she knew anything more. I knew if Tristan sensed my worry, he would want to know what was wrong. He would make me tell him all about the dream. And then he would be the one worried and scared.

So I faked good cheer, plastered a smile on my face and went about my day.

After lunch we had Music class. The classroom was filled with instruments placed randomly on shelves, and there was a small stage at the far side of the room, directly opposite the door. Chairs circled the stage and a big piano was placed right in the middle of it.

I was immediately drawn to the piano. It had been such a long time since I'd last played on one like this! Piano lessons had been my mother's idea. She'd said I would regret it if I passed my life without knowing how to play at least one musical instrument. But I think the truth was that she only wanted me to because my dad used to play too. He had a band once, and played professionally for some time. So I chose piano lessons first, because she liked it, and guitar lessons second, because I liked it. This was way before I fell in love with martial arts. There was also my photography addiction period, my drawing lessons enterprise and my dance classes disaster. Boy! Dance classes were a train wreck. I wasn't meant to dance, for sure.

I walked over to the stage and studied the piano, passing my hands over its smooth, shining black surface, while Tristan and Seth were looking at the guitars. Seth handed a guitar to Tristan as they talked quietly to each other.

I sat on the piano bench and punched a few random keys.

"You better step away from the piano, Joe! Only Professor Rubick plays it. He's rather possessive of the thing. He says we 'murder sound' when we try to play piano," Seth said with a short laugh. "You should see his face when someone tries the violin! He looks like he's about to die!"

Seth approached the stage and sat on a bench right in front of the piano, chuckling at fond memories of Professor Rubick's despair. Tristan was right beside him, pulling another bench close to us. He had the black guitar still in his hands.

"You guys have violins lessons?" I asked, excited. "I

always wanted to learn how to play the violin! It looks rather hard, though…"

"Yeah, well, that's because it is. And no, you'll probably have to learn the little drums first in the class…maybe later he may let you try the guitar. If you don't attempt to 'murder sound', that is." Seth laughed some more, but stopped abruptly when he heard Tristan playing the guitar at his side.

I raised my eyebrows too. I didn't know Tristan could play the guitar! And he was good, too! But I guess it made sense, since he'd been a teen when rock 'n' roll was born. I could even picture him in my mind, with his leather jacket, greased hair and a guitar on his lap. There was so much I still didn't know about him…and I was even more surprised when I realized he was playing Seth's song! The one I had helped put together in my first week at school. How on earth did he know that?

"I didn't know you played guitar, man!" Seth said at the same time as I exclaimed, "How do you know this song, Tristan?"

Tristan continued playing chords while he answered us both. "You never asked and I heard it yesterday at Seth's band rehearsal. They played it like a hundred times to get it right. I kinda memorized a few parts…"

I was a little jealous. Seth had never asked me to go to a rehearsal, and Tristan already got invited. I think Seth saw the jealousy on my face, because he hastily added, "We looked for you, but you were at Martial Arts class! And it wasn't even a proper rehearsal, since Josh and Sam weren't there," he mumbled apologetically.

Tristan continued playing softly, humming along, lost in his own world. He looked up and smiled at us. His eyes shone a soft violet color, because of the violet T-shirt he was wearing. I suppressed a strong urge to sigh loudly at the sight of his smile.

"Sorry, don't remember the lyrics much, only the chorus," he said, getting back to humming and looking down at the guitar. Dark locks of hair fell over his face when he looked down, making me want to brush them back and tuck them behind his ears. Maybe I just wanted any excuse to touch his handsome face.

I looked down, feeling ashamed for having these kinds of thoughts. This was probably just the binding spell working its devious grasp on me again. I should learn to control it, to tame these weird urges I was feeling all the time around him. It was very disturbing!

Seth joined in then, singing the lyrics that Tristan didn't know. I looked up, startled. I had never heard Seth singing before. He was good! He had this electric, energizing quality in his voice; it made you want to sing along. He rocked!

Then Tristan started to sing along with Seth in the chorus part. I was even more astonished. Tristan had such a rich, deep, low voice. It was husky and sad, a hint of darkness behind it; it was like a soft stroke on your face, a rough whisper in your ear. It was breathtaking. Seth stopped and just stood there quietly, listening to Tristan sing his song. I decided to join in with the piano, with the little I had heard and the parts I remembered from the afternoon when I'd rearranged Seth's song. My piano lessons were a bit rusty, but I could play well enough to tag along.

I kept playing without looking up, focusing all my attention on Tristan's voice and the lead of his guitar's soft notes. It sounded like an acoustic version of the song, simpler and more melodic than it was originally intended to be. I didn't know if Seth was going to like it much that way.

When the song ended, Tristan and I both looked up at last, our eyes locking. Seth was looking at Tristan and then back at me with wide eyes. I guess we'd managed to impress him, then! I smiled softly at Tristan, and something strong flashed back at me inside his eyes. A mix of... longing? With something else, something I had seen before.

Before I could follow that thought, Seth's voice cut in. "Wow. That was..." he began, but was interrupted by Professor Rubick's voice from the other side of the room.

"That was quite good!" Professor Rubick bellowed, walking over to join us. The music teacher had small round glasses resting on a stubby nose, and he was wearing casual jeans with a long-sleeved cream shirt. He was tall, and had a trimmed dark beard that matched his brown hair. A few signs of baldness were starting to show on the top of his head.

The room was suddenly filling with students while he approached the centre of the stage. "What was it that you two were playing?" he asked me.

I stepped out from behind the piano and Tristan stood up, leaning the guitar on the bench. "It's Seth's song, sir," I said. "I was trying it out on the piano, just for fun. I think it's quite good too! I can't wait to hear the whole band playing it!"

"Really? Seth's song?" Professor Rubick asked. "You have always struggled with your lyrics, Seth, but that was really good. You need to trim a little around the edges, but the guitar part was rather good. The piano needs a little more practice, though. You sounded a little rusty, missy," he said, looking at me.

"I could not agree with you more, sir," I said, nodding my head.

"I'm sorry, Professor. It's not actually my song," Seth chipped in. I glared at him, trying to make him stop talking, but he ignored my warning look. "It's Joey's song, sir. She wrote almost the whole thing, she deserves the credit."

A few students were picking random instruments from the walls and starting to play a few screeching tunes. At first I thought they were tuning their instruments, warming up to play, but the chaotic notes and sharp screeches were only getting worse and louder by the minute.

I saw Tristan flinching at the horrible noises around us, and I tried my best to put on a straight face, but wasn't succeeding much. Now I understood why there were so few names on the Music class list! Staying here for a couple of hours was going to be pure torture! Seth could've warned us about this, the numbnuts!

Professor Rubick seemed to understand our worried glances. "Yes. Sorry about that." He looked apologetically at his students. "So, Joey, is it? Since you two seem to be advanced students, perhaps we could work out some kind of arrangement. The same one I have with Seth and his band. We have a special deal so they don't have to attend my classes here. But they still need to work on music, though," Professor Rubick said firmly.

"Arrangement, sir?" Tristan and I asked at the same time. We were up for anything that could take us out of here!

"Yes. You two can join in Seth's band, how about that? But wait! There's a catch. Each one of you needs to deliver me an original song by the end of term. Joey can help you guys with yours, since she already managed a song in just one week!" he said, getting excited. "Oh! This is going to be such an interesting project! I can't wait to see what you boys will come up with!"

"But...but...sir!" Seth intervened. "I need to talk to the rest of guys first! I don't own the band, they all have to agree with new members..."

"Well, you talk with them and let me know! It's that, or this..." Professor Rubick gestured to the chaotic commotion thumping around us.

Tristan and I looked desperately at Seth. Anything was better than another minute in this hell! Poor Professor Rubick. I wondered how he coped with those lessons. You had to really love teaching to endure long hours of horror in this room with these students!

We huddled next to Seth, while Professor Rubick shouted at the other students to stop playing the instruments for the love of all that is good in the world.

"Come on, man! We'll just sit quietly at rehearsals and watch you guys play. You won't even know we're there!" Tristan pleaded. He looked like he would do just about anything to avoid attending this class!

Seth looked at both of our desperate faces, and sighed in defeat. "Okay. I'll talk to the guys. Come on. Let's meet them in the practice room," he said, waving us to follow him.

We gave Professor Rubick a thumbs-up and darted out of the room, clapping our hands over our ears.

"Thanks so much, Seth. We promise we won't disturb you!" I said in relief as we followed Seth down the hallway.

"Hey, don't thank me yet. I still need the guys' permission! If they don't agree, the deal is off, sorry!" he said in a worried tone.

"Come on! They don't like us, is that it?" I asked by Seth's side.

Josh seemed to be quite easygoing, and we were training buddies at M.A. Harry might have a problem with us, because we were new people and he seemed really shy. I didn't have a clue about Sam, since I hadn't met him yet.

"Well...I don't think they are going to mind about Tristan. Not after they hear him sing. But, you, Joey, I don't know...because you're, you know, a girl and all. The only girl," Seth mumbled.

Oh. So it was a boy band. Boys only. Crap.

"I could be your songwriter, help you with some new song ideas," I suggested, trying to sound like I didn't care much about being in the band. But I couldn't hide the disappointment in my voice.

Seth took a quick glance at me and saw how much I wanted to be in the band. "But then we won't have your wicked piano skills on board," he said, smiling warmly at me. "Do you think you can play again on the piano for the band to hear? It was amazing hearing you two together!"

"Sure," I said, "Let me just practice a little more, take a few lessons with Professor Rubick, then my piano won't sound so sucky."

Seth laughed. "It wasn't 'sucky'. You were really good! You too, man," he said, clapping Tristan's shoulder.

Soon we arrived at the practice room. It was on the farthest east side of the school building, in a big stone-walled room. It was crowded with boxes and all sorts of repaired furniture, tables, chairs and benches. It was a junkyard of old furniture, but the guys had arranged things in a way that actually looked sort of cool. The room smelled of pinewood and dust.

Harry was already there, waiting, sitting on some boxes, his wild, dark-red hair falling over his pale face. Josh was also there, with his usual black T-shirt and black mohawk, setting his drums in place. They turned as soon as they heard us walk into the room.

"Hey, everybody, we have some company!" Seth shouted cheerfully. "Joe, Tristan, you two have met Harry, bass man, and Josh there, drummer boy. The gloomy stranger on the other side of the room, plugging in his guitar, is Sam Hunt. Lead guitar and lead singer. Sammy, my man, how ya doing?"

A tall, strong boy stood up and smiled at us. He had curly brown hair and deep, dark-blue eyes. He wasn't as tall as Josh, but he was larger and stronger. And he had the most open, warm smile ever. Nothing about him was gloomy; he was absolutely vibrant and full of cheer. He came over to us, laughing loudly.

"So, these are the infamous Grays!" Sam said, shaking Tristan's hand vigorously and turning to me. "Nice to finally meet you! Seth's been babbling about you non-stop. It's Tristan this, Joey that, all day long! I was wondering when you were going to show up!" he said, giving me a huge hug, which surprised me a little.

And I'd been worried Sam would have a problem with us! He was so nice!

Sam, Tristan and I chatted for a while, and I grew fonder of Sam by the minute. He was funny, kind and obviously the joker of the band. He made everybody laugh with such ease! He was just naturally funny, a born entertainer. Harry laughed at almost everything Sam did or said. And Harry's laugh was really contagious. Once you heard him laughing, you couldn't stop yourself laughing too.

Then Seth called the band to a corner to discuss our situation, and I stood in the other corner with Tristan, looking around the room. I could hear only parts of the conversation.

"*You should have heard them. It was freaking amazing...*"

"*Professor Rubick actually liked them? Wow, that's a first...*"

"*I'm telling you, man, he has a REALLY good vocal...*"

"*...she plays the piano! It'd be great in some of our songs...*"

"*...but she's a girl, dude. What if someone asks about the name?*"

"*If we change the name...*"

"*We're NOT changing the name!*"

Apparently, there was a name-changing discussion happening over there. After a few minutes, they seemed to have reached agreement. They all turned in our direction, and Seth walked over to us with a poker face on. "That's settled, then! Tristan, you're definitely in!" Seth said, clapping Tristan's back with a wide grin.

"Great! I'll just stay out of your way, you won't even know I'm here!" Tristan breathed, relieved to get rid of music classes.

"Sorry, dude, but you can't stay in the corner just watching, you'll have to sing too. And work on your lyrics. You heard the professor: each one of us must come up with a new song." Seth smiled evilly at him.

Tristan nodded with a happy smile.

"What about me?" I asked Seth anxiously "They didn't let me in, right? That's okay, Seth, you tried," I said shuffling my feet. I was a little bit disappointed, though.

"Oh, you're in too, Joey. But you will have to just be our composer, because they don't want to change the band's name. I think they're being stupid. We don't need to be all boys playing in the band just because of the name of the band. It's not a literal thing, it's just an idea. And you do rock with your piano skills! It was brilliant! We should be begging you to join in!" he said, giving the others a pointed glare. Then he gave me a welcome hug.

I smiled while I hugged Seth. Tristan was looking at us kind of seriously, with a weird expression on his face, but when he caught me looking at him he averted his eyes, fast. I wondered why...

"I'm really glad to have you on board, Joe Gray!" Seth said into my ear. Then he turned to the band and shouted at them. "HEY! She even has a boy's name, so it all still looks certified on paper and you don't need to worry about changing the band's name!"

"What is the band's name, by the way?" I asked, intrigued.

Seth was strapping on his guitar on and walking into their practice area. "How about we give Joey here a pre-view of her song?" he said, winking at the rest of the band.

They were all set at their marks and ready to play. I sat on the floor next to Tristan, waiting to finally hear my song played for the first time! I was so excited!

"I hope you like it, Joey! And welcome to The Lost Boys!" he said, striking the first chord.

Chapter Eighteen

The Spell Bond

The song was good, but the band was amazing!

They were all really good musicians! Like, nearly-ready-to-record-an-album kind of good! I thought they were just a bunch of kids joking around with some instruments, but I was so wrong! No wonder they had pulled that arrangement with Professor Rubick. They really deserved it! I was so excited after hearing their rehearsal that I ran to my room and started working on some new songs right away. I wanted them to know that I'd do my best to earn my place in the band. I'd compose my ass off!

I spent the rest of the week, and my whole weekend, working on lyrics and melodies. Tristan helped a lot with the melodies and harmony composition. He was really good at blending and mixing those parts.

I called my mom and told her Tristan and I had to stay at school that weekend because of an intense load of homework, but really I'd stayed only to work on my songs. I felt guilty at first, because she sounded so upset that I wouldn't be visiting her, and I could tell that she missed me a lot, but I was really excited about the band. All I could think about was music 24/7. It was like a light had turned on inside of me and I couldn't stop glowing.

Seth was as excited as I was about working together on new songs for the band. He said it was good to find someone as passionate about it as he was. So Tristan, Seth and I spent the whole weekend working on new songs. Tiffany was really happy that all of us were staying for the weekend too. Many of the students, mostly the ones with family living close to the school, went home to spend time with their parents. Josh, Sam and Harry sometimes went to visit their parents in Esperanza, sometimes they stayed at Sagan; it depended on their mood. Tiffany and Seth were the only ones who almost never went to see their parents, since they lived in another state, and visiting was difficult and took too much time and effort.

During that first weekend with Tristan, and the next week that followed, I got to know every one of my new friends better. By the end of the second week, it was like we'd known each other for centuries; like we were childhood best friends. I couldn't explain the instant connection, I just felt really blessed to have found them.

Sam, with his curly brown hair and midnight-blue eyes, was a sweetheart since day one. He was so much fun to be around with that goofy, cheerful way about him; a natural joker on any occasion. He had good looks, the most melodic, beautiful voice, and could make you laugh with incredible ease.

Josh was always around Sam. Or vice-versa. If you looked for one, you found the other too. Josh, with his light-blue eyes and black mohawk, was as strong in mind as in spirit, and the most loyal friend. He made you feel secure and calm, a steady arm in a wavering storm. Josh also had good looks, coolness and the most wicked drumming skills of all time.

Harry, with his lovely emerald green eyes and spiked red hair, was out of this world. He was incredibly beautiful, and the walking metaphor for his crimson and green tattoo of cold waves crashing over fiercely flaming fire. He was really shy and quiet at first, but once you got to know him better you realized he was also wild, unpredictable and incredibly passionate, all at the same time. Harry was extraordinary!

Then there was Seth. Seth and his blond locks of hair over the most kind and loving hazel eyes. There weren't enough words to describe Seth's friendship and kindness…He was the brightest light in the darkest tunnel, a shining spirit. It was an honor to be his friend.

And I couldn't forget about my one and only "girl" friend! In just a couple of weeks, Tiffany had become irreplaceable. Tiff with her supermodel good looks, expensive clothes, cheerful attitude and vibrant soul. Little by little I'd allowed myself to be more free and open with her, and she in return started to let her guard down around me. Each day I got more of a glimpse into how honest, kind and generous she really was inside. I saw in her eyes all the time how much she feared that nobody would ever care for her, or love her for who she was; that her parents' money was always in the way, always blocking her path to real happiness, to real friends, and true love.

So I did my best to always let her know how much I valued her friendship, for her company alone. I never asked her for favors, special treatments, or recommendations. I didn't want to know about anything related to her surname. She whined whenever I didn't let her have her way on things, but I think she respected me more because of it. I was the only one who didn't let her boss me around. She was my friend, but she wasn't gonna tell me what to do: she didn't own me! That was what true friends were all about. We supported each other in our choices, but we didn't impose our needs on the other.

Tristan and Seth had developed the same close relationship as me and Tiff had. They were always together, chatting, studying, laughing and having fun. I even felt a little jealous of their bond sometimes, like it was somehow a threat to the connection Tristan and I had.

My fear was always that, although my bond with Tristan was strong, as it had been made by magic, it might not be real at all. And Seth's bond was the real deal, no parlor tricks, no magic involved; it was true friendship. They were together all the time and Tristan was picking up a lot of Seth's mannerisms. He'd changed his way of speaking by observing Seth and the boys in the band. He was using their cool handshakes, and some new slang even I didn't know. He was updating himself pretty fast. He even went for a modern haircut!

Tristan looked incredible! I couldn't believe his radical make-over. In just a few weeks he had changed from this quiet, old-fashioned, "swell" kid to this amazing "rocking" guy.

That weekend I planned to go visit my mother. I asked Tristan if he minded staying at the school, because I wanted to ask Tiffany to come with me. It would be a girls' weekend/slumber party of sorts.

He smiled and said it was no problem, and that he would hang out with Seth at school; he'd make it a boys' weekend for them too. He asked me to give my mother a hug from him, and to tell her he'd continue keeping her posted on everything. On that point, I raised an inquiring eyebrow.

"Yeah, well, I call her every so often to tell how things are going," he explained, chuckling.

"You do?" I asked, bewildered.

"Yes, she made me promise! And I wouldn't have to if you called her yourself once in a while, you know?"

"Oh, that is such bull! I call her all the freaking time!" I said, making him flinch twice. He always flinched whenever I cursed or did something bad mannered. He couldn't help himself; it was like a body reflex or something.

"Not as often as she'd like, and she worries," he said, chiding me.

"Come on, Tris. I'll call her every single day, if that's what she wants! And besides, she could live life a little and stop worrying about me!" I snapped, annoyed.

"Okay, all right. I'm not getting in the middle of this. You two girls can sort it out when you get home," he said, throwing his arms up in a gesture of surrender, and walking off to find Seth.

Mom welcomed Tiffany and me with open arms, and I smartly avoided saying Tiff's family name during the whole time we were there, so my mom treated her just like any of my friends. She even made us wash the dishes after dinner! I washed and Tiffany had to dry and put them away. A fantastic new experience for her. She kept smiling at my mom like she was the best mom in the whole world for making us do this!

Tiffany and my mom ganged up on me and dragged me to the mall to pick some new clothes on Saturday. I tried to protest, but it was hopeless. Tiff said it was time I stopped dressing like a boy and started wearing dresses, skirts, and some color. My mom elected her my new best friend.

On Sunday I snuck out while Tiffany was occupied talking fashion with my mom, and I paid a quick visit to Miss Violet. I really needed to talk to her about all those weird dreams I'd been having lately. She received me with a warm smile and we talked in her cozy living room while we had a cup of tea. I told her all about the cloaked man and all the cryptic things he had said to me.

I had been feeling a little tired all day long, unable to shake a gnawing headache that had started earlier in the week. Recounting my nightmares tired me out even more, and Miss Violet kept asking me to repeat my dreams over and over again. I saw that she was worried, but she tried to disguise it by avoiding looking directly at me. After a long hour of talking, Miss Violet told me she was going to study "my case" with her witch friends, and would keep me posted on whatever they discovered, and that I shouldn't worry about it for now. I left her house in a hurry, because I didn't want Tiff to notice I was gone. Explaining to her where I'd been and what I'd been doing would be a bit difficult.

Tiffany and I got back to school late Sunday afternoon. I hugged Tiff and headed to my room with a weary heart and a pounding headache. All I wanted for the night was a nice hot bath and an early night. I was so tired!

When I opened the door, Seth glanced up. He was sitting on his bed, a deep worried frown on his face. "Hey, Joey! Thank God you're back. I was about to call you." He seemed flustered.

"Hi, Seth. What's wrong?" I asked. I could see the concern flooding out of his eyes.

"Tristan's been really sick today. He doesn't want me to

take him to the infirmary. He said it's nothing, but he looks real sick!"

Tristan was lying on his bed, covers up to his neck and eyes closed. He looked really bad, sweat pouring out of him, his face pale as death. I remembered the last time I'd seen him like this. New Year. The night of the spell. I threw my bags on the floor and hurried to Tristan's bed. "How long has he been like this?" I asked Seth.

"Yesterday he just looked really tired. He mentioned he'd been wondering during the week if he was getting a cold or something. Today he woke up pretty bad. He had a light fever but his temperature has been rising since then. Maybe we should call a nurse?" Seth said, running his hands through his blond hair in distress.

"No nurses," I said at the same time as Tristan. His eyes were slightly open now. The brightness of the room seemed to be hurting him, so I turned the lights off, leaving only the lamp over my night-stand on.

"You two and this 'no nurses' nonsense," Seth mumbled at his bedside, aggravated.

"Don't worry, Seth. He'll be okay," I said, sitting by Tristan's side. "He's always like this with the flu. Tomorrow he'll be all good again, you'll see."

I passed my hand over Tristan's forehead. He was burning up! The moment the palm of my hand touched his forehead, sharp pinpricks of energy shot into my fingertips like needle stabs. A wave of heat spread out of my hands, making me feel like I was dipping frozen fingers in to steaming hot water. It didn't hurt, but it felt really strange. My headache stopped pounding immediately. Tristan sighed and closed his eyes in relief, relaxing beneath his covers. "See, he's already feeling better!" I pointed out to

Seth. I know I was! It was amazing; Tristan really did look instantly better.

Seth eyed him suspiciously for a moment then shrugged, realizing he had been worrying for no reason after all. "All right. Well, I'll go grab some dinner, then, since you're here with him now. Do you want me to bring you anything?" Seth asked, heading for the door.

"Yeah, a juice box and any sandwich would be great! Thanks, Seth!"

"No problem. If you need me, ring me and I'll be right back."

"Okay. Thanks, we'll be fine. Don't worry, go have your dinner!"

Seth left us and I took off my shoes, climbing into bed with Tristan. I snuck inside his covers, but remained seated, resting my back against the headboard. I put my arm over his head, trying to be as close to him as possible. I could feel the side of my leg touching his body, the tingling sensation reverberating through us. He mumbled something and turned to his side, wrapping his arm tightly around me. I sat there for a long time, watching him.

Seth returned after a while with my dinner, and I ate it in bed with Tristan. I hoped Seth would think I was only being a caring sister right now. Each passing day was turning out to be harder and harder to cover up our lie. Especially for someone observing things closely, like a room-mate.

I don't remember when I fell asleep that night, but I woke up next day real early, lying in Tristan's arms. It felt so good having him this close to me that I wished I could spend the rest of my life there.

Then I remembered Seth. I stiffened immediately but, when I looked over, he was sleeping heavily, bundled inside his covers. I let out a sigh of relief and turned to look at Tristan. God, he looked so handsome asleep...I tried to focus on the more important matter at hands: I needed to get out of his bed. Like, right now!

I moved slowly, trying to dislodge his arm, but the movement woke him up. He blinked a couple of times, registering his arms around me. He started to smirk, but then he saw my worried face as I silently mouthed "Seth!" at him. He looked over at Seth's bed and quickly released me.

I climbed out of his bed fast and went to mine. Tristan was yawning and rubbing his eyes. He looked much better – in fact, he looked completely fine. I whispered in the lowest voice I could manage, "Are you okay?"

He looked at me groggily and nodded. "Yeah. I feel fine now. Yesterday I felt like cra– I mean, I felt awful," he said, correcting his language.

I rolled my eyes. "Tristan, you can say *'crap'* to me, for God's sake!" I hissed. "I'm gonna take a bath now, but I need to talk to you about this spell thing. Wait for me before you leave for classes, so we can talk, okay?"

He nodded and pulled up his covers again, getting back to sleep while I tiptoed to the bathroom.

I finished my long, steaming bath at the same time as Seth's alarm beeped loudly. The boys got up grudgingly and went about their daily wake-up routine.

Seth was impressed by Tristan's quick recovery, but I reassured him it was a normal occurrence, and that Tristan's "colds" were always like that. Seth seemed to buy that explanation.

"You do look a lot better," I said, when Tristan emerged from the bathroom.

"I'm fine. Thanks for staying with me all night," he said, sitting on his bed.

"That's no problem. I'm glad you're okay. Miss Violet was right, though. She said this would happen again..."

"Why do you think that is? I mean, why now, all of a sudden?" Tristan asked thoughtfully.

"I don't know. I was thinking about it. Maybe it's because I was away at the weekend?" I hazarded.

Tristan pondered the idea for a second. "No. I don't think that's it. You were away before, your first week at school. Nothing happened then. And I started feeling this way during the week. About Tuesday, I guess."

I bit my lips, thinking hard. "Well, maybe we need to think about what these two occasions have in common...First time it happened was New Year, right? What about Tuesday? That was..."

"February, first," Tristan completed. "Maybe it's at every start of every month?" he ventured.

"Maybe. It makes sense. We'll have to wait until next month to find out for sure," I mumbled, looking at the calendar hanging by my desk.

I hoped we were wrong about this, though. Otherwise we'd have to go through this again at the start of every month. This did not sound good! At least I'd only felt a little tired this time, not violently ill like the first time it had happened...But Tristan was as sick as before.

What what would happen if we were apart during the first days of the month? If we couldn't be together?

This thing was starting to get really complicated. Haunting nightmares with this creepy cloaked being, magic spells compromising my feelings, weird bonds making us ill...

Tristan was looking at me with worried eyes. I was glad I hadn't told him about Vigil; he'd be even more worried if he knew. I realized I hadn't spoken for some time now, lost in my own thoughts. "Listen, let's not worry about this for now, okay? We'll figure this out later. The important thing is that you're feeling better. Let's get you some breakfast," I said, standing up and reaching out my hand to him.

He smiled and took my hand, but I knew he was still worried.

"I didn't have the chance to tell you about my weekend!" I said, holding his hand and walking with him out of the room. "You think you had a bad day yesterday? My mom and Tiffany took me shopping!" I said, shivering as I remembered the horrors of the trip.

He smiled at me again, and this time his smile reached his gray eyes, the fear of moments ago replaced by warmth and happiness.

We were going to be fine. We'd be fine as long as we were together.

Chapter Nineteen

The Bet

After proving my worth, delivering so many amazing lyrics, melodies and song suggestions for the band, I was now an official member of The Lost Boys.

Well, I was actually a Lost Girl, but you get the idea. I was putting the final touches to my first official song, and working simultaneously on three others for Harry, Sam and Josh now. I was having a hard time picking one theme for Tristan, though. We still had a lot of work to do.

By the end of the week Tiffany surprised me first thing in the morning in front of my locker, practically jumping up and down in excitement. "So, Joey! Are you anxious about tonight?" she squealed in her high-pitched voice.

"No. What's happening tonight?" I asked calmly. Clueless, that was me.

She gave me a scowl. "Are you serious? Everybody's been talking about this party all week long!"

Oh. Yeah. The sort-of-Valentine's party: with Valentine's Day being on Monday, the plan was to "celebrate" this side of the weekend instead...though, in all likelihood, it was more a case of any excuse for a party. I'd overheard the boys babbling something about it, but I hadn't really been paying attention. The truth was, I wasn't very good at parties. I always found a way to embarrass myself, and people usually stared uncomfortably at me and tried to avoid me because I said the most inappropriate things. I guess I was too blunt and too honest, and that was a major party killer.

"Oh, yes, I've heard about it…but I don't think…" I started to say when Tiffany interrupted me.

"Great! Fantastic! And don't you dare say you're not going, because you are, and that's final. We need to pick your outfit! You're so lucky I went shopping with you this last weekend, otherwise you'd only have those old sports clothes to wear! Oh! And you MUST wear that new purple top I picked out for you!" she said excitedly.

"Really, Tiff, I'm not good at parties…"

"I don't care if you are the worst ever in the whole wide world at parties, Joe Gray. You are going! And in the purple top!" she said, stomping her foot. Gosh, she was so bossy!

"Okay. All right," I agreed, giving up.

She smiled at me, happy she had won the battle, and then she spent the whole day talking about the damn party. And I spent the whole day dreading the evening to come.

At least I managed to forget about it through part of the afternoon, because of my music lesson with Professor Rubick. I was picking things up really fast and my piano didn't sound so rusty any more.

When class was over, I headed to my dorm room. Seth and Tristan were inside, with the rest of the boys spread around the room. Tristan was on his bed with my iPod plugged in his ears, shaking his head in synch with the beat of whatever song he was listening to, and Seth was lying on his bed strumming his guitar. I plodded inside the room and slouched on to my bed, pushing Harry out of the way because he was spread wide across the whole mattress. Seth stopped playing for a second, and Tristan took out his earphones when he saw me walk in.

"Hey," I greeted them sourly. "Harry, scoot over, will ya?"

"Jeez, Miss Sunshine. What's with the long face today?" Harry asked, shuffling across my bed and leaning against me.

Harry was a very touchy-feely person. He liked hugging, holding hands and leaning close. And it wasn't just with me; he acted this way with the rest of the band too. But he only acted like this with people he really liked and felt comfortable with. He was very shy and reserved with people he didn't know or trust. Harry's hugs were the best thing in the world. I don't know why, but they always gave me this warm, fuzzy feeling inside. It was quite addictive.

"It's nothing," I mumbled, leaning my head on Harry's shoulder. "I just really don't wanna go to this party tonight."

"Tiff is *ordering* you to go, isn't she?" Seth said, chuckling over on his bed.

"Yep," I confessed.

"So, don't let her boss you around! If you don't want to go, then don't go!" he said, getting back to playing his guitar.

"No way! You totally have to go, Joe!" Harry gasped next to me. "It's your first party at the school! It'll be so much fun! We're all going to be there, right, guys?"

"I'll definitely be there," Josh said, standing up and stretching, the muscles on his arms bulging over his black T-shirt. Josh was really fit. I tried hard not to stare.

"Me too," said Sam, standing up as well. "In fact, we should head over to our room and get ready! You two take for ever to get ready!" he complained with an eye-roll.

"Okay, then, let's go," Josh agreed, heading to the door.

Harry stood up, his red hair all ruffled up, and followed Josh and Sam. "See you there, then, Joey!" he said, waving at me. "I'll come with Tiffany to get you if you dare chicken out!"

I grunted under my breath. Great, now there were two of them forcing me to go to this party! "Are you going too, Seth?" I asked.

"I don't know. I'm not much of a party guy. What do you think, Tristan? Are you up for it?"

"Sure. Why not?" Tristan said, shrugging.

Great. Everybody was going. Now I had no way out of it. Especially as, at that moment, Tiff walked in.

"Hey, girl! Come on, grab your clothes, we're dressing in my room!" she ordered, waving me to hurry up.

"Aaaawww man!" I whined, and stood up reluctantly. Tristan and Seth chuckled at my childish antics.

Then Seth got up, saying he'd better start getting ready too, and Tiff obviously had to throw in a snarky remark about how Seth had finally stopped being such an "*indoor geek*", and then Seth was like, "*What's that supposed to mean?*" and Tiff bit back at him, "*You know you never go to any parties, Seth!*" and he was like, "*That's so not true!*" which made me snort out loud because he had *just said* a minute ago how he wasn't much of a party guy, and then he looked at me with murderous daggers in his eyes and I had to give him a pleading, sincere, apologizing look while Tiffany mocked him some more.

I shoved my clothes into my backpack in dead silence

after that. I didn't want to get in the middle of any of their fights.

Tiffany and Seth were constantly arguing over the smallest, silliest, random things. They enjoyed teasing each other like nothing else. It was a constant poking, provoking, sneering, scowling and mocking each other all the time. And when I say "all the time", I mean it! There wasn't a single occasion they were in the same room together that an argument wasn't born. At first I thought Seth was still miffed about Tiffany's bullying me during my first week, but then I realized he just simply enjoyed teasing her. It was his thing.

Tristan and I were used to it by now. So we usually just rolled our eyes and let them argue it out, until they got tired of it and made up.

Seth stomped back to his bed then, saying he wasn't in the mood for parties any more, and that he was fine being an "indoor geek", thank you very much. He grabbed a book and stared at the pages, pretending he wasn't noticing anyone in the room any more.

Tiffany tried to apologize to him, but Seth was fake-focusing all his attention on his book. She looked at us quite crestfallen when she realized what she had done. I think she'd been really happy that Seth was coming to the party, until she had gone and screwed things up. Tristan smiled at her and said he would take care of things, winking playfully. He'd convince Seth to go to the party later, then.

I followed Tiffany out of the room, walking like a woman going to her own hanging. Surprisingly, I had never been to Tiff's room before. When I entered her third-floor room, I was awestruck! Her room was twice the size of ours, with one king-size bed in the middle, a spare single bed to one side, lots of wardrobes around the room, a big mirror on the wall, a flat TV screen in the corner, and a small kitchen area that had a mini bar and also a portable stove on the countertop.

"Are all the girls' dorm rooms like this?" I asked, momentarily regretting my decision to room with the boys.

Tiffany shrugged and pushed me quickly into her bathroom, where I gasped in amazement. The bathroom was gigantic, with a beautiful pearly white tub and a big marble sink. Everything looked sparkly and sophisticated. I jumped, startled, when Tiff banged on the door, yelling that she wasn't hearing any shower running.

I stopped gawking at the place and hurried the hell up to get ready. After a quick shower, I walked into her room to get dressed and let Tiff help me with my make-up. I stared at my reflection in the huge mirror on the wall. A scared girl looked back at me, feeling slightly awkward with her new look.

I had on a tight top and black jeans with black pumps. I'd put my foot down about my pony-tail. Tiff wanted me to let my hair loose, but the dark-purple lipstick and black mascara she'd insisted on applying were already too much of a change for me to handle. Plus the purple top she had picked for me had a little too much cleavage showing for my taste too. So Tiff gave up on the hair, because she knew that in life you have to win some and lose some.

My stomach was twisting with nervousness as we arrived at the party. The outside space where the party was being held was already packed with students, everybody chatting and mingling. I could already see Sam, surrounded by a large group of people. He looked like he was telling a funny story and everyone was hanging on his every word.

Surprisingly, Josh was over the other side of the party, looking all cool and sexy in a black T-shirt over loose black jeans. He was talking to three girls who were giggling and batting their eyelashes at him. I realized Josh partied alone and preferred the *female-only* kind of audience.

I didn't need to search for Harry, because his high laughter caught my ears before my eyes could find him. I followed his voice to the middle of a group of skater-looking boys. He looked like he was having a lot of fun. Then he caught me looking at him and waved excitedly, coming over to greet us. "Finally! I was about to come get you! I thought you had cold feet!" he said, smiling at me.

"Oh, my feet are as cold as they can get!" I joked.

"You two look bewitchingly good, if I may say!" Harry said, whistling at the both of us. Tiff made a funny curtsey and I blushed intensely.

"You look smoking hot too, honey bun!" Tiff said, winking at him and admiring his salmon T-shirt and baggy shorts combo. "Come on, Joey, let me introduce you to everybody!" Tiff said, pushing me forward. "We'll catch up with you later, Harry-Berry!" Harry laughed and waved us goodbye, getting back to his friends.

I was really insecure and uncomfortable when Tiff introduced me to her friends. They were all polite to me, but I still could see the *"What's up with this girl?"* look in of their eyes. At some point I lost track of Tiff's whereabouts and just wandered aimlessly through the crowd. Then all of a sudden I felt a pair of hands grabbing my waist from behind, making me jump. I twisted around and saw an amused Tristan holding me in his arms.

"Hey, Buttons! I told Seth I was pretty sure it was you, but he said I was seeing things. So I came to see for myself," he said, giving me one of his bright sparkling smiles.

Lately Tristan had gotten into the habit of calling me Buttons, because once he'd said I looked "cute as a button" and I'd burst out laughing. It was such an old people's phrase, like something Miss Violet would say. Since then he'd stopped using it but had shortened it to Buttons whenever we were alone, as a private nickname. I loved it when he did. "You look so different!" he said in quiet surprise.

"Yeah, this is me after being subjected to Tiff's extreme make-over," I muttered apologetically, and smiled awkwardly at him. "I feel weird."

"No, no. You look…" he began, and paused as his eyes wandered from my eyes down to my cleavage "…lovely. Different, but lovely." His eyes suddenly darkened and his voice turned a little huskier than usual.

I didn't have time to blush, or even to enjoy his compliment, because I caught sight of Seth coming our way. So I pushed Tris away fast, making him lose his grip on my waist. He looked surprised but then realized what I was doing when I greeted Seth in a slightly freaked-out voice. "Heeeyy, Seeeeth! You're here! You came!" I said, stepping away from Tristan and giving Seth a hug.

"Hey, Joey! Yeah, I'm here. Tristan wouldn't shut up until I agreed to come, so I gave up. And, wow, you look great!" he said, looking me up and down with an appreciative grin.

Tristan was right by his side, doing the exact same thing, but then he caught Seth's expression and punched him in the arm. "Hey! Watch it! Stop looking at my sister like that!" he warned Seth.

"Sorry, man, I was just admiring, but in a respectful kind of way!" Seth said, holding his hands up, but then he glanced over my shoulder and his jaw dropped. I heard Tiffany's voice coming from behind me. So he had seen Tiff coming. She could make any boy's jaw drop, all right.

"Hey, guys! You all came!" she said excitedly.

"Yes, I might lose my geek-card over this, but I thought, what the hell, let's go to this party and risk losing my reputation, then!" Seth teased her.

She blushed a little, but did not lose her composure. "Oh, you can always replace your geek-card for this 'awesome-party-goer' one that I have right here in my purse! It's for exclusive members only, and you totally earned it tonight! Looking good, Seth, my boy," she said, teasing him back.

He laughed and looked shyly at her. It was his way of saying he had forgiven her for earlier.

Seth was wearing a pair of dark-gray jeans with a black long-sleeved shirt that hugged his lower torso nicely. His shirt was slightly open, exposing his neck and a little of his chest. He looked really hot. Tiffany seemed to agree, because her eyes burned as she watched Seth.

Then my gaze swept back to Tristan. If I thought Seth looked hot, I'd have to come up with an entire new word to describe Tristan! He was wearing a white buttoned-up shirt over light-blue jeans that fit him to perfection, but my eyes couldn't leave his face. His mouth quirked in a crooked, sexy smile. I was utterly surprised to realise that Tristan had been staring at me all along. Why anyone would look at me when Tiffany Worthington stood beside me in the most stunning, tight little black dress of the century? Was he freaking blind or something?

Then we heard Sam shouting, calling out for Tristan

somewhere in the middle of the crowd. Apparently, he needed Tristan's contribution to the tale he was telling at the moment. "Okay, I need to go or he won't stop shouting. I'll be right back!" Tristan said, chuckling and a little embarrassed, sliding into the crowd of people around us.

I took the opportunity to say I was going to look for Harry, and excused myself. Seth and Tiffany looked like they needed some time alone.

I continued wandering around the party, still feeling awkward and out of place, when two Barbie girls from Tiffany's cheer squad tackled me, blocking my way.

"Hey, Gray! How are ya?" one of them asked. I had no idea what her name was.

"Hey…*you*. I'm fine," I said suspiciously.

"So, you look different tonight! Tiff's been giving you a little help, hasn't she?" the other mocked, condescendingly.

"Yes, she is the best," I said sincerely. I didn't mind telling them Tiff helped me get ready for tonight. It was quite obvious anyway. "We got dressed in her room and she helped me out with all the pampering stuff."

"You were in her room?" they both squealed at the same time, clearly astonished.

"She actually asked you to go to her room? Like *inside* her room?" they asked again. "She never let's anyone in her room! Like, never, ever! What's it like in there?"

"It's, you know, roomy," I said vaguely. If Tiff never asked anyone to go in there, it's because she liked her privacy. I wasn't about to expose it to anyone, then.

They rolled their eyes at my vagueness, understanding I wasn't going to give anything up.

"So, Gray. What's the deal with your hunky brother?" one of them asked, changing the subject. I guess that was the real reason they'd stopped me in the first place, to ask me about Tristan. Urgh.

"What about him?" I said through pursed lips.

"What's his type? Is he into blondes? Or brunettes?" they asked eagerly.

I really didn't want to have this conversation. In fact, I was tempted to tell them he was gay or something like that. But that would be right. I couldn't do that to him. Or could I? No! No. I couldn't. They stared back expectantly.

What was I going to say? That I was really hoping his type of girl would be short, dark-haired, with black eyes, who liked martial arts and music, and who had a cute nicknames like, oh, let's say, Buttons?

"Um…I don't know, I don't think he has a type," I mumbled.

They jumped in excitement. "Oh, so we have a shot with him! I will totally win this bet, Caroline!" one of them said with a happy squeal.

"Na-ha! I will! He's going to be mine, you'll see!" Caroline retorted.

"Bet? What bet?" I asked, frowning.

They looked at me with matching sneers.

"I guess there's no problem you knowing…As long as you promise you won't tell him anything?" Caroline asked. She was the prettier of the two, all wavy blonde hair and big round blue eyes. I hated her already.

"Sure," I lied. Like I was going to keep a promise to the pompom squad! I mentally snorted at that.

"There's a bet going on, about who's gonna snap up Tristan tonight!" Caroline said.

"We know he's not with anyone, so it's open season on Tristan!" her friend squeaked.

"He's so dreamy! And such a gentleman, he treats us girls like princesses," Caroline confessed. "He opens doors so we can pass, pushes chairs for us to sit, kisses our hands. He's not like any of those lame guys I ever dated."

"Plus, he's smoking hot! Did you see how rock hard his ass looked in those jeans, Caroline? And those soft lips? I wonder how they taste…"

"Okay! That's enough!" I said, raising my hands in disgust. "Look, I've got to go. Best of luck trying to snap up your Prince Charming there," I growled, really upset.

Good God. Tristan open season! Yuck!

I hoped those girls tripped over their high heels and broke their necks! The party went downhill for me after that. Wherever I looked, I saw Tristan surrounded by beautiful, slutty girls, forever touching his arms, fighting for his attention, giggling and flirting shamelessly like they were all in heat over him. A few were coming on very strong, batting eyelashes, draping themselves over him and whispering in his ear. It made my blood boil! So I walked as far away from him as I could. This was turning out to be the worst party ever! I was set on going back to my room when Tiffany found me again and grabbed me by the arm, getting back to introducing me to her friends. It was torture, I tell you! I swear to God I was going to flip any minute now.

And people kept looking at me weirdly. I don't know why! Was it my make-over? Did I look that different? The boys who came to talk to me looked at me in the most odd way, and then glanced around and took off fast. What's up with that? The fifth time it happened Tiffany noticed it too, and looked at me with a frown, trying to understand what the problem was. We were clueless.

So she said she was going to mingle and try to find out

what was going on, then report back to me. I really didn't care any more. I just wanted to go back to my room! I was about to try to leave again when Harry appeared out of nowhere, and pulled me away from the mass of people. "Come here, Joey! I've got something to show you!" he said, with a mischievous glint in his emerald eyes.

Chapter Twenty

The Secret Terrace

I let myself be pulled towards the school building, with Harry tugging at my arm.

He kept glancing around to see if anyone was watching us. I wondered what he was up to as we passed through a little hidden door by the corner of the stone wall and climbed up some uneven stone steps. He opened a heavy iron door and we walked through on to a large, square balcony, almost like a terrace, except we were one storey up.

He motioned for me to follow him to the edge of the terrace. I followed right behind him, slowly and a little uncertain because there was only the moonlight illuminating the small space.

He stopped by the ledge and leaned his arms on it, observing the view. I did the same and we watched in silence as people chatted at the party below us.

"I like coming in here when they throw parties on this side of the building," Harry said. "See? We can watch everything and they can't see us up here." Harry pointed out some people at the party.

The balcony was positioned in a way that it was easy for

us, up above, to see everything, but difficult for the people below to see us. The lack of light helped too. We were fairly close to the party; we could even hear what some people were talking about. It was the perfect place to observe: a voyeur's paradise.

"It's so peaceful in here," I mumbled to myself. We could just relax and watch everything without the bother of actually being at the party.

"You looked like you weren't enjoying yourself much," Harry said, chuckling. "I get tired of those *party people* sometimes too. They try too hard to fit in, to be the prettiest, the coolest... I thought you might like it better up here."

"This is great, Harry!" I said. "Thanks for showing me this place. I promise I won't tell anybody."

"Good. Once word is out, it'd be hard to keep it a secret," he said. "It's just you and the band who knows about it. They always know that when I disappear from a party, I'm chilling out up here." I turned around and slumped slowly to the floor, leaning my back against the stone wall and glancing up at the sky. It was such a clear night, full of stars with a bright moon over our heads. It felt so much better looking up at the sky than down below. That party was tiresome. I sighed, relieved to be in a quiet place with no one around to judge me, or look at me in a weird way.

"You *really* don't care much for parties, huh?" Harry asked, slumping down into the other corner wall near to me.

"Well, everybody was kind of avoiding me there... I guess I don't know how to act much in these things... I feel a bit phony. People can tell I'm being fake, I guess," I mumbled, suddenly upset.

"You don't need to be fake. You were doing just fine!"

Harry said, laughing a little. His green eyes sparkled when he smiled. He looked so calm and peaceful now, so different from how he'd been at the party a few minutes ago.

"Yes, well. I just...I don't know, Harry. It looks so easy when you guys do it. Tiffany is Miss Popularity. Sam is so easygoing and fun to be around, people just crowd around him. Tristan has his magic charisma and Seth knows everybody, even the janitors! And girls swarm round Josh like bees to honey!"

Still looking up at the dark sky, I said, "I'm never going to be good at this party game."

"I'm not good at it too. But I don't care," Harry said with a shrug. "I'm just here to enjoy the company of my friends, have some laughs and some fun."

I scoffed at him, laughing. "Come on! You're not good at it?"

Harry just looked at me, frowning. "Yeah, why do you think I have my hide-out place up here? To hide. From people!" he explained with a mocking glare.

"Harry, you have your hiding place because you want some time alone; it's not because you don't fit in! You're amazing! I can't believe you don't know how much people follow your every move, listen to everything you say! All the guys want to be like you! You're so happy and carefree," I said, looking at him.

"Come on, now, happy and carefree? You're just throwing out random words," he said, amused. He thought I was making fun of him, by the look on his face.

"I'm not joking, Harry. You have this inherent happiness in you. Anyone can see that, no matter where you are, you're happy because you're comfortable with who you are! And you really don't care what anyone thinks or says about you. And you enjoy the little things in life and make them look so beautiful and important," I said seriously so he could see I wasn't joking. "People want to be near you just to get a glimpse of that feeling. It's genuine and honest and amazing! I wish I had the same free spirit you have. It's liberating."

I finished my ramblings and stared at my feet, fumbling with a small pebble on the floor. Harry was silent for some time, absorbing what I had just said. Or maybe he was just thinking I was crazy with my ramblings...

"That was...thanks, Joey. No one ever said anything like that to me before. It's usually, *'Harry you're crazy!'* or *'Harry, you're weird!'*" he said, adopting a funny squeaky voice, sounding like one of the pompom squad girls. He had probably heard things like that from them before.

I glanced up and saw him watching me with a shy smile, locks of soft red hair falling over his handsome thin face.

"Can I ask you a question, Joey?"

"Yeah, Harry. Sure."

"The first time we met, back in your room, remember? Why were you looking at me all funny like that? I thought you were thinking I was a freak or something," he mumbled, and looked startled when I started laughing out loud.

"No, Harry. I was just...surprised! You were the first person, well, the only person, actually, who hasn't made fun of my name. I was surprised, that's all. I meant to ask you about that, by the way. Why didn't you?" I poked his shoes lightly with my foot.

"There's nothing wrong with your name," he said honestly. He really meant it. I saw it in his eyes.

I couldn't help but smile. "See? That's why you're so

amazing, Harry," I muttered to myself, but he heard me and smiled too.

"Come on, Joe Gray, we've chilled enough up here! Let's get you back to that party and let people know how awesome you really are too!" Harry stood up and held out his hand to me. "And do what you want to do! Have some fun! Laugh with your friends! Don't worry about what any of those people think!"

I smiled and took Harry's hand, pushing myself off the ground at the same time that he pulled me up, which made me stand a little too fast. I stumbled, falling against his chest. His hands automatically went to my waist, trying to stop me from losing my balance. When I realized I hadn't fallen, I looked up. My face was only inches from his, and I could see his green eyes up close. Really up close. He had this amazing blue hue in the middle of the green, which gave his irises this incredible green color, like water in a rock pool, or a crystal emerald stone. It was so uncanny and his gaze was so intense!

His thin lips curled into a small smile, and my eyes drifted from his eyes to his lips. His lip ring glinted in the moonlight and I immediately thought about Tristan and his heartwarming smile. Slowly, I stepped away from Harry, feeling really guilty about allowing this little moment to have happened between us.

God! I hope Harry wasn't thinking I was making a move on him! We were all alone up on this terrace, in the complete dark, on a romantic moonlit night, and I was just going on and on about how amazing I thought he was! I felt like I was cheating on Tristan, even though we didn't have anything going on…I felt so awkward and guilty that Harry must have seen the embarrassment glowing brightly on my face.

"Couldn't wait to fall into my arms, huh?" he joked with a teasing smile.

"Harry...I- I'm sorry, I'm not...I don't..." I stuttered, pulling away from him fast.

"That's cool, Joey, I was just kidding!" he said, chuckling "I know you're taken."

"I-I- huh?"

"You have a boyfriend. He's probably from your old town, right? Long-distance relationships are hard," he said, looking up at the sky, contemplating the moon.

"I-I..." I couldn't manage to say anything. I was too stunned to come up with any lie right now.

"That's okay. You have this *'I'm-committed-to-a-relationship'* vibe going on. I usually pick up on these things sooner. Relax, I just brought you up here to chill, nothing more," he said, motioning to the door, smiling. "We better get back to the party now, or people will start thinking something was going on here and Tristan would kick my ass! He looks like the jealous-brother type. He's been checking on you all night!"

"H-he has?" I said, trying to conceal the surprise in my voice.

"Hell, yeah! And he did NOT look happy when a guy tried to approach you. He was giving them quite the evil glare...Hey, you said people were avoiding you there, that might be the reason why. At least for the male ones," he said, laughing at his discovery.

"Shut up, Harry, he was not! He was too busy with all those bimbo girls all night long! He didn't even know where I was..." I said, trailing down the stairs behind Harry.

"Well, I was right by his side and he kept glancing around

and asking about you all the time. But now that you've mentioned it, those girls were acting a little weird. I overheard something going on, some sort of bet. I dunno... I'll find out about that soon enough, don't worry."

We walked outside the school building and I was less upset now that I knew Tristan had been looking for me. I went back to the party holding Harry's hand. The band and Tristan were used to Harry holding hands and hugging all the time, but not everyone was aware of his particular touching habits, so there were a few raised eyebrows and glances towards us.

I didn't care any more. I had decided to accept Harry's suggestion: I was going to enjoy this damn party no matter what, and I wasn't going to worry about what anyone thought of me! I looked up and saw Tiff waving at me, smiling. I smiled back at her, truly happy.

"I'll go find out about those weird girls, Joey," Harry said. "You go ahead and have some fun, okay?"

I turned to him and hugged him tight. The warm, fuzzy feeling I had every time I hugged Harry came back, spreading happiness inside. "Okay, I will. And thanks so much, Harry!" I said.

"What for?" he asked, amused and surprised.

"For being my friend. You're awesome!" I said, kissing his cheek and ruffling his red hair with my hand. He didn't care about messing up his hair; it was always a mess, anyway. If I tried to do that with Seth's hair, I would be in so much trouble! Harry winked at me and took off, blending into the crowd.

After that enlightening conversation with Harry, everything changed for me. I was looking at things now from a different point of view. I was going to enjoy myself! I was going to have some fun with my friends, and laugh, and dance and forget about everyone else!

I hugged Tiff and thanked her for helping me dress up, and asked her to come dance with me. She looked surprised at my change of attitude, but then she beamed and hugged me back, pushing me to the dance area, which was a spot of grass near the sound speakers. I knew people were looking at me and I didn't care! To hell with them! I danced and danced with Tiff, shaking my body and laughing out loud. Then Tiffany asked for a time out to get some drinks, and I went to find Sam. I tackled him with a hug and tickled him just to hear him laughing, then hugged Josh too. That earned me a few envious stares from all the girls around them. They were my friends, my band; I could tickle and hug them whenever I wanted to! Then Harry appeared in our circle, beaming at all of us. I went to ruffle his hair again and hugged him once more.

The Beach Boys were blasting out, and I loved their songs so much, it kind of reminded me a bit of Harry's mood, so when he noticed I was stomping my feet along to the beat, he grabbed me by the waist and twirled me fast and started dancing with me in his crazy moves! Seth and Tiff arrived together, and Sam was already jumping around wildly with Harry, goofing around and following the music, singing along.

We had the most fun circle going on at the party! When the music ended, I grabbed my knees for support, panting and trying to catch my breath. I was desperately in need of something cold to drink, so I headed towards the refreshments, smiling happily and singing to myself.

I was scanning the table for something to drink when I heard someone clearing their throat. I looked up in the direction of the sound. It was Tristan. He was leaning against the wall, his arms crossed over his chest, looking at me intently with an indecipherable smirk on his face. I had a hard time pinpointing his exact location against the wall; it was like he was blending in with the texture of the stone. I squinted my eyes. He was using his special "fading" ability; that was why I was having difficulty focusing on him.

"Hey, I was wondering about where you were!" I said, smiling at him. "Tris, can you stop doing that, it makes my eyes watery."

"Not here, people will see me here and I'm trying to lay low. Walk with me?" he said, pointing towards the corridor that led away from the party.

"Sure," I said, walking by his side.

We walked a long way in silence before he decided to stop to rest on a low wall. Suddenly, I missed our good old days of long walks in the cemetery, when I had him all to myself. Lately I hardly got to see him at all; he was always away, busy with something...

"I see you're enjoying the party," he said, turning his "fading" off and sitting down on the wall, his long legs stretched out.

"I wasn't really. I was hating it. But then Harry talked to me and cheered me up...and I decided to change my attitude and enjoy the party. How about you? Why were you doing your 'fading' thing?"

"God! I needed to. There are some crazy girls here today! They wouldn't leave me alone one second, it was infuriating!" he said, frowning.

"Come on! Are you complaining about having lots of girls hanging all over you? Really?" I mocked him.

"It's not like that. They were really clingy...and kind of annoying. I don't like that at all," he said, shivering and making a funny face. "They were acting like crazy too! Modern girls are so...forward at times!"

I chuckled. "Yeah, I know, girls can flirt and hit on guys these days. It's not a 'men-only' thing any more, Tris. Plus, they have a bet thing going on, you know? About who's going to hook up with you tonight. That's why there's all the craziness around you."

"I know. You heard about it, huh?" he said, shaking his head in disbelief. "Do you know there's a bet on you too?"

"Yea, what?" I stopped chuckling and stared at him, wide-eyed.

"Oh, so you don't know about that! The bet is on both of the 'Grays', little sis. The girls are betting on me and the guys are betting on you: who's going to be the lucky guy to lay hands on you," he said, a grim look on his face.

"I-I...WHAT? Who the hell is making these bets!" I yelled, baffled. "But you must've heard it wrong, there were no guys coming after me. They were all acting really weird, looking at me like I was some sort of freak or something!"

"Yeah, sorry about that," he said, smiling and looking down to the ground. "Josh, Sam and Seth were kind of threatening everybody, saying if any scumbag got near you, he'd have to deal with them later."

That explained the weird behavior of the guys at the party. My boys were harassing people for my sake. They were so sweet! "And you? Did you do something too?" I asked, cocking an eyebrow at him.

"You mean, did I threaten to beat people up too? No, I didn't." He smiled cryptically and avoided eye contact.

"Oh. Okay," I said, a little deflated. He obviously didn't care.

"I just stared at all of them with a really, really disappointed face. And I may have implied that whoever touched you, would be kind of on my black list. Forever," he added, smirking evilly.

"Tristan!" I laughed out loud, deeply pleased.

"What? I'm sorry about that," he said teasingly, not one single ounce of sorrow in his eyes.

"Well, I guess that explains a lot," I muttered to myself.

"Apparently, Harry has won the bet, though," Tristan mumbled. There was doubt in his voice, just a little sadness behind it.

"What are you talking about? Did you hook up with Harry, then?" I asked, teasing him.

"Um…You guys disappeared for a while, there…and then you were back holding hands and stuff," he mumbled, looking uncomfortable and avoiding my eyes. So he had really been keeping close watch on me all night. And here I was, thinking he didn't care! I smiled and leaned my head on his shoulder. He was jealous of Harry.

"Harry is my friend, Tris. He saw that I was upset at the party, and tried to cheer me up. He also gave me some tips about how to enjoy a party properly, to stop worrying about what people think of me. Harry is awesome. But he's just my friend," I said seriously.

Although I couldn't see Tristan's face, I knew that he was smiling now. We stood still for a while in silence, enjoying each other's company. He kept stroking the back of my hands with his thumb and had leaned closer to me. I could feel the heat coming out of his body and a few butterflies fluttered in my belly. What was this cologne he was wearing? He smelled so good!

"Why on earth would you be worried about what people are thinking about you at this party? You're amazing. Everybody can see that," he said quietly.

I was glad he couldn't see me blushing. At times I have some serious low self-esteem issues, and it was hard for me to believe in that… "Thanks, Tris. You're amazing too," I said shyly.

After a time I noticed Tristan was getting anxious about something. He kept tensing up, like he was preparing to do or say something, but didn't have the nerve to act on it. Maybe he wanted to get back to the party and I was holding him back. I was beginning to get a little anxious myself. "Tris, what's wrong? You seem upset." I lifted my head off his shoulder.

"Nothing's wrong. I'm not upset."

I turned to look at him but he kept his gaze down, staring hard at the stone wall. I sighed loudly. "Tris, you promised you wouldn't do that any more," I said quietly. "I told you I can't read you like that, just by looking at you. It takes a lot of effort and concentration. Please. I hate it when you avoid looking at me. It makes me feel like you're mad at me. Or that you don't like me." I felt really bad for lying. I even tried to turn this thing off, block it somehow so I wouldn't be lying after all, but I couldn't.

"I'm sorry, Joey. I didn't mean to make you feel like that," Tristan said, looking up at last.

And when his eyes met mine, I held my breath and grabbed the wall for support. Because the intensity of his gaze was mind-blowing.

It was like he had been storing up all of his emotions,

and now the barrier was breaking down. It was impossible to block all of that out, even if I tried with all my might.

Waves of emotions flooded from his eyes, overflowing uncontrollably. I watched as guilt flickered in them. Guilt for making me think he didn't like me, crashing over jealousy of all the other boys near me at the party, over anger and sadness of thinking Harry had won me, all mixed with admiration of the new way I looked, and fear that someone might notice how badly he wanted me.

I tried to breathe while his emotions washed over me. I saw lust in his eyes at seeing my body while I danced, and nervousness about wanting to make a move, and fear of being rejected, arousal now at feeling my skin against his, the need to kiss me right now! I was frozen, desperately trying to cover up all I was seeing in his eyes. I couldn't even think straight, for that matter, mostly because all the desire and longing I could see in him mirrored my own feelings.

Before I could regain some shred of control, Tristan leaned slowly closer. Everything happened in slow motion. I could feel his hot breath and his piercing gray eyes boring into mine. There was only an inch of space between our lips and the distance seemed unbearable. I tried to close the gap but I couldn't move.

Then Tristan leaned in teasingly, brushing his lips so softly to mine that I almost thought I was imagining it. I didn't know how much longer I could hold my breath, but I feared I might break the spell if I exhaled. I felt his lips curve in a smile, and saw his eyes crinkling, as he leaned in, closing the last fraction of an inch between us. I felt the heat and the softness of his lips over mine for the first time, and tiny tingling pinpricks of heat.

I had never been kissed like this before in my life. It made all my previous experiences fade in comparison, weak shadows of what a kiss was really supposed to be like.

His lips were everything I'd imagined, and more.

It felt like magic.

The most absolute perfect thing.

And then it was over.

People started arriving down the corridor, shouting and laughing loudly, making Tristan jerk his head away from me, surprised by their sudden arrival.

I felt lightheaded, like I was coming down from a high. I blinked, confused, slowly coming out of my dazed state. Had Tristan just kissed me? Because it felt so unreal...so unworldly. Or had I just imagined it all? The fading tingling in my lips told me otherwise. It had happened. It wasn't a dream.

He looked at me with a glint in his gray eyes, and smiled. God! I couldn't get enough of his smiles! People kept passing by us, chatting and laughing. Where were they going?

"Do you want to go someplace else?" Tristan asked quietly, his voice raspy and low, making me snap my eyes away from the clusters of passing students back to him. I blushed all shades of red when I understood he wanted more time alone with me. His eyes darkened, fixing on me, making my heart go haywire. He wanted more than a few seconds of a kiss.

I opened my mouth but nothing came out. I was speechless and overwhelmed. If one kiss had turned me into this incoherent mess, can you imagine what a whole lot more of his lips on me would do? My head kept shouting at me to take it slow, to do the right thing and call it a night.

But I just went ahead and nodded at Tristan, smiling at him shyly.

Take that, stupid head! Hah! I mentally poked my tongue out to my brain. Apparently, my heart was in charge of things tonight. It wanted some more time alone with Tristan too; it also wanted more of his kiss. But before we could stand up, Seth, Tiff and Sam appeared in the corridor, talking happily to each other.

They spotted us sitting there and headed our way. Tristan sagged when he saw them approaching, frustration rolling off him in waves. Alone time seemed to be farther and farther away from our grasp...

"Hey, man, we were looking all over for you! You disappeared!" Seth said, beaming at Tristan. "Sam was even saying you must have been hooking up with a girl somewhere."

"I've been here with Joey," Tristan said, smiling to the ground. I noticed he had this habit of telling the truth without actually saying the truth. It was kind of clever of him.

"What's going on, guys?" I risked asking, my voice coming out a little quivery. I still hadn't recovered fully from my incoherent jelly state. "Why everybody's heading this way?"

"Party's over," Tiff said, leaning on Seth and taking her high heels off. "Oh God, that feels good. Shoes were killing me. Pooh."

Sam sniggered teasingly. "Have you noticed how women always make these orgasmic moans whenever they take their heels off?" He chuckled loudly. "And the more uncomfortable the shoes, the more orgasmic the sound?"

At Sam's side, Seth started laughing hard. "Oh man! That is so true!" he said, high-fiving Sam.

They were almost choking with laughter. Tiffany, however, seemed oblivious.

"My toes just feel too good to care about them," she said, shrugging, and wiggled her toes on the cold floor. "I'm calling it a night, guys! I'll see you tomorrow." She waved us goodbye then walked back to her dorm room.

Sam wiped tears of laughter from his deep-blue eyes. "I'm going to head to bed too. Night all!" he said, with a wave.

It was just me, Tristan and Seth, then. Seth turned to leave and looked at us, waiting.

"Aren't you coming? You heard them, party's over. Let's go."

I shrugged and stood up. What were we going to say? No, we are staying here some more, because we want to be alone and make out a little bit, so please, leave us alone now? Tristan sighed loudly and followed us down the corridor. I could still feel his frustration flooding off him while he walked by my side, even though his eyes were glued to the floor the whole time.

"So, where are Harry and Josh? They left the party early?" Tristan asked, making small talk with Seth. I focused on their chat, to distract my mind from that kiss.

"Oh, those two are still partying out there somewhere," Seth said, chuckling. "Josh is always the last to return to the dorms at night. And Harry has his 'boyish charms' and the 'I'm so shy' sweet face of his. It's a freaking gold mine! No chick resists him. Ever."

The boys chatted amiably as we headed back to our dorm, but I remained silent. There was a lot that I needed to process about the night. About my feelings, and what I'd seen in Tristan's eyes. Which part of that kiss was really us? Which part was the spell that bound us? I remembered the pinpricks of heat on my lips when we touched...Was that magic and, if so, was anything that was happening between us real at all?

I was the first to the bathroom, the first to get dressed in my comfy pajamas and the first in bed. When Seth retreated to the bathroom, Tristan took the opportunity of us being alone to sit on my bed.

"Are you okay, Joey? You look a little worried."

"Yeah, no. I...I'm just a little confused. I mean..." I burrowed deeper into my bed. Okay, understatement of the year. I was freaking out.

"About us?" he said, biting his lips. It looked so damn sexy. I wished I could be biting those lips. "I'm not. Things are pretty clear to me," he said.

"R-really?"

"How about we do this. Let's take things slow. How does that sound?" he said, putting his hand over mine.

"Okay. I think. Sounds good..."

We locked eyes again and there was a sizzling buzz shooting electricity between us. He started leaning closer to me, but Seth came out of the bathroom, making him lean back hastily. Frustration and annoyance flickered in his eyes for a brief second, but it was replaced by a humorous glint.

"Yeah, slow. Maybe this is for the best," he mumbled to himself, and shook his head. "Good night, then, Buttons." He gave me a chaste peck on my forehead and walked over to his bed, smiling softly.

Chapter Twenty-One
Sky

I woke up lying on soft, warm, silvery sand.

Okay, I was having that same weird dream again, I thought to myself. It was the same moonless night in that infinite desert and the same goth-looking girl was sitting next to me. I sat up and turned towards her.

"Hi again."

The girl greeted me back. She had her legs crossed in a meditation pose, her hands folded loosely in her lap. "Why do you keep coming back here, Joe?" Goth Girl asked. "I told you before, you're easy to track here."

"I don't know why I'm here. Why are you?" I retorted, a little miffed. Why did she keep telling me to leave all the time?

"This is sort of a 'workplace' for me," she said calmly.

"Well…your job must be really boring, then, huh?" I asked, looking around at the endless desert sand. This place looked as dead as it could be.

"It can get a little repetitive sometimes," she said, following my gaze, but then she turned back to focus on me. "But sometimes unexpected things can happen." She added thoughtfully, "Like when you called me. That was an interesting evening for me."

"I called you?" I asked suspiciously.

"Yes. That night at the cemetery, you called me."

Apprehension gripped my stomach. "What night?" I asked, but I already feared the answer.

"New Year's Eve. But you know that."

"I-I didn't call you. There seems to be a misunderstanding..."

"Sure you did. You and Tristan." She smiled softly.

"I-we...d-didn't," I stuttered. But then I remembered what Miss Violet had said. There were seven people that night. The three old ladies, Mom and me making five, Tristan being the sixth. And the seventh? She beamed, watching as realization dawned: "You were the seventh? Wait, who are you?" I asked, starting to get a little scared now.

She seemed to ponder that question. "You called me and you don't know who I am?" she asked, confused. "And you keep coming here but you don't know why, or how you are doing it? Not many people come here voluntarily, you know. And, please, do have in mind that he can also find you very easily in here too," she said, looking at the horizon.

"He?"

"Yes. He's been searching for you for a while. But then he stopped. Very odd..." she said talking to herself. "It's not like him to give up like that. He can be so relentless, so stubborn."

I tried to make sense of her words. Someone looking for me. Relentless. "Do you mean Vigil?" I asked. It could only be him that she was talking about. "I mean, I don't know his real name, so I just call him Vigil. He already found me."

She frowned then her expression changed to one of amusement. "You actually named him?" she said with a big grin. "That should be interesting to watch! And you said he found you?"

"Yes. He keeps crashing into my dreams. Kind of like you and this place…" I mumbled, looking at her in annoyance. "But I always wake up and there's nothing he can do about it. Plus, last time I sort of punched him and it looked like it hurt him. So maybe he stopped after that…"

"Punched him, you say? You sure are entertaining. That explains his absence. He'll be back, though."

"I hope not," I muttered to myself. Even in his fragile, pale, thin boyish incarnation, he was scary as hell.

"He will. You can count on that. It will be fun to see this," she said.

"Well, as long as I'm entertaining you, that's all right, then," I replied, annoyed at the way she was looking at me like I was some sort of circus freak show.

"Oh! You're tremendously entertaining. I do hope you can come see me again! But enough of that. It's time to wake up, Joe."

"What? Wait! You still haven't told me who you are!" The sky above us suddenly seemed brighter. It looked like the sun was coming up – clearly my time here was running out. 'Tell me your name?" I asked in a hurry, hoping she'd answer at least one of my questions.

She smiled. "I have many names."

She was almost as cryptic as Vigil. Could this girl give me at least *one* straight answer?

"Why don't you go ahead and make one up for me?

Since you are already so good at giving names!" she said, winking playfully at me.

I didn't have time to answer her, though, because the sound of Seth's alarm clock burst through the scene. I blinked slowly, trying to adjust to the bright daylight washing over my eyes. For a second I thought about a name, while I was still slumbering in that intermediary state of half-consciousness.

Sky. Her name is Sky.

"That's a good one!" I heard her whisper in my ear, and then I woke up completely, and the dream faded from my mind like twirling leaves scattered by the wind.

The sound of his alarm woke Seth up too.

He wanted to rehearse the new songs today, even though it was Saturday. He'd decided that two days a week to practice wasn't good enough for "the band", so we were rehearsing three afternoons in the week, and now apparently we were going to practice all weekend too. Seth was riding us pretty hard with all the band practice, but I didn't mind; rehearsal time was like the most amazing time ever for me!

Since waking up, I'd tried to avoid looking at Tristan. Every time our eyes accidentally met, I blushed like a thirteen-year-old; it was extremely aggravating! I felt so stupid, being all girly like that! Why did he have that effect on me?

Josh and Sam were already in the practice room when we arrived. We chatted a while about the events of the party, and then I sat in my favorite spot, right in front of the instruments area where I could lean against a bunch of boxes. I took out my lyrics book and some pencils from my backpack, getting ready to start work.

Tristan glanced my way, while the boys were setting out

their guitars and drums. Then he walked over to me and, before I could start blushing again, he sat down by my side.

"So, did you sleep well?" he asked a little nervously, looking at my notebook.

"Yeah. You?" I asked. *Stop blushing, Joey. Stop blushing. Stop blushing.*

"Yeah. But I got a little worried this morning, though."

"Worried?" I asked shakily. *Keep it simple, short replies, and do not blush.*

He gave me a nervous sideways glance. "I was worried that I may have stepped over some boundaries last night. I didn't ask you if I could do what I did...if it was all right. I didn't mean to disrespect you," he said, and blushed. "If I did, please forgive me, Joey. I didn't want to make you feel uncomfortable, like you seem to be now."

"No! No, no. You didn't! I-I mean, I'm not. You don't make me feel uncomfortable, Tris!" I said.

Tristan was so sweet, with his polite, old-fashioned ways, worried that he had ruined my honor just because of one kiss. One amazing, obliterating, mind-blowing kiss...

Before he could say anything in response, Harry barged into the room, his bass strapped to his back.

"Yellow, peeps! Ledger is in the house! You can all chill now!" Harry greeted everyone happily.

"Harry, you're always the last one here, man! Every time, every rehearsal! What took you so long?" Seth complained.

"Whoa. Why all the sulking, Mr. Grumpy Face?" Harry retorted jokingly. "You should be more cheerful today, since last night you got some action, and all..."

Seth went all red in the face. "I-I did not! I don't know what you're talking about. Shut up, Harry!" Seth snapped, looking all flustered.

Harry laughed, took his bass off his back and settled it down. "Seth, dude! You know I can always tell when someone has seen some action! It's my super power," he said, surveying the room.

I was glad Harry hadn't so much glanced in my direction yet. I was sure I would turn a new shade of red if he guessed that Tristan and I had also seen "some action" last night. I looked down at my notepad embarrassed. After a few seconds of uncomfortable silence, I heard Harry again. I didn't dare look up.

"You know who else got lucky? Smirking Josh over there in the corner. Oh! Tristan my man, too! Way to go, Tristan! And, aw, sorry, Sammy. Maybe next time, huh?" Harry said, making a sad face at Sam.

It was Sam's turn to turn red. "Shut up, Harry! You are just making this stuff up!" Sam grunted as Josh chuckled.

"I'm not. You all know it! I can totally tell who's been getting some or not." Harry sniffed loudly, putting his bass down. "And I don't understand why Seth is so worked up about it; he's usually the last one to hook up. You shouldn't be ashamed, bro! It is actually a good thing, you know? Unless...it was a shameful hook-up? Who was it, Seth?"

"It was nobody, Harry. Would you just shut it and get ready to rehearse?" Seth muttered crossly.

"Okay, Okay! Don't need to bite my head off!" Harry said, opening his bass case. "How about you, Joey? Did you have a good time at the party last night?"

I glanced up and, panicking, looked around the room. Sam was sniggering at Harry over the other side.

"What? Can't you tell? Don't you have this *hook-up-radar* super power?" Sam teased him.

"I asked her if she had a good time, not if she had hooked

up. Keep your mind out of the gutter, dude! Plus, my powers don't work on girls. They mess up all my signals, it's the damnedest thing!" Harry said, squinting his eyes at me.

"Stop staring at me, Harry!" I said, squinting back at him and mentally muttering, *"Don't blush now, Joey, just don't freakin' blush now!"* to myself.

Thank God, Tristan came to my rescue then, telling the band to start rehearsals. We had a long practice session, but in the end all our efforts really paid off. The songs were starting to sound more finished now and we were playing our instruments in a much more refined way.

We had also started to give small performances every Wednesday at Professor's Rubick's classes. Since a well-performed prank had got us noticed at school, we'd attracted a regular gathering of people showing up to listen, too, not just our friends and classmates.

Our little unnoticed band was finally starting to get noticed inside Sagan's grounds.

Chapter Twenty-Two

Under Pressure

Monday morning I woke up with a little bit of a headache. I was walking to my locker to gather some books for my first morning class, when one of the cheer squad girls called after me. Caroline, I think, was her name. She was the blonde perky girl who'd been dead set on having Tristan at that party. I remembered hating her. Vividly.

I sighed when she stopped in front of me. I wasn't in the mood for conversation. My head started to hurt slightly more in her presence.

"Hey, Gray!" she said, putting a hand on one hip.

"Hi... *you*," I said, a little annoyed, pretending I didn't remember her name.

She gave me a glare because she was probably not used to people forgetting her name. She was quite popular around the school. "So, we *kinda* need your official state-ment so we can close the bet," she said with a huff.

Ah. The bet. I wasn't one bit surprised that she was the one in charge of that stupid deal.

"Yes. We need you to confirm the hook-up, so we can deliver the prize," her friend said, picking at a nail.

"What prize?"

She gave an annoyed sigh, rolling her eyes. "Jeez, you really don't know anything, do you? The person that hooked up with you at the party gets a whole week of physics homework done by Dwight for free."

Dwight, I knew, was the school nerd; Seth had told me the guy had a lucrative business going, charging people for homework.

"A whole week of physics homework? That's a lot." I hadn't realized I was worth that much. I think she noticed where my thoughts were heading, so she quickly set me straight, putting me back where I belong: Loserville.

"Yeah, well, we first set the prize up for Tristan's hook-up. He's totally worth a whole week of any homework. Hell, he's worth a whole *month* of homework!" she said, getting all excited, but then she noticed my disgruntled face and returned to the point. "And since we had already set his prize for a week, we thought we had to set the same for you...so you wouldn't feel too bad, and all."

"Gosh. Thanks so much. I don't feel bad at all *now*," I muttered sarcastically.

She shrugged, meaning she really didn't care how I was feeling.

"So, should I take Harry's homework, then? He still hasn't come to collect. It's so typical of him, always forgetting things..." She shook her head in disapproval.

"Wait, what? Harry?" I asked, puzzled.

"Yes, Harry Ledger. Red hair. Pierced lip. Crazy tattoo, hot and weird. Harry. I'm sure you remember him, the party wasn't *that* long ago!" she said with a smirk.

"I know who Harry is!" I snapped, annoyed "I don't... we didn't...there was no hook-up with Harry!" I said in a hushed voice, and looked around to see if there was anyone overhearing us.

She cocked an eyebrow, not believing me at all. "Come on, Gray. Don't play coy now. We all saw you two that night, holding hands, dancing. You were all over each other. The whole school is talking about it. Let him have his prize!"

I was baffled. "I-I-I . . . There was NO hookup!" I shouted, stamping my foot. "And even if there had been, it's none of your goddamn business! And these bets are awful! You are all awful people! You want some gossip to spread around? Spread this one: if I ever hear that someone has made a bet on me again, I'll kick their ass! Got it?" I snapped, and stomped off to my next class.

I was early and the classroom was empty, which was fine by me; I really didn't want to talk to anyone anyway. My head was throbbing. I was rubbing my temples in aggravation when Tiffany walked in.

"Hey, Joey! I saw you storming madly through the corridors. What's happened? Something wrong?" she asked in concern, sitting by my side.

"No, it's just . . . I hate people!" I grunted menacingly.

She chuckled at my general display of hatred. "Care to elaborate? People in general or someone specific?"

I sighed, holding my head in my hands. "People here at this school. Did you know everybody's been talking about me and Harry getting together?" I said, exasperated.

"Yeah, I heard about that at breakfast. So? What's the matter?"

"The matter is that we didn't! It's a lie!" I snapped.

"I see. I just don't get why you are so upset about it. Harry is a really great guy, and he follows you around like a lost puppy. Maybe you should give him a chance," she suggested.

"Harry is my friend," I said quickly.

"Yes. But he could be more." Tiff raised an eyebrow, looking me directly in the eyes. "Unless there's something you're not telling me...some other reason why you won't even consider being with him." She leaned over, close to me. "I always get this feeling you're hiding something from me, Joe. I thought that, with time, you'd trust me and tell me what it is...It's the reason you won't give Harry a chance, isn't it?"

I avoided looking at her and fumbled with the hem of my shirt instead. "I'm not hiding anything, Tiff. I really like Harry, but just as a friend!" I said, trying to sound convincing, but I wasn't fooling anyone here.

"Come on, Joey. I tell you everything that's going on with me! You can trust me! I know there's something," she said pushing harder.

"I'm telling you the truth, Tiff. Really," I said nervously.

She stared at me for a few seconds in silence. "Fine. If you want to be like that, be like that, then." She looked hurt. "I thought you were my friend."

"Tiff, come on! Please..." I began, but she just stood up and went to sit far away from me.

Students started to arrive, and the teacher followed right behind. The class started and I didn't have a chance to talk to Tiff again. She didn't look my way the whole class, and when it was over, she just stood up and left. She was really hurt and I couldn't blame her. She knew I was hiding something from her. Keeping my secret was starting to have a price. And it seemed the price was going to be Tiffany's friendship.

I walked out of class in a very bad mood. The day couldn't get any worse. First I'd heard about the nasty rumor about me and Harry, and now my best friend wasn't talking to me any more. Then I glanced up and saw Tristan walking my way, a worried expression on his face. That was it. He had heard the gossip going around school and was angry and had come here to tell me he hated me and never wanted to see me again.

He stopped in front of me, glancing sideways to see if anybody was listening. Okay. He didn't look angry. I was just over-reacting. He looked…concerned and anxious. Not mad. That was good. Not mad was a good thing.

"Hey, Joey," he greeted in a tense voice, and managed a weak smile. "What's wrong? You look awful."

"Gosh. Thanks very much. It's always nice to hear a compliment in the morning," I muttered darkly. I didn't know why I was snapping at everyone today! The headache definitely wasn't helping.

"I didn't mean…You just look kind of in pain. Are you okay?" he said, trying to apologize.

"Sorry, Tris, it's just a headache, but I'll be fine. You look worried…" I said, trying to rub the headache away.

"Listen, I need to talk to you…" he said, then stopped and looked hesitantly to one side "…later. Can I meet you after morning classes, by the big oak tree?" he said, his eyes flicking back and forth.

"Sure. What's the matter?" I said, trying to get some clue about what he wanted to talk about.

"We can talk later, okay?" he said, waving to one of his basketball friends at the end of the corridor. "Come on, I'll walk you to your next class."

"No, that's fine. You don't need to walk me, I'm not a

baby," I snapped again. "I mean, I'm fine here. Your friend is calling you, you can go." I waved him away. This headache was putting me in such a foul mood.

He looked uncertainly at me, and nodded. "Okay. I'll see you after classes, then," he said, walking away.

When I turned around to walk to my next class I spotted a wild-spiked redhead bouncing around in the middle of the crowd. "HARRY!" I yelled, to get his attention, and flinched with the sharp pain that resulted. Curses! No yelling, Joey.

"Hi, Joey! What's up?" Harry asked, all innocent, when he reached me.

I grabbed his arm and pushed him against the wall, where we could have a more private conversation.

"Don't go all *'Hi, Joey'* on me, Harry!" I grunted. He looked startled at my harshness "Have you heard what people are saying about us all over school? Did you have anything to do with it?" I interrogated him.

He raised his eyebrows, curious now. "No! I haven't heard anything! What's going on?"

I looked into his green eyes. He wasn't lying; he really had no idea. I'd noticed Harry never lied to me. That was...kind of sweet of him. I shook my head, trying to get back on track. "Okay. So...you haven't heard people are saying we hooked up at the party? That you won the bet, and all..."

A wide grin spread across his face then. "Get out of here! Really? All right!" he said, all smug.

"No. No. *No*. Not 'all right', Harry! Stop grinning. This is not funny!" I said, real upset.

"Come on, Joey! It's a little funny. Well, for me it is," he said, chuckling. "I can't believe I won the bet!" He jumped up and down, making a squeaky voice. "Wait! What have I won, exactly?"

I rolled my eyes. "You didn't win any stupid bet, Harry. And it was a week of Dwight doing your physics homework. Just so you know what you didn't win," I said, grabbing him by the arms, making him stop his little excited jumps. "I already told them we didn't hook up!"

Harry looked crestfallen, pouting his bottom lip. "Awww, Joey! You took a whole week of physics homework from me? That's just so wrong of you!" he said, crossing his arms, upset. "Couldn't you just lie about it, just this one time? I really hate physics!" he whined.

"No! I could not! And you'd better start telling people the truth, Harry!" I said, glaring menacingly at him.

"All right! All right! Don't need to use the Evil Eye on me! I'll tell everybody, don't worry! You need to take a chill pill!" he said, uncrossing his arms and giving me a worried look. "Are you okay? You look awful, you know?"

I let out a heavy sigh, hunching my shoulders down. "Thank you, Harry. You sure know how to make a girl feel better," I muttered, in a bad mood; being told I looked awful twice in one day was doing nothing for my self-esteem. "I'm just having the worst day. And my head is killing me. I guess I'll go to the infirmary, grab some aspirin. I'll see you later." I walked away tiredly.

On the way to the infirmary, I watched Tiffany pass by me, pretending she was deeply engaged in a conversation with Caroline. I felt awful. I never realized how much Tiff's cheerful mood and positive presence meant to me. Now that I didn't have it, I missed it so much!

I badly wanted to tell her the truth about me and Tristan. Then I would never have to worry about pretending I didn't like him in front of her, and I could talk to her about it, and stop with all the lies. I was so lost in my gloomy thoughts that I didn't pay attention to where I was going as I bumped into someone, hard. I staggered back and looked up in surprise to see a pretty brown-haired girl giving me a scared look.

"Oh, sorry, I wasn't looking where I was going," I began, but the girl interrupted me, taking a small frightened step back.

"Gray!" she exclaimed in shock, as if my name was some sort of curse. "P-please don't hit me!" she squeaked, panicking.

"I— What?" I stammered. "I wasn't going to hit you!"

She seemed not to hear what I was saying. "It's not my fault, you know! You don't need to hit me just because of Harry! He never told me you guys were together! I should have known, no boy that pretty is good news!" she said in a crazy rant. "I swear I didn't know he had a girlfriend the night of the party! He's such a man whore!"

Oh. I see. I remember Seth telling me Harry and Josh were still partying somewhere that night, and how girls never resisted Harry and his innocent good looks. Innocent, yeah, right! Apparently this was the girl who'd had him "occupied" that night. She was pretty. Harry had good taste.

"And now everybody's giving me crap about how you're going to kick my ass!" The girl continued to freak out, stepping away from me. "Because Harry is yours and you're some judo queen and you even kicked Bradley's ass, and now you're going to kick my ass. And all the cheer squad is scared of you, and... please don't hurt me!" she rambled on, clearly terrified of me.

If my head hadn't been throbbing that much, I would

have found this thing amusing, but I guess I wasn't in the mood for any enjoyment. And what about the way people were acting? Like I was some sort of scary bully that beat people up all the time! I'd never touched anybody in this school, for God's sake! I just stood up for myself when I had to, and I didn't take crap from anyone! Is that such a bad thing?

"Look...you." I didn't know her name. "First. Harry is not '*mine*'. I'm not his girlfriend. We're just friends," I stated seriously. "Second, he's not a man whore. He was only with you that night. We didn't hook up at the party. Third. I'm only going to kick 'some ass' if anyone dares to make bets on me again. And fourth...I'm not going to hit you, so please stop flinching, for God's sake!" I huffed, by now annoyed with the frightened girl.

She blinked uncertainly at me. "R-really" she stuttered. "So...Harry likes me?"

I frowned as an unsettling jealousy lurched unexpectedly inside my chest. Where did *that* come from? "I didn't say that," I snapped. "I don't know, do I? But we're not together, that's all. And I don't go around punching people, you know? I'm actually a very mellow person!"

She snorted loudly, then coughed, trying to cover up her lack of faith in my mellowness. "Hum, yeah, yeah. Right. Everybody knows you're...very...*mellow*." She attempted a serious expression.

"Oh, shut up!" I said, aggravated, and stormed away, leaving a very relieved, frightened girl behind. My head hurt too much to keep trying to be nice.

I was almost at the infirmary door when Bradley passed by me, smirking.

"Gray! Looking good! Heard about you and Harry! Did

his lip ring feel good?" he said, making a disgusting move with his tongue before walking away, laughing.

I growled viciously at his retreating back and headed for the infirmary's door, my headache pounding twice as hard now after his gross gesture.

I got some aspirin from the nurse and stayed at the infirmary for the rest of the morning, just resting. It took some time for my head to stop throbbing. But I still felt like crap. I was sure people were still gossiping non-stop about me; Tiffany still wasn't talking to me; Tristan still wanted to talk about something, and it didn't sound like it was going to be a good thing.

At least I had finally got rid of my stabbing headache.

I realized that the final class of the morning had ended a couple of minutes ago, so I headed to the school garden to meet up with Tristan, but he caught up with me before I could even reach the end of the hallway.

"Hey, Joey! I'm glad I found you," he said, but his eyes looked worried.

"Yeah, I was just heading to the oak tree where you said to meet you," I said, returning to my nervous state.

"Great! Come on, I wanted to talk to you as soon as possible. I don't want you going to our room just yet…" His eyes darted around the hallway. "You haven't seen Seth today, have you?"

"No. I've been in the infirmary most of the morning, why?" I asked as we walked outside with him.

Tristan paused, looking at me in alarm. "Infirmary? What's wrong? I knew I shouldn't have left you earlier today! You aren't well!" he said, stopping in front of me and putting his hands under my chin, studying my face with a frown.

"I'm fine, Tris. It was just a headache," I said, feeling my cheeks tingle at the contact between his fingers and my skin. "It's gone now. I'm much better."

He stared at me for a few seconds, trying to see if I was being honest.

"I swear I'm fine, Tris!" I smiled at him. The fact that he still cared about me warmed my heart. He wasn't mad about the rumors surrounding me and Harry. I felt so relieved that I blurted it out before I could stop myself. "I'm glad you're not mad at me..."

He frowned again, his gray eyes sparkling with a hint of curiosity. "Mad at you? Why would I be mad at you?"

"Well, you must have heard people talking..."

"Talking?"

"About me...and Harry?" I probed cautiously. "They've been saying that Harry and I hooked up."

He frowned, but then a small smile played at the corner of his lips. "Yeah, I heard about it." He grabbed my hand and resumed walking towards the oak tree. "Harry was the one who told me, actually. He was worried that, and I quote, 'I might hear from someone else and get mad and go berserk on him.' He was a little miffed that you couldn't play along and get him out of a week's homework, though. He kept repeating that part. Over and over again." Tristan chuckled.

When we arrived at the big oak tree, Tristan kept checking to see if there was anyone around, and then he turned to me, anxiety pouring off him. "Good, we're clear! So, listen, I really need to ask you something, Joey. It's very important," he said in an urgent tone. "And you really need to agree on this," he pleaded. "Because if you don't, you might have to go out with Seth and that would be really, *really* bad!"

"What are you talking about, Tris?" I asked, amused. "What's this nonsense now? First I'm hooking up with Harry, now I have to go out with Seth. This day is getting really weird!"

He let out an exasperated breath and swept his hands through his hair in agitation. "I'm serious, Joey. Do you think I'd joke about something like this?"

"About what, for crying out loud?" I said, throwing my arms up in the air.

"We need to tell Seth the truth! About you and me!" he blurted out.

"What?" I managed to say.

"We need to tell Seth that you're not my sister. That I'm not your brother. And we are...you know." He mumbled the last part, blushing a faint shade of pink.

I cocked an eyebrow at him. "Actually, I *don't* know. What are we again?" I asked with a smirk. This ought to be good to hear.

The faint shade of pink turned into a deep, fierce crimson. "I– I, we, I, you *know*," he stuttered, and then got all flustered. "What is with people trying to hassle me today? Are you all trying to make me lose my mind, is that it?" he said in a despairing voice.

I patted his shoulder, trying to calm him down. "Okay, okay! All right, sorry about that. Stay calm, I'm just teasing you!" I said, smiling at his flushed face. "Now, please, tell me about this going out with Seth thing."

He pouted at me. "This isn't funny. Seth's been on my back all day, you know? Asking about you, what you like, what you don't like. He wouldn't shut up about you!" Tristan exclaimed, getting all worked up again "Then he told me he's going to ask you out today. On a date. So you see, we need to tell him. It's the only way out of this. He said he wouldn't take no for an answer; he was pretty set on taking you out. And he can't!"

I looked at Tristan's flustered face. He was so cute having a jealous fit!

"He can't? Why is that?" I asked, leaning against the trunk of the oak tree, teasing him again. I just loved so much seeing him blush that I couldn't help myself!

He stared at me and his eyes darkened to a deep gray. A lascivious smile quirked the corner of his mouth, and he leaned closer to me until his body was pressed dangerously close to mine. I guessed he was done being shy!

"Can't you tell why? Maybe I should just show you, then." He put a hand either side of my head on the oak trunk. He looked around again, just in case there was anyone watching, and then edged his face, slowly, closer to mine, making my throat go dry in a second. Okay. The teasing came back to bite me in the ass! He wasn't stuttering or blushing any more. Now he was smiling sexily, and leaning really close, and smelling really great, and I was the one blushing fervently while he licked his soft lips, his mouth slightly open, hovering only an inch away.

"What?" he whispered in a husky voice. "No smart come-backs now?"

My heart was beating so fast I was sure he could hear it! Which made me blush even more. And he wasn't actually doing anything. He made me react like that just by standing close to me.

Then we heard a girl shouting from not far away, and I jumped, snapping myself out of his wicked spell. "Tristan! People can catch us here!" I whimpered, scared. He gave me a playful smile. Then he winked, and leaned back, stepping a little away from me. He crossed his arms over his big chest and raised an amused eyebrow.

"You look cute when you blush. I shall try and make you do it more often." He smirked sexily. "So, do you agree? We'll tell Seth about us today?" he asked once again.

I cleared my throat and tried to slow my heartbeat before I answered him. "Hmm. Okay. But only if we can tell Tiffany too. Seth and Tiff are our best friends. I think we can trust them. And Tiff knows I'm keeping a secret, and she's really upset that I don't trust her. I don't want to lose her friendship! We tell Seth only if we can tell Tiffany as well. That's the deal. Take it or leave it," I said, crossing my arms too.

"Your mom is going to be upset with us for telling everybody about this," he pondered.

"They're not *everybody*. They're our best friends! I know we can trust them. Mom doesn't even need to know about this," I argued. "Can you manage not telling her this on *all* your frequent phone calls to her?" I remarked sarcastically.

"Okay. Deal. We'll tell them," he said, with a huge grin on his handsome face. "Can we do it now? I can't wait to wipe that smirk off Seth's face every time he mentions you!"

"Okay. I'll get Tiffany. We'll meet up in our room! Wait for me so we can tell them both together!" I said, running off to get Tiff.

In just a few minutes I had a disgruntled Tiffany by the arm and was dragging her to my room, despite her harsh complaints. I pushed her inside and saw Seth lounging on his bed reading a book, while Tristan waited for me on his bed, pretending to be breezy but unable to conceal from me the anxiety flashing in his eyes.

Seth looked up curiously from his book as I walked in after Tiffany, locking the door behind me.

"Okay, Joey. I do not appreciate being man-handled like that all the way down here," Tiffany complained, crossing her arms, really upset. "I'm not in the mood for games. And I'm done with the pretending-to-be-friends act. So, if you'll excuse me, I have a lot of things to attend to…"

"Tiff, will you sit down and listen, please! We have something to tell you guys." I pushed Tiffany on to my bed and went to sit by Tristan's side. "Seth, could you come over here. We want you both to hear this."

Seth raised his eyebrows and went to sit by Tiffany's side on my bed, facing us.

"So, since you two are our best friends, we reckon it's time to tell you the truth. You were right, Tiff. I was hiding something from you, and you're my best friend, and I really trust you. We both trust you guys," I said, looking them in the eyes.

Tiffany squealed, grabbing Seth's arm. "I knew it and I told you, Seth! I told you if we worked together we could squeeze the truth out of these two!" she exclaimed, beaming proudly at her Sherlock insights.

"Working together?" I asked in surprise.

Seth rolled his eyes at Tiffany. "Well, we were doing quite well until you blew our cover just now, Tiffany! They haven't actually told us anything yet, you know."

She looked at us, startled. "Oh. Right. But they just admitted they have a secret. You are still going to tell us the secret, right, Joey?" she asked cautiously.

"Yeah, Tiff. But first, what's going on here?" I asked, pointing at her and Seth.

She smiled again, and nudged Seth in the ribs. "Well,

we've been talking a lot these days, and we both have been suspicious about you two. You are always acting really weird around each other, and all the silent glances and whispered conversations made us wonder something was up. So we come up with a plan," she said, putting her arm around Seth's shoulder. "Seth here was going to push on the 'dating Joey' thing. That would put a pressure on Tristan to tell him what's going on between you two. If that failed, I was going to bring out the 'best friend card' with you, Joey. We expected you or Tristan would crack soon. And it worked!" she said, making a "*Voilá!*" hand gesture.

"So, what's this big secret of yours?" Seth asked, smiling reassuringly at us. "We do appreciate you telling us, even though we had to force it out of you. But you can really trust us. We'll keep your secret, we promise."

"We had a guess about what it could be," Tiff continued, deeply into her detective role play. "We figured you two used to have a crush when you first met, but you didn't know you were related back then, but then you found out and it's all very forbidden and you can't tell anybody of fear of what people might think! It's very soap-operary of you…" She rambled on excitedly.

I rolled my eyes at her guess. Then I frowned, making a face. I mean, seriously? Forbidden love? "Okay. Tiff. No. No! And, ew! You were really thinking that about us? Ew. No! So, here's the thing," I said, taking a long breath. "Tristan is not my brother. Not even my half-brother. And I'm not his sister. We had to lie to get him enrolled at the school with me. We're not related. He's…a good friend of my family," I said, looking at Tristan. I thought the ghost story could wait a while longer. One big revelation at a time.

Tristan smiled softly at me and held my hand, lacing his fingers between mine. I smiled back at him. It felt so good to be able to hold his hand without worrying if there was someone looking.

Seth and Tiff looked at us holding hands and exchanged glances.

"Oh, I see. But you can't really tell anybody ... about ... oh, that sucks!" Seth exclaimed.

"And you can't tell anyone about this! Or they could throw Tristan out of the school! I'm serious!" I said.

"That's it? That's all? That is the big secret you were keeping from us?" Tiffany scowled. "That's no big deal! My theory was so much better! And far more shocking!" she said, pouting at having guessed wrong.

"Sorry to disappoint you, Tiff. I'm really glad to get this off my chest. And that you're not mad at me any more ... right?" I said, giving her my best puppy-dog eyes.

She smiled at me, and came to sit by my side. "You didn't need to hide this from me, Joey! You're my best friend and I love you; you can trust me with anything!" She gave me a tight hug.

"So ... this means I can still ask Joey out, right?" Seth asked, standing up and smirking evilly at me. "Because now I don't even need to worry about her over-protective big brother kicking my ass any more!"

Tristan stood up and wrapped a muscled arm around Seth's neck, squeezing it lightly. "Oh, you still need to worry about that!" Tristan grinned at us and started pushing Seth ahead of him out of the room. "If you girls excuse us, I have to do some ass kicking outside. We'll be back in a moment."

Seth grimaced, trying to wriggle out of Tristan's grasp,

but with no success. He let himself be dragged outside, waving goodbye at us. I guess it was a male way of saying they needed alone time to talk. It was great because it gave me the chance to talk in private with Tiffany too. It felt so great to be able to talk to her about what was happening! Now Tristan and I didn't need to worry about pretending any more, not in the privacy of our room, and not in front of our best friends. That made all the difference in the world and my heart felt a whole lot lighter.

Chapter Twenty-Three

Ugly Duck Syndrome

The days that followed our *Big Revelation* were amazing!

I felt a whole lot more at ease in our room after that. Seth acted pretty normal around us, except for a little joke here and there, but the rest of the time he just resumed his usual behavior like nothing had happened.

It was great to be able to confide more intimate things with Tiffany now. When I told her about the kiss on the night of the party, she was all squealing and euphoric about it, which made me feel excited too! It felt so good to be able to share that moment with her. I wondered if Tristan had told Seth about that night too, and if he had, I wondered what he'd said. But I guessed this was one of those special things you only share with your best friend.

After a few days I started noticing that Tristan was around more. Before our kiss, he was constantly busy with all sorts of different activities, always rushing off to experience all the school had to offer. He had clearly been making up for lost time – all those decades in the cemetery with nothing to do and other ghosts his only company. But after the party, he started hanging out more in the room, even if it was just lying on his bed listening to music and keeping me company while I did my homework, or listening to me babble on about stupid little things that happened in my day. It was great having him all to myself again! It was a very selfish feeling, but I didn't care. He was sharing his time with *me* now, rather than endless school activities. It made me feel special, somehow.

He would always sit with me at lunch breaks; he carried my food tray (despite my protests as I felt kind of useless not being able to carry my own tray with my own food!); he carried my books for me and offered me his arm when he walked me to classes. I liked having him more present in my life, but I felt a little weird about all the pampering stuff he did all the time for me. But I had to remember he was from a time when people were a lot more polite. And he was gallant and courteous with all the girls, not only me. His attentive graciousness was the major reason the girls at school were all head over heels for him.

Tristan also acquired the most unsettling habit, after that day at the oak tree, of trying to make me blush. It always involved some illicit, sudden body proximity: sometimes he tried to make me blush with a soft stroke of his hands over my cheeks, or a sexy smile; other times with a teasing wink. I think he was trying to drive me crazy. And he was succeeding, I might add.

One of his favorite private games was to trace his fingers lightly over my arm. He was very cautious when he did it, always careful to ensure nobody was watching. His touch was the most amazing and unsettling thing in the world, because it made me feel charged but also jittery and tense at the same time. Sometimes I wondered if he knew the effect his touch had on me, how just a soft brush of his fingerprints could discharge such an intense, vibrant jolt of pure electricity through all my nerve endings. It was an inebriating feeling. I almost hated to feel that way, but craved it at the same time, anxiously waiting for the moment when his skin would brush against mine again.

He never tried to kiss me again, though...which then made me feel stupid for agreeing to take things slow.

Sometimes I wished I could have the courage to make a move myself. But I didn't have the guts to do it. I rehearsed and rehearsed, trying to gather some courage, but in the end I always chickened out. Or just froze. Although I hadn't mastered the courage to make a more assertive move, Tristan's constant attention made my confidence grow. Surprisingly, I also found myself wanting to wear more than just plain shirts or baggy jeans. Not just for Tristan's benefit, but for my own. I felt different inside, and I wanted that difference to show on the outside as well. I wanted the world to see how happy I was feeling, and my old clothes didn't seem a good enough statement.

Tiffany caught me one day rummaging through my wardrobe. A pile of loose T-shirts was scattered over my bed. I was beginning to despair at my grim clothing panorama at that point. Tiffany sat on my bed, leaning her head on her shoulder, watching me curiously.

"So, I see you finally decided to get rid of your old wardrobe, huh? About time!" She smirked.

I sighed loudly, and looked at my clothes, exasperated. "There's no hope for me. Everything I try looks hideous on me!" I whined, and slumped hopelessly on my bed.

"You are always putting yourself down. Why do you do this to yourself?" she asked, amused, getting up and going over to my open drawers.

"I don't do anything. It's not my fault I look horrible in those fashionable clothes you wear! I guess dressing up is not for me..." I mumbled, defeated.

"That's just silly. Of course it is for you. You looked great the night of the party! Everybody said so. Tristan couldn't resist you!" she said, winking.

I blushed and shuffled my feet, staring at the floor. "He did say I looked good that night..."

"Exactly! But the thing is...you always look good. You are very beautiful. You have this amazing long black glossy hair, and those big black eyes of yours. You have beautiful pale skin, plump lips and a great figure; you're so pretty! You just try really hard to hide it, and I don't know why. It's like you try your best to cover up and disappear behind all your baggy clothes, and then when you actually succeed and nobody notices you, you get all bummed and sad about it!" she said, getting irritated. "So stop doing it and start getting noticed! Boys should be crawling over you! And they will be, once you decide to show who you really are! You just have this Ugly Duck Syndrome, but don't you worry, cos I'm the cure, baby!" she said, winking at me again. "Come on, I'll help you out with your clothes!"

"Thanks, Tiff. You're the best friend in the whole world," I said gratefully.

"Hey, Tristan won't know what's hit him when he sees the new you!" she said, beaming happily. "You know all the boys were talking about you all night at the Valentine's party, right?"

"They were?" I asked suspiciously.

"If it wasn't for 'your band' threatening everybody that got near you, you'd have been a big hit!" she said reassuringly.

"Everybody just wanted to win a free week of homework..."

"There you go again, putting yourself down! Stop it!"

"Well, it is true!" I snapped. "It was just about that stupid bet!"

"Okay. So, I'll prove you wrong. The Spring Ball is next month! I'll make sure there's no betting going on that night! And you'll see how you'll fare." She crossed her arms defiantly.

"Spring Ball?"

"Yes, we have a school dance every other semester, a Spring Ball and a Winter Ball. There's a big dance, people dress up all fancy; it's very formal at first, but at the end of the night the teachers leave and we have the fun part of the party!" she said, clapping her hands, excited. I smiled at her.

Lately, I had been rethinking a lot of things about myself and about my life, and I felt it really was time for a change. This dance might be a good opportunity to launch the new Joey on the world. And who knew, it could even end up being fun. And I already had the most perfect outfit: the red dress my mom had given me for my birthday, and that I'd thought I would never wear. Maybe it was time for never to become now.

Tiff also helped me sort out more stylish outfits for the school week ahead – donating some of her outfits as well as showing me better ways to put together the clothes I had. On Monday, I woke before Seth's alarm and took my new outfit to the bathroom with me. I felt a little nervous about the drastic change in outfit: instead of loose pants, I had on a tight pair of dark jeans with a vivid red tank-top, and my hair was loose instead of in my usual pony-tail. When I emerged from the bathroom, Seth glanced my way with raised eyebrows, but I think he caught my worried expression and decided to drop any of his teasing remarks. Which I was very thankful for; I was already nervous as it was.

When Tristan looked up, he wasn't as subtle as Seth had been, though. He gave a long, audible intake of breath, followed by a even longer and louder exhaling. Inevitably, I turned red in the face. Obviously.

"Yeah. Yeah. Tiffany is giving me some make-over therapy sessions, helping me get rid of my old baggy clothes and get over my fear of exposure. Who knew I had issues with that, right?" I said, smiling weakly at him.

He smiled back, putting his gray hoodie on. "By all means, expose away. Whatever she's doing to you, tell her to keep doing it!" he said, still with raised eyebrows.

He was wearing my favorite ocean-blue T-shirt under his hoodie, the first new shirt he'd worn after coming back from the dead. It made his eyes sparkle with such an insanely beautiful vivid blue! I loved Tristan with blue eyes.

"I love this T-shirt," I mumbled, looking at his eyes instead of his top.

He glanced down, and smiled. "I've noticed."

Seth cackled at the other side of the room. "Why do you think he wears it so much?" he pointed out, putting his sneakers on.

"I do not! Shut up, man!" Tristan complained, blushing a little and throwing Seth's backpack at him. Seth caught it in the air and stood up, chuckling, ready to leave.

"Okay, love birds. I'm getting some breakfast. Who's coming?"

We all left for breakfast. Tristan held the door for me, and bowed slightly after I passed. I shook my head, laughing. He really couldn't help himself with all that chivalry stuff!

***

Over the next few days, I risked more daring outfits: a few tighter jeans, colorful tank-tops and tight shirts, all thoughtful presents from Tiffany. I even started to let my hair down once or twice. The response from the boys at school was immediate. I was a little surprised by it. Okay. That's not true. I was a lot surprised by it! Tiffany would only shake her head and laugh at my shocked face and intense blush every time a boy turned his head to watch me go by. She was having the time of her life treating my Ugly Duck Syndrome, as she'd termed it, with her pretty-swan shock treatment!

Tristan started noticing the sudden male attention directed at me as well. I could see the conflict in his eyes. On the one hand, he was enjoying the way I looked in my tight jeans and tank-tops. What boy didn't like looking at figure-hugging clothes and exposed skin?

But on the other hand, he wasn't pleased with the looks other boys were starting to give me. I could see the protective glares he shot out while he walked with me through the corridors.

Harry, Josh, Sam and Seth wouldn't stop harassing me about my new clothes, telling me one of The Lost Boys was definitely starting to get all girly on them. The more I blushed, the more they teased me. Tiff always had to intervene, and they'd shut up about it, but not for long. And then, to my utmost shock, boys started asking me to go to the Spring Ball with them! I was so surprised the first time it happened, that I just turned around and ran away, leaving the poor boy standing there. Tiff had to rescue me five minutes later, hyperventilating in the bathroom. I hadn't been expecting that to happen! I didn't want to go to the dance with anyone but Tristan! And I couldn't go with Tristan, because what weirdo would refuse everybody else's company in order to go with their own brother?

So I spent the whole week avoiding all boys. Every time a male turned my way or indicated he was about to start talking, I would run for the hills! I'll bet people were thinking I was crazy now. I was sure acting like it. I even considered going back to my loose T-shirts and baggy jeans. But Tiffany talked me out of it, not allowing me to turn back into a duck after all of her efforts to make me into a swan.

It was the last week of the month already, and I was so engrossed with new outfits, and avoiding dance invitations, and music practice, lessons and school, that I completely forgot about my past nightmares with Vigil. Until he came back.

He was still in his pale, skinny, fragile young body. Every night he would cautiously try to approach me, but I never allowed him to say anything. As soon as I realized he was there, trying to reach me in my dreams, I would close my eyes and intone an endless *"Wake up wake up wake up wake up"* until I woke up. I felt relieved the first time I managed to break Vigil's connection that way, but after the fourth time he crashed into my dreams, it became a tiresome ordeal. Goth Girl Sky was right: Vigil was relentless.

I decided to call Miss Violet and tell her about Vigil's attempts to make contact. She sounded worried on the phone and said she was trying hard to find a way to help Tristan and me. She promised to get in touch as soon as she had something valuable to share.

Then, on Tuesday morning, Tristan started to feel strange again. I checked the calendar, dreading what I would see.

And there it was: the first day of the month. Tristan was right about the monthly cycle hit for the spell. As soon as he started to feel the symptoms, I climbed into bed to stay close to him all afternoon, pretending I was reading a book. Because we stayed together, Tristan didn't get as sick as he had before.

I pointed that out to Tristan and made a joke about it being his "time of the month" problem now. He looked so mortified at my playful pun that I had to promise him never to joke about it again, and profusely apologizing over and over again. I learned that boys don't like jokes about periods, especially boys from the twentieth century.

Seth didn't even really notice Tristan wasn't feeling well that day; since I stayed next to him all the time, he managed to stay in a relatively good shape. The whole process was also a lot easier to endure because we didn't need to cover up being together in front of Seth any more.

When the day was over, I waited until Seth was deeply asleep to snuggle comfortably under the covers with Tristan. I woke up the next day with Tristan's heavy arm wrapped around my waist again. I could feel the beaded bracelet on his wrist as his hand gently enveloped mine, as he always did when we slept in the same bed. I could seriously get used to this... waking up in his arms, feeling the warmth of his body next to mine and his breath so close, not to mention his amazing smell lingering all over me. Yep. Not too hard to tolerate at all.

Tristan had a smell that was hard to describe, since it was a thing you have to... well, smell, to know it. It had a hint of vanilla, and carnations, and something sweet mixed with something undistinguishable... But it did something inexplicable to me. It filled me with this wonderful, intoxicating feeling. I wished I could bottle it up and carry around with me all the time. Every time he got too close, I had to suppress the urge to sink my face in his neck and sniff the hell out of him! I wondered if smell was something you could run out of. Or if I could sniff him so much that I'd wear it out until he ended up odorless.

In fact, I realized how badly I had it for Tristan one day after school, when Tiffany flopped down heavily beside me at our customary meeting place under the big oak tree.

"I knew I would find you here!" she exclaimed happily, smoothing her clothes as she sat on the grass by my side.

I smiled and nodded at her. "I'm waiting for Tristan. He said he wanted to show me a new place he's discovered around here. He wanted to hang out or something," I told her.

She made a deflated face and gave me a tiny pout. "Aw, boo! I wanted you to come with me into Saint Pete today!" she said, referring to the small nearby town. You're always hanging out with Tristan!" she complained.

I laughed at her exaggeration. "I'm not!" I protested.

"Yeah, you are. You're *always* with him!" She huffed but then switched to a goofy grin. "But that's all right, you two are the cutest thing together! He looks so happy when he's with you, and you get all starry eyed, it's so adorable!" she quipped, mimicking my moony eyes and battling her lashes.

"Shut up, Tiff! I do not!" I chuckled, embarrassed.

"You do too!" she scoffed. "You really like him, huh?" she questioned, a serious tone in her voice.

I pondered the question for a minute, biting my lip. I had been thinking about this since Tristan had kissed me that night at the party. I kept wondering about what I'd felt that night, and what I had been feeling ever since. I wondered about our strange connection, and the effect this spell had on us. Was it ruling our decisions, playing with our real feelings?

The real questions here was: what was real and what was magic? Was the binding spell that had brought Tristan back to life forcing things to happen between us that neither of us really felt? I remembered the strange urge to hug him when he first arrived at school; the surge of electricity between us. I was pretty certain that had been the bonding spell. I also remembered our first kiss, and how I had felt the same jolt of electricity, the tingling in our lips. That kiss had felt so magical, so out of this world. Surely it had some magic involved in it? Or did first kisses – good first kisses – always feel that way? I thought about all the kisses I had shared before. There hadn't been any fireworks, any tingles at all. Was the magic bond I had with Tristan making it so?

But then I thought about the way I felt around Tristan now. And I knew it wasn't just about a magic spell, a forced bond making me feel the way I did. I liked being with him. I liked his smiles and the way they made his eyes glint with a light of their own. I liked the sound of his laughter; it made something reverberate inside my heart. I liked his mysterious scent, and the way he tilted his head down when he was embarrassed so his hair could fall over his face and hide his eyes. I liked how caring and honest he was, how kindly he treated everyone around him. He had such a beautiful heart, such a unique and special soul. All of this had nothing to do with a magic spell or Tris being an ex-ghost. It was all part of who Tristan was. And that was why I loved him so.

"You want to know the honest truth, Tiff? I don't think I

just like him," I mumbled, staring at the sky. "I think I *love* him," I confessed, mostly to myself at that moment.

Tiffany let out a small gasp, her green eyes wide in shock at this sudden revelation. Before she could process what she had heard, or say something back, Tristan's voice cut in, catching us completely off guard and making us both snap our heads back in surprise.

"Hey, Joey?" His voice was somewhat tense.

"Oh, h-hey, Tris," I stammered, trying to recover. I realized he might have heard what I had just said, and I started panicking.

"Sorry, Joe, but I just came by to say I can't hang out today. I have to take a rain check on our walk; something came up and I can't get out of it. We can reschedule for some other time, okay?" he said in a bit of a hurry.

"It's o-okay. Some other time," I agreed, and he nodded before turning away and speeding off towards the school building.

Tiffany and I watched him retreat in silence. I was fumbling anxiously with the hem of my shirt and Tiff was clasping her chest with one hand, still trying to recover from the shock.

"Do you think he overheard us?" I asked her in a small voice.

She blinked and turned to me with a sympathetic smile. "I really don't know, Joey."

I slapped my face and sighed loudly. "Talk about the worst timing ever!" I grunted. "How freaked out do you think he'll be?"

She shrugged. "If it was any other boy, I would say a whole damn lot. But Tristan is…different. He may not react the way we think he will."

"You really think so?" I asked in a hopeful voice, raising my head a little.

"Yeah. I really do. Let's just wait it out and see what happens, okay? Who knows? He might even tell you he loves you too. The way he looks at you...I wouldn't be surprised," she replied with a smile. "Come on. Your afternoon has just opened up. Let's go into Saint Pete and take your mind off this." She beckoned to me, already on her feet.

I followed Tiffany with a weary heart, and a feeling of dread in the pit of my stomach telling me that something bad was bound to happen.

Then the week carried on as usual. Classes, teachers, lessons, Harry being silly, Josh giving me some tips on martial arts moves, Sammy's new joke updates. And Tristan went back to his normal self: pompom squad Caroline drooling all over him at third class; me, pissed off with Caroline for drooling all over him in third class; then lunch break.

Seth, Harry and I were having lunch in the cafeteria, talking about our new songs and waiting for the rest of the gang to show up. Tiff was doing her social networking thing all around the room, chatting to her various friends, though she always ended up at our table. She was talking excitedly with Bradley, at the other side of the food counter, and Brad was laughing loudly at something she was saying. Seth glanced over at them, and frowned, giving them a dark glare before resuming munching his food.

After a few minutes, Tiffany walked back to our table and sat down, greeting us cheerfully. She took a sip of her juice and started talking excitedly about the Spring Ball. I wasn't paying much attention to what she was saying at first. I usually tuned out when Tiffany was going on and on about dresses and shoes and stuff like that, and since the unfortunate incident by the oak tree, I also couldn't think about much else. But before I knew it, all hell broke loose around the table. Seth and Tiff had started another one of their quarrels. I'm not sure how things escalated so fast, but by the time I noticed, they were already at each other's throats.

"I don't know how *that* has anything to do with you!" Tiff yelled angrily.

"Hey, whatever!" Seth said, shrugging, clearly upset. "Just go back to your gossiping friends there! You know Brad only talks to you because he grovels for any scraps related to your parents! He probably didn't even understand your jokes; he was only laughing to keep you happy! He's such an ass kisser!" Seth hissed, and started making annoying kissing noises.

"Don't put me in the middle of your fight with Brad! It's not my fault you were kicked off his basketball team! And it's not gossiping, it's called having a social life, just so you know!" she bellowed.

"I wasn't kicked off the team! I quit! He begged me to come back, just so '*you*' know!" Seth barked back. "And you could try being less '*social*' sometimes!"

"What's that supposed to mean?" she snapped angrily, catching on his innuendo.

"Oh, you know what it means! You're such a people pleaser! And you only talk to half of your so-called *friends* because your parents impose them on you! If they weren't kids of your father's business associates, you would never even glance their way!"

Tiffany snorted at him, crossing her arms over her chest. "You're only jealous because you don't have a social life like I do! It's not my fault you're such a nerd and barely leave your room! Don't blame me for being such a loser!"

"Fine! I won't!" Seth shouted, pulling himself up from his seat, angrily. "Glad you finally got that off your chest! You don't need to worry about hanging with a loser any more! I'll save your reputation and just leave, how's that sound? No need to thank me, your highness!" he growled, and stormed off.

Harry was looking wide-eyed at them, and then he glanced my way, gulping hard. "That was...intense. I'm sorry, I don't do well in tense environments. I completely lost my appetite. I think I'm gonna go now," he said, and stood up, then walked away.

"Harry!" I called after him, but he didn't even turn to look at me; he just threw his hands up in the air and left the cafeteria. Harry got really upset about fights.

"Tiff...what just happened there?" I asked, bewildered.

She sunk her face between her hands, and hunched her shoulders down, blonde curls falling all over her face.

"I-I don't know! He was so mean to me...and I was so mad! And he kept yelling!" she said, sobbing a little.

I scuttled close to her, patting her on the back. "Hey...there, there. I don't know what's happening with you two! You can't stay together in the same room without fighting! You were really hard on him with the loser thing, Tiff. You shouldn't have said that..."

"I know! I couldn't stop myself! I just wanted to hurt him! I'm so sorry, Joey! What can I do now? He'll hate me for ever!" she said, sobbing harder.

I wiped the tears off her face. "Look, you have to go talk to him. Like, right now! Just go and say what you just said to me, he'll understand."

"No, he won't," she whined quietly. "He hates me."

"No, he does not hate you, Tiff. He's an amazing guy, and he'll forgive you, trust me on this. He needs to do some apologizing to you too," I said reassuringly. "Okay? Then go now," I said, shooing her.

She stood up reluctantly and headed to our room.

Sam, Tristan and Josh showed up a little after that, oblivious to the raging war that had happened at that very same table only a few minutes before. I had already finished eating my food when they arrived, and I kept them company for a while, but Tristan's awkwardness around me now left me in a constant state of embarrassment, and Tiff and Seth's fight had put me in a jittery state. I was really worried they might be fighting again in our room. So I excused myself and went to check on them.

I couldn't let this bickering continue any more. Even if I had to lock them in our room until they worked things out, I wasn't leaving them until they'd kissed and made up! I walked through the school hallways in a worried gloomy mood. I was so deep in thought about what I was going to say to Tiff and Seth, that when I got to the room, I didn't even knock on the door before stepping inside.

And my jaw dropped a hundred feet down to the floor then: Seth and Tiff were in the middle of the bedroom, in the most intense make-out session of the decade! Scratch that. Of the century! Their lips were locked together, hands roaming everywhere. It was...I didn't know what it was! Unexpected, for one thing. Shocking. Definitely. I was also a little embarrassed. There was some serious heavy petting going on there. They should get a room. Oh. Wait...

I coughed loudly. They jumped apart, startled and

surprised. Hell, I was the surprised one, pals! Tiffany blushed from head to toe, and Seth looked away, patting his messy blond locks of hair, all embarrassed.

"Okay. Guess you guys kissed and made out – I mean up!" I mumbled, without realizing I was saying it out loud.

Tiff blushed even more, and Seth smirked just a tiny fraction.

"I was actually worried you guys might be killing each other in here right now, but I guess I couldn't have been more wrong, huh?" I said, squinting my eyes at the two of them. "Oh, I see now what happened back there! Seth was jealous of you, Tiff! Because you were all chatty with Brad McSmelly!" I said, realization dawning on me.

Seth hunched on his bed, scowling at me for outing his jealous fit. Tiff sat next to him and began to smirk, but I continued talking.

"And you, Tiff, were all so sad and crying because you like him and you thought he hated you!" I said, wiping the smirk off her face. She froze and scowled at me too for outing her earlier breakdown. Then she shuffled her feet and stared at the floor.

"You were crying?" Seth asked quietly by her side.

She nodded slightly, all embarrassed. I thought Seth was going to start teasing her about this all over again, but he surprised me once more.

"I'm sorry," he said gently, putting his hand over her hand on the bed.

She looked at him and smiled softly. "I'm sorry, too," she said.

"Aaaaww, that is so sweet!" I said, sitting on my bed in front of them. "So, you guys are like, together now? Oh, please, please, please say yes! Then we won't have any more of you two fighting all the time!" I said, clasping my hands together.

"I doubt we'll stop fighting," Seth said thoughtfully. "But at least if we start dating, we could have make-up sex after the fights. That's a plus, what do you think?" Seth asked her jokingly.

She rolled her eyes, annoyed. "We are not having make-up sex, Seth. We are not having anything at all!" she said, glaring at him.

"That's what you said after our first kiss at the party, and look at us now, kissing again," Seth remarked, amused.

"Yeah!" I said, trying to help him win the argument "Wait. Kiss at the party? Are you saying this wasn't the first time it's happened?" I scowled.

Tiff winced, giving Seth quite the glare. He wasn't supposed to tell me that!

"Tiffany!!" I yelled at her. "And you gave me such crap about being a true friend, saying you tell me everything that happens to you! No secrets between us, my ass!" I scolded.

I was really mad. I curse a lot when I'm mad. Tristan would be flinching non-stop if he were in the room right now. He hated when people cursed around him, especially me.

"I-I'm so sorry, Joey! It was a one-time-only thing!" she mumbled.

"Well, obviously not," I snorted, looking at Seth now.

"What? She told me not to say anything," he said, shrugging. "She's ashamed of it. She doesn't want anything to do with a nerd." He looked upset again now.

"I thought you didn't want anything to do with me," Tiff mumbled.

"Yeah. Right. What guy doesn't want a tall, blonde,

gorgeous, sexy, smart, funny girl, right?" he said sarcastically, with a heavy frown.

She glanced over at him, a little surprised but happy. "You know...I kind of like my men sexy, and blond and geeky," she said, looking directly at him, making him lose the frown and smile at her.

"Aaaaww, that's so sweet!" I giggled from my bed.

They both grabbed a pillow each and tossed them at my head.

"Joey, can you please cut it out!" they both yelled at me.

"And leave, so we can have our make-up sex!" Seth added as an afterthought.

"Seth!" Tiff yelled, and tried to punch him lightly on the arm, but he grabbed her hand and pulled her closer, wrapping his arm around her waist.

"I can see that the fighting thing isn't going to change," I mumbled to myself.

"No. Seriously, Joe. Get out," Seth commanded, looking at Tiffany with hungry eyes.

"Okay. Okay. I'm going. Jeez. Just promise you won't try to kill each other after I leave," I said, walking over to the door.

"We'll try," they both said, eyes locked on each other now. I hurried to get out of the room and leave them alone. I could see that killing wasn't exactly what was in their minds right now. And I didn't need to worry about helping those two. They were doing just fine on their own.

Chapter Twenty-Four

Spring Ball

Seth took Tiffany out on an official date the following night.

It was so funny seeing them all excited about going out. They were together all the time, at school, at the lunch table, lazing around in my room, but apparently being together on a date was a totally different way of hanging out.

I stayed up until late that night, waiting with Tristan for Seth to get back. It was like we were anxious parents waiting for their son.

Since Tristan was acting like nothing had happened back at the oak tree that afternoon, I decided it was best not to mention it at all. He probably hadn't heard anything anyway. Though sometimes I caught him taking quick peeks in my direction, but he always had a faint smile on his lips, and I knew that, whatever it meant, it wasn't making him upset, but happy.

When Seth finally got back, he had a big smile plastered on his face.

He looked so happy as he told us all about his romantic date with Tiffany. Before Tristan, I had never really understood what the fuss was about with romance. I thought it was a silly, unimportant thing to be concerned about. I also had never known what desire truly meant. And now I was in love for the first time in my life. Even if I didn't know for sure if he knew. Or indeed how he felt about me.

The rest of the week passed by in a dance-preparation frenzy. Everybody seemed so excited about it, while I still had no clue about who I was going with. I was still dodging all approaches, but Saturday was getting near and I hadn't found a solution to my problem. Tristan hadn't mentioned it either. I was slowly realizing I was going to end up at the dance on my own, the rate things were going.

Two days before the Ball I bumped into Seth on the way back to our room, and he told me I'd just missed my grandmother. After a few questions, I found out that my "grandmother" was actually old Miss Violet. I was really bummed about missing her, especially as she must have found out something about our situation. Seth told me that Tristan had looked for me all over the school, but couldn't find me.

When I walked into my room I found Tristan sitting on his bed, staring at the floor with a haunted look in his eyes.

"Hey, Seth told me you were looking for me. I missed Miss Violet's visit. Is something wrong?" I asked, startled by the grim look on his face.

"You tell me," he said shortly. His tone was sharp. Cutting.

"Y-you're angry," I stated.

"How clever of you," he snapped.

"Tris, I don't know what the problem—"

"You lied to me," he said, cutting me off.

I stared at him in surprise. Then I thought about my

last call to Miss Violet, asking her to help me with my nightmares.

"Miss Violet told you. That I'm still having dreams," I realized slowly.

"Why didn't you tell me?" he asked sharply. He sounded betrayed.

"I-I'm so sorry, Tris. I didn't want to upset you," I mumbled, but he cut me off again.

"You've been dreaming about him all this time; he's carried on haunting you in your sleep. *He's hunting you.* And he's doing all this because of me! To get to me! And you thought it was best not to tell me?" he said angrily, his voice raised.

"Tris, no, you don't understand! I was just trying to protect you!"

"Exactly! I should be the one trying to protect you! You don't trust me. You asked an old lady to help you, but not me."

"No, Tris, you're getting this all wrong!"

He stood up abruptly, his fists clenched, a dark look shading his eyes. "You know what? I don't want to talk about this any more. I need some air." But he stopped in the doorway, his face troubled, a hundred thoughts and emotions racing through his eyes. "I think we need to rethink things about us," he said, and he still sounded a little angry, but so, so sad.

"Tris, please...you're over-reacting! You can't say that just because I didn't tell you about some stupid dreams!" I pleaded, and for a second something else flashed in his eyes. Something he wasn't telling me. "What did Miss Violet say to you? Did she find out about something?"

He clenched his jaw and avoided looking straight at me.

"She said she's really sorry and that there is really nothing she can do to help. You can call her and hear it for yourself, since it's painfully clear you don't trust me," he snapped, and then he left, banging the door shut.

I sat on my bed in a shocked state. I didn't know what to do, what to say to make things better again. I had really screwed things up by hiding this from him all this time. I tried to find him at dinner, but he didn't show up, and I waited in our room until really late, lying in bed, staring at the ceiling in the dark, my heart as heavy as if lead had been poured over it. He finally came home really late in the night and went to bed without speaking at all. I bit my lips in the dark, trying hard not to cry. This was all a big misunderstanding! I would talk to him tomorrow, clear this whole mess up. That's what I told myself again and again and again until I drifted into yet another restless night of sleep.

I couldn't have been more wrong. Next day things were not better. I tried to talk to Tristan before breakfast, but he wouldn't let me. He closed himself down so fiercely I couldn't even read anything from his eyes any more. All I could see was a cold empty stare on the brief occasions he glanced my way.

He was absent most of the day, and I got to see him only in our shared classes, when he chose to sit in a distant corner, far away from me. He even skipped band rehearsals and again only came back to our room really late at night, once he could be sure I would already be in bed. He seemed a shadow of his former self, his posture weighed down by worry, and the only time his face changed from a blank stare was to show a troubled, anxious expression. He seemed so lost, so alone; it made my heart ache. But he still wouldn't let me say a word to him, not even in apology.

The day of the Spring Ball took me by surprise, so focused was I on my problems with Tristan. Tiffany noticed something was wrong between us, but she didn't press to know more. I guess she presumed that Tristan had told me he didn't love me back. I couldn't tell her the reason for our fight anyway. She didn't know the real truth of how Tristan had come into my life.

I spent the whole day in Tiffany's room, watching her trying on dresses for the ball. She was so excited about going with Seth. Seeing her happiness made my heart a little lighter. When she had finished picking out a beautiful cream lace dress, with shoes, purse and jewelry to match, I told her my bad news.

"Tiff, I hope you'll forgive me, but I think I'm not going to the dance," I said, lying face down on her bed. She immediately pouted at me.

"Aw, Joey. Come on! You too? You guys are acting silly over this fight!" she said, putting her hands on her hips, upset. "Tristan is not going too. He told Seth he didn't have a suit, so I got him a suit and he still said he wasn't going. That's when Seth found out about your fight. He's been trying to talk to Tristan, but Seth tells me he's been pretty reclusive and quiet. Like you," she said, sitting on the bed. I started to protest, but she cut me off. "I know you don't want to talk about it, I get it. I just want you to know I'm here for you if you ever need me, okay?" she said, putting her hand over mine.

"Thanks, Tiff," I muttered. "But it's not like I was going to go with Tristan anyway. You know we couldn't do that when the school thinks we're related. And I'd feel weird going with anyone else."

"Well, Harry, Sam and Josh told me they'd dump their dates in a second if you chose to go with any one of them!" she said, smiling at me.

"Oh. Good to know they care about me that much. I wouldn't do that to their dates, though!" I smiled weakly at her. "I don't know, I'll decide what I'm going to do later, okay? I'll go take a shower now, cool my head a bit, and I'll come back here to see you all dressed up, all right?"

I got back to an empty room. Of course, Tristan wasn't there. The room was the perfect symbol of the way I was feeling lately. Empty and lonely. I took my shower in a dazed, numb state.

I wasn't going to cry over this, though. I wasn't the weepy type of girl. And it was a stupid thing to cry about anyway. I was sure Tristan was going to come around sooner or later, and we'd talk things through and everything would be fine again. I left the bathroom dressed in my loose sweats, and watched Seth preen himself to the point of exhaustion. But he looked incredible in the end, so it was really worth all his effort. He wore a black tailored suit, a dark-blue shirt with a light-blue tie. His blond hair was, as usual, impeccably groomed and styled. Tiffany would be even more head over heels with him than ever.

The dance was about to start, so I walked over with Seth to pick up Tiffany. I wanted to see Tiff's face when she got a good look at Seth all dressed up, fancy and gorgeous! I smiled, thinking about the rest of the boys dressed up and handsome. It was a pity I wasn't going to be there to see it.

Seth knocked on Tiff's dorm room and we waited patiently. When she opened the door, both my jaw and Seth's dropped to the ground. Tiffany looked absolutely incredible! She looked like a princess out of a fairytale!

Her blonde curls were even curlier, and her lips had a pink gloss that made them look even plumper. Seth gasped and choked and stuttered some compliment, while trying not to grin like a complete idiot. They were so adorable together – the best-looking couple I had ever seen!

Before they left for the dance, Tiff made one last attempt to get me to come, pointing at my dress laid out on her bed, but I shook my head sadly. After they left, I sat on her bed, aware of the soft music coming from downstairs already.

I replayed everything that had happened to me these past days, while the music drifted through the windows. I don't know exactly when or what made me change my mind. But suddenly, all I knew was that I wasn't going to sit around and sulk, all alone in Tiff's room. I was missing out the opportunity of enjoying this! That wasn't what my mother had taught me. She had taught me to enjoy all life's possibilities. And that was just what I was going to do! I didn't need a date to go to this dance.

Before I could change my mind, I slipped on my beautiful red dress. Tonight wasn't going to be about getting dressed up for Tristan, or for any other guy. Tonight was going to be about me. I was getting dressed up for myself. And I didn't care if people stared because I was by myself. If Tristan wasn't going to be my date, then I was better off alone.

Tiffany had left out a beautiful red-stoned necklace, with matching red earrings, for me to borrow. I put them on and let my hair down, also putting on a ruby lipstick the same color as my dress.

As I passed through the big doors to the ballroom, I was really nervous, but kind of excited. I breathed deeply as I stepped inside the room. I spotted Tiffany and Seth from the entrance. They had turned to look in my direction, and then, it was just like one of those scenes in the movies where the whole room goes quiet when the heroine walks in. Everybody turned to look at me as I walked through the doors. Embarrassed, I gave Tiff a small smile before walking to where she was standing, without giving a second glance to the crowd staring silently at me. Tiff was grinning widely at me, and after a while people stopped staring and went back to enjoying the party. However, I was aware that a few gazes still lingered, people whispering things, probably about the lameness of attending the party alone.

"Thanks so much for your help!" I whispered in Tiff's ear as I hugged her. "And thanks for lending me your jewelry. It's beautiful," I said, holding the stone of my necklace. She nodded, beaming.

"So, how do I look?" I said, stepping in front of Seth and hugging him tight. He had an awestruck expression on his face.

"You're kidding me, right? Did you not see the reaction from everyone here? You look...incredible!"

"Yes, you do!" Tiff said, nudging Seth but smiling all the same. "I'm almost feeling jealous," she teased.

I looked around us. A few people were still glancing and whispering, but there was admiration and envy shining in their eyes. I guess I should take that as a complement, then.

Seth snapped his fingers all of a sudden, like he had just remembered something. "I gotta go but I'll be right back!" he said, already walking away from us before either of us could say anything.

Tiff grabbed my hand and twirled me around, making my round skirt flow around my knees. My dress wasn't as long as Tiffany's – it ended right below the knees – but it showed a lot more of cleavage…

"You know, one of us should be doing that to her," Josh said, walking towards us. He was referring to the twirling move. Sam and Harry were right behind him, both with a glint in their eyes.

"Oh my God! Look at you!" I squealed when I turned to look at them. "You all look amazing, and so handsome in your suits!" I said, taking a step back to get a good look. They stared back at me, wicked smiles on their lips.

The Lost Boys were all wearing dark suits, with different shirt colors. Josh was the most tidy of them, with his buttoned suit, white shirt and tie, and formal shoes. Sammy wasn't wearing a tie, and had discarded his jacket already. Harry was also jacketless and the only one wearing sneakers. He was wearing a dark-red shirt that matched his hair, and black formal trousers. He had already rolled up his sleeves to his elbows, in a very sexy, casual look. They were all still staring really hard at me. Especially around the cleavage area. Boys.

"So, can I have your word that I'll get a dance with each one of you tonight?" I asked, hugging them each in turn.

"Only if I'm the first, and only if it's right now!" Harry said, linking his arm through mine and pulling me to the dance floor.

"What? Like right now?" I asked.

"Yeah, right now! Do you have something else to do?" he said, smiling at me. "If I don't grab you now, I will never have a chance later. I'll have to fight for you with all the other guys in here!"

"But… but Harry, what about your date? Don't you have to ask her first, or something?"

"Why? I'm not married to her! And all my babes know *my band mates* come first," he said, pulling me closer to him. It was a slow dance. "After all, I've already ditched her once tonight to dance with Josh! *My band* is always priority number one," he said, winking playfully.

"*Your band*. Right," I said, chuckling quietly at Harry considering me the same as Josh.

I danced with Harry for two dances, a slow one and a fast one, and then it was Sam's turn, followed by Josh. My Lost Boys were amazing! All my worries disappeared when I was around them. I was having a great time, but still Tristan was constantly in my thoughts, even while I danced with my friends.

After a whole lot of dancing, I called a break and tried to find a chair to sit and rest for a while, but someone pulled my arm, making me stumble back to the dance floor. "Hey, don't I get a dance too?" Seth said, smiling kindly at me as he wrapped his arm around my waist. "I heard all band members had a chance of dancing with you tonight."

"Of course! Did you get permission from your date?" I asked playfully.

He laughed loudly. "Actually, yes I did," he said, nodding in Tiff's direction. "I have complete permission on the Worthington front."

We danced a fast number and then the music ended, and a slow one began right on sequence. Seth glanced quickly around the room, then twirled me around the dance floor yet again. "Just one more dance, and I'll let you go," he promised. He had a devious look playing in his hazel eyes. We had been slow dancing for only a minute or so, when Tiffany bumped into us, hard.

"Oops! I'm so sorry, guys!" she said, beaming. She also

had a glint in her eyes. "Gosh, I hope I'm not intruding, but I need to talk to Seth urgently." It was then that I noticed her dance partner – Tristan! "Here, Tristan, why don't you continue this dance with Joey while I talk to Seth. It's very important! I'll see you guys later!" she said, pushing him forward, while Seth gave me a slight nudge forward too. I stumbled and fell towards a surprised Tristan, my hands outstretched against his big chest.

I stared at him, wide-eyed. He looked so incredibly handsome in a black tailored suit and black tie. All words escaped me. I was still leaning against him, hands over his chest. Then I remembered he was mad at me, and pulled my hands away from him, taking a defensive step back-wards. He was looking away, frowning at Tiffany and Seth's retreating backs, but then he finally turned back to me.

He looked surprised for a moment, and then admiration flashed in his eyes, the blank stare gone.

"So. I think we should be dancing?" he said quietly, his gaze roaming over me before slowly ascending to look deeply into my eyes. He seemed to have forgotten our fight momentarily, because his eyes burned with desire.

"Sure. If you want to," I mumbled, feeling heat spread over my face. He took a step forward and placed his hands lightly on my waist, while I rested my hands on his shoulders.

"Seth came to our room to tell me that I needed to come to the ball, or else Tiffany would be really upset with me, you know, for fixing me up with this suit for nothing," he said in a low voice, shaking his head as he finally under-stood the set-up. "Did you have anything to do with that?"

"No! Of course not! I had no idea what they were up to!" I said, affronted at his accusation.

We both tensed up, remembering the harsh exchange of words from days ago.

Then he started dancing with me and, once again, worry and doubt marked his face in turn. He looked guilty, like he wasn't supposed to be doing this. But the longing was too strong and he was losing the fight. I was afraid he might leave at any minute now, but he continued moving and I followed his lead. We were the only ones on the floor dancing in an old-fashioned waltz to the slow dance, but he didn't seem to notice, or to care.

"You look beautiful," he said quietly, almost as if talking to himself.

"Thank you," I whispered back.

The song talked about love and addiction, about people getting under each other's skin. It was as if the lyrics were speaking directly to us. They spoke of lovers reuiniting, about how words can cut you deep inside, and how silence can be even worse, and haunt you for ever.

We continued dancing so slowly, and everything else around us seemed to melt away, fading from sight. I no longer cared that everyone thought we were supposed to be siblings. There was only him and me on that dance floor, our eyes locked; only his body close to mine, his smell intoxicating me. Only his face leaning close, his jaw brushing so lightly against my cheek, his warm breath touching my neck, teasing me, torturing me, making me shiver in joy.

The music ended and Tristan remained pressed against me, really close for a few more seconds, like he was resisting waking up from a dream, but then he slowly pulled away, standing still and breathless in the middle of the dance floor, his eyes filled with regret. "We shouldn't have done this. I have to go," he said hoarsely, forcing his voice to be emotionless and cold again. He turned around and left me there, alone on the dance floor.

It took me a few seconds to realize that he had left, and then I blinked quickly, snapping out of my stupor. I ran, following his steps like a prince in a fairytale. "Tristan, stop!" I yelled at him, catching him up outside the ballroom doors. How could he just leave me there? After he'd danced with me like that; after he had looked at me the way he had? How could he say we shouldn't be together, pretend he didn't care about me? Who was the big liar now?

I grabbed his arm, making him turn around to face me.

"Joe, what do you think you are doing?" he growled, yanking his arm from my grasp, as if my touch could burn him.

"Why are you acting this way?" I yelled at him. I looked around and cursed under my breath. People were starting to glance curiously in our direction. I was making a scene. We needed a place to talk. A private place. I grabbed his arm again and pulled him outside with me to the school grounds.

A few minutes later we entered the small terrace that Harry had once shown me. Yellow light poured softly onto the stone floor, spilling from windows in the building above us. I shut the small iron door behind Tristan.

"We can talk freely here, without worrying that anyone will hear us," I said, turning to look at him.

He shrugged his shoulders, his face masked with a blank expression, like he didn't care if anyone heard us or not. "We don't have anything to talk about. I don't see why we had to come all this way for nothing..."

"Yes, we do have to talk, Tristan!" I huffed, stamping

my foot. "You can't keep treating me like this! I've already told you I'm sorry I didn't tell you that my nightmares had continued! I didn't want to worry you, that's all!"

"Look, Joe. This is all very simple. You lied to me. You said they'd stopped. It's very clear you don't trust me. So let's stop pretending, okay? *This* is never going to work! *We* are never going to work! Why don't you get that?" he blurted out, passing his hand over his head, frustrated.

"We are never going to work just because I didn't tell you about my dreams? That doesn't make any sense!" I snapped, getting even more frustrated than he looked.

"Yes. We're not meant to be together!" he said, stepping closer. "I didn't want to say it like this, but you've given me no choice!" he said, losing his temper and then he let out a long sigh. "Let's just... go back to the way we used to be, you know, just being friends. Pretend you are my sister, I'm your brother, and we're good friends. Let's stay that way."

"You don't mean that," I said, dropping my arms to my side. "I know you don't mean that, Tris! Why else were you dancing that way with me, if you truly didn't want anything to do with me?"

He stuck his hands into his pockets, in a defensive stance. "That was a mistake. It won't happen again. It was just... the spell talking, and I was caught up in the moment, that's all. It didn't mean anything." He looked anywhere but at me.

He was only a few feet away from me. I walked slowly towards him, my voice shaky with tension. "Tris, please... Just look me in the eyes and say that again, and mean it. I know you can't, I know that's not what you want," I pleaded.

He snapped his eyes open, staring fiercely at me. "Look

you in the eyes? So you can see if I'm telling you the truth, Joe? Is that it?" he spat out in fury. He stared at me and we both knew then that I could see everything he was feeling. He felt cheated, betrayed, robbed from his private feelings. "I wish I had this little ability of yours, so I would've known a long time ago how big of a liar *you* really are! Do you want to know if I'm lying to you right now? Take a good look! *We cannot be together!* Can you see if I really mean it?" He stepped closer, stopping an inch away from my face. His anger caused me to step backwards, flinching until I was stopped by the iron door behind me. I looked into his eyes, and saw that he really meant it. Every word he had said. He thought we shouldn't be together.

Tears filled my eyes, threatening to fall. "So you never wanted to be with me? Why did you make me believe that you cared?" I asked shakily. I could feel a single tear streaking down my cheek, and I hated that I couldn't stop it from falling. I didn't want to cry. Not like this. Not right now. Not in front of him.

His eyes were still locked with mine when I asked him one more time. "Why did you let me love you?" I whispered, so sadly that I could feel the frail question breaking his heart and my own at the same time.

His gray eyes shone furiously with pain. "I didn't *let you* do anything. You did it all on your own," he said coldly.

"You shouldn't have let things escalate to this, Joey," he said, and looked away, his voice turning a little softer, like he regretted saying it, or regretted acknowledging this fact. "It's best that we stop this right now, don't let it go further than already has. I just don't feel the same about you," he said quietly, his voice too stern.

"The way you danced with me in that ballroom wasn't

like someone who doesn't care," I said through clenched teeth. I had seen the passion in his eyes while we danced. I had felt it.

"Why do you keep insisting on this?" he pleaded, lowering his head in anguish.

"Because you're hiding something." His eyes flickered at me for a second, but he soon averted his gaze as if mine scorched through him.

But before he did I saw fear, despair and one thing that puzzled me. At first. I thought it was only my own emotion reflecting in his gray eyes. Then I knew. It was his emotion. Buried deep inside, covered by the all the pain. I saw love.

"You are lying. I can see it. You care. More than that," I affirmed to myself, but he heard me because he was too close to me. Anger came back into his eyes, taking over all his face, filling up his bright eyes in a piercing, dangerous stare.

He grabbed my wrists tight and pushed me back against the iron door. I was so shocked that I couldn't react; I couldn't say anything. I never thought he would be capable of hurting me like this. With all my training, all my hours of martial arts, I felt so impotent now, unable to react. Because it came from someone I'd never expect to do that. From the boy I loved.

"You've always been able to read me just by looking at me, haven't you? You lied to me all this time – and you accuse me of being a liar? Can't you see? There is no trust here. There is no future for us. How can you think this could ever work?" he said desperately, still holding me.

"Tris! P-please…" I whimpered. He would hate me for ever now that he knew I could always read him. I could always see the truth in his eyes.

His eyes glistened with betrayal and hurt and unshed

tears. The sight of his pain took all the fight out of me. "I'm s-so so sorry I lied...I never meant to hurt you," I whispered as I sobbed. "I love you."

His eyes searched desperately for something inside of mine, too many emotions flickering on his face. I couldn't read him any more; it was too much to process, too fast, too intense, too overwhelming, too painful. Before I could say anything else, he crushed my lips with his, taking me completely by surprise. I was shocked by the urgency with which his mouth claimed mine. For a second I was frozen with the shock, but then my body reacted; the sensation of his kiss was uncanny and I gave in to it, and him.

I tasted his hungry lips, his need, his longing; I could feel his desire in the palm of his hands, searching me, his whole body pressing hard against me, grabbing and touching, pushing me up hard against the door, making my skin hot with pinpricks of energy wherever his hands touched me. It was nothing like our first kiss, that almost chaste, soft and tender kiss of long ago. Tonight he was kissing me like he was a drowning man and I was his last chance of air. Like it was our last time. It was a desperate, hopeless kiss.

He broke away, gasping and looking shocked at what he had just done. His eyes were filled with heartbreaking sadness, and he shook his head lightly, as if trying to dislodge all the pain from it.

I reached my hand out to him, trying to make him see that everything would be okay, as long as we were together, but he flinched and stepped away, walking to the far end of the terrace, as far away from me as he possibly could, his back turned. He grabbed the stone ledge with both hands. He was shaking, like he was struggling with a demon inside, tearing him apart.

A few seconds passed and I couldn't take the silence any more, or the distance between us. So I started to walk towards him. I wanted to hold him in my arms, to make all his pain go away, to stop all the hurting.

Before I got too close, he turned to me quickly, his face and eyes completely void of any emotion. He had closed down again, blocking everything from me; his blank stare was like a slap.

"I'm sorry, Joe. But this can't go on. We can't be together. You need to accept this," he said coldly, firmly and steady.

"W-what? No! Tristan, please! No! I will never lie to you again! I promise! Please!" I begged, walking towards him again. I didn't care any more if I was crying, if I sounded pathetic, weak, begging for a chance. I'd beg! I'd do whatever it takes! He shook his head and passed by me without a second glance. He was walking away from me, from us. He was leaving me.

"Tristan, please! Don't do this! I'll tell you everything!" I said, while tears streamed down my face.

He turned to look at me, but his eyes were still emotionless, cold frozen gray stones. Diamond eyes, sparkling mesmerizing jewels with nothing but coldness inside.

"I'm sorry. It's best that we stop this now. You'll see that this was the right thing for us," he said, trying to convince me. "You think you love me now, but you'll forget about me soon enough. We were just not meant to be together, Joey," he said, the finality and certainty on his voice breaking my heart into a million tiny pieces.

"Tris...please. I love you. I know you love me too. I can see it in your eyes..."

"You're right. I love you too. But love is not enough," he said, turning to leave.

"If you turn your back on me now, when I need you the most…"

"Then what?"

"Then there's no going back after this, Tristan!" I begged him for the last time.

"Good. That's the way it should be." He opened the door and walked away, leaving me behind on the terrace, broken and alone.

Chapter Twenty-Five

No Going Back

I walked to Tiffany's room and sat outside her door on the cold stone floor, waiting for her. I didn't want to go back to the ball, or to my room, and risk bumping into Tristan in either place.

The corridor was dark and empty. I don't know how long I stayed there on the floor, but I was glad that, when Tiffany found me, at least I wasn't crying any more. I hated when anyone saw me crying. She let me into her room, concern filling her face. I slept the night in her room. Well, I tried to sleep, but managed only to lie awake, thinking about Tristan and everything that had happened that night.

Next day was Sunday and I stayed in Tiffany's room all day, curled up in bed. I didn't want to see or talk to anyone. I was lost. I couldn't stop thinking about Tristan's words; they kept bouncing in my head, driving me crazy. *We are not meant to be together...*

Sunday evening I gathered the courage to leave Tiff's room and went to have dinner with her and Seth. I hadn't eaten all day, despite Tiff offering me snacks. My stomach had just twisted and turned inside, refusing food. When we got to the cafeteria, I saw that Seth was really worried. He said they hadn't seen Tristan since the dance. I couldn't help but feel concerned.

Just when I was about to suggest we start looking for him, he entered the dining hall, with Caroline at his side. She was laughing and giggling, leaning against him with her arm wrapped around his arm. He glanced at our table but moved on quickly, selecting his food and taking it to the other side of the room, sitting with his back to us. He looked relatively normal, maybe a little tired, but not a drop of worry or sorrow showed on his face.

Seth and Tiff exchanged worried glances. We could hear Caroline giggling in the distance and I felt livid. I stood up and excused myself, walking as far away as I could from the ghastly scene. What was he doing with her? My heart had twisted watching Caroline leaning teasingly over him. I stayed in Tiffany's room again that night, but I pretended to be already asleep when she got back from dinner. I didn't want to talk about what had happened, about what it could possibly mean. The possibilities were all too horrible for me to face. But I bit my lips and clenched my fists tight, holding the tears inside.

I eventually managed to get a couple of hours of sleep, drifting off in exhaustion by the early hours. On Monday morning I felt like a truck had hit me. My body ached all over. Tiffany eyed me warily all the way down to the cafeteria, but she didn't risk talking to me yet. I was glad. She made me eat something for breakfast, so I forced down some juice and whatever she put in front of me, so I could get out of there and go to class.

We were walking down the hallway to our first class when we spotted Tristan by his locker. He was talking to

Caroline, who was leaning against the lockers at his side. She was smiling and blushing, blonde hair flowing over her shoulders, a pink tank-top only just covering her curves. She looked beautiful. She always looked beautiful. Tristan leaned closer to her, making her gasp in wonderment at what he was about to do.

I gasped too and held my breath, watching the scene unfold before my stunned eyes. I watched as Tristan kissed her and she wrapped her arms around his neck and kissed him back, in utter bliss.

It felt like I'd stopped breathing. For a second, the world stopped moving. And when it restarted, everything crashed and broke inside me. Tristan had moved on. There was no going back from this. *We were not meant to be together.*

I watched as he broke the kiss and smiled at Caroline, the way he used to do at me, and then walked away, arms draped around her waist. Everybody was staring at them, and gossiping about the big news. *Caroline had finally caught Tristan Gray.* Tiffany grabbed my arm and pulled me inside the bathroom. I hadn't even realized she was beside me this whole time.

She tried talking to me, and I pretended I was listening, but nothing mattered any more. I watched Tiffany talk, looking at me with worry flashing in her eyes. Everything around me felt weird and unreal. Like it was all a dream. A really bad dream.

I turned and left the bathroom in a haze. I remember vaguely walking to my first class, and sitting in my chair, and staring at the teacher and the blackboard. But I went through lessons that day on autopilot.

After classes I retreated to my own room. Tiffany and Seth turned up, and chatted for a while. But I was glad when they left. I wanted to be alone. I opened my note-pad and scribbled in it all afternoon. I had a new song to write. A new song I wanted The Lost Boys to sing. The lyrics poured out of me as I replayed everything that had happened on that terrace. Every line, every word, every emotion: everything Tristan had said to me.

"I'm sorry but I never meant to hurt you." (I could hear the guitars strumming in my head, along with the lyrics.)

"There's tears in your eyes, they fall as you cry, but it's getting late." (I imagined Tristan's quiet voice whispering the song to me.)

"I say it's not meant to be, that is our fate, and it's getting late."

The next lines were for me to sing.

"There's something you're hiding from me, but I cannot see. You're bright, sharp, cold. Cutting through the night, blinding my every sight." (With Harry, deep bass, pounding on every word like a heartbeat.)

"You have to understand, we're not meant to be. Babe, can't you see?" (I could hear Seth's vibrant voice.)

"It's like a long note of a violin, vibrating over a sad night. It's like a falling star descending from the darkest sky. Babe, can't you see? Your sorrow is like mine. Its music is the night."

And the next lines were for Seth.

"You left me now, when I needed you the most, you let me down. Babe can't you see? There's nothing left for me."

And Tristan.

"Now there's no going back, that is our fate. And now is too late."

I finished the song and it was night already. I remembered

I had to eat, so I made myself head to the cafeteria. I wasn't going to impose on Tiffany another night, so I slept in my room. Tristan showed up really late that night, when the lights were out and Seth was already deep in sleep. He walked slowly and silently to his bed, taking only his shoes off and lying down with his clothes on, turning his back to me again.

"You don't need to keep doing this," I said quietly to him, from the safety of my bed.

He tensed and turned around cautiously. I couldn't see his face in the dark room.

"Staying out all day, and only getting back really late at night, when we are all sleeping. You can come and go as you like. It's your room too," I said without emotion, staring at the ceiling.

He didn't respond for a while, but then said softly, "I'm sorry about the way I treated you that night, Joey. That was not the way to treat anyone, and I apologize. I shouldn't have done some things...I shouldn't have said some things, either. But the fact remains so. It's best that we're not romantically involved," he said to the dark room. "I hope we can still be friends." When I didn't respond, he sighed and resumed his position, facing the wall.

"I see that you have already moved on," I blurted out.

"Yes," he replied quietly, still facing the wall. "You should move on too."

I didn't know what to say after that, so I just lay there in silence for a long time, staring at the ceiling, replaying in my mind him kissing Caroline at the lockers. Anger filled my heart, washing everything else away, flooding and invading. I wanted to get up and pound into Tristan for doing this to me; I wanted him to feel all the pain he was causing me. Then, as suddenly as it came, the raw anger was replaced by cold numbness.

I passed the next few days in this jumble of emotions. Detachment and anger taking turns to play inside me. It seemed that Tristan and Caroline were officially dating now. They were always together, everywhere I looked, holding hands, kissing, leaning over each other, cuddling, touching. Caroline was in heaven. All the girls in school shot envious glares at her, and congratulated her on her victory at winning the most wanted boy in the school.

I tried to avoid them both as much as I could. I focused on school activities, on my homework, on band rehearsals, to get my mind off my problems. If I kept really busy, maybe it wouldn't hurt as much.

I showed the rest of The Lost Boys my new song on Tuesday, and they were really impressed. Seth complimented me the most, but I could see the worry in his eyes. He knew the story behind those lyrics. The boys were keen to rehearse the new song so we could play it next day at music class. We were playing for Professor Rubick's class every week now, presenting a new song or showing how the old ones were coming along. When music class started the next day, there was quite a crowd waiting to hear us play. Tristan hadn't shown up at band practice, but he had to attend the music lesson, or run the risk of failing Professor Rubick's class.

He arrived with Caroline at his side.

Josh had his drums all set up, and Seth, Harry and Sam were ready to play. I sat at my piano and Professor Rubick bellowed to the room, asking for silence. Tristan was sitting very close to the stage area, not exactly blending in with the crowd, but also not quite with the band on stage. He was watching me with his now habitual blank stare. Professor Rubick shouted once again, and everybody fell quiet. I stood up and presented our new song.

"Thanks, Professor Rubick. We have a new song to show you. It's only a first draft, and we haven't had much time to rehearse it, but I hope you like it," I said, looking towards where the professor was standing at the front of the stage, quite close to Tristan.

"Wonderful. Whose song is it?" Professor Rubick asked. Each one of us in the band was supposed to work on their own song in order to pass the end-of-term exam.

"I wrote some of the song, sir. But I'll have to say it's mostly Tristan's work," I said, sitting on my bench. Tristan looked at me, startled. He wasn't expecting that. But I wasn't lying. It was really mostly his work. I had literally used a lot of lines from his speech on the terrace, the night of the Spring Ball.

Then we started playing and I watched as Tristan's face turned from mystified to livid. We finished playing and the room exploded in cheers. People really liked the new song. It was sad and beautiful. But Tristan just stood up and left without a word, leaving a clueless, confused Caroline trailing behind in his wake.

I was very pleased with the reaction of the crowd, but mostly with Tristan's response. He was truly upset. Good. It meant that, underneath his cool, uncaring demeanor, he still felt something, even if his eyes didn't show it to me any more.

He got an A plus on the song that day, and he wasn't even there to hear about it.

For the next few weeks, Tristan avoided us, though Seth tried to talk to him numerous times. He just shot him down at every attempt. I still had a few short conversations late at night with him, but it always ended the same way. With him telling me I needed to accept his decision. That he was happy with Caroline now, and it was time for me to move on and forget about him.

But I was used to fighting for what I wanted. Every time I thought about giving up, profound anger burst through me. I alternated between this and a deep melancholic numbness. Fire and cold. It made me think of Harry's tattoo. Fierce waves crashing over burning melting fire. Two forces that seemed to want to consume me until there was nothing left.

Then one day I was about to exit one of the stalls in the girls' bathroom, when I overheard Caroline and one of her cheerleader friends coming in. I retreated back inside, eavesdropping on their conversation.

"I can't believe you, Caroline!" her friend giggled obnoxiously. "So, you two finally did it? It's been a month already and you haven't got into his pants all this time! That's a record!" Another friend giggled from the other side of the bathroom.

"Well, you know Tristy, he's so shy and polite! He wanted to show me some respect, which I truly appreciate! But enough of respecting already, right? His kisses alone were making me go crazy!" Caroline said, while I bit my lips in disgust.

"So, how was it?" her friend asked. I wanted to be deaf right about now. I clenched my hands over my ears, but I still could hear their high-pitched voices.

"He's the best I've ever had!" Caroline shrieked.

"Tell me everything!?" the other shrieked back.

I wanted to die. I really wanted to die right there and

then, while Caroline described in excruciating detail to her friend everything Tristan had done to her. How incredible he looked naked. How amazing sex with him was. When they left the bathroom, I stayed there for a few hours, trying to regain what was left of my sanity. It was the final blow for me. I was officially giving up on him.

He was with Caroline now. He was having sex with her. He really had moved on. We were not meant to be together.

That day I passed by my room and gathered a bunch of clothes and stuffed them all inside my backpack. Tristan walked into the room and looked startled. He saw the look on my face and stopped dead in his tracks.

"Joe? Are you okay? Something happened?" he asked, and his eyes flashed with worry.

I was beyond despair now. I must've looked like a deranged, crazy, lost girl.

"You wanted me to leave you alone, didn't you?" I shouted at him. "So I'm leaving you alone. I'm moving on, like you wanted me to! And I'm moving out! You don't need to ever talk to me again! I hope you have a nice life!" I stormed out of the room with my backpack clutched in my hands, leaving an awestruck Tristan behind.

I went straight to Tiffany's room and asked if I could move in with her, and I breathed a sigh of relief when she said she had already offered me like a hundred times already and I had never said anything back. I guess I hadn't been listening when she asked. I spent the rest of the month living with Tiff. I couldn't thank her enough for being there for me. For helping me get through this. She made me feel loved and cared for, and helped me get back on my feet again. I was truly blessed to have her friendship.

The other Lost Boys also noticed something was wrong

with me, but they didn't press to know what was happening. Seth was always present, always watchful and alert to see if I needed anything, if there was anything he could do to make me feel better. Sam healed my heart, making me laugh and raising my spirit with his positive energy. Josh was my steady arm in a wavering storm. Always firm, strong and calm; we talked a lot about all kinds of things, about life, heartache, friendship. And then there was my Harry.

How can I describe what Harry did for me? He was so unique, and kind and sweet. His hugs made me feel warm inside, and his presence made me feel at peace. I don't know how he did it, but whenever he was with me, I just felt happy, like he could cast all my pain away with his comforting embrace. I loved all my Lost Boys with all my heart. With them at my side, I could face anything. My friends were all that mattered to me now.

Then it was Friday again and classes were over. I was glad I hadn't bumped into Tristan for some time now. I walked through the hallways, considering going to visit my mom that weekend. We had band practice on Saturday, but I was planning to skip that, because I hadn't seen my mom in ages. I needed to grab my bag and some last remaining clothes from my old room first. And I sure could do with some time away from Tristan and Caroline too.

I bumped into a panicky Seth on the way to our room. He looked at me, frowning, sweat pouring over his forehead. He was really worried and scared.

"Seth! What's the matter? What happened?" I asked apprehensively.

He shuffled his feet, and ran his hands through his hair. It must really be serious for him to mess his hair and not care.

"I'm on my way to the infirmary, Joey! I don't know what else to do any more!" he said in despair.

"What's going on?"

"It's . . . Tristan," he said, and paused, looking worriedly at me. "I know you two aren't speaking . . . and he made me promise not to call you, or to tell you anything! But he's been really sick since this morning . . . and he's getting worse! He has a fever and he's started hallucinating, babbling nonsense about ghosts and gray cloaks and death. I'm freaking out here – and he won't let me call anyone!"

I looked over at my cell phone to see the date. The first of April. *Crap*. I'd completely forgotten about it! I had been so depressed, lately, that I hadn't equated my own extra tiredness with the spell bond.

"Everything is going to be okay, Seth!" I said putting my hands on his shoulders. "You don't need to go to the infirmary, trust me. Tristan will be fine. I need to see him now. Come with me." He followed me reluctantly. I ran to our room and stumbled inside. Tristan and I had spent almost a month apart. I didn't know how badly that could have affected his condition. And the stupid idiot wouldn't let Seth call me!

He was lying on his bed, trembling and deathly pale, sweat pouring over his face. He looked as bad as he had on New Year's Day. His eyes were closed and his jaw was clenched tight in pain. I looked over to Seth. He was watching us with scared, wide eyes. This was the second time Seth had witnessed Tris getting sick, and I needed to think fast how to explain it now to him to stop him calling the nurse.

Chapter Twenty-Six

The Plan

"Okay. Seth. Everything is going to be all right, okay? Tristan just forgot to take his medication. He doesn't want anyone to know about his illness," I said, making up the lie out of the blue. It probably had a lot of loose ends, but I didn't have time to think things through right now. "I'll get it now and he'll be fine, okay?"

I faked grabbing something inside Tristan's chest of drawers, took a glass of water from his night-stand, and sat on his bed. I pushed his bedclothes down to the waistline, revealing his bare chest. He didn't have any clothes on. Then I remembered Seth telling me he'd had to give him a cold shower to lower his temperature. I extended my hand and put my palm on his chest. A violent jolt of stabbing energy pierced through my hand to his chest. He grunted in pain, his jaw clenched.

I remained there a few minutes like that, and then I cupped his chin in my hand, tilting it slightly up so he could take a sip from the glass of water. I pretended to give him a pill and made him drink the water. Seth was walking back and forth in the room, too freaked out to notice much anyway.

"Seth, listen. He took his medicine and he'll be fine now. You should have called me earlier!" I said, frowning at him, disappointment showing all over my face.

"I'm so sorry, Joey! He made me swear!" Seth said guiltily.

Stupid idiot! He would have been dead – again – if I hadn't come by our room! What was he thinking?

"I'm going to stay with him now. Look, he already looks better, see?" I said, sitting on the bed really close to him, with my hands still over his chest. The energy continued flowing between my hand and his skin. He had stopped trembling, but sweat still poured off his forehead.

"Listen, can you go to Tiffany's room and tell her I'm staying here tonight? " I asked Seth.

"Sure. No problem. I'll go right now." He paused as he looked at Tristan. "Incredible. He does really look better. That is some magic pill you gave him. Text me if you need me, okay?" he said, leaving us alone.

I smiled, thinking about Seth's chosen words. Magic pill indeed.

Tristan turned his head and mumbled something incoherent, his eyes still shut tight. I put my other hand over his forehead. God! He was still burning up! We needed to lower his temperature, or he would start convulsing soon. I took off his blankets, leaving him with only a thin blue sheet covering him below the waistline. He grunted and recoiled, turning on to his side, shivering.

"I'm so sorry but I need to lower your temperature," I whispered, lying down by his side and putting my arm around his head, and my other hand over his chest.

He continued shivering and mumbling things I couldn't quite discern. I glanced quickly at his naked torso, his ribcage showing behind his muscles, his strong arms contracting and relaxing spasmodically. I remember Caroline's words, describing how amazing he looked naked, and she was right. I shook my head, dismissing this thought. I shouldn't be remembering this; I shouldn't be looking at him like this now.

And I knew I should be mad at him, but I didn't even care about our fight any more, or that he was with Caroline now. He was sick and needed my help. That's all I needed to focus on.

A few hours passed, and Seth didn't return. I remained at Tristan's side, making as much skin contact with him as I possibly could. The pinpricks of energy continued in a steady sharp beat, the intensity of the flow never fading. Which got me worried. It had never been this way. Usually, it was a stronger jolt, and then it gradually subsided. But now it felt strong and sharp all the time. Maybe it was because he needed more of it? Because this was the fourth time it had happened? Why didn't he bloody call me? Stupid idiot, I thought again.

He stirred and clenched his fists, mumbling something weakly. "Sorry...no...don't tell her..."

"What's that, Tris?" I whispered, leaning in to hear him better.

"Don't tell Joe!" he mumbled again, a little more audible now. "She can't help...She can't help me at New Year's..." he mumbled.

"Because at New Year..." I said, feeding him a line to see if he continued speaking.

"She won't stop him any more..." he mumbled. This was becoming very interesting. My head was racing. Was this what he had been hiding?

"At New Year's she won't be able to stop Vigil?" I guessed cautiously.

"She can't…The bond won't work any more," he said, tossing his head again. He was getting really agitated now. "New Year's…I die."

My heart was in my mouth at that point. Why would he keep this a secret?

"Miss Violet told you that?" I whispered. He'd told me Miss Violet had said there was nothing she could do to help my nightmares, but clearly she had told Tristan so much more than that. Tristan continued mumbling in his half-conscious state. "She can't help…No one can…"

I frowned at him, even though he had his eyes closed and couldn't see me doing it. "Well, that's just…stupid. You give up way too easily, Tristan." I scowled.

Then his words came back to me, the ones he'd said at the terrace on the night of the Spring Ball. He had said we *cannot* be together. He never said he didn't want to be with me! He never said it was his choice. He asked me to look in his eyes to see if he really meant it, and he did. He really thought we could not be together, because he was going to die at the end of the year!

He'd wanted us to get back to the way we used to be, just being friends. Why? He thought it was the best thing for me, and that I would see that some day…

God! How could I not see what he'd been saying to me that night? It was right in front of me! He had said he loved me that night. But love wasn't enough. Because this was going to happen to us whether we wanted it to or not, because it was beyond him to prevent it, and love wasn't enough!

"Tris…you are trying to make Joey forget about you,

to move on with her life, without you. And then she won't hurt too much when you're gone. Is that what are you trying to do?" I asked, watching his reaction closely.

He grimaced and tossed his head on the pillow, struggling with some inner fight. He seemed in serious pain. It broke my heart seeing this.

"I don't want her hurting . . . because of me. She hates me now . . . I made her hate me," he whispered in a heartbreaking voice. "We were . . . going too fast . . . too much . . . pain, in the end . . ." His voice choked and he couldn't continue talking. He was breathing heavily, his eyelids shut tight, but still a tear escaped his eyes, trailing slowly down at the side of his face.

Did he really think he could make me forget about him like that? There was no way I was going to let him die! There was always a way. And we were going to find it!

I leaned really close to him, wiping the tear from his cheek and clasping both of my hands around his face. "Shhhh, Tris, it's all right. Everything will be all right. You don't need to worry about this any more, okay? You need to relax and rest now," I said, pressing my lips softly to his forehead. "And Joey doesn't hate you. She could never hate you. New Year is ages away, but you have to remember: life is full of possibilities," I whispered in his ear.

I saw a single drop splashing on to his chest and I realized it was a tear. Mine. I was crying over him. Tears of relief and happiness. I rested my head on his chest and smiled. I could hear his fast heartbeat, drumming loudly against my ear. It was the most amazing sound I have ever heard. He put his hand softly over my neck and I felt a faint tingling sensation on my skin because of the contact.

The heartache of the past month melted at the steady

beat of his heart, the warmth of his skin against my face and the touch of his hand on my neck. All this time he'd only been trying to protect me. He was trying to save me from hurting in the end. In the most unbelievably stupid possible way, I might add. Idiot! A flash of him kissing Caroline passed through my mind, and I lifted my face slowly and looked at him.

"Tristan...do you...love Caroline?" I whispered. I had to know. I had to be sure. What better time than right now when he was deliriously honest?

He had his eyes still closed, and I watched as he made a disgusted frown, like he was tasting the worst lemon in the world. I smiled widely. That was a good enough answer for me.

He seemed to get calmer after that. His breathing slowed down and he drifted into sleep. Sometimes he would wake up, mumbling incoherent nonsense, and then he'd drift back to sleep again. One time he awoke, tossing his head from side to side, and grabbed the sheets with his clenched fists. "No, no, not the clowns!" he kept muttering under his breath.

I raised my eyebrows and smiled. Was he still feverish?

"Don't worry about the clowns, Tris," I said passing my hand over his head. He was slightly less feverish now.

"But...but they'll get here! It's so...unnatural..." he continued rambling. Unnatural clowns. I chuckled. Teasing him about this later was going to be so much fun!

I stifled a laugh. He seemed to be getting seriously agitated over this. Was he really freaking out over clowns? Everybody has an irrational fear, I guess...

"Don't worry, Tris. I'll take care of those clowns for you. You don't have to worry about them any more," I said reassuringly.

"Okay," he mumbled, turning over.

He had his eyes still closed, but there was a small smile on his lips now. He looked so beautiful. So...sweet. I gave in to an impulse, and kissed him lightly. When I broke the kiss, he sighed softly and whispered so quietly I wouldn't have heard if I hadn't been so close to him.

"...love you, Joe," I heard him say. I realized this was the second time he had said he loved me. Only the first time he'd done so, he'd broken my heart. And now he was kind of delirious. But still...twice it was. Maybe the third time would be for real, with no lies, no subterfuge, no fever, no hallucinations. Third time's the charm, wasn't that what people said? I needed to make the third time happen.

But first things first. To begin with, I needed to make him confess all when he was himself again. I'd make him buckle and cave and confess he loved me. I already had the most brilliant plan. I almost didn't get any sleep that night, thinking about my evil plot to make Tristan crack. His fever vanished in the middle of the night, and he slept like a rock after that. When morning came, I was already up and about, rummaging in my bag. Tristan stirred in his bed and woke up sluggishly, leaning on his elbows and blinking at me, truly confused. He opened his mouth and then closed it again, without saying anything.

"Hey! You're up," I greeted, and walked over him, sitting on his bed. He continued blinking at me. "How do you feel? Better now?" I asked.

He tried to lean away from me and flinched, grimacing in pain. I guess he was still paying the price for our separation.

"Well, I guess not that better, huh?" I teased him. "Good, that serves you right for not calling me earlier!" I said, putting the palm of my hands to his face. I couldn't feel any pinpricks any more. I guessed that whatever needed to be recharged was fully charged now.

He eyed me cautiously. He didn't understand my sudden change of mood. He looked like he didn't remember a thing about last night, either.

"I'm going to see Mom today. Would you like to send her a hug?" I asked, standing up and walking over to my suitcase.

"Huh?" was all he could say.

"Rose. Remember her? I'm off to see her for the weekend. As long as you feel well enough? I'll say you sent her a hug, okay?"

"Okay," he mumbled, still trying to figure out what the hell was happening.

"And please don't be that stupid again and not call me next month. You weren't being very smart keeping this from me," I said. I guess he would take it that I was talking about his monthly illness. But I was also talking about everything else. See? I could do this double-meaning stuff that he excelled at too! Take that, mysterious-ex-ghost-boy! I chuckled quietly to myself and grabbed my bag, turning to leave.

"And, since I'll be gone this weekend, band practice is today at four. Now your fever has broken, you're well enough to be there. Two Grays missing won't be acceptable, and you're in the band too, even if you seem to be forgetting about it. They've been asking about you all the time. They miss you," I said, opening the door.

He sat on the bed, baffled. "They...d-do?" He really looked surprised.

What? Did he think they didn't care about him? That

just because we'd had a fight, his friends had forgotten him? He was my Tristan, and he was adorable and sweet and all, but it turns out he was such an idiot too. I'll have to remember to smack him in the head repeatedly when all this secret business was over.

I shook my head, chuckling again, making him even more baffled. "Of course they do, Tris! They are your friends! And your band. So be there. Four o'clock. And practice. I gotta go, see you Sunday," I said, and walked out, laughing a little. He looked so cute when he was clueless!

I went to Tiffany's room to finish packing. While I stuffed my clothes into the bag, I told her about my evil plan. I actually needed her help to get things into motion.

"You're gonna what?" she shouted, surprised.

"You heard me. And I need your help to do it. You're going to be my special adviser," I said beaming at her. I was in a very cheerful mood today.

"Are you serious, Joey? You're gonna seduce him until he caves and admits he has feelings for you? He's with Caroline now!" she said gently.

"Not for long. I'll make sure of that. Come on! You know me. I'm ... persistent," I said.

She laughed loudly. "Yeah, that's a swift way of putting it. You're the most stubborn, strong-minded person I have ever known!" She shook her head, amused.

"Well, thanks ... I guess. But I still need your help. Boys go wild about you ... I need to learn a few of your tricks to pester Tristan now!" I said with a laugh.

"Okay. I'll do my best to help you. I already told I could have Caroline expelled if you wanted to! You didn't even let me kick her out of cheer squad!" she whined.

"No, Tiff. It's not her fault. She's just head over heels for him, but let's be fair, what girl wouldn't be? He's the one to blame! He's the one who must suffer! " I said, smiling evilly.

"That reminds me...and I'm just realizing this now, but Seth didn't return to our room at all! Where did he...? Wait! Did he stay here all night? Did you and he...? Did you guys?" I said, squinting my eyes hard at her. She turned a deep shade of red. "Oh my God," I mumbled.

"I was going to tell you! It's just...I'm kind of...embarrassed about it...ahem." She coughed and blushed again.

"Embarrassed? About what, pray tell?" I asked, raising an eyebrow.

"Well...I sort of tackled him last night," she mumbled, shuffling her feet.

"Tackled?"

"I jumped his bones, okay? There! I said it! Happy now! I'm a big pervert!" she shouted, throwing her hands up in the air for dramatic effect. She was such a drama queen!

"He snuck into my room all worried, and I convinced him to stay for the night, to give you guys some privacy. But then he was all cute, and geeky, and I love when he gets geeky on me" She blushed again. "So I jumped on him. And he spent the night. And I can't believe I actually did this! He's gonna pester me for ever now, saying I can't resist him and can't keep my hands off him..."

"Well, he does have a point," I said, stifling a laugh.

Tiffany ended up coming with me to my mom's house for the weekend, and she even helped me go shopping for some new special outfits for my evil plan.

We had fun with my mom and when we got back late at Sunday, I grabbed all my clothes that were in her room and moved back in to the boys' dorm room. Seth and

Tristan were in our room chilling out. I guess band practice on Saturday had done Tristan some good; he looked a lot happier having his friends back. I guess he'd been feeling lonely this past month. But then I remembered he had Caroline to keep him company, and I didn't feel that sad about his loneliness any more.

As soon as I stepped into the room the atmosphere changed, and they both tensed, anticipating the possibility of another fight. They didn't know I was done fighting. I had my evil plan now.

"Hi, boys! Missed me much?" I entered beaming widely at them. Tristan eyed me suspiciously from his bed. He was trying to figure out my game. "How was band rehearsal? Did you guys work on my new song? It still has a lot of tweaks to be done." I dumped my bag on the bed.

"Yeah, we worked on it a little. Harry wasn't in the mood to play...He gets awfully lazy when you're not there, you know?" Seth answered.

"Oh, I'll have a word with him about it, don't worry!" I said, winking at Seth.

Tristan started to rise from his bed, getting ready to leave. "Tristan, you don't need to leave because of me. We need to get past this. In fact, I want to apologize for any yelling I may have done. I'm moving back in now, and I wanted to tell you I'm okay with you and Caroline, so stay, will you? There's no need for you to leave every time I'm around now!" I said, still in a cheerful mood.

I was really impressed with my acting skills! I didn't even stutter or pause after saying Caroline's name!

"Hey! I even got you guys presents!" I said, opening my bag. "This is for you, Tris. I think you needed another one of these." I tossed him the package. He eyed me even more suspiciously before opening it. I had bought him another blue T-shirt, this one a very deep, dark blue. "It might make your eyes look as blue as Sammy's," I said, smiling at him.

"And this one is for you, Seth!" I said, tossing him his present. "It's actually from Tiffany. She told me to give it to you and record your reaction, so... wait just a second, need to grab my camera to film this!" I pointed my cell phone in his direction.

He looked at me with an even more suspicious, puzzled look than Tristan's.

"Hey, I'm just the messenger. Just open the thing already!" I said, laughing.

He unwrapped it and took out silk Superman boxer briefs. He looked at them, wide-eyed, and then at me, and turned all pink. His mouth was hanging open too. I cracked up laughing at his face. He turned a deep shade of red, pink, purple and then violet. It was freaking hilarious! Those two crazy blonds belong with each other, all right!

He stuffed the underwear back in the box, and frowned at me. "Joey! Cut it out! And please, don't let this video end up on YouTube, or I will kill you! You hear me?" he shouted.

I laughed even louder. Tristan was trying to be serious, but the corner of his lips twitched slightly.

"Okay, then. I need to grab some dinner. Who's coming?" I asked, after I managed to stop laughing. I closed my bag and headed to the door.

Tristan shook his head and leaned back on his bed. "I'm not hungry. Maybe I'll grab some with Caroline later," he said, testing me.

"Okay. Have fun," I said, smiling softly. "Oh, wait, I

need to take my cell phone and show this to Tiffany at dinner!" I said, turning back to grab my phone.

"Oh, no you won't!" Seth shouted, running after me. "And don't you dare show this to anyone else, Joey!"

We ran outside the room together, leaving Tristan behind. I sprinted fast, holding my cell phone tight in my hand with Seth went running after me. He eventually caught up with me, and snatched the phone out of my hands, deleting the video. At dinner he acted all cool and thanked Tiffany for his sexy gift, and I laughed the whole time, because I knew what his true first reaction was. Tiff and Seth kept teasing each other during the whole meal. It was a fun night. Not as much fun as the week was going to be, though. I had my evil plan to work on now! I was going to drive Tristan crazy. I felt a little mean about Caroline, but I knew now he didn't love her. He loved me.

Chapter Twenty-Seven

Game On!

Monday came and *The Plan* was set into motion. I had Tiffany's coaching during our weekend at home and a new killer wardrobe to add to my arsenal. I had bought some low-cut shirts, and even a few dresses.

I also bought a few outfits in a "rock chick" style, for band performances and rehearsals. I was more comfortable keeping the tomboy attitude in place for shows, but this was at least a little sexier. I liked those outfits far more than the dresses, because they were more my style. But this week I wasn't going for tomboy; I was going for driving boys crazy!

I would tease, and flirt and provoke Tristan in every possible way, until he cracked and caved, and confessed he was crazy about me! And after that he would have to confess his idiotic plan to make me move on and forget about him. But I decided to start gently at first, so as not to make Tristan suspicious. I put on my brand new low-cut cherry tank-top for first class, and my tight black jeans, and cherry lip-gloss. I was kind of nervous about doing the teasing thing because it was so out of my comfort zone, and totally uncharted territory, but I guess all's fair in love and war. I had watched Tiffany doing this very same thing with Seth a lot of times before, so all I needed to do was copy her moves and see how I faired. I was no Tiffany in the looks department, but I had something to work with.

Tristan was already inside the classroom, sitting and talking to Tiffany about something. I sat by his side, and greeted him with a soft smile, winking playfully at Tiffany. Tristan turned his head and looked at me with this usual blank stare. That was my cue to "accidentally" drop my pencil on the floor, and then lean over slowly to pick it up, exposing a lot more of my cleavage area.

I felt so stupid doing this! It was never going to work! I fought back the urge to blush or giggle, but when I looked up, I saw Tristan's eyes glued to my chest, the blank stare completely gone from his eyes. Then he snapped his eyes up, lingering momentarily over by my lips. I guess the cherry lip-gloss was a hit too, because his eyes shone intensely for a brief second. Then he blinked and diverted his gaze fast, staring hard at the blackboard.

Holy crap! It had totally worked! He was really checking out my boobs! I glanced quickly at Tiffany, and she was stifling a laugh on the other side of him, and then she gave me a nod of approval. I had passed my first test!

So the *lean-in-cleavage-move* totally worked. I stared ahead, smiling widely. This was going to be so easy! I couldn't believe it had actually worked! But I tried again later at the lunch table, and I actually caught Tristan *and* Sammy glancing down, and Josh stretching his neck a little, trying to sneak a peek.

Boys… It was so easy messing up with them! If only I'd known this before. It was like their brains shut down at the slightest possibility of breasts showing up. I have to admit, though, that I had my own brain shutdown when Tristan had kissed me. But that was different...somehow...I think. Okay. Not so different, after all. But I was glad to know I had the same effect on him.

That afternoon we had band practice. I changed into my tomboy/rocker girl attire for the rehearsal: baggy low-slung pants and a black tie over a tight white tank-top, leather wristband and Converse shoes. I walked into the room and Harry was the first to compliment me.

"Hey, Joey! Looking sexy and delicious!" he yelled from the other side of the room. He was barefoot and shirtless, for some reason, his red and green tattoo curling up in his arm and half his chest. I was always amazed by how good Harry's tattoo looked on him. The others greeted me and complimented me too.

"Thanks, guys. I'm testing some new outfits for Wednesday's presentation! I'm glad you like it!" I said, waving at them. "Oh, man, have you guys been stripping Harry again?" I said, watching Harry putting his T-shirt back on.

Seth, Josh and Sam sniggered. They were constantly forcing Harry to strip to embarrass him. They picked on him because he was the youngest and the smallest – and he got the most embarrassed at being stripped down to his underwear! It was like brothers teasing a younger sibling. I had watched them doing this to him a lot of times already, and I always turned my back when they reached the critical moment, for decency's sake.

Harry walked in my direction, sniffing loudly. "I might as well walk around naked all the time to save them the trouble!" he grumbled, annoyed.

"Guys, you should at least take turns who to strip! Picking on Harry all the time isn't fair!" I berated them.

"So, maybe we should take a turn with you, then, Joe! You look good in those clothes, but I'll bet you'll look even better without them!" Sam hinted, smirking at me.

"Hey, you are all free to try to strip me!" I said, shrugging. They all stopped and stared at me.

"No way! Are you serious? You should've mentioned this before!" Josh said from behind his drums. They were all smirking evilly and walking closer to me. Except Harry and Tristan; they just stood still and watched.

I gave Josh a beatific smile. "I said you can *try* to strip me. I didn't say I was going to let you."

"That's good enough for me!" Sam said, reaching out to grab my hands. It was a rookie's mistake. I side-stepped him and grabbed his wrist instead, twisting it lightly and making Sam grunt in pain.

"Come on, Sammy! Did you forget about my martial arts classes?" I said, walking behind him and pushing his back, making him stumble forward and away from me. Seth and Josh tried it too, but it was easy escaping their grasp. Josh was a little more difficult, but I managed to skip away from him too. They all tried a couple of times again, individually and together, and I wriggled free each and every time.

They gave up after a while, panting and sweating. "Okay, we give up. We might as well keep to picking on Harry, then," Josh said, holding his hands on his legs and panting. Then he stood up and started walking in Harry's direction. Sam and Seth smirked too, coming to Josh's aid.

"Hey! Come on, guys! Again? No fair!" Harry shouted, trying to evade Josh's grasp. He wasn't fast enough, though. I waited until they'd completed the dirty job, while Harry struggled and laughed and shouted at them. They liked to tickle Harry to hear him laugh and wiggle more during strip sessions. Harry was very ticklish and his high-pitched laughs were funny!

After the rumpus subdued, we started working on our songs, and a sweaty Harry started getting dressed again, muttering darkly under his breath. I chuckled and opened my notepad. I could have helped Harry, but seeing him getting stripped was always too damn entertaining for me. Not to mention that it was always a nice view. I glanced at Tristan and he was looking at me and Harry, all serious and in a foul mood. I smiled to myself. Jealousy was actually a good color on him.

I had a new song that I was working on, and I was helping Josh and Sam with theirs too. Tristan was scribbling a song of his own, leaning over a pile of boxes at the other side of the room. I wondered what his song was about... I guess I would have to wait until he was ready to show it to us.

After a while I stopped what I was doing and walked over to Sam, looking over at the pile of papers around him. "Sam, do you want me to give some tweaks to your song?" I asked, leaning over him.

He smiled warmly at me. "Sure, Joe! You can *tweak my song* as much as you want!" he teased. The other boys starting cracking up at that the innuendo. I rolled my eyes at them.

"Man! What is up with you today, Sammy? You're way over-excited!" I said, exasperated, but I smiled at him nevertheless. His flirting was kind of flattering.

"Sorry, Joey! You just look too good in those new outfits! I can't help myself!" he said, chuckling and putting his arm around my waist, pulling me closer to him. I laughed and rested my head on his broad shoulder.

"Yes, Joey! I need you to *tweak* my song as well!" Josh shouted, laughing at Seth's side. Seth and Harry were still cracking up over this. Boys.

"Yeah, yeah, I'll be there in a minute!" I said, waving at them in annoyance, and looking at Sam's lyrics. I glanced over at Tristan and he still had a dead-serious expression on his face.

I whispered to Sam that I would be right back and stood up, walking over to the other side of the room, where Tristan was slouched. He watched me approach with a frown, and closed his notebook when I got right in front of him. I leaned over, resting my hands on my knees, and looked him straight in the eyes. Caution and suspicion flashed inside. But then his eyes slowly descended to my neck and a little lower. Heat burned in his eyes for a split second. Yep. Cleavage-move still working good!

"So, Tristan," I purred softly at him. "Do you want me to give a *tweak to your song* too? I'll do my best to make you pleased."

He snapped his eyes back at me, with raised eyebrows and a hanging mouth.

"Uh…" was all he managed to say.

I smiled teasingly at him. "No? Well, let me know if you change your mind. I'm at your service," I said, and turned to leave, walking back to the other side of the room where Sam was sitting. I crouched by Sam's side and saw Tristan with his mouth still hung open, staring at me. It was like he needed a brain reboot to start operating properly again. Evil plan was on full blast!

Later that evening I tried a new approach. After taking a

nice warm bath, I rubbed scented lotion all over my body. Then I put on some small, soft white cotton shorts and a white tank-top, letting my hair fall slightly over my chest. I watched myself in the mirror. There was a lot of leg and skin showing. I usually slept in baggy sweats and long T-shirts, like the boys did. I was glad it was very warm inside the room, otherwise the small PJs were going to look a bit off. I bit my lips, wondering how Tristan was going to react to this new sleeping outfit. Well, I wasn't going to find out hanging in the bathroom. I walked outside and thanked the angels because the lights in the room were already off; only my night-stand lamp was lit. I felt a lot more confident with semi-darkness hiding my embarrassment. In this gloom, Tristan might not be able to see me blushing.

Seth was just about to sit on his bed, and actually managed to miss the mattress and slip on to the ground when he saw me passing by. Tiffany had helped me pick out the cotton shorts and top, and she was curious to know about Tristan's reaction, but I thought I better keep Seth's to myself...But right now I needed to focus harder on trying not to blush. Or trip over.

Tristan was already under his covers. He was in the middle of a yawn when he caught a glimpse of me, which made him shut his mouth tight and stare silently at me. The look on his face alone was priceless! I walked over to his bed and sat by his side.

"Tris, I was just thinking in the bathroom...What do you think about this new lotion I'm using? Is the smell too strong?" I said, extending my arm right up to his nose.

He stared silently at me until he realized I was waiting for an answer.

"It's…a bit much," he mumbled. It had a *bit-much-I-can't-handle-this-it's-driving-me-crazy* sort of meaning, though. There he goes again with his double-meaning answers! He was a very clever boy, telling the truth and not telling the truth at the same time.

"You think?" I said, sniffing my arm inquisitively. "Seth, what do you think?" I said, standing up and going to Seth's bed. He had managed to compose himself in the mean time, and was fairly normal again when I extended my arm up his nose.

He inhaled and exhaled slowly. "I think it smells awesome!" he said, smiling. "It's so great having a girl in the room! It's lavender, lilies and vanilla scents all around… When I had to share the room last year with Harry and Sammy, it was the battle of funky smells here!" he said, making a funny face.

I chuckled and went to my bed. "Well, it's a tie. One vote pro, one con. I'll ask Tiff tomorrow to settle this thing, then," I said, and climbed under my covers. "Good night, boys."

Tristan tossed and turned that whole night, unable to sleep after that. He looked like a fish out of water, flipping in his bed so many times. It was great! It was about time for him to have some restless nights as well.

The next couple of days were filled with round after round of more torture and tease. I didn't feel guilty for making him suffer – I wanted to see him hot and bothered.

On Wednesday morning I noticed Seth leaving the room earlier, to meet up with Tiffany and hang with her a little before classes. I took the opportunity with Tristan still sleeping, and headed to the bathroom, taking a quick bath. I was preparing a major Round Four knock-out for this morning!

Tristan was leaning over Seth's bed switching off his alarm, blinking sleepily with his hair all crumpled, when I timed my entrance, wrapped only in my small towel, hair all wet and water dripping slightly over my back and chest. We usually got dressed inside the bathroom, but today I thought it would be best if I "forgot" my clothes over my bed. Tristan turned his head towards me, eyes wide open, suddenly completely awake. I felt his eyes roaming my body and I didn't allow myself to blush. "Morning, Tris!" I greeted him nonchalantly. "Forgot my clothes here," I said, walking over to my bed. I felt his eyes following me all the way, burning into my back. Then I sat on the mattress, wrapping the towel more close to my body, and crossing my legs slowly. I grabbed my clothes with one hand and looked at him for the first time. His eyes flashed with complete lust for a second. It was almost like there was fire glowing from inside.

I smiled at him. "You can use to the bathroom now, I'll get dressed in here," I said softly.

He just stood there speechless. I was having that effect on him quite a lot lately!

"Go on, now!" I said, waving him away and flapping my shirt in the air, and then I looked up at him again, with a curious expression on my face. "Come on, Tris! It's almost like you want to stay and watch me get dressed!" I inquired, smirking teasingly.

That made him snap out of his trance, blush intensely and turn around fast, heading for the bathroom, almost hitting the wall near the door at the last second. I giggled quietly and almost felt sorry for him. Almost.

He still insisted on dating Caroline, though. But I could see his heart wasn't into lying and pretending any more. I was breaking his resolve. Seeing him with Caroline still made my insides twist, and bile rise in my mouth every time she touched him intimately, but I sucked it up and pretended it didn't bother me at all. I was starting to get really good at acting...

Then it was time for the presentation at music class. I arrived a little late and saw that the boys were already inside, all set and ready to play. Tristan was on the stage today and Caroline stood, watching him with googly eyes. I frowned, glancing up at the stage area. Tristan was looking at me intently. I put on my fake smile. The room was full of people. Each time we did a music presentation, more and more kids showed up to listen. I noticed a few even knew the lyrics from our older songs already; they mouthed the words as we sang. I guessed The Lost Boys were getting to be a bit of a hit, at least on campus.

"Kids! Everybody quiet now!" Professor Rubick shouted. "I hear the band has a new song today. I'm very pleased with you, boys...and girl," he said, looking at me sitting by the piano "You are managing to come up with so many amazing songs! So, let's hear it, then, shall we?" he said, clapping his hands. Everybody cheered on cue. I looked up at Seth, confused. I didn't know about any new song for today. What was he talking about? Seth shrugged and gave me an apologetic look. Then he grabbed a sheet of paper and walked over to the piano, handing the paper to me.

"I'm so sorry, Joe. We rehearsed this while you were home at the weekend, and...it's Tristan's song," he said, looking at me guiltily and then back at Tristan. "So sorry," he mumbled, and got back to his place on stage.

I glanced at the sheet of paper in my hand. It was the

part I needed to play in the song. Then Josh started playing his drums, and I hurried to play along with him. Tristan started singing then, and I finally understand what Seth was so sorry about. The song was about me.

About the way my smile made him feel, how much pain it caused to him, and about lovers and lies. He sang about how much he didn't want things to end this way, but there was no other way to go. It was a song about how much it hurt to be heartbroken, to love and to lose. Tristan sang that he was better off without me; that I could leave at any time because he was tired of all the fights. It was such a heart-breaking song, full of pain and despair. When it was over, Tristan looked so sad, staring at the floor. The room erupted with clapping and cheering, but he seemed unaware of the success of his music. He didn't care because his heart was broken.

Harry, Josh and Sam were oblivious to what was happening on stage; they looked happy with their performance and the reaction of the audience.

Caroline jumped on stage and hugged Tristan, and at first he didn't respond. But then he seemed to remind himself of his act, and he reluctantly put his arm around her, glancing sideways at me. Seth came over, worry filling his eyes. I stood up and walked out from behind the piano, giving him a hug.

"That's okay, Seth. Everything's fine. Don't you worry about me, okay?" I said, parting the hug and smiling softly at him. "It was a beautiful song. Tristan should be proud of it. It's one of our best songs, if not the best," I said sincerely. "I wish I'd had a little time to practice it, though, but we can rehearse it more later."

Seth looked at me in relief. "Really?"

"Yes. It's really great. And the part when you and Tristan sang together was the best bit! You two were great!" I said, putting my hand on his shoulder.

"Thanks, Joey." He smiled. "You are so amazing. I wish he could see that too," he said, glancing Tristan's way.

Tristan was watching our exchange with an indecipherable expression. I shrugged and went to hug the other boys. I wasn't really upset over the song. Tristan was still trying to push me away, the best he could. I knew he didn't mean it. It was time for a few more rounds of my master plan until I landed my final blow.

That night we all went celebrate the success of Tristan's new song in a small bar in Saint Pete, the small town close to school grounds. Seth had inside connections with the owner of the bar (I told you that boy knew everyone, everywhere!) and since the place was fairly empty, the owner let us in to celebrate there that night, with the condition that we didn't drink anything alcoholic. Tristan brought Caroline along, and Sammy invited a girl named Melinda to come with us. I debuted one of my new dresses that night, a low-cut little black dress. I felt really fancy in it. Tiffany lent me a pair of her high-heeled black sandals. They were tremendously sexy, but equally painful. I let my hair down too, and put on a dark-red lipstick. I got a lot of compliments from everybody, but none from Tristan.

I had an amazing time, laughing and dancing with my boys. Sammy was courting Melinda all night long, and Josh couldn't stop flirting with lots of girls in the bar. Seth had Tiffany in his arms all night, and Tristan just hunched in his chair and sulked the whole time, while Caroline tried to get him to dance with her, to no avail. A few guys I didn't know even came to flirt with me and asked to buy me drinks, but the boys always intervened at that point, pulling me away. They were awfully over-protective of me, which was sweet of them, but a bit annoying as well.

On the ride back to the school, I got in the back of Sammy's car with Harry and Caroline, who sat between us, since she was the shortest and wouldn't block Sam's rear-view mirror. Tristan sat in the passenger seat while Sam drove, chatting and laughing with me and Harry, both boys teasing me about how good I looked. But Tristan and Caroline just sat there in silence, sulking in their seats. Caroline was fuming over the way Tristan had been treating her all night, and I even felt kind of bad for her. He was being a real lousy date tonight. Guilt gnawed at me, because Caroline didn't deserve to be treated like that, and it was my plan that was putting Tristan in such a foul mood; but then I remembered it was his idea to fake-date her in the first place, and I pushed the guilt down until I couldn't feel it any more.

When we arrived back at school and Sam had parked the car, Tristan was the first to get out, acting like he had a thunder cloud over his head. He banged the door and stalked off. He didn't even wait for Caroline. She rushed after him.

"Jeez, what's up with Tristan tonight, man? He was a serious pain!" Harry asked, and Sam just shrugged his shoulders, clueless. "I guess Caroline isn't putting out, man, the way he's all tensed up like that. That's some major sexual tension there. He seriously needs to let off some steam, if you know what I mean!" Sam sniggered at Harry, and then he caught my frown and coughed loudly to cover it up. Boys!

I bade them goodnight and walked back to my room barefoot, having slipped off the killer high heels. I was glad

I was getting under Tristan's skin like that. It meant my plan was working. When I stepped inside the dorm room, he was already there, slouched on his bed alone, playing one of Sam's portable videogames. Thank God he'd managed to wriggle free from Caroline's grasp. He clearly wasn't in the mood for cheerleading tonight. I smiled to myself as I walked to my bed.

He was still in a foul mood, a huge scowl plastered on his face. I bet myself he would start picking a fight with me any time soon, as he had been attempting to do all the previous nights of the week. "Didn't want to spend the night over at Harry's?" he sniped at me in a mocking tone.

"Nah, he was tired. He wasn't going to satisfy me the way I deserve, tonight!" I said teasingly. "So I thought it would be best to leave him to rest for now. Maybe tomorrow," I said suggestively.

He grunted and stared at his computer game, punching the buttons with vengeance. He was rubbish at videogames, a real modern novelty in his eyes, but he continued trying to understand how the things worked, no matter how many times he died in the game.

I walked over to him and sat right by his side on his bed. "Tris, would you help me get out of this dress? I can't reach the zipper," I said, turning my back to him.

He paused his game and muttered something under his breath, betraying his irritation with my request. I pretended I didn't understand all his quiet growling and grabbed my hair, pulling it all to the front, leaving the back of the dress clear to him. One of his hands reached over and rested against my lower back, putting a gentle pressure on the fabric of the dress, and his other hand tugged at my neckline, next to the zipper.

I had never been so aware of his touch as I was at that moment, the heat of his hands hovering over my back. He grabbed the zipper and gave a slight tug, sliding it down. I could feel the palm of his hands brushing softly over my skin, so slowly, hesitantly, like he was afraid of what he was doing. The faint tingling sensation spread wherever his hand touched my skin, sending shivers down my spine. I had forgotten how his touch made me feel. Suddenly my plan didn't seem so safe any more. I was feeling way out of control here. I felt his hand give the final pull, and the zipper slid fast down the last remaining inches of the dress, exposing my entire bare back to him.

I heard him catch his breath and then silent tension filled the room like a thick fog. I stood up slowly and turned around, clutching the front of my dress so it wouldn't slip off me. Tristan looked like he was still holding his breath.

"T-thanks," I managed to stutter shakily.

It took a while for him to respond. "No problem," he said, in a low hoarse voice, lust filling his eyes. Then he grabbed his videogame like it was a life-saver on a sinking ship, and then he resumed his game. Literally and meta-phorically speaking.

I mentally cursed. I had almost slipped up there, and he was still playing his silly act, still in control. I went to the bathroom with wobbly legs and changed into my short white cotton PJs. When I came out, he didn't even acknowl-edge me. So I just shrugged and decided to call it quits for tonight. I stopped trying to look sexy, lost the hip-swaying moves and just walked over to my bed, getting ready to go to sleep.

Man, I was so tired! I yawned loudly, arching my back and stretching out my arms, feeling the tension in my muscles disappear. I relaxed and dropped my arms, blinking lazily at the floor. My stretching had made my tight top lift up a little, showing off my belly and hips. I was about to push my top back down, when I glanced up at Tristan.

He had stopped playing and was staring me down. His look was so intense that it had caught me off guard, his eyes burning with a fierce hunger. "Tris...are you all right?" I asked, before I could stop myself.

He took a sharp intake of air in raw agony, and my heart filled with pure satisfaction. There was so much need and desire in his eyes. Then he blinked a couple of times and tossed his videogame onto the bed. "I'm fine," he snapped. "I just need...a shower. That's all." He stormed off to the bathroom. Lately he seemed to be needing a lot of long showers. I'll bet they were all cold ones. So...Stretching, huh? How about that...I needed to tell Tiffany about this new discovery. I also needed to push Tristan a little harder; I needed to step up my game. I needed to land my last punch. Saturday was going to be knock-out day!

Chapter Twenty-Eight

Poker Game

On Saturday I put the last part of my evil plan in motion. Well, I hoped it would be the last, I didn't know how much longer I could endure this silly game. I had convinced Tiffany and all the boys to participate in our own poker game night. Tristan and some boys usually had a poker game once a month, but it was a boys-only type of event, and it was mainly engineered by Bradley. That fact alone made me shiver and run away from it as fast as I could. Spending a night of gambling with Bradley and his moronic friends was definitely not my definition of a good time. Plus, girls were not allowed at Bradley's poker nights.

But Tristan was the golden boy of the team now, and he had to attend the games every month. He sometimes took Sammy and Josh with him. Seth refused to go because he had his ongoing feud with Bradley. Harry was forbidden to attend poker nights since *The Incident*. They didn't like to talk about it much, but from what I could gather, the major problem with Harry and poker was that he was totally unpredictable. He was the master of bluffing, mostly because he didn't pay attention to what was going on around him, and had no clue about the rules of the game.

And the other big problem was that, despite this, he had an almost supernatural lucky streak. Harry usually bankrupted everyone at the table. And to top it all, he made fun of the sore losers quite vehemently. After some hours of relentless money loss, things had gotten out of control on the night in question. It had all ended in a fist fight, with Harry banned from poker nights permanently. So I convinced everyone to have our private, special poker night, Lost Boys only! And Tiffany could come too, because she was a Lost Boy's girlfriend, and she was the only one who could arrange to get the key for the recreation room. Now, the special thing about our night was that we were going to play strip poker. Yep. You heard me right. As in, poker with stripping!

Josh was the first to accept. He was awfully competitive, and I knew he would immediately accept anything involving a dare. Sam and Seth tried to protest a little, but they caved after a few minutes of Josh calling them chicken. Harry just shrugged, like it was no big deal for him about the poker or the stripping. The boys had stripped Harry so many times before that it wasn't big news for him to end up naked any more. He was just thrilled about being allowed to play poker again.

The winner of the round got to pick the person who was going to have to take off a piece of clothing. The best part was that, with so many boys playing the game, the opportunities for getting to strip would be many, increasing my chances of succeeding with my evil plan because:

1. I could tease Tristan with my nakedness, piling on the pressure.

2. I could make Tristan rage with jealousy over the boys ogling me naked, and me admiring them.

3. Then I could make him crack, lose his precious self-control and stop with the stupid pretending.

Of course, I was planning to stop playing before I got down to my underwear. But Tris didn't know that. He was going to flip when he saw me losing items of clothing, one after another! I was sure as hell he was going to crack tonight.

I was kind of nervous about it, though. If someone caught us there, it was a sure-fire way to be expelled. Being out of the dorms at late hours, gambling and a bunch of half-naked kids locked up in a room... Tiffany reassured me that we wouldn't get caught. They had Bradley's poker nights at the school all the time, and no one had ever caught them.

When we arrived at the rec room that night, the boys were already inside, talking excitedly. Tiffany was all perky and pretty, wearing a scarf, earrings, a small cute beret, a jacket, bracelets and so many pieces of clothing that it was kind of funny. Josh caught on at once.

"No way that's going to count, Miss Worthington! You have to be wearing the same amount of clothes as all of us!" he said, walking towards us. "Otherwise it'll take a week to get you naked. See Joey here? She's wearing the same thing as us: jeans, shirt and shoes. Three pieces is more than enough!"

"Oh, all right!" Tiffany snapped at Josh, pouting.

I didn't remind Josh that girls also wore bras – he didn't know I wasn't playing to win. Evil plan required a lot of skin showing. If Tristan didn't cave tonight, then... I didn't know what else to do any more...

Tristan was slouching on the old couch next to the game table, playing Sam's videogame again. He was plugged into that thing lately like it was his life-support machine.

"Come on, Tristan! It's time to play some strip poker!" Josh bellowed to him. Tristan glanced up quickly and frowned.

"Strip poker? I thought you said this was going to be a normal poker night."

"It is a normal poker night. But with stripping," Josh replied smugly, and when he saw the glare Tristan was shooting his way he added quickly, "Come on, if I'd told you about it, you would never have come. Stop being so prudish, man. Let's have some fun!"

"Strip poker's not for me. Sorry, Josh. I'll pass on this one. The ladies should have the decency to do the same," he added, giving Tiffany and me a pointed glare before staring back at the videogame while everybody took their seats around the game table.

"Aw, come on, you play with that idiot Bradley and not with us?" Seth complained, offended.

"Yeah, what's that all about?" Sam joined in the protests. "You're always saying life's too short and that we should make the most of it while we can, and now you won't even play a little game with us?" Harry pointed out, pulling out a chair out for Tristan. I walked behind Tristan's couch and leaned over him, wrapping my arms around his neck and resting my hands on his broad chest. I felt him tense instantly beneath my hands.

"Come on, Tris. Play with your friends!" I said, brushing my lips lightly near to his ear.

I could almost feel his heart thumping beneath my hands while the boys mocked him. He tried to hide a shiver that ran through his body as my fingers played over his large chest, and a small grunt escaped his throat. He was so uncomfortable with me that close, that I think he agreed just to get the hell away from me.

"Fine! I'll play." He hissed, getting off the couch like it was on fire, or something. I could see Tiffany giggling from her seat on the other side of the table.

The game got going and we all made our best poker faces, trying to win the first round of the game, but to no avail because of Harry's lucky streak. He won, making everybody at the table groan loudly.

Harry looked around the table, smiling, trying to decide who he was going to choose for the first strip session. I was sure he was going to pick me, but he grinned evilly at Josh while he pointed an accusing finger at him. "Josh, my man, payback's a bitch! It's your turn to taste your own medicine! Let's see how you feel naked!" Josh smiled kindly and took his shoes off. "Harry, only you would pick a dude to strip with two gorgeous girls playing!" he said, chuckling. Tiff and I blushed a little. Josh was such a charmer. The next round Tiffany won, and pointed at me.

"You're the one whose idea this was! Not so funny any more, huh?" she teased, mocking me, but she was just helping me speed things up in the game. I gave her a mean smile while the boys made catcalls.

"Dude, wouldn't it be awesome if there was a cat fight here tonight? Can you imagine Joey and Tiff in a messy tangle, rolling on the floor? That'd be so hot!" Josh said, provoking Seth again and preparing to get punched. But Seth only stared at Tiffany and me with a dreamy expression on his face.

"Seth!" Tiff shouted, slapping him on the arm. "You are totally imagining the scene in your head right now, aren't you? You boys are such pervs!" she scoffed with a glare.

"All right, everybody! There are NOT going to be any cat fights here today, so settle down," I bellowed, laughing at all of them. There was a series of 'awww' and 'maaan' around the table from all the boys.

The next two rounds Harry won again, and everyone groaned. He picked Josh again, and Josh had to take off his socks and shirt. I was fairly used to seeing Josh shirtless, because of M.A. classes; he always ended up without a shirt there. But his bare muscular chest was always a sight to behold, nevertheless. Tiff stared at his pecks and put on a dreamy face, making Seth nudge her in the ribs, a heavy scowl on his face.

"What?" she asked, all innocent. "I was just imagining you and Josh arm wrestling naked in here..."

All the boys made disgusted noises at that, and I laughed loudly. Then I happened to win the next round. I looked at my boys, a dubious expression on my face. "Hmm, which one to pick...which one...Can't be Seth, I already see him naked all the time in my room," I teased. Tiffany looked at us wide-eyed, and Tristan looked equally surprised.

"No! You *do not*!" Seth shouted in panic. "She's just kidding, Tiff! I don't...Joey, tell her, for God's sake!" he pleaded, shifting on his seat.

"I'm just joking, Tiff!" I said, chuckling loudly. "I don't get to see him even without his socks off!" I said, laughing. Tiff relaxed and smiled contently at Seth, who let out a sigh of relief.

I looked around and decided to make Tristan a little more jealous. I pointed to Josh for my pick for the round. "Sorry, Josh. Let us see those pants off."

He smiled and winked at me. "Always wanted to see me in my underwear, haven't you, Gray?" he teased, and took off his pants, while everybody cheered at him. He was wearing a pair of black cotton boxer shorts. He looked really good. I tried hard not to stare as he undressed, but I took a quick few peeks whenever I noticed Tristan looking my way.

Next couple of rounds Josh won, and he pointed vindictively at me both times. "What goes around comes around," he teased, waving for me to start stripping. I smiled at him and took my shoes and socks off. Then next round Harry won again. Apparently, watching me take my shoes off brought Harry's priorities back on line, and he picked me to strip this time instead of Josh.

I had come prepared and was wearing a sexy new black lace bra. Everybody on the table kept cheering and whistling loudly while I took my shirt off. I didn't dare to look Tristan's way. Oddly enough, the boys' catcalls didn't make me nervous, but just the thought of Tristan looking at me made butterflies clamour inside my stomach. When Harry won again the next round, the only thought occupying his red head at that moment was the one where he got to see me naked. He pointed at me with a half-giggle, half-smirk, and the boys cheered like crazy. I took off my jeans, revealing matching panties. I then bowed to the table of my clapping friends. Then Tristan stood up with a seriously disgruntled face and excused himself, heading to the bathroom at the far end of the rec room. He looked livid with jealousy.

While he was there, I took the opportunity to step away from the game table.

"So, guys, I think I'll call it a night!" I said to a group of very disappointed boys.

"What? You're quitting?" they all asked in unison.

"Yeah, I am! I have to draw the line at undergarments,

here!" I said, chuckling. "I'm not going to risk losing next round. Harry will probably win again and I'm not taking anything else off!"

They all protested vehemently, and then Tiffany came up with the most brilliant idea of all time. "Joey, why don't you stay and play some more with us? We all promise not to pick you to strip any more, right, guys?" she said looking at the boys. "Plus, it will be hilarious if we don't tell Tristan about this deal! He'll freak out so much thinking that his, um, half-sister's at risk of being naked here.'

Everybody laughed, finding Tiffany's idea indeed very entertaining, and they all agreed to play along. When Tristan got back from the bathroom, everybody had a straight face on. I sat back and called out for another round.

"You're still playing?" Tristan asked, surprised. He'd thought I was going to quit for sure now I was down to my underwear.

"Yeah, sure! I like to live dangerously!" I said, winking at him. "And it's not like I have a boyfriend or anything like that." I shrugged nonchalantly.

He clenched his jaw and balled his hands into fists. Sam and Harry giggled quietly as we started playing again, and I could see that Tristan was doing his best to win this round. He didn't want the chance of someone else winning and picking me to strip again. But, what a shocker (and note the sarcasm), against all odds Harry won again. I think he cheated somehow; it wasn't possible for someone to win all the time like that! He grinned at me quite evilly, but before he could open his mouth, Tristan stood up abruptly and walked over to me with a murderous frown etched on his face.

"That's it. Game over for you, miss!" he said, picking

my clothes off the floor and grabbing me by the arm. Everybody cracked up laughing like maniacs at Tristan's outburst. Of course, most of the boys thought it was Tristan being a protective big brother, but I rejoiced knowing there was nothing brotherly about his outburst. I smiled and waved a quick goodbye at everybody, while I let myself be dragged out of the room by a furious Tristan.

He pulled me angrily with him halfway down the corridor outside, before stopping and tossing me my clothes. "Here! Put these on," he ordered menacingly. He scowled at me, waiting for me to get dressed. I usually don't appreciate anyone ordering me what to do and bossing me around like that, but his stare was making me really self-conscious, and I was suddenly very aware of being almost completely naked in front of him.

"Fine!" I snapped, grabbing my clothes and putting my shirt back on. When I tried to shove one leg into my jeans, I lost my balance and stumbled backwards. Tristan grabbed me firmly by the arm before I could fall, making me tumble into his arms. The direct contact with me under such revealing circumstances made him bristle and get even more worked up.

"Good God! I can't believe you! Stripping off like that!" he snapped, pushing me away like touching me had burned him somehow. "What's the matter with you? Have you no decency?" he spat out, disgusted.

I yanked myself angrily away from his grasp and headed back to our room. He followed me warily. "What the hell is the matter with you?" I hissed as soon as we entered our room. "You're the one embarrassing me in front of all my friends here! What's your problem?"

"You shouldn't be mad, I'm just looking out for you. I

promised your mother I'd look after you," he said, more calmly.

I snorted loudly. "Yeah, because you're only doing this out of the goodness of your innocent little fucking heart!" I spat out at him. I saw him twitch when I cursed. I knew how much he hated it, and I was glad to throw as much swearing as possible in his face!

"Exactly," he agreed, pretending he didn't get my sarcasm. "What would your mother think, seeing you behave like this?" he added reproachfully.

"She would think I was having a great time with my friends before you came in and ruined everything!" I retorted mockingly.

He just raised an eyebrow, a smug expression on his face. "Come on, Joey. Just calm down and go to sleep, and you'll see I'm right about this when you wake up tomorrow," he instructed me.

"Fine! I'll go to sleep, then!" I shouted, taking my shirt off and tossing it hard at his chest.

Startled, he uncrossed his arms, watching my shirt land at his feet. "W-what are you doing?" he stammered, eyes wide like a deer caught in headlights.

"What do you think? I'm taking my clothes off so I can go to bed! Or do you want me to sleep in these uncomfortable things all night?" I said, taking my jeans off now. "If that's all right with you, sir! Wouldn't like this to be reported to my *mother*!" I scowled and tossed my jeans at his chest too.

Then I stopped, panting hard, and glared at him. He stared back for a couple of seconds, then turned to his bed, grabbing the first shirt he saw on the bed and tossing it over to me with an upset look on his face. "Here, cover yourself up! What's up with you today? Taking your clothes off all the time!" he grunted, turning to look to the wall by his side.

"You're the one excessively concerned with being righteous, Mr. Prude!" I shouted, and turned my back to him, taking my bra off and slipping his shirt on. That new bra was killing me! New clothes sucked! Sexy clothes sucked more! Tristan sucked more than anything!!

"There!" I shouted again. I didn't care any more if people could hear us fighting. They could all go to hell! And Tristan could go to hell with them!

I looked down and realized he had tossed me his favorite blue T-shirt. It was way too big for me, hanging to the middle of my thighs. The fabric of the shirt was really soft, light and slightly cold to the touch. And it smelled of him. I cursed silently. Like I was going to be able to sleep now, with this shirt smelling like him! Just freaking fantastic!

"Are you fucking happy now?" I shouted at him, walking over to the head of my bed. He looked at me with a mean look in his eyes. Then he started to walk in my direction, with a vengeful purpose in his stride. I gulped. Maybe I should have shut the hell up. He looked so scary that I took a step back... Had I finally made him snap, but in the wrong way?

"Stop cursing, Joe," he said quietly, in a menacing whisper. It wasn't a request. "You know how much it upsets me," he growled. He freaking growled at me!

That made me snap out of my wimpy, feeble state of mind. I will not be threatened *or* growled at! I'm not scared of anything or anyone!

"Yeah? Make me! I can take you without breaking a sweat, pal!" I snapped at him, but I knew I was pushing my luck.

He took another step closer and I stepped backwards involuntarily, bumping into the wall. There was nowhere left to run. The corner of his mouth curled up in a victorious smirk. "Not scared, huh?" he jeered in satisfaction.

I squinted my eyes. Was he making fun of me? So he thinks he's all big and strong, and mean, and I'm all scared! I'll show him! I flared my nostrils, like a raging bull seeing a red flag. Then I leaned the remaining inch closer to his face without breaking visual contact.

"Asshole. Fuck. You," I said through gritted teeth. He didn't like me cussing? Take that, then! Right in his prudish twentieth-century face!

"So. Damn. Stubborn," he replied in a hoarse voice while he grabbed my wrists and held them against the wall. I didn't have time to snap anything back at him, because he pushed me against the wall and kissed me.

He freaking kissed me!

I was so shocked, I didn't respond at first. Although my mind was still in a shocked state, my mouth seemed to be a faster thinker, because it responded to Tristan of its own accord. Before I knew it, I was kissing him with the same eagerness and passion that he was kissing me. I wasn't thinking straight any more; everything was a foggy blur, like I had been drinking gallons of alcohol all night. I could hardly breathe as he devoured me. I could feel every inch of him pressed against me, hard. I could feel how badly he wanted me right then, the urgency, the complete need. God! His lips were so soft, and he tasted so sweet...His hands were snaking below my – his – T-shirt, making my thoughts melt beneath the heat of his fingertips. I wanted him to touch me everywhere, an urgency filling my whole body, but I knew there was something that needed to be done, to be said...What was it? The plan...to make him crack. He needed to confess!

I pulled my lips away and struggled to think straight. "Tris...please, stop," I gasped.

He grunted in protest, breathing heavily against my neck in short labored gasps.

"What are you doing? Didn't you say we can't be together?" I asked in a trembling voice.

He buried his face in my hair, trailing deep hard kisses on my neck, trying to avoid my eyes. "Yes. No. We can't," he replied, and his voice sounded strained, heavy with desire.

"So why are you doing this?" I whispered, though I couldn't stop running my fingers through his hair, making him shiver and press harder against me. His lips on my skin were scorching! He licked all the length of my neck and stopped at my earlobe, nibbling and biting it softly, making me whimper in pleasure.

"God, Joey! You're driving me insane here!" he said in a whisper full of despair.

I don't recall much of what happened after that. I was drowning in Tristan's arms and I would die of happiness. I could no longer elaborate any form of coherent thought. I could only feel his soft, strong hands on me, everywhere on my body, his heat burning me, the taste of his mouth and his amazing scent suffocating me. I didn't care about anything else in the world; the only thing I needed was Tristan with me, right there, right then.

I don't remember when we ended up in my bed, or how we were both naked when we got there – or when it was that Tristan went and got protection from his bedside drawer. All I remember was the weight of his heavy body pressing against mine, leaving no space between us. And then everything was going so fast; he had me scorching beneath his fingertips, so much pleasure under his urgent touch, leaving me burning, breathless and spinning out of control, clutching at him like I was in the middle of a fierce storm and he was my shelter. And then the Earth trembled and shattered all around us.

This sense of peace and completeness overtook me after the ecstasy started to die down. I remembered the fireworks of so long ago, at a dark cemetery, in a midnight black sky. I remembered his hands enclosing mine, and his soft whisper in my ears on that night. *"Don't be afraid. You'll be fine."* And I'd known I would be, because he was with me. He was mine and I was his, for that brief, intense, amazing and scary moment. And now he was mine once again.

Nobody could ever take this away from me. No lies could ever taint it.

I was his and he was mine.

But I could sense his uneasiness as he moved away from me and sat on the edge of the bed, naked, hands covering his face, head hung low. There was still so much despair in him...I couldn't bear to watch him torturing himself. Before I could reach out to him or say anything, he stood up and put his black sweat pants on. And then he left the room, without saying a word.

Chapter Twenty-Nine

Love Lullaby

Yes. He just walked out. I often wondered about that moment, later on in my life. What if I had never followed him that night? What if I had stayed in that room? What would my life have turned out to be then? It's funny how one single decision can turn our lives around, and make so much difference to our future.

All I knew was that I needed to go after him. The bond we already had from before was now a hundred times intensified after what we had just shared together. I could feel him completely, all his emotions; I could feel his despair for having given in to his need, his undeniable love for me filling every inch of his soul, and the excruciating pain when he thought about losing me.

Maybe if his emotions weren't flooding over me like a cracked dam, I wouldn't have followed him. But I had never been more certain about anything in my entire life. He loved me. There was no denying in it. He wouldn't dare to claim anything else.

So the minute he left, I slipped into my underwear and his T-shirt and rushed out of the room after him. I saw his dark silhouette way ahead, turning downstairs. I couldn't just shout because I would wake up the entire floor, but I ran as lightly and silently as I could, trying to reach him, but he was freakishly fast! There was a full moon in the sky tonight, so I could see everything quite well, the soft moonlight bathing the grass with its bright glow. I glanced around and the place seemed deserted. I took my chances and shouted at him.

"Tristan! Stop!"

He froze mid-step, and turned slowly to look at me. The look in his eyes confirmed what I was already feeling through our bond. Despair, love, pain...but I also caught something more: surprise and confusion, like someone suddenly waking up from a dream.

"Joey?" he asked in a dazed whisper. I focused hard on his eyes and reached out, trying to capture what he was feeling. There was...a lot of confusion. He was freaking out badly. That's why he'd just stood up and left the room like that. His protective walls were crumbling down. Recollection passed in his eyes and he seemed to gather his thoughts well enough to remember what had just happened between us. "J-Joe, are you okay?" he whispered, walking closer to me. He looked genuinely concerned. I wanted to make him crack, but not like this! He was seriously worrying me now.

I remembered I was only dressed in his T-shirt when a cold wind swept by us. Tristan was only in his sweat pants, bare-chested and barefoot. I could see goosebumps all over his skin, but he didn't seem to care. I shivered and crossed my arms over my chest. He knitted his brows even more, worry taking over his whole stance now. He must have taken my shivering as something other than cold.

"I'm so sorry, Joe," he said gently. "Did...did I hurt you? I couldn't stop myself...Was it...was it your first...?" He trailed off, unable to continue the question.

I frowned, trying to follow his jumbled train of thought, and then realization dawned. "Oh! No! No, no! I'm all right. It wasn't my first...time." I smiled awkwardly at him. I was glad it hadn't been. It had avoided that whole pain/awkwardness issue. Tom, my first and only boyfriend, had taken care of that. Tonight I had felt nothing but over-whelming pleasure. It wasn't even fair to compare it with my first time, really.

I heard him sigh in relief and then saw him frown in upset again. "Is it weird that I feel relieved that it wasn't, and I didn't hurt you? And awful at the same time because now I keep picturing you and some other guy," he mumbled, looking down at the grass. "I know I'm being old-fashioned but girls in my day...'

He stopped when he saw my face. "I know it's a different time now,' he concluded lamely.

I smiled and took his hands. "Stop being silly, Tris," I said quietly. "And I mean not just now, but in every possible way. You have been very silly lately." I was thinking more in terms of "utterly-beyond-reason stupid", but I thought it wasn't the time for bluntness right now. He was already in a shaky condition as it was.

The soft tingling sensation flowed between our inter-laced fingers. He stared down at our hands, wonder and sorrow filling his eyes, making them bright with tears. "Tris, you do realize you just stood up and left me there," I said cautiously.

"I-I...did? I'm so sorry," he whispered, as if he was tired to the bones of fighting his feelings. "I can't stand this, Joey, not after what happened tonight. I can't lie to you any more, not after this," he said, letting go of my hands and kneeling in front of me, his head hung low, defeated to his core.

I kneeled down in front of him, real close, putting my hand over his heart. His skin burned beneath my fingers. "So don't," I said softly.

I wished I could take all his pain away with my bare hands, plunge inside his heart and pull it all out, free him from his suffering. I wished it with all my heart.

He tensed up again, and looked at me, a little startled, and then he put his hand over mine, over his heart, and nodded. "I know. I can feel it," he whispered. He could feel the bond between us, all the emotions I was feeling. His bright gray eyes sparkled with tears. "I don't want us to be only friends. I never did," he confessed. I wondered if he would tell me his secret now. He stared at me for a long time in silence, before he dared to speak again.

"You already know." It was a statement, not a question. "How did you find out?" he said in a shaky, low voice. He was talking about his secret.

I sighed heavily and smiled at him. "You told me, Tris," I said, and watched his eyes widen in surprise. "When you had that high fever, on the first day of the month. You were sort of...delirious. You told me everything then."

"But-but, it can't be...I don't remember saying any- thing," he muttered to himself.

"You told me about New Year, and you also told me about your fear of clowns," I said, trying to make my point.

He tensed and looked at me suspiciously. "Nobody knows about that," he whispered in fright.

"Yeah, well...it's no big deal. Everybody has their fears. I'm afraid of ghosts," I said, shrugging.

He eyed me in disbelief. "Are you kidding me? Ghosts?"

"Ironic, right?" I chuckled.

"So you knew I was lying. That's why you have been acting so weird these past few days," he stated. "You were trying to...punish me?" There wasn't a trace of condemnation in his voice. He thought he deserved it. I could see it in his eyes. He thought everything that was happening was his fault. He was the one that had closed the spell bond that night at the cemetery. He had brought this on us.

"Not punish. I was only trying to force you, you know, to tell me the truth. That's all," I said, looking him in the eyes. He wasn't avoiding looking at me any more. He wasn't trying to hide anything from me any more.

"But you knew the truth already," he said, confused.

"I needed you to tell me yourself. I needed you to confess so you'll stop pushing me away. Stop this *stupid* act of yours." I put fierce emphasis on the "stupid" part.

I watched his face contort in pain again. "I...I'm sorry. I didn't know what else to do...I never meant to hurt you. I never meant for any of this to happen," he said, emotion catching his voice. "I was just trying to protect you from hurting more because of me. If we remained just friends, you wouldn't hurt as much when..." And he trailed off, unable to finish the sentence.

My hand was over his chest, and I could feel the shocking force of his sorrow through my fingers, the intensity of his torment. It made my heart whimper. I leaned in and held him in my arms protectively. "I know, Tris. Please...everything will be all right now," I said quietly in his ear.

"No, it won't. Miss Violet came and told me everything she'd managed to uncover. The only thing keeping this Vigil guy away from me is you. And also this," he said, pointing to his beaded wristband. "Our magic bond gives you power to guard me. But once the year is over, the bond will vanish and you won't be able to save me. My time – my extra time – on Earth will be up. Vigil will get to me, then, magic amulet or not." His voice was strained and sad.

"Look, I've been thinking about this deadline since I found out. I can help you, Tris. I know I can!"

He shook his head, not accepting my wishful thinking. "Joey…it's not that easy."

"I didn't say it's going to be easy. I'm saying it can be done. You can't lose faith so fast! I can hurt him," I told him firmly, and he glanced up, suspicion and surprise in his eyes. "I can hurt Vigil. He wasn't expecting it either – he was as surprised as you are right now – but I have hurt him once, in one of my dreams. I know I can do it again. Maybe I can get rid of him somehow. It is worth a shot. There's a lot we can try before you think of giving up, Tris."

"You…you really think so?" he asked quietly, his voice still full of doubt, but also with a trace of hope.

"I know so," I said with conviction. "We could have been working on it already, if you hadn't been acting like a fool all this time, pushing me away from your life, pretending that I meant nothing to you," I said reproachfully. "Besides, it's too late for us to be 'just friends'. You can't protect me from what I feel about you. It won't change what I feel about you."

He glanced down, so much sadness marking his face. "I was just trying to protect you from hurting, but I have been hurting you all along with this, haven't I?" he murmured.

"Yes," I answered truthfully. There was no way to sugar-coat this answer.

"I thought you were going to get over me fast...and forget all about me."

I cupped his face and tilted it up so I could look him straight in the eyes. "There's no getting over you. I could never forget you. Not in this life. Not in a thousand life-times." I heard an echo in my head; I'd said these words to Tristan once before, back in the cemetery.

He blinked a couple of times, eyes brimming with tears. "I'm so sorry...for all the pain I've caused you," he said, pulling me close and holding me in his arms.

I curled against his chest, basking in the warmth of his embrace.

"You probably wish that you had never met me that day in the cemetery. If you had never got lost there, your life would be so much easier now," he said, his voice leaden with emotion.

I pushed him hard on the chest. "Don't ever say that! You are the best thing that has ever happened to me! Can't you see how amazing you are, how special you are to me? I would never wish for that! Never!" I said angrily. Tears threatened, but I held them in.

He blinked at me, surprised at my angry outburst. But understanding flashed in his eyes and they sparkled with admiration and love. "I'm sorry. You're right, Joe." He reached out cautiously to me and I let him pull me back into his arms again. "Please say you forgive me...for everything," he whispered in my ear.

I nodded silently, and then pulled away to look him in the eyes. "Let's make a promise now, okay? We always tell the truth to each other, no matter what."

"No matter what," he vowed, smiling softly at me.

I hugged him tight again, to seal our vow. "As long as

we are together, everything will be fine," I said in a frail whisper. I grazed my fingers through his hair, and held him tight, feeling the warmth radiating from his body like my own private sun. If only he could feel how badly I loved him right then. If only he could feel...

I heard his soft voice vibrating in the air, thick and charged with emotion, while his face was buried in my neck.

"I love you so much, Joe."

I smiled against his skin. Third time's the charm.

"I love you too, Tris," I whispered back. "So, so, much."

I could feel him relaxing in my embrace, his pain melting away through my arms, leaving only love behind. "I've loved you since the first day I saw you, that bright afternoon at the cemetery. You were the most beautiful thing I have ever seen, all messed up and covered in dirt," he confessed, chuckling lightly, still with his face buried in my neck. "You had so much life in your eyes, so much light. You glowed like a rising star. I couldn't believe it when you talked to me that day! It was the happiest day of my life – and my death – the day I met you." He stroked his hand over my hair. "You stole my heart that day."

"I did no such thing! I don't ever steal!" I said, smiling.

He chuckled and shook his head. "Yes, you did. You completely stole my heart. But if you prefer, I'm willingly giving it to you, right here, right now. I can't ever claim it back now, it's yours, rightfully owned." He smiled, clasping my hands tight. I'd missed his smiles. I'd missed his laughter. I'd missed his touch. I'd missed him so much. And now I had him back. I had his heart. Rightfully owned.

I leaned in and kissed him softly on the lips. I'd missed his lips too. "Thank you. I will treasure it for ever," I said, smiling under his mouth. Then I parted the kiss and looked at him. "Do you want to know when I gave you my heart, then?" I inquired teasingly. "That same day at the cemetery. When you smiled at me from the top of your tomb. It was the most breathtaking smile I had ever seen," I confessed. "You had my heart right there and then."

"So...love at first sight, huh?" he murmured eerily, gazing into my eyes.

"I don't believe in that fairytale nonsense," I mumbled.

"I didn't either..." he said with a steady gaze "...until I met you." He leaned in slowly and kissed me deeply, taking my breath away again, while a gust of wind swept over us, making me shiver in his arms. That's when I remembered we were in the middle of the freaking school grounds, with hundreds of windows in the building facing our way. Anyone could be watching us kissing here!

"Shit! I mean, darn it!" I exclaimed, jumping away from him. "I just remembered we are kind in the middle of the yard here, and you know, I'm kind of half-naked, and so are you, not to mention all the kissing..." I trailed off, embarrassed.

He tossed his head back and laughed, and some leaves twirled around us. I think there was some sort of magic in that laugh of his. Magic seemed to be engraved deep in his core. Then he extended his hand to me, and we walked back to our room, holding hands in silence. I kept praying no one would catch us walking through those dark cold corridors that late at night. It was Saturday, and there was a chance of bumping into students getting back from dates out. Absent-mindedly, Tristan kept stroking the back of my hands with his thumb. It was a thing he used to do when he was deep in thought. I wondered what he could be thinking about.

I was still shivering when we got to our room, but as soon as I closed the door, he turned and picked me up, bridal style, walking towards his bed. "What are you doing?" I yelped, surprised.

"There's no one to see us in here. Seth's at Tiffany's, so I'm free to do this now," he said, smiling. He put me on his bed so carefully, like I was going to break, and lay down by my side, pulling the covers over us and wrapping his arms around me again. "I'll keep you warm," he mused softly into my ear.

I giggled and relaxed in his arms. His bed smelled of him. His sheets smelled of him, the T-shirt I was wearing too. Not to mention Tristan holding me tight in his arms. I was overdosing in Tristan's scent. It was exhilarating! I smiled contently and sighed, feeling the warmth returning to my whole body. In a few seconds I had stopped shivering.

"Better?" he asked softly.

"If I say yes, are you going to send me back to my bed?" I joked.

He chuckled. "If you want to, you can go to your bed, yes." He shrugged and I frowned in disappointment. "I'm cool sleeping there too. Wherever you are is fine by me," he said, laughing and making me scoff at his teasing. I almost believed he wanted me out of his bed! Jerk!

He shifted slightly to his side, propping himself up on an elbow while he wrapped his other arm around my waist. We lay in his bed in the dark and in silence, but I could sense his brain working hard beside me. I started to get worried with all this hard thinking he was doing.

"Tris?"

"Yeah?" he replied softly.

"You're not thinking about another stupid plan to push

me away again, are you?" I asked, my heart constricting at the thought. "Do you regret what happened tonight?"

I felt him pull me even closer, tightening his grip on me. "No. I don't regret it, Joey. How could I regret the best night of my life?" he said quietly, and placed his lips over my forehead. "Don't worry, Joey, I'm not thinking about any plan...but if I do think of one, I'll make sure to run it by you first to see if you approve, okay? That way, you'll be able to veto the stupid ones." He grinned.

"Okay. Sounds good to me," I said, burying my face on his chest.

Then I remembered another very important question. "Hum...Tristan?" I called out in a serious voice now.

I felt him tensing up, because I'd called him by his full name. "Yes?" His tone was a little worried.

"What about Caroline?" I asked, dropping the bomb. I might as well know about it now.

He remained in tense silence for a couple of minutes, and then he sighed loudly. I could actually hear the mechanisms of his brain whirring and clicking in the dark, trying to think of the best way to say this to me. "This will sound bad for me, but, I promised you the truth. And the truth is I was only using her, to make you forget about me and move on with your life. I knew that if you thought I was with somebody else, you'd...give up on me. "

I did a little happy dance inside my head. "So...you don't really have feelings for her?"

"God! No! She's so shallow and clingy! She's the opposite of everything I like. She's the opposite of you."

A huge smile spread over my face. "And you guys never...'*you know*'?" I asked, making air quotes with my fingers. That was the million-dollar question. I had to know for sure. I watched him frowning at me in the dark. The moonlight drifting through the window gave me a good view of his features. I could also see his bright gray eyes clearly, and I was watching intently for his answer.

"Never, what?" he repeated, trying to understand, and then finally he did. "Oh, okay. *'You know'* – got it! No. We did not! We didn't do anything," he stated firmly.

"Because she was saying some pretty wild things about what you guys had been doing…you know…" I told him, still looking directly into his eyes.

I could actually see him blushing in the dark now. He coughed, really embarrassed. "She was? God, no wonder you were that mad at me! Now I understand all the torture you put me through, if you really thought I had…but no! No. I only kissed her properly once, when I knew you were looking at our way, by the lockers. And then we held hands and hung out sometimes, but even that was excruciating to me! She is such a pain in the a—" And then he stopped abruptly, remembering his "no cursing" rule, and continued in more educated terms. "Sorry about that. I meant to say, she was very…annoying."

I smiled, seeing him blush again. He blushed even more when he cursed by accident. It was the cutest thing. I didn't say anything after that, and he glanced at me in concern. He clasped his hands around my face, making me look him directly in the eyes.

"I swear to you, Joe. Nothing has ever happened between me and Caroline. Can you see? That I'm telling you the truth?" he asked, anguished. "I'm actually grateful for your ability now, that you can see that I'm telling you the truth!"

"Yeah. I see it," I said sadly. "I'm sorry about lying to you about that, Tris. I just don't know how to switch it off, and I didn't want you to always be afraid to look me in the eyes. It killed me every time you avoided looking at me, for fear I might read what you were feeling. That really sucks. I'm so sorry," I mumbled, and looked down.

He nudged my chin up with his thumb, making me look at him again. "You don't have to be sorry for your gift, Joe. It makes you even more special than you already are. I'm the idiotic one that has been lying to you, and didn't want to get caught. But that's in the past. I won't ever be afraid to look at you again, because I'll always tell you the truth from now on, no matter what, remember?" he said, smiling sincerely.

He leaned in to give me a soft kiss. "I'll break up with her tomorrow," he said slowly, tucking a lock of hair behind my ear.

"And do it nicely, because she may be annoying and a pain in the ass, but she's done nothing to deserve to be treated so badly by you or me, specially not over this stupid plan of yours!" I warned him. No one could ever say I was not a fair person.

"Yes, ma'am," he said, stroking my hair.

I looked up to see if he was making fun of me, but he just smiled kindly, so I snuggled back against his chest. I suddenly felt tired to death. It had been such an overwhelming night, so emotionally draining. Everything was so intense. I was exhausted.

"Joey?" he asked softly.

"Hmm?"

"I don't know how is this supposed to be done now, but... you said you love me. And I love you. And after what happened tonight... I know I might not have much time left, but I have to ask you. Will you marry me?"

I choked out loud and turned to look him straight in the eyes, cupping his face gently between my hands.

"Tris, we have a lot of dating to do before we start thinking about marriage, all right? Marriage is for much, much later. Trust me on this," I said calmly, trying to make him understand.

He sighed loudly. "I'm being old-fashioned again, aren't I?"

"Yes, very much so. But it's okay, you'll get the hang of modernity eventually."

"Okay," he said with a cute pout.

"Let's not talk about serious stuff any more tonight, all right? I'm so tired," I mumbled, my voice coming out a little muffled.

"Yes, ma'am," he said again, and kissed the top of my head.

He cradled me into sleep then, passing his fingers through my hair gently and humming a soft lullaby close to my ear. I was asleep before he ended his song.

Chapter Thirty

Secret's Out

I woke up to the sound of voices in the room. I remained still, lying on my side with my eyes closed, trying to discern the source of the noise. My brain still felt sluggish and blurred. One of the voices in the room was definitely Tiffany's; I'd know her high-pitched tone anywhere. The other one was...Seth. It sounded like him. My brain began to function in a faster mode, the cotton-candy feeling disappearing like a weak fog.

I also suddenly realized I wasn't in my bed. This one seemed different somehow, softer. It smelled of Tristan. Then I registered his heavy arm draped around me, his hands enclosing mine, his face leaning behind my neck. I was in his bed. I'd slept in his bed! I remembered the previous night and a smile appeared involuntarily on my lips.

"See? She's waking up!" Tiffany's voice was so up-close that I stiffened and opened my eyes, startled.

"Hey, honeydew!" she greeted in a low whisper, trying not to disturb Tristan behind me. "I gather you had a nice evening after all! I was worried about you two all night, cos you left the poker game in such a storming way! But I guess everything worked out fine, right?" she said with a wide grin.

I just stared at her and blinked, trying to gather my thoughts.

"Okay. I think that's enough, Tiff," Seth intervened. "You were worried, we came, we checked them out. Everything's fine. Let's leave them alone now," he said, amused, trying to drag her away from the bed.

"But...but...we hardly talked! She didn't say anything yet! I need to know!" she whined, while being pulled by Seth. Then she wriggled free and ran fast towards me again, her blonde curls bouncing widely with her long steps.

"Hey, Joey, listen," she whispered urgently, while Seth walked back to retrieve her. "We're going to have a picnic-lunch-thing at midday, by the big oak tree. We're waiting for you two, okay?" Seth grabbed her arm and pulled her away softly again. "If you don't show up, I'm coming to get you! You hear? I'm waiting on you! I need to know ev-er-y-thing!" she squealed in Seth's arms.

I raised my head a little, and saw Seth smiling and shaking his head in amusement, with Tiff firmly in his grasp, and then they stepped outside and he closed the door softly behind them. Tiffany was really dying to hear what had happened last night. She couldn't even wait until I was up, for crying out loud!

I shifted slowly in bed, trying to look at Tristan. He sighed deeply and moved over, releasing me from his hold and lying on his stomach, his face turned to the wall. I could only see his jawline now, but almost nothing of his face. I turned to him and wrapped my arm around his smooth chest. He looked so peaceful sleeping, his breathing deep and slow, making his chest rise and fall in a quiet, steady rhythm. Last night had been such turmoil that I hadn't had the chance to enjoy the full view that was Tristan's bare chest. Now I had time enough to appreciate it all. I traced my fingers softly over his chest and down his ribcage, and then shifted sideways to his hips, outlining all his muscles. I wanted to memorize each and every one of them, every curve, every line, every single part of him.

I traced my fingertips softly over his stomach. His breathing rhythm changed when I started playing with the small, soft trail of dark hair that started right below his belly button.

"You keep touching me like that, Joe Gray, and I won't be held responsible for my actions," Tristan said quietly, turning his head to face me. He gave me a mischievous, crooked smile, squinting his eyes a little because of the bright light in the room.

"I'm sorry, I didn't mean to wake you." I blushed and took my hand off of him.

"You didn't," he said softly, and then his eyes adjusted to the light in the room and he opened them completely. His gray eyes were so bright, they almost looked like glowing silver rings; the effect was mesmerizing.

"I woke up with Tiffany and Seth bustling around the room and talking to you. At first I thought I was dreaming," he said, laughing. "But Tiff wouldn't shut up and then I felt you touching me. I thought it was about time to wake up," he said, with a playful side smile on his lips.

"Yeah, Tiff woke me up too," I mumbled, a little unsettled by the way he was looking at me. "Did you…um, sleep well?"

"I think it was the best night of sleep I have ever had,"

he said, looking dreamily at the ceiling. Then he glanced down and caught me staring at his chest. *Drooling over* was perhaps more accurate.

"Enjoying the view?" he teased, his eyes burning as he watched me. "Because I'm sure enjoying mine," he said, pointedly staring at the front of my shirt.

I tried to avoid blushing and failed miserably. "I wasn't staring!" I quickly denied, which made my lie even more transparent. I pushed the sheets away and stood up, all flustered.

Tristan chuckled at my mortification and leaned over, grabbing me by my waist and pulling me back into bed with him. "I'm sorry, Joey. I didn't mean to make you embarrassed. But you have been driving me crazy all these days, walking around in tiny towels, low dresses and tight jeans!" he said, pulling me into his arms, bridal style again. "Not to mention you have the most beautiful legs I have ever seen, and you look out-of-this-world-good in my T-shirt." He buried his face in my neck and trailed soft kisses all over it.

I shivered and tried to squirm out of his grasp, afraid that he might catch on and make fun of me.

"All right! Okay! Stop it now. I need to go to the bathroom, and brush my teeth, and tame my hair, and take a shower, and...stuff." Flustered, I wriggled out of his lap and got out of bed. "Apparently, we have a lunch appointment at the oak tree. Tiffany said she'll come and get us if we're late!" I warned, leaving him pouting on the bed.

"Do we really have to go? Can't we just stay here in bed all day long?" he asked in a hopeful voice.

"No, we can't, Cocoa Puffs," I said, grazing my fingers through his hair.

He glanced up with a quirked inquisitive eyebrow. "Cocoa Puffs?"

"Yeah, I think I need to have a cute nickname for you, since you have one for me." I smiled teasingly. "And Cocoa Puffs is my favorite thing in the mornings," I said, pinching his cheeks, looking down at him hungrily so he would know he was my favorite thing in mornings too. "Plus, Cocoa is awesome because I love chocolate, and since you sometimes disappear into thin air, Puffs is quite fitting for you, don't you think?"

He eyed me playfully, trying to stifle a laugh. "Since we are in the cereal-naming basis, couldn't your favorite be Tony the Tiger?" he said, chuckling hard now. "Or Lucky Charms, or Captain Crunch! You can call me Tiger, Charms or Captain!" And he cracked up laughing at his own puns. One of Tristan's favorite things about the twenty-first century was the amazing range of cereals he got to enjoy – he was like a big kid whenever Mom and I dragged him grocery shopping.

His face brightened again. "Maybe I can join you in the shower...to speed things up?" he suggested, full of eagerness and mischief.

I laughed at his hopeful voice. "I don't think so, mister." I tsked him, pushing him back on to his bed. "You already got lucky yesterday, but you owe me a proper date, you know? With dinner, movie, the whole shenanigans!" I chuckled, pointing my finger at him. "You caught me off guard yesterday, but don't think I'm usually that easy!"

He blushed, a little embarrassed, and fumbled with his feet. "I-I don't...You're right. I haven't been treating you right, Joey. I will give you the best date you ever had!" he promised me with a bright smile.

We both showered and dressed, but just as we were about to leave, Tristan's face turned serious. "I was wondering if maybe now would be a good time for us to tell the whole truth about me and the magic 'situation' we're in. To Seth, Josh, Sam, Harry and Tiffany. We can tell Seth and Tiff today at lunch. And we can tell the rest of the guys we're not brother and sister too," he blurted out, an anxious look on his face.

I stared at Tristan in silence, not knowing exactly what to say. "We know we can trust them. They're like family, right?" he added. "I'm just sick of lying, Joey. I don't want lie to them anymore. I don't want to lie to people I care about any more," he pleaded wholeheartedly.

I nodded, giving him a reassuring smile. "All right. They are family. We can trust them with this. And I'm sick of lying too. Let's do this," I agreed. To hell with all the secrets!

We headed to the oak tree, Tristan walking beside me with a sprint in his feet. He seemed very happy now that we were telling our friends everything. It seemed like a huge weight was lifted from his shoulders.

I could already see Seth sitting on the grass below the big oak tree, just a few feet away from us, with Tiffany right in front of him, with her back to us.

As we reached them, Tristan greeted Seth with their cool male handshake thing, but before we could all sit down, Tiffany jumped in with, "Okay, boys, you go along and buy us some food now." That was my Tiff. Bossy to the core. "We'll be here, you know, talking about random things, like school, grades, homework, *whathappenedwithyoutwolastnight*, essays for the semester, that sort of things," she said sneakily.

Seth laughed and signaled to Tristan. "Okay, girl talk time, we'd better hurry off now."

"Actually, we sort of have something really important to talk to you guys about first," Tristan said, with a hesitant smile as we both sat down on the grass next to Tiffany. Seth gave us a curious look before sitting beside his anxious girlfriend. Tristan cleared his throat, and then he told then everything, while I leaned against the oak tree, watching them.

Their reactions raged from disbelief, to worry, reluctance, awe and finally settling for simple acceptance at the end. Seth's eyes were a little wide and scared, but he seemed to genuinely accept everything we'd told them, while Tiffany looked mostly confused. There was this huge sense of relief after Tristan was done explaining things, like it was somehow easier to breathe now. I was actually really surprised at how easy this whole "secret reveal" had been. I always imagined that nobody in their right mind would ever believe us. But Seth and Tiffany accepted this extraordinary tale with such open hearts and minds, it was uncanny!

"Thank you so much for being our friends, for believing in us, for wanting to help us," I said. "I can't believe how lucky we are to have you in our lives," I said in a choked voice. I was trying really hard not to cry. "And thank you for not thinking we are crazy people telling freaky ghost stories."

"It's all right, Joey. We believe in you. This actually explains a lot of questions we've been asking since we've met you two...and it's so surreal, it must be true!" Seth said, wrapping an arm around me and looking curiously at Tristan. "But this sure explains Tristan's weird illness every month, and your scary nightmares. Also Tristan's wacky way of speaking, his old-fashioned habits, his complete and utter lack of technology knowledge...Yeah, it explains a lot," he mused thoughtfully.

"Hey!" Tristan complained, a little miffed. "I think I'm 'modernizing' pretty well here! No one seems to be noticing that," he grumbled, with an adorable pout. I tried hard not to giggle.

"Yeah, right. You're still complete rubbish at Xbox! And sometimes you say things like 'swell', especially when you're too excited over something. I thought it was the weirdest thing ever, but now that you've explained, it makes perfect sense," Seth said, while we all laughed hard at Tristan's flustered face.

We ate lunch then, sitting in the shade of the big oak tree, answering a bunch of questions they still had about Tristan and his past, our New Year's story and everything that had happened after that. After a while we were laughing and feeling a lot more cheerful. Tristan sat glued to my side with a soft smile on his lips, while I leaned my head on his shoulder, and Seth and Tiffany bickered relentlessly over stupid little things. Watching my two friends snapping at each other, while Tristan stood protectively by my side, made me feel like everything was right in the world again.

Seth watched me lean against Tristan, and smiled. "I'm glad this stupid fight is over. I'm glad Joey put some sense back in that thick head of yours, man!" he said cheerfully to Tristan.

"I'm glad too," Tristan replied, smiling.

"So, Joey, come on, tell me what happened last night after you guys left?" Tiffany asked excitedly. That was the part she'd been really dying to hear about. She was squirming, looking at me expectantly like she was about to explode with anxiousness.

I rolled my eyes at her lack of tact. "Well, we had a huge fight, then I made him confess and quit his stupid plan of pushing me away, for once and for all. And that's because ..." I trailed off and gave Tristan a pointed glare, egging him on to continue my sentence.

"Because 'it was the stupidest plan ever in the entire history of the whole wide world'," he chorused, rolling his eyes with a faint smile.

"Okay. There are a few Lost Boys that need to know all about this secret tale too," I said, standing up. "Let's call them into our room now, shall we?"

"I don't know how we are going to make them believe us," I muttered worriedly at Tristan. "What if they don't accept it as easily as Tiff and Seth?" Twenty minutes had passed and I was still trying to gather courage to enter our room. Tristan was by my side, trying to be supportive. I could hear the boys' voices muffled inside the bedroom. Tiffany's high-pitched squeals, Sam's loud laughs and Josh's grave tone. Seth and Harry were inside too.

"They will, don't worry, Joey. Let's just do it, already!" he said, opening the door impatiently. Tristan pushed me inside and closed the door behind him.

"Hey, Grays! What took you so long! We've been waiting here for you two for ages! What's this serious talk about?" Sam asked, sitting on the floor by the foot of Seth's bed, wearing his customary brown flannel shirt. Seth was leaning against his headboard, holding Tiff in his arms, and they both had knowing looks on their faces.

"Yeah! Seth practically barked at us to come right away! What's the big emergency?" Harry asked, sprawled over my bed. Harry was always on my bed, taking up all the space, the numbnuts. He was wearing his baggy skater shorts with a large T-shirt, his hair as wild as usual.

"It's no emergency," Tristan said, going to sit on his bed at the other side of the room. "We just wanted to talk to you guys." If he was nervous, he didn't show any signs of it. I had a butterfly riot in my stomach. Josh was in front of Tristan's bed, fumbling inside the drawers, looking for something to eat. He had on his usual black T-shirt and dark jeans. "So, spill it, man!" Josh said, munching an ancient-looking cookie. That boy would eat just about anything.

Tristan eyed me, raising both eyebrows. I was still frozen in my spot by the door.

Well, the hell with it. It was now or never, right? I walked over to Tristan's bed and sat on his lap. Tristan wrapped his arms around my waist and I turned my face, smiling at him. He leaned in and gave me a hard kiss on the lips. It wasn't hot enough to be considered distasteful, but deep enough to leave no doubt about it being an "unbrotherly" kiss. I guessed that would be a good conversation starter!

Silence descended in the room like someone had just hit the mute button. I felt Tristan chuckling beneath my lips. "This is going to be fun," he mused softly, ending the kiss and turning to look at the reactions in the room. I turned too, and watched three shocked faces staring at us, and two smiley ones. Harry had his mouth open, Sam had wide eyes and raised eyebrows, and Josh was frowning slightly.

"I knew something was going on between you two!" Josh was the first to speak. "I told you guys! And you wouldn't believe me!" He made a smug gesture.

"Yeah, man, you told us they were hiding something.

Uh, but did you seriously think of *that*?" Sam retorted in a freaked-out voice.

Harry was staring at me in shock, but when he caught me looking back, he diverted his gaze, embarrassed. "Yeah, that was seriously freaky, even for me," he mumbled, obviously uncomfortable.

"Before anyone else freaks out, I have something to say!" Tristan said. "Joey is not my sister, and I'm definitely *not* her brother, okay?" He held up his hands.

"Come again?"

"Say what?"

"I'm sorry, what?"

The three boys replied at the same time.

"We had to lie to get Tristan accepted at the school," I explained. "It was the only way to get him in."

"Joey's mom was cool enough to help me with this," Tristan said, and then he turned to look at me. "I cannot thank her enough for all she has done for me," he said softly. "I also need to thank her for having you. She gave the world the best gift ever," he whispered the last line into my ear. I blushed and smiled and then he kissed me again softly on the lips.

"Oh, man! This is so messed up!" Sam shouted from the floor. "I know you just told us you're not related, but it's still so weird to watch you two...you know. Give us some time to adjust before you go swapping spit like that!"

Josh, Seth and Tiffany laughed at how freaked out Sam was about all this. Harry was still silent on my bed, watching everybody with cautious eyes.

"Hey, so that's what the fuss was all about earlier in the year?" Josh said. He was a fast thinker. "We thought Joey had broken up with her boyfriend at her old school, and was very down for a while. We tried to cheer her up, and all," he said.

"Oh, man! That's right! That's when Tristan dropped out of rehearsals! It all makes sense now!" Sam said, all excited, like he was solving a mystery murder crime.

"And the songs you two have been doing! Don't take me wrong, they're brilliant, but now that we can put the puzzle together, it's kind of funny...I mean, sorry, not the fighting part, the story behind the lyrics part," Josh said apologetically when he saw us frowning at him. Then he looked up at Tiff and Seth, and put yet another piece of the puzzle together. "Hey! And the golden couple over there knew about it all along, didn't they?" Josh shouted, getting as excited with his discoveries as Sammy had been a minute ago.

Sam turned around to glare at Seth, and put his hand to his chest, faking hurt. "Oh, the betrayal!" he said theatrically.

"Sorry, dude. They made me swear. I couldn't tell." Seth held up his hands.

"What about Caroline?" Harry asked quietly, for the first time.

Tristan's arm tensed around my waist, and his jaw clenched a little. "That was...a mistake," he said quietly.

"But everything is fine now," I cut in. I didn't want *that* to be discussed in front of everybody. "And we thought it was time to tell you guys the truth, because we know you all can keep our secret."

"Of course, you can trust us, Joey!" Sam said seriously.

"Always," Josh added, and Harry nodded reassuringly as well.

"Okay. Good. I'm glad you are coping well with this," Tristan said, smiling at the room. "Because now comes the really big revelation." He made me sit by his side.

And then he told them about our history, the same way he had done with Seth and Tiffany by the oak tree. He told them everything. The whole truth.

At first they looked at us incredulously, making funny remarks and joking around. They weren't believing any of what Tristan was telling them. Harry kept glancing at us and then at Seth to see his reaction, and when Seth stared back solemnly, he was left all confused about what to think.

After a while they realized we weren't laughing. Then they started throwing questions at us, and we tried to answer them the best we could. The truth was, there were lots of things we didn't know how to explain and some parts of the story were still a mystery to us as well. The only thing Tristan didn't tell them about was about my ability to tell if someone was lying. I guess he thought it was my secret and not his to tell. I was glad he hadn't told them. I couldn't bear my friends being afraid to look me in the eyes.

But even so, Tristan glanced at me and I could read the question in his eyes. He wanted me to check how the boys were feeling. I surveyed the room. They wanted to believe, but the whole story was too fantastical for their skeptical minds to cope with. I looked at Tristan sadly and shook my head in a negative gesture. He sighed heavily and stood up. "Okay. I reckon this supernatural stuff is a little hard to swallow. I may have to do something more drastic to make you believe. This is just a special 'treat' I got to bring from Dead Land. It's a ghost trick of sorts." He walked to the middle of the room, so everybody could see him properly.

What was he talking abou— Oh no! He wasn't! Before I could say anything, he faded out of sight.

Chapter Thirty-One

Finding Death

Well, at least for the people in the room he did. For me, Tristan turned into that partially faded state, like he was part of the background somehow. But if I focused a little, I could discern his form clearly. Not for the first time I wondered why I was the only one able to see him like that. Was it yet another peculiar quirk of our magic bond? But even before the spell, when he was still a ghost, I was always able to see Tristan, even though I couldn't see the other ghosts in the cemetery. Maybe Tristan and I shared something deeper than a magic spell: an ancient connection? Maybe our souls were linked and I would always be able to see him, no matter what.

The second he disappeared out of sight, Harry let out a small yelp. Sam stood up fast, ready to sprint for the door if he needed to; and Josh, his eyes wide, blurted out a disbelieving, *"What the hell?"* Tiffany just held Seth's arms in a deadly grip, frozen in fear. Even Seth looked surprised. He and Tiff had previously accepted Tristan's story unconditionally and without proof, but now they were able to see *for real* what Tristan had been talking about all along.

While our friends stood in this half-frozen, half-ready-to-flee stance, Tristan walked towards me and turned his fading off as he sat down by my side.

"Holy crap!" Harry was first to speak.

"Almost had a heart attack here, but definitely believing it now, dude." Sam was sitting slowly back down on my bed, gasping with his hand over his chest.

"This. Is. So. Freakin'. Cool," was Josh's reaction. "Seriously, how did you NOT tell us that you can do this before, man? It's like you're one of the X-Men, or something! Does anybody else here have any superpowers they haven't been telling us about?" He glared at the rest of the boys.

"Nope. Not that I know about," Sam said. "Wait! Does super-human good looks count? Cos I'm certainly guilty of that one!" Sam winked playfully at Josh, who just rolled his eyes at him.

"And Harry has his freaky 'super-hook-up-radar thing'," he added thoughtfully.

"Yeah. That is freaky," Seth agreed with Sam. "He's never once got it wrong..."

Everybody turned their heads suspiciously towards Harry, who just reclined against the headboard, shrugging. "Don't hate me cos I'm special," he said mockingly.

Everybody laughed at Harry's theatrics and seemed to relax again. After that little display of supernatural powers, a new round of questions was launched at Tristan. He tried to answer the best he could, but most of his replies were along the lines of *"Don't really know"* or *"Can't really say"* and sometimes *"I'm not sure."*

After that the boys stopped their interrogation and switched to high praise for his superpower special ability thing. He just listened to the boys joking around, and smiled contentedly at their excited faces. I could see sincere affection in Tristan's eyes, how much he cared for our friends. And the rest of The Lost Boys clearly felt the same about him. I couldn't help but smile. Not in a million years would I have imagined myself being part of such an amazing group of friends, and part of a band with them, too. How cool was that? I felt Tristan's hand squeezing mine softly, and I turned to look at him. Once again I was blown away by the intensity of his piercing gaze. He grasped my chin lightly with the tip of his fingers, making me tilt my head up a little, and leaned in to give me a soft kiss. I was so engulfed by his kiss that I completely forgot about anything else. I could happily spend all eternity lost in his kisses. They made me forget about the rest of the world.

But then Sam's voice cut in sharply, startling us and making us part.

"Hey! You two, cut it out! Some of us still haven't adjusted to this new relationship yet!" Sam shouted from my bed. "So no kissing for at least the next twenty-four hours!" he said, frowning and making a parting gesture with his arms.

Tristan chuckled and leaned back on his headboard, pulling me with him and wrapping his arms around my waist. "How about hugging. Is that allowed?" he asked, resting his chin on my shoulder.

Sam pondered the question for a second and sniffed loudly. "I suppose a little hugging is acceptable. But please keep the lovey-dovey stuff to a minimum. It's very unsettling," he said, making everybody crack up laughing all over again.

The boys started pondering the many ways of turning

Tristan's fading ability to their advantage, suggesting he could sneak inside the staff room and have a quick look at test sheets.

Tristan chuckled lightly at their absurd requests but shook his head at all suggestions thrown his way.

I laughed hard at his refusals. It was like trying to convince Superman to do something against the law. It just wasn't going to happen. Not in a million years.

Seth was apparently the only one on Tristan's side. "You're right, man. Don't do it! With great power comes great responsibility!" Seth said, quoting the famous line from *Spider-Man*. He was such a geek. And so was I, because I knew where that line came from.

"Could you be more lame, dude?" Harry scoffed.

"How do you put up with him being so nerdy, Tiffany?" Josh asked, shaking his head vigorously.

Tiffany paused, looking at the ceiling thoughtfully. "Oh, I tolerate all his geekiness because he is so good in bed, you know?" she said, smiling sexily.

Seth choked and turned all red in the face, taken completely by surprise at Tiffany's out-of-the-blue confession.

Everybody in the room, including myself, gawked at her. Tiffany loved seeing Seth blush. And he was so pale and blond; it was true entertainment seeing his face turning full-on beet red in a matter of seconds. Seth got a round of applause and compliments from the guys after that, making him turn an even darker shade of red. It was hilarious to watch!

We kept talking for a long time in our room after that. The boys also offered to help us by researching Tristan's situation online and in the school library. I was overwhelmed by their support: they were determined to do whatever was necessary to help us get through this. They were confident about finding a way out of this deadline deal. I felt confidence rising inside of me as well. We could do this! We could find a way!

In the middle of the afternoon, Harry offered to get everybody some snacks and sodas from the cafeteria, and I volunteered to help him carry the food. I had been watching Harry for a while, and there was something he was trying to hide, something that was bothering him, but I couldn't figure out what it was. So I took the opportunity to ask him while we were walking through the school corridors.

He glanced quickly at me and then went back to staring right ahead. "No. Nothing's wrong," he said, but the smile never reached his green eyes.

"Come on, Harry. You can tell me. You look upset...and sad," I said, reading it in his eyes.

He stopped slowly and turned to me. "I guess I'm still a little surprised, that's all. I just need some time to let it all sink in."

"I'm sorry to drop the bomb on you guys like that. We should have told you little by little."

"Nah, that's okay. I'm glad you told us everything." He shuffled his feet "So...you and Tristan, huh? I should have seen it, the way you two looked at each other. It's so obvious now," he mused. There it was again. The hint of sadness behind his eyes. "And here I was thinking he was just a jealous brother, when he was in fact a jealous boyfriend." He chuckled lightly.

"Harry," I said, smiling softly at him, and then I saw it. Love and hope and then defeat and resignation. He was giving up on the possibility that something might happen between us. I truly hated my gift of empathy then. I didn't want to violate his private feelings like that. I wished I hadn't seen the secrets in his eyes. "Harry...I-I hope you know how much you mean to me," I managed to say. "You're one of my best friends and I love you so much. Your friendship means the world to me."

He smiled in response and I threw my arms around him, hugging him tight. He tensed in surprise first, but then he slowly relaxed and hugged me back. "Of course, Joe," he said quietly, and then he quickly broke away and coughed, slightly embarrassed. "Come on, you're way too emotional today, Joey. You're almost acting like a girl! Let's go get these snacks, okay?" he teased, walking ahead of me.

I followed him with a heavy heart, and after that day I never once mentioned what I'd seen in Harry's eyes, to anyone.

That night I slept in Tristan's arms and dreamed I was walking through the cemetery lanes, back in Esperanza. Everything looked familiar, but at the same time strange. There were still the angel statues and big heavy-stoned crosses, a few scattered trees between graves and the usual grass and weeds growing between the cracks in the paving. But when I started to look more carefully, some things were out of proportion and bent in wrong angles. The light seemed weird too, too foggy to be identified as any particular time of the day. It was the kind of light you only get in dreams.

As soon as I realized I was dreaming, I tensed up. It was Vigil's favorite place to try to contact me. As soon as this thought popped in my head, I saw his slim figure hunched on the nearest wooden bench. He looked sideways at me, not daring to stare directly. He was trying out a nonchalant, non-threatening pose.

My first instinctive reaction was to shut my eyes tight and try my *"wakeupwakeupwakeup"* mantra, to break Vigil's connection. But then I remembered we needed to gather as much information about Tristan's situation as possible. The library and internet were all well and good, but who would know more than Vigil himself? So instead of shutting myself off from him, I walked straight over and sat on his bench, but as far away from him as I could, just to be on the safe side.

He looked startled at my approach and was even more shocked when I started up a conversation with him.

"Go ahead, Vigil, talk," I said a little too sharply.

"E-excuse me?"

"You obviously want to talk to me. You have been trying to contact me in my dreams for a long time now. If you wanted to do something to hurt me, you would probably have done it by now, so I gather you won't, or perhaps you can't. So. Talk. I'm all ears," I stated.

"I-I do wish to talk with you," he said, a little uncertain.

"Yes, Captain Obvious," I retorted sarcastically.

He frowned, not understanding me.

I was starting to notice Vigil didn't grasp sarcasm very well. I needed to be more straightforward when I was talking to him. "I mean, yes, I know that. Go on," I corrected myself, and waited for him to continue.

He eyed me suspiciously, a little fearfully, as if I was about to strike him again. I was also starting to notice I could read him more easily now. The first times we had met, I could barely detect a smidgen of emotion coming from him. But with each encounter, he seemed to be letting more show.

"I want you to know that it is not my intention to hurt

anyone. As I've told you, I am just trying to make things right. Is that such a bad thing?" he stated calmly.

I tried to follow his line of reasoning. "Your job is to send Tristan back to being a ghost, or worse. Who says that is the right thing to do?" I questioned.

"I do." he said it like it was the most obvious thing in the world. "It is my job to know this."

"And if you're wrong? What if he belongs here, with me. With the living, I mean," I said, correcting myself just in time.

"I am never wrong."

"What if you are this time?"

"I am not. This is what I need to do."

I sighed, frustrated. "Is there anything I can do to make you change your mind?" I asked. It was worth to try. "I can help you, you know, with your job? You said it's your job to fix things, to put things back in their right places. I gather you must have to deal with a lot of problems, a lot of...unexpected things," I said.

From what I could observe, Vigil was a sucker for rules, a control-freak. And dealing with unexpected events all over the universe must require being adaptable. Something he lacked big time. I continued my proposal. "I could help you with that; I could be your 'human adviser' for unpredictable matters. I could help you understand."

"Human beings are a very chaotic life form," he pondered.

"Yes, we are. And you know what they say: you need to think like a thief to catch a thief. With my help, you could be the best at what you do. I will help you, if you let Tristan go," I said.

That was my only hope. He must have chosen a male

appearance for a reason; he identified with maleness more. And there was one thing a lot of men craved – power.

He seemed to be deep in thought for a second, but then he shook his head. "I am sorry. I cannot. I have to fix it. I must find...*Tristan*," he said stoically.

Crap. He was a stubborn thing! So, perhaps he wasn't motivated by power. "Then, can I talk with your supervisor?" I asked, thinking of my mom. Whenever she had received bad customer service, she would throw out that line.

"What?" he spat out, a little disconcerted.

See? Unexpected. Take that, Mr. Unbendable! He was so not ready to deal with humans! "Your boss, the guy who makes up all this stupid rules you follow so dearly. The one you report to. Management," I explained.

"There are many like myself out there: my 'colleagues', as you might call them, and a few higher than us." he said with a disgruntled sniff.

Ah. Touched a nerve there, have we? He didn't like having to answer to someone. Maybe it was all about power after all. "Can I talk to one of them, please? If I convince them to let Tristan out of this, you'll have to obey, right?"

He seemed reluctant to answer now.

"Come on, Vigil. Play fair. I have the right to talk to your boss. I bet there's even a rule saying so," I risked.

He pursed his lips, which meant I was right on the money with that one! Mental high five for me! "You have already talked to a higher power. I have witnessed you twice now," he said.

"I have? When? Who?" I asked in surprise. The only strange, unearthly being I remembered talking to was him. Then Goth Girl drifted into my head for a split of a second. Sky. "You mean Sky?" I ventured.

"Sky?" he mused, with a sneer. "You and your strange, silly human habit of naming us. Most of your kind call her Death."

I stared at him with my jaw hanging open. "Come again?" I said in a choked voice.

"The creature you call 'Sky' is Death," he replied.

I had not seen that one coming!

He rolled his eyes, annoyed at my slowness. He seemed to be absorbing a lot of human emotions at quite a fast speed. Curious. Maybe I was rubbing off on him. Emotions can be contagious? I shook my head, trying to dislodge the silly jumble of thoughts and focus on the most freaking important one. "Death?" I repeated. "As in The Grim Reaper? The Collector of Souls? The tall bony dude dressed all in black with the sickle thingy?" I expanded, just to be sure.

"Yes. Death has many . . . personas."

"Get out of here!" I said, flabbergasted.

He flinched, slightly puzzled, and looked at me warily. I forgot he took things too literally.

"Sorry, what I meant to say was, I can't believe this!" I explained.

That little glint of fear was back in his eyes. I almost felt sorry for him but then I remembered how scary he had been the first couple of times we'd met. I should always keep that in mind and not let myself be misled by his more human frailties.

"So, if I talk with Sky, I mean Death . . ." Boy, that was a weird sentence. ". . . and she agrees to let Tristan off the hook, you'll have to obey?" I asked slowly.

"Yes," he agreed, warily.

"Great! So, when can I see her again? I always find her in that desert place. Is she there now?"

"Yes. *'She'* can often be found there. It's the transition space between the world of the living and the dead."

"Cool." It sounded like some cosmic waiting room or what my mother might have called Limbo. "How do I get there?"

He turned to look at me again and his eyes were dark as the blackest night. "You have to die to get there."

I looked at him in shock. "I h-have to die? But...but...I have been there, like, twice already!" I said, a little freaked out.

"Yes. And you have died both of those times, then. It's the only way...for humans, that is," he said with an all too human smirk.

"I don't understand. I'm certainly not dead...right?" I asked, a little uncertain now, and pinched myself to see if I was real or not. I had met Sky in my dreams – could a person die in their dreams and not know?

He rolled his eyes again. "You are definitely not dead. But you must have been at those times you met 'her', even if only for a second. It's a little tricky, but a few humans manage to do so once in a while," he said thoughtfully.

"Wait. Are you saying I *'died'* for a time, talked to *'Death'* and then came back to the living, twice already?" I asked.

"Yes. I don't recommend it, though," he said quietly.

"What do you mean?"

"It's tricky, meeting with Death. You were lucky before. Sometimes the human body just gives up and you do not come back. A heavy price to pay."

"Are you saying I can really die...if I try to do this again?" I asked shakily.

"Yes. That is a possibility."

"Is there any other way?"

"No. There is no other way. To meet Death, a human being must die."

"Okay. I'll take my chances and talk to Sky, then. How do I get there?" I asked.

"You have to find your way back there like you have done before. Just remember, the longer you stay in there, the riskier it gets for you – and the harder it will be for you to come back," he warned.

"Oh. Okay. Thank you for talking to me, Vigil. I appreciate you telling me all this," I said, and I don't know why on earth I did what I did next, but before I could stop myself, I just leaned in and hugged him as a thank you gesture. As I let him go I felt a little awkward. Vigil seemed shocked beyond all reason. A little embarrassed, I stepped back, giving him some distance.

"Can I have your word you'll stop hunting Tristan down until I talk to Sky?" I asked politely.

He was staring at the ground, with a disconcerted look on his face. "Tristan has a protective spell blocking me from finding him in the physical world," he said almost to himself. "Or even through his dreams. I will wait until you meet Death. But if I don't hear from you by the next New Year, your connection with him will cease to exist and you won't be able to protect him any more...I'll find him then. And fix this. It's only a matter of time," he proclaimed eerily.

I shuddered. There was nothing I could do to stop the New Year coming. But I knew what I had to do now. I needed to meet Sky and pray that I was clever enough to persuade her against taking Tristan from me. Ironically, Death was my only hope.

Chapter Thirty-Two

Break-Up

The next day I was woken by Seth's alarm clock as usual.

Tristan grunted by my side, untangling himself from me, and that's when I realized I had spent the night in his bed …again. It was becoming quite the habit. I smiled at the fact and rubbed my eyes, trying to sweep the sleepiness away. Dreaming of Vigil always made me tired the next day; it was like he drained me of all my energy. Then I remembered our discussion…and what I had to do. I had to meet Death now if I wanted a chance to save Tristan. He wasn't going to like hearing about my dream, but I had promised him there would be no more secrets between us. When I told him and Seth about our encounter, it was like I had punched Tristan in the stomach.

"No fucking way, Joey!" Man, he was really upset if he was cursing!

"Tris, listen. I have to do this," I insisted.

"Absolutely not, Joey!" he exclaimed, exasperated. His eyes were full of fear and worry. Then he shook his head and sighed deeply, trying to cool his temper down a bit. Next time he spoke he wasn't so loud. "Please, Joey. I can't let you put yourself at risk for me. If something happens to you..." he said, and his voice broke down at the end. "Promise me you won't do this?"

I needed to be strong now. For the both of us. I couldn't let myself be swayed by his pleadings. I needed to do this. "I'm sorry, Tristan. I can't promise you that. And I need your support on this. We can do this!" I said encouragingly, trying to convince him.

"No, Joe! It's too dangerous. I...I forbid you!" he said, crossing his arms, angry and upset again.

I raised an amused eyebrow. *Forbid me?* Seriously? Didn't he know me at all by now? "Okay, Tristan. I wasn't actually asking your permission, you know? I'm just telling you what's going to happen, because I promised you I wouldn't keep any secrets from you again. So, either you help me do this, or I'll do it by myself." He stared at me in silence for a long time. I stared right back. I was wickedly good at the stare game. And I could beat him on the stubborn front by miles.

After a few minutes he rolled his eyes, breaking eye contact. "So...damn...stubborn," I heard him grunt under his breath. "But can't I go in your place and talk to her?" he suggested.

"I don't think you can. You've never been to that desert place, have you?" I asked. "I'm not sure how I got there myself, but I think I can maybe dream my way back again, if I try hard enough," I said hesitantly. That was for sure a huge "maybe". "And somehow, instinctively, I've learned the trick to get back alive. And you haven't."

He sagged, hanging his head in defeat.

Seth sat beside me and wrapped his arm around my shoulder. "We'll help you, Joe. Like you say, you've already done this twice and you're okay. Let's help her get prepared for this, right, Tristan?" he said, looking up.

"Yes. Fine," Tristan said sharply, shaking his head, still upset.

We got dressed and headed together to class. I wasn't paying much attention to anything during the lesson, immersed in thoughts about meeting Sky. Tristan was also in a thoughtful, distant mood too. After our first class was over, Tristan parted ways saying he needed to take care of things with Caroline.

I met up with Tiffany and got to tell her about everything that had happened. I knew Seth was going to tell her anyway, but I wanted her to know about it from me first. She looked a little scared, but tried to sound reassuring and positive for my sake, just like Seth had done.

I was really anxious to meet Tristan and talk to him again when lunch break came around. I wanted to know how his conversation with Caroline had gone. I hoped she hadn't taken the break-up too hard. It wasn't her fault for getting tangled up in this mess that Tristan and I had created. And I still felt a twinge of guilt for my part in it, but there wasn't anything I could do to soften the blow now. The right thing for Tristan to do was to let her down, as gently as he could.

I didn't need to wait long to hear news about their break-up, though. I got to hear it all straight from the source when, only halfway to the cafeteria, I got tackled by a hysterical Caroline.

"Joey! You have to help me, please!" she sobbed shamelessly. "Tristan just broke up with me! I-I don't understand!" I shifted on my spot, at a loss to what to say. This was so awkward; how was I supposed to comfort her when I knew I was the one to blame for this?

"He told me things weren't working out for us, that I deserved someone better than him. But I don't want another boyfriend! I want him! He's the hottest, most popular guy in school! I don't want to date some loser!" she whined, and stomped her feet in a tantrum.

"Ah, maybe it really is for the best, Caroline," I tried to reason with her. "Maybe you're better off with someone else. He doesn't seem to appreciate you..." I said, trying to bite back any sarcastic comment, because I was trying to make her feel better, no matter how annoying she could be.

She snorted venomously. "Damn right. Do you know how many times Bradley Finn has begged me to be his girlfriend? But I turned him down because of Tristan! And now the boy has the audacity to dump me?" she growled viciously.

"You really should give Bradley a chance, then..." I tried to suggest, but she cut me off.

"You have to help me get him back, Joey! He's your brother. You can talk to him, make him see he needs to be with me! I'll do anything!" she begged me. "I'll even stop complaining about him being so polite and shy! If all he wants is to hold hands, then it's fine by me!"

"I'm sorry, Caroline. I don't meddle in Tristan's relationships," I said as calmly as I could. "It's his decision, we should respect what he wants. You should move on, look for someone better, like he said. I'm sorry, but I have to go." She seemed completely baffled that I was refusing to obey her every wish.

"I'll get him back, I don't need you anyway." And she stomped away in righteous fury.

I managed to walk a few feet through the hallway before

Bradley stopped short in front of me, purposely blocking my path with a devious sneer on his bulky face.

I rolled my eyes and huffed, aggravated. I wasn't in the mood for Bradley's stupidity today. He, however, caught me eye-balling him and flashed me a wide, provocative grin.

"Hey, Joe Gray! Looking good!" he said with a wink. That was weird. Since Tristan's arrival at the school, Bradley had stopped bullying me, because he didn't want to upset his basketball star buddy. But what he was doing right now wasn't bullying; this was different. Was this ... flirting?

I shivered slightly at the thought. "Can't say the same to you, Brad. You look awful as always," I snapped back. I hoped that would make him upset. Angry was certainly a better mode for him than flirtatious.

But to my most complete surprise, he just laughed out loud in a playful mood. "Oh! You're so feisty! I like them feisty!" he said, still with that unsettling grin on his face.

"Do you like 'them' with a foot up your ass too?" I asked, annoyed.

He sniggered and pretended he didn't hear my last snarky remark. "You totally made me change my mind about you at the dance, Gray. You looked like a total babe that night! And lately you have been nothing but eye-candy," he said with a lascivious grin.

Oh, dear. Triple Yuck! "You know, Brad, I've just heard Caroline isn't with Tristan any more," I began. Maybe I could play matchmaker here and get both of them off my back. That would make my life so much easier.

"Really?" Bradley said, and then paused thoughtfully to weigh up his options. "I hadn't heard that. Well, in that case, I'll have to put you on hold for a while, Gray. You're a babe, but Caroline is smoking hot! I think I'll have another go at her, then!" he stated with a clever smirk.

"You do that. I'll be waiting here, holding my breath, Bradley," I said, but he didn't seem to catch the sarcasm.

"All right, then, Gray. If things don't go well with Caroline, you're next in line!" He gave me a cheeky wink that made me feel slightly nauseated, and then he sauntered away. I practically ran to the cafeteria after that; I didn't want to bump into anyone else in the hallway.

Chapter Thirty-Three

The Date

The rest of the week passed by in a crazy haze. Tristan announced he was going to take me on a proper date and I decided to focus all my attention on that instead of dwelling on my impending meeting with Death...Sky. Tristan had been walking around with a smirk at the corner of his mouth during the whole week too. I could tell he had a wicked plan in motion, and I was dying to figure out what it was. I knew it had something to do with our date on Friday. I'd tried to fish for information whenever I got the chance, but Tristan just chuckled at my curiosity.

I tried tackling Seth, sure that Tristan must have confided his plans to him for sure. Seth hazarded a guess that Tristan was probably going to take me to the same fancy restaurant in Saint Pete where he'd his first date with Tiffany.

Friday came and at six p.m. I started getting ready for my date. I took my shower thinking about the evening to come. I was a little disappointed by Tristan's plans, to tell you the truth. Posh dinners meant uncomfortable clothes to me, and painful high heels, and awkwardness because I didn't know how to behave in such top-notch places. I know most guys think that an ideal date for girls means expensive dinners and red roses, but that was such a cliché and not like me at all! Well, Tristan was just trying to do his best, I guess, and I had to remember he came from a different time. I better master my fake-surprised face and appreciate the date. He was going to all this trouble because of me, and the least I could do was enjoy the evening with him, right?

He was going to be there and that was the important part; that was all that mattered to me. It was my first official date with the boy of my dreams, after all. I was heading to my wardrobe to select a suitable outfit when Tristan walked into the room, all cheerful and bustling with eagerness.

He was wearing my favorite blue T-shirt, and jeans that hugged his body in all the right places. "Hey, my tangerine girl!" he cheered and walked over, wrapping his arms around my waist and kissing me deeply. "I've missed you!" he said, putting me back down on the floor after the kiss.

"You're the one who kept disappearing all day long, mister!" I scoffed, and then added hurriedly, "You're early, you know, I'm not dressed yet! "

"Of course you're dressed, Joey. See? These are clothes," he said, pulling the hem of my T-shirt to demonstrate the obvious. "Oh, I see! You're talking about getting dressed for the date!" He faked like he had forgotten all about it and laughed at my annoyed face. "First I need you to come with me! You can get dressed after that. Come on!" he said, pushing me out of the room.

Tristan grabbed my hand and walked with me quickly down the hallways until we were outside the school.

"Tris, were the hell are we going?" I whispered, while he glanced around to see if there was anyone watching us.

"I wanted to talk to you, you know, in private. Our room

is Seth's room too," he explained, stopping to look at me "That small terrace you brought me to the night of the dance was around here somewhere, right? Can we go there for a little bit? To talk?"

I tensed up immediately at the mention of the secret terrace. The memory of that night was still fresh in my head, and the "talk" we'd had then had been the most painful one I have ever had in my life. I didn't want to re-live any of that, ever again. I looked at him suspiciously and nervously, but I saw nothing but happiness shining inside his eyes. "What sort of talk?" I asked worriedly.

"Yeah, just, you know…talk…a little," he said, leaning against me in such a provocative sexy way I almost tackled him right there in front of everyone. And I realized he was so lying with his "talk" excuse! His eyes totally betrayed him! He wanted to do other private things with me than talk!

I smirked at him, amused. Well, now I understood the sudden need for a secluded private place. All week long we had been busy with school and band rehearsals. And Seth was often in the room, and sometimes Tiffany, Harry, Josh and Sammy were around. Given our date was going to be in a restaurant full of people, we certainly wouldn't have any privacy there for sure. We might as well enjoy this couple of hours alone while we could, right?

"Come on," I said, pulling him by the hand in the direction of the small hidden iron door by the side of the school building. Harry's secret terrace was saving the day, I thought, smiling to myself. I got to the top of the stairs in a few seconds and opened the iron door with a small push, stumbling on to the terrace out of breath. And then I gasped in shock. The place had been transformed!

There were two blankets put together in the middle of the terrace, and a picnic basket placed right by its side. A couple of candles lay in the middle, with a little vase filled with white lilies next to them. A small boom box had been placed in the corner of the terrace, with Tristan's guitar case by its side. There was also a big backpack resting in another corner.

The sun was setting, giving the place an eerie, magical look, helped by the edges of the terrace being lit by hundreds of small tea-light candles. I was so surprised I couldn't even speak! I just stood there with my mouth hanging open. Tristan wrapped his arms around my waist and rested his chin on my shoulder.

"Did I manage to surprise you?" he said quietly by my ear. "It's a tricky thing to accomplish with a girl that can read your thoughts with a quick glance into your eyes."

"I-I-Y-you...yes!" was all I could reply. So that was why he had been avoiding me all day long!

"Good," he said, chuckling, satisfied with my reaction. Then he placed a soft kiss on my neck, and another one higher up, below my ear, making me shiver lightly.

"But...but...what about the posh restaurant thing?" I asked, completely confused. He laughed, making me want to melt right there on the spot. "I never said I was going to take you to any fancy restaurant," he said with a chuckle. "I know your idea of a good time does not include putting on uncomfortable clothes and spending time in a formal setting with so many people around. You'd hate a date like that so much!" he said, and led me to sit on the blanket.

The terrace was getting darker by the minute; the sun had already disappeared behind the horizon but the candles glowed so beautifully on the terrace, bathing a soft warm yellow light over the lilies at the centre.

"How did you know lilies are my favorite flowers?" I asked, surprised again.

"Well, it doesn't take a mastermind to figure that one out! You always make us stop by the garden next to the auditorium, on the lilies patch. I assumed you liked them," he said, laughter lines playing around his beautiful gray eyes.

"Yeah, I love them. They are beautiful." I looked at the small cluster of white lilies, nested nicely in front of me. "They have the most amazing scent."

He gave me one of those quiet, sexy smiles of his again. Then he leaned in and kissed me slowly. "Hmm, tangerine," he whispered teasingly. I was wearing my tangerine lip-gloss, and the smoldering tone in his voice told me he liked it, making me feel giddy.

"Speaking of which," he said, pulling away to stand up and grab his guitar. He sat again, this time in front of me, and patted a place next to him for me to sit. Then he placed the guitar on his lap, strumming a little on it. "This is a song from back in the days, you know, when I was alive. I don't think you know it, but I really like this song. It makes me think of you, so I thought I should sing it for you tonight," he said and starting playing.

It was a song about summer, and love and the scent of tangerines in the air. It was a really sweet old song. This was the best date ever! I couldn't believe I got to have a private musical performance from Tristan. His voice was so amazing; it was raspy, low and a little sad, and so damn sexy!

When he'd finished singing I took his guitar from his

hands, putting it to one side, and kissed him like it was our last chance to kiss on Earth!

"Wow, I should sing for you more often!" he said with a cheeky smile when we finally parted for breath.

"You would always get this kind of response from me if you did!" I said, laughing at his slightly flustered face.

"Well, I'll keep that always in mind, Miss Gray!" He winked and then grabbed the basket by his side. "Now, let's dig in to the main course, madam," he said, pulling a bunch of stuff out of the picnic basket. He took out a bottle of wine and two glasses. Then some sandwiches and many assorted foods including chocolates and candies. I chuckled at his food choices.

"I have been talking the whole week with the cafeteria lady. Susie. I told her I was trying to win a girl over, and Susie was thrilled to hear all about it. Apparently, she is a huge sucker for romantic stories. She got me the wine and glasses because I told her it was a very special occasion," he said, pointing to the bottle. "She was dying to know who the girl was," he confessed with a chuckle.

"This is the best dinner ever!" I said, taking another big bite out of my sandwich as I listened to his story. "Thank you so much for not taking me to a posh restaurant!"

He laughed hard. "Yes, who wants a five-star restaurant if you can have fast food sandwiches instead!" He shook his head at my silliness. "I'm glad, though, because if you did like expensive meals, I would be at a loss! I don't know how to act in posh places either," he said, smiling and pouring us some wine.

"This is perfect, Tris. I love it."

We ate for a while and drank our wine, talking excitedly about our new songs, and the band. We purposefully avoided any topics like Sky or the New Year deadline Tristan was under. By some unspoken agreement we had decided tonight was a time to be happy, to be together, to enjoy life to its fullest. Tristan had put his guitar back in its case and had turned the boom box on, but very low so we wouldn't attract any attention to the terrace. But it was nice having low, soft music in the background while we talked. Then the song that we'd danced to on the night of the Spring Ball started playing, and after a few seconds Tristan recognized the music.

He stood up, pulling me into his arms, and started slow-dancing with me. When we had first danced to this song we had been fighting. Now I was in heaven.

"This is how that dance was supposed to be," he whispered as he pulled me close against him. "I ruined it that night but it's never too late to right a wrong, is it?" he said, and leaned in, kissing up and down my neck.

I was glad he was holding me tight against him, other-wise my legs would have given up on me. I was melting in his arms and I felt slightly dizzy. And I'd only had one glass of wine. His mouth left my neck for a while, and he gently brushed his lips against my cheek. His lips felt like they were pure scorching fire, pinpricks of heat burning my skin wherever they touched me. My lips eagerly searched for his and when I found them, I kissed him madly and forgot about the world.

"Joey, we should slow down, I'm barely managing to control myself here," he warned in his incredibly sexy voice. "I promised I was going to treat you right on this date, and you're making me seriously consider breaking my word, here."

"Oh, I'm sorry," I said, stepping away from him, giggling

a little. "Come on, sit down with me," I compromised. We watched the sky in a comfortable silence for a while, each of us deep in our own private thoughts. He linked his hand with mine and intertwined our fingers. This was one of the things I loved the most about being with Tristan. We could be together for longs periods of time without feeling the need to speak.

Finally it was getting late so Tristan started packing up all his stuff. He turned the music off, put the candles away and the rest of the food back in the basket. I guess my amazing date was coming to an end. It had been magical. I'd loved every second of it.

"This was the best date I have ever had," I told him.

"I'm glad you liked it, Joey," he said truthfully.

"Like it? I loved it! I wish it could never end…"

He smiled and remained silent, gazing at the sky with me.

"It's getting really late, we should head back to our room," he said reluctantly at last.

"Can we just stay here for a little while more?" I asked softly. He just smiled his sexy smile again and lay down beside me. It was such a beautiful, warm night.

"You know," he said slowly, "life with you is full of possibilities. I think you're extraordinary. And you are so beautiful, but you don't know it, which makes you even more stunning. You're strong, and brave, but sweet and kind at the same time. And you never cease to amaze me," he said before lapsing into thoughtful silence again.

But I decided it wasn't the time for words in any case; it was time for action.

"Okay, Tristan. Take off your clothes," I commanded firmly. He chuckled, thinking I was just joking around. "I'm not kidding. Start stripping, mister," I repeated seriously. "I have no words to tell you how I feel, so I'm going to show you."

He smirked, still thinking I was joking. I had to prove to him I was serious so I lunged at him and kissed him like he was the last drop of water in the middle of a scorching hot desert. My hands were everywhere on him and I couldn't get enough of how good he felt under my fingers. He kissed me back with so much hunger that we both had to part after a few minutes, gasping desperately for air.

"Can you, please, take your clothes off now?" I asked, laughing at his ragged breathing. His shirt was off before I could finish the sentence. I laughed even more at his speed and readiness. I took my top off too, and started kissing him back. In a few seconds we were both naked. This time we didn't rush things as we had our first time together. This time we weren't fighting or angry. This time was sweet and loving.

I would never forget this terrace, but the memory of our first fight here was completely obliterated by the wonder of our first date now. I was glad Tristan had had the foresight to have condoms in his back pocket, and that he had put out some of the candles. I was glad for the darkness. It felt comfortable and soothing, like a nice soft blanket wrapped over us.

Afterwards, as I lay in his arms, we watched the night sky in companionable silence. When he noticed me shivering a little, he grabbed the big backpack behind us and pulled out a small soft blanket.

I snuggled close to him under the blanket, resting my head against his chest. After a while he started talking, his voice rumbling softly under my ear. He talked about his plans for the future, how much he loved playing music, writing lyrics and melodies, and how amazing it would be if maybe we could do this for a living some day. He talked about places he wanted to go and see with me, languages he wanted to learn to speak, so many wonderful things he still wanted to do.

It felt good knowing he thought about the future like that. It meant he wasn't giving up, that he really hoped we could figure something out for the end of the year. It meant that he wanted a future; that he wanted to live. I told him then about how my dad had been in a band when he was young, that he'd played in bars to earn a living for some time, and it was in one of those bars that he'd met my mom for the first time. I told him how he had died when I was only three years old and that I didn't remember his face, but sometimes I thought I remembered his voice singing to me. How it had been just my mom and me since then, and how she'd refused to let sorrow take over her life and had forged her rule to always be open to new things. She'd even made me learn how to play the piano and the guitar because of my dad and his love of music; she wanted to pass to me some of that love, some of his soul. I knew that was why music always particularly touched my heart. These past months had been a rediscovery of that connection. Being in The Lost Boys had made me feel closer to my dad, made me feel I hadn't lost him completely. Playing music felt like being home again.

I had never talked about this with anyone before. It felt good to talk about it with Tristan for the first time, like a little knot in my chest dissolved and faded away.

Later, we returned to our room. Seth was already deeply asleep. All we could see was the tip of his blond hair over the top of his blankets. Tristan pressed a finger to his lips and we put all our stuff on the floor carefully, so we wouldn't wake Seth up. Tristan started taking all his clothes off again, except only his boxers, and slipped quickly under his covers. Then he stretched his arm to me and mouthed a silent "come".

I walked over to his bed and he pulled me to lay with him, and then he turned on to his side. Our bodies fell immediately into that familiar position, his arm wrapped around me, his hand enclosing mine and his face snuggled behind my neck. It felt like two pieces of a puzzle clicking together in all the right places. He sighed deeply and I felt his warm breath over my neck. Just like home.

Chapter Thirty-Four

Surprise Meeting

When I woke up, my face was buried in soft, warm, glittery sand. I shot upright as if a bolt of lightning had hit me, and saw a moonless sky above my head. Holy crap, this was Sky's desert again: Death's domain. Tristan and I had agreed I wouldn't try this before we'd had a chance to plan things, but I'd made it here unintentionally.

How was I supposed to find Sky in this forsaken place? Should I try to call her? Was it a wise thing to do? What if there were other creatures hiding here? Waiting for a weak, dumb prey to start shouting, announcing its next meal?

I took a deep breath, trying to calm myself down, when Sky's voice greeted me from behind, making me jump. "Hello, Joe."

I flipped myself around, almost losing my balance, but caught myself just in time. "Jeez, Louise! You scared me half to death...Huh...I mean..." I trailed off. Not a good opener to a conversation with Death, I reckoned. Gosh, this "talking with Death" business was turning out to be a lot more complicated than I'd expected.

"You came to visit me!" she said, smiling. "I don't ever

get visitors...Well, not willing ones," she mused. "And everybody's always in such a rush," she complained.

"Maybe it's because the place is a little...barren?" I suggested weakly, trying to make conversation.

The visiting topic seemed to be a sore spot for her. Who knew Death could be lonely? That was...well, unexpected. But if you thought about it, it kind of made sense. No one in his right mind would like to hang around Death to "chat".

"Yes, I suppose you are right. The place isn't very 'lively', is it?" She smiled at the view. "It has been like this for, oh, I don't know, millennia?" she said. "But enough of this talk! Come, sit!" She indicated a mound of glittery sand. I sat close to her, turning a little so I could see her face. She looked so young, younger than me. I supposed that, just because she was Death, she didn't have to look all crinkled and old, or be just a skeleton. That would be stereotyping Her long black hair fell over her shoulders and down to her waist. It was very beautiful, as was her angelic pale face and her round cheeks and plump lips. She was still wearing her dark clothes, and necklaces everywhere. Her deep black eyes watched me curiously as I watched her.

"I guess you know who am I now," she said.

"Oh, yes." I nodded. "Why you didn't tell me?"

She thought for a while before answering me. "I didn't want to rush things for you."

"Oh. Okay. I guess..." I said, peeking slyly at her.

"And you are wondering why I look like this," she said, noticing me staring. "Everybody sees me differently in here. If you find me terrifying, I would probably look scary to you. A dark creature wrapped in a dark hooded cloak with nothing but bones inside." She shrugged, like it didn't bother her at all what she looked like. "If you're not scared, you'll project something else. I rather like the look you give me. It's quite... what's the word I'm looking for? Dashing?" she offered, smiling warmly at me.

"Are you saying I make you look like that?" I asked, puzzled.

"Human personification; it's all in your minds. You can be very creative and imaginative when you want to be. When you're not killing things, that is. You're very good at that; gives me loads of work to do in here," she said, a hint of annoyance in her voice now.

"Uh... sorry," I apologized, on behalf of all humankind.

She waved her hand at me, dismissing the topic. "So, Joe. How's *'Vigil'* doing? Any more punches?" she asked, excited now. I'd forgotten about that. She thought I was very... entertaining. It was like she was asking for the next episode of a soap opera.

"No, no more punches. We just talk nowadays," I answered. "Actually, that was why I came here. I need to talk to you about Vigil," I said, getting to the point. "He said you're his boss..." I began.

She frowned and cut in. "I am certainly not. I don't have anything to do with any of those gray things!" she said, affronted.

"He told me you... outrank him."

"Well, yes. That is correct."

"So, you're *kind* of his boss, if you're higher up in the command chain?" I asked, trying to get my point made.

"I'm as high as it goes, Joe," she stated bluntly.

"So, if you told him to do something, he'd have to obey, right?" I asked eagerly. She just shrugged her shoulders, not really getting where I was going with this. "So, if you told Vigil to let Tristan be, he'd have to obey."

"I don't think it works that way, Joe," she said, finally understanding where I was aiming for. "I don't decide who lives or who dies."

"Come on, now! You, like, kill people every day! You're *Death*!" I countered.

"I haven't killed anyone in my whole life!" she said, crossing her arms over her chest defensively. "I just show them the path between worlds."

"B-but…" I stuttered, at a loss. What could I possibly say to convince Death to let Tristan live? She was our only hope, and it was turning out to be a total dead end, no pun intended. A burning bright light was starting to rise on the horizon. Sky glanced at it and turned to face me again.

"It's time for you to leave, Joe. You can't stay here much longer," she said seriously.

"Listen, are you saying there's nothing you can do to help Tristan?" I asked in a despairing voice, brushing aside her warning.

"I didn't say that."

"What are you saying, then?" I huffed, annoyed at her cryptic answers. "Are you going to help us or not, Sky?" I pleaded again. "You're our only hope!"

"I'm so sorry, Joe. I can't meddle in Vigil's affairs. I'm really sorry, but that's the way it is." The bright light continued ascending in the sky, its light making the sand glitter like it was billions of shining stars exploding. The luminosity was so intense, it was burning my eyes, making my head hurt.

"No! There is always a way!" I cried out. I was feeling so tired; my arms were heavy, like chunks of lead. I swayed a little, sitting on the sand by her side, my eyelids getting heavier by the second.

"Joe, you can't fall asleep in here. You fall asleep, you never wake up again, do you understand?" she warned me.

I forced my eyes open, but it was so hard to stay awake. It was like the coming morning was draining all of my energy, leaving me as barren as this waste land.

"You shouldn't have stayed this long," she stated seriously.

"How long have I been here?"

She pondered her answer as the morning drew near. "Time is relative between our worlds. One minute of your world can be hours here," she pointed out. "But the most important rule of this place is that you cannot stay after the waking sun. You have to go now," she urged me again.

"Can I come back again?" I asked urgently. I hadn't got what I came for – a way for Tristan to live.

"As much as I enjoy your visits, Gray, I don't advise it. It is a tricky affair, counting on your guardian spell to protect you in here. But no human spell can save you from this sun, Joe. And that is why you need to leave now."

"You have to help us first!" I begged.

"Why? Why would I help you?"

I stared at her for a moment before answering, "Because...because I-I love him," I said, crying, despair filling my heart.

"Yes, I have heard that plea before, Joe. From many others. Love is very common of your race. I don't blame you for trying to stay together. I have seen many before you, and I will see many after you're gone. When he leaves, it will hurt. But this pain will pass," she said, wiping a tear from my face with her long, slender fingers. "You have to go now," she informed me one last time.

The scorching sun of fire was almost in the middle of the

sky, burning everything in its wake. The heat felt like it was burning me from inside, making my blood boil. I slumped over the hot sand, too tired to sit any more. I just wanted to curl up and sleep. I remembered Tristan's voice somewhere in time. It seemed like so long ago since I last heard his voice...I felt like I had been here for centuries.

"Wake up now, Joe," Sky said, walking slowly over to me, her heavy black boots crunching on the melting sand.

"I-I...don't know how," I whispered, trying to keep my eyelids open, trying to resist sleep. Numbness was taking over my whole body. I could feel tears streaming down my face. They were burning hot over my skin.

Sky kneeled in front of me, and just seconds before I closed my eyes, she pressed her thumb over my forehead. A sharp piercing pain shot through my head, making me flinch, and all my body seemed to be washed away by a cold rushing sensation.

The next thing I remembered was opening my eyes in a dark room. My room. All my instincts were shouting for me to stay still and remain calm, to get back to reality slowly, but I panicked and bolted up, gasping for air. I clutched my throat with one hand, searching desperately for help with the other. I found Tristan lying by my side and gripped him hard, but I couldn't speak! I still could feel the scorching heat from the desert place, burning me from inside.

Everything hurt. I fell back down on the mattress and my body convulsed as I shut my eyes tight, because of the blinding headache piercing my skull. My stomach twisted inside, making me feel sick. I cried out in pain and heard Tristan's trembling voice telling me to breathe. Just keep breathing. Relax. Calm down. Everything was going to be all right.

I felt his body holding me, his voice drifting inside my

head, his touch making the pain in my body slowly melt away. I sighed and relaxed; I wasn't suffocating any more. I could breathe!

"Joey? Joey? Can you hear me? God, please, let her be okay!" I heard him whispering over me. I breathed for a while before answering him.

"I'm fine," I mumbled, slowly trying to open my eyes. My voice sounded crooked and parched. For now, I was focusing all my energy on breathing. Slowly, deeply, inhale, exhale...

"What happened?" he asked me anxiously. His voice sounded anguished, shattered. He was suffering, seeing me in pain like that. "Was it Vigil? Did he hurt you, in your dreams? I'm going to kill him," I heard him growl, with so much fear and anger in his voice. I fluttered my eyes open and looked at him.

"I think I'm okay now," I said weakly. "It wasn't Vigil. God, my head, it hurts so much," I said, grabbing my throbbing head. A wave of nausea hit me like a punch in the stomach and I stood up fast, trying to walk to the bathroom. I didn't want to throw up in the middle of the room! My legs gave away and I would have fallen to the ground if it weren't for Tristan's speed. He grabbed me before I hit the floor, his face a mask of worry.

"Bathroom...feeling sick...fast," I managed to say, and he carried me there quickly, putting me carefully on the floor by the toilet. Another wave of nausea hit me and I threw up for the longest minute of my life. I felt his hands pulling my hair away from my face, his body pressing into mine, giving me support to remain upright. After a while, I stopped throwing up and felt a little better, so I tried to move away, but Tristan stopped me.

"Take it easy. Sit still for a while," he said, wiping the sweat off my face. Seth's hands appeared at my side, holding a glass of water for me to drink. I took it with shaking hands and drank a few gulps.

I looked at both boys. There was so much fear in their eyes.

"I'm sorry to scare you like this," I murmured. I was feeling so tired, like I had just run an entire marathon. I have never been sick like this before. This was the price for staying in the desert place for too long. Heavily taxed and duly collected.

"What happened, Joe?" Tristan asked, frightened.

"You're going to be mad at me," I began, and then, sitting there on the cold, tiled bathroom floor, I told him everything about my visit with Sky. I cried the whole time. When I'd finished telling him all that had happened, he hugged me close to him, and rocked me softly with his body, saying that everything was going to be all right. But how could he say that? We had lost our only hope! Sky couldn't, or wouldn't, save him.

"We will figure something out, Joey. Please, stop crying. It hurts me so much to see you crying," he whispered in a heartbreaking sob as he held me in his arms. "I still have hope. There is always a way. You can't lose faith like that."

His words kept bouncing in my head. It was the same thing I'd said to Death in the end. *There's always a way.* Perhaps it was only a lie we kept telling ourselves to keep going. Or was it a real possibility? Whatever it might be, all I knew was that I wasn't done fighting yet. Tristan was right. I shouldn't be upset like this, like I had just giving up on everything. Giving up on him. So I stopped crying and hugged him back. I could feel his relief seeping through his arms into me.

"I'm so sorry, Tris. I don't know what came over me." I lifted my head to meet his eyes. "I will never lose faith in us. You're right, there's always a way." I repeated his words and smiled at him. "I would kiss you right now, but I don't think it's a good thing, cos, you know, the barfing and all . . ." I mumbled in embarrassment.

He laughed quietly at my silliness. "Okay. We can leave the kissing for later. Just promise me you won't try that stunt again," Tristan pleaded.

"Oh, I don't plan on doing that ever again, if I can help it! It was brutal. And it's not like I planned it; it was totally an accident that I ended up there tonight!" I said, trying to get up but stopping, cringing, when pain still shot through my body. Tristan grabbed me and carried me to my bed, laying me down carefully like I was made of crystal.

"Try to get some rest now, Joey," he said, brushing his fingers slowly through my hair, and I drifted almost immediately into a blessedly uninterrupted and uneventful sleep.

Chapter Thirty-Five

Graduation

The next day I woke up feeling like a freaking train had hit me. Twice. My body ached all over; I think even my hair hurt, if that were actually possible. Tristan didn't let me get out of bed. He told me we were calling in sick today. I raised my eyebrow at the "we" part, but he said he was staying to take care of me. And he wasn't *asking*, he was *telling* me, he said with quite the imperative voice. He was kind of sexy when he got all bossy like that. I was too weak to contradict him anyway, so I snuggled back under my blankets.

I spent the whole day drifting in and out of sleep, and my stomach still hurt a little whenever I was awake. Sometimes Tristan would wake me to give me something to eat, or one of the boys or Tiffany would come and check on me between classes. At the end of the school day, Harry came in and sat by my side, hugging me for a long time. I guess Seth had pretty much scared him to death with his tale of my desert expedition. When I woke up, Harry wasn't there any more, and instead Sammy was in the room, sitting on the floor and leaning by my bed, reading a book. Every time I turned over on my bed, I caught one of the boys around the room, doing something and keeping me company. Tristan was always a constant. Always there, always vigilant, never leaving my side.

It took me two days to get back on my feet. My little "adventure" had taught me a hard lesson: you don't overdo time in Death's domain and leave unscathed. I was lucky I had walked out with merely sore limbs and a weak stomach. It could have been so much worse.

By Wednesday, I was feeling normal again and insisted on going out despite Tristan's protests. School routine would make me feel more normal too, helping me divert my mind from grim future predictions and depressing thoughts.

I talked with my mom a lot during that week too. I guess I was feeling a little homesick, and hearing her voice helped get better and heal faster. I told her about the grim news on Tristan's deadline. I bet hearing all that terrible news had her really worried, but she never let it show, keeping her voice calm and reassuring as she tried to keep my spirits up during the whole time we talked.

Weeks passed and graduation loomed. Tristan, the boys and I talked endlessly between classes and rehearsals, trying to come up with a way to allow Tristan to remain living past the next New Year. But we were dealing with the unknown – it wasn't as if you could Google "How to keep a ghost alive permanently"! All our research so far had proved futile, including Miss Violet's occult leads. I tried to remain positive, though: after graduation, we'd still have half a year left before New Year.

We only had a few more weeks before we would get our final results, and then we'd have to start thinking about what came next. I had no idea whatsoever. I only knew

Tristan's problem was top priority now. And if I had to put my studies on hold until everything was sorted, then so be it. I couldn't think of university applications or any plans for the future besides trying to find a solution for Tristan's deadline. I was glad my mother wasn't pressuring me about my studies and career choices.

All of our new original songs for music class were finished and practiced to exhaustion. We still needed to perform them one last time for Professor Rubick, and then wait for our grades, but we were confident we'd score the highest marks: we had worked very hard on those songs. Rehearsals were the only time we saw Tristan truly happy, so we practiced as often as possible, even though we didn't really need to. Playing was the one thing keeping us all sane during this madness of magic deadlines.

Exams passed in the blink of an eye. We were constantly busy, rehearsing even more now because now we'd been booked for our first ever gig, as the band playing at graduation! So we spent all our time focusing on our show for the closing ceremony celebration and working on our stage performance. We didn't worry about our outfits, since Tiffany was in charge of that and we trusted she would ace them. I wasn't over-anxious about my exam results, but the show was worrying me.

Before I knew it, the day of the concert was upon us. Graduation had been really emotional, especially for our parents, who cried openly during the entire ceremony. My mother had managed a front seat and smiled at Tristan and me so proudly it almost made me start crying as well. I got to see all the boys' parents and family, too, after the diplomas were delivered. It had been exciting, exhausting and overwhelming all at the same time.

I was heading to my room to start getting dressed for the show, when I saw Tristan talking with a short, middle-aged man in the hallway. Tristan was speaking calmly, while the man replied excitedly, waving his hands a lot, clearly impressed by Tristan or what he was saying. I tried to sneak closer to catch what they were talking about, but before I got halfway there the man waved Tristan goodbye and took off fast. Tristan turned around, saw me approaching and walked towards me.

"Hey!" I greeted him.

"Hey, Tangerine!" he said with a smile. Tangerine was his nickname for me when we were in public. He only called me Buttons in private. Before I could ask what the guy had wanted, both of our cell phones rang with new messages.

"Tiffany," we both said at the same time as we checked our phones and discovered we each had the same text:

get your @$$es up here ASAP!! need 2 get U ready 4 the show! @ your room! XoXo.

We ran to our room as fast as we could, passing a few students who waved at us, excited about our upcoming show.

"So who was that?" I asked as I ran, panting at Tristan's side.

"What? Oh, yeah. That was Lisa's father. You know Lisa? She's been in all our rehearsals, remember? She has that weird spiked blue hair, kinda hard to miss," he explained when he noticed my puzzled face. "She must talk about us all the time, and her dad was curious about us."

I grunted under my breath. *"Us."* Right. She must talk about *Tristan* all the time, was more likely! She probably had their wedding planned already! The Lost Boys were starting to attract groupies!

When we arrived at our room, Tiffany was bustling with clothes and face paints everywhere. She'd done a tremendous job with the outfits; they were all amazing! She was really talented!

Tristan didn't allow much customizing on him, so he ended up the most "normal" looking of all of us. He had on his jeans and T-shirt, all black, and Tiffany had managed to convince him to wear some more beaded wristbands, mostly in gray and black. He had a short necklace string on his neck with a black stone, too. It looked sexy on him.

Josh was dressed in black jeans too, but with an olive T-shirt and ragged vest, and lots of necklaces and cloth wristbands. He looked tough and dangerous. Sammy and Seth wore gray jeans, brown-and-green shirts and vests. They also had beaded wristbands, and leather necklaces threaded with twigs, stones and feathers. They looked like a collection of wild adventurers!

Tiffany had created different "war paint" on each of our faces, mostly in black, gray and olive green; only Harry and I had orange and red marks. He wore his customary olive baggy shorts and his chest was bare save for a ragged vest, showing off his green and red tattoo. He was wearing lots of cool necklaces and wristbands, too.

And then there was me. Tiffany had chosen olive shorts for me, just like Harry's, a red tank-top and my well-worn black boots. I had the coolest necklaces and wristbands of them all, because Tiffany was a tad biased and had picked the better-looking ones for me, the only girl in the band.

She'd insisted I leave my hair down, but had made lots of thin braids with tiny sparkly beads tied all around them. Then she made small marks with orange paint on my arms, my nose and cheekbones. It looked so cool! I beamed proudly at my reflection. I had never been much into dressing up, but I was having the time of my life with this! After she was done accessorizing, Tiffany left us to go in search of the best spot in the front row to record us playing. Then it was show time!

We all high-fived each other and headed to the auditorium, everybody cheering, feeling excited and a little nervous as well. The tension built up the closer we got to the stage door. There wasn't any sound coming from inside, though. Weird. We opened the door a little and peeked inside. The lights were all on, but the room was empty. There wasn't anyone in there. We all entered, our shoulders hunched. We looked around, trying to at least find our instruments. We had made a last soundcheck the previous night, and left our guitars, bass and drums all ready in there, but we couldn't find any of them anywhere.

"Maybe it's cancelled? And they forgot to tell us?" Harry suggested.

"Maybe they have changed the day? Maybe it's tomorrow..." Sam added.

"I'm sure everything is fine," Tristan reasoned, "We should find Professor Rubick. He'll know what's going on."

We were huddled in a circle, discussing where to look for Professor Rubick first, when Tiffany bustled into the room, flushed and out of breath.

"There you are! What's the hold-up, people? There's a show to do, and you're all here, chatting like you have all the time in the world! Come on!"

"Uh, Tiff? What's going on? Why there isn't anyone in here?" I spoke on behalf of the band.

"Because the show is *outside*!" she said, exasperated.

"What? Nobody told us!" Seth exclaimed in surprise.

"There were too many people wanting to see you guys, and there wasn't enough room in the auditorium! And the crowd is getting impatient! Hurry up! Let's go!" she said, clapping her hands urgently as she dashed out.

We all ran after her, with wide eyes and shocked faces. As soon we started to get near the west wing of the building, we could hear the noise of the crowd. All the boys looked nervous, except Tristan, who was smiling like he was having the time of his life. How could he be so cool about it? The noise was getting louder and louder by the second. And I was getting more anxious by the second too.

"Professor Rubick's been freaking out at the amount of people that showed up to see you! It's not just kids from our school, too." Tiff chuckled, gazing at the distance. "Okay, then. I'll be right at the front, recording the show! Rock on, Lost Boys!" she cheered, then kissed Seth hard and gave a quick peck on the lips to all the boys, including me at the end of the line. Then she darted outside.

"Did you all see that? She just kissed Joey on the lips!" Sam said, all excited.

I turned to see all the boys staring at me with glazed, dreamy expressions. "Huh. Only boys could get hung up on that, with all this happening right outside!" I said, nervously gesturing towards the noise coming from the entrance. That seemed to snap them all back to reality.

Tristan turned to look at us, smiling broadly. "Come on! This is going to be great! We have nothing to worry about! Let's just go and have some fun!" he said, all cheerful.

"How are you not freaking out over this?" I asked, a little scared.

He shrugged calmly, still smiling. "I'm just not. I just enjoy each day as if it were my last, that's all. It takes the edge off, you should all try it!" And then he looked intently at me. "And you are Joe Gray! You don't scare easily, remember?" he said with a wink.

We all stared at him still with worried faces.

"Look, it's like this," he said. "The best thing that can happen is people will like us. The worst, people won't. What's so horrible about that? Who cares what they think? We are here to do something we love to do. So let's just go up there and do it already!" He clapped his hand firmly on Seth's back before heading outside. Well, he already had the rock star attitude nailed down, that was for sure!

Harry seemed to be thinking on the same lines because he grinned and shouted, "Hell, yeah!" before following Tristan. And then we heard him yelling outside, "Don't need to shout any more, The Lost Boys are in da hooouse!"

We all laughed hard and followed in his footsteps, ready to face a loud, electrified crowd.

I don't remember much of the show, apart from the noise and cheers. I do remember stepping up on stage and looking out at a whole lot more people than I'd been expecting, and seeing Tristan smiling reassuringly at me. As soon the boys picked up their guitars, the crowd began to cheer even louder. We heard Josh banging his drumsticks three times, our cue to start the first song. The rest was a blur.

I also remember stepping down off the stage, and walking inside the building again, to avoid the mass of people crushing us. Girls huddled around me, shouting and asking questions. I don't remember what they asked and what

I said. It was all totally insane and surreal and very, very chaotic. Then our parents came over to congratulate us – the Hunts, Ledgers and the Harts. My mom was also there, shouting something and hugging me with a big grin on her face. Professor Rubick did almost all the talking with our families. He was beaming with so much pride. It took almost an hour for the rumpus to subdue and the crowd to disperse a little. I left my mom talking with the other parents and went in search for my band.

I found Tiffany first. She hugged me tight, saying I had kicked ass up there, and we walked slowly out of the mess of people. We spotted Seth far away at the school front doors. He was talking to the same middle-aged man that Tristan had been talking to earlier – Lisa's father, I remembered. We were walking in their direction when the man shook Seth's hand vigorously, and scurried quickly away before we could reach them.

When we got to Seth, he turned to look at us with a blank, unfocused stare. He looked pale and in deep shock. Something had happened. I couldn't get a good read of his eyes because he had a jumble of emotions crashing inside. I put my hand on his shoulder and shook him gently, trying to nudge him back to reality. He was staring behind me to a spot on the horizon, gazing at nowhere in the distance.

"Seth! Are you all right? What happened?" I asked. Tiffany was looking worriedly at him too. He finally shifted his gaze, focusing on me for the first time.

"Uh ... hey, Joey. When did you get here?"

I glanced at Tiffany in concern. "Seth, is everything all right?"

"Uh, it's ..." he mumbled incoherently, and then he shook his head lightly. "You're never gonna believe this ..."

Chapter Thirty-Six

Recording

"What? Believe what, Seth?" I asked again, getting impatient now. He stared down at his hands. He held a small, silver-edged business card between his fingers, and he kept flipping it over, again and again.

"I'll have to get my dad to look at this," he said again in wonder.

"Seth, come on! Talk to me. Is this something to do with Lisa's father? The guy you were talking to just now?" It had to be.

Seth glanced up, looking at me curiously. "You mean Mr. Silver?" he asked. "You know him?"

"No. I saw him speaking with Tristan earlier..." I said.

"That was Scott Silver," Seth told me, with admiration in his voice.

"You mean, *the* Scott Silver?" Tiffany asked, looking stunned.

Seth turned to her, squinting his eyes suspiciously. "Did you have anything to do with this, Tiffany?" he suddenly accused.

"What? With what?" I asked cluelessly, getting frustrated.

Tiffany grabbed my arm excitedly. "Scott Silver is a big music producer! He owns several record companies!" she explained, her voice getting high-pitched. "What did he say to you, Seth?"

"He just offered The Lost Boys a record deal," Seth told us plainly.

I gaped at him in total shock.

"Tiff, did you ask him to do this?" Seth repeated sharply. He hated asking Tiffany for any favors. It was a big issue between them.

"I swear to God I didn't do anything!" Tiffany bellowed, offended. "I know his name, but I've never actually met the man! My father knows him, but you *forbade* me to try anything, so I never did!" she said, emphasizing the "forbade" part, because she was always a little miffed when anyone ordered her around. Worthingtons weren't used to it!

Tristan appeared behind us then, looking at our little group with curious eyes. "Hey, there you are. I've been looking all over for you!" he said, wrapping an arm around my waist.

"So this means you guys have a record deal, then?" Tiff squealed loudly.

"Ah, you talked to Mr. Silver, then?" Tristan asked, grinning. Everybody stopped abruptly and gawked at Tristan. "He came and talked to me this morning. Joey was there, she saw us, right?" he said, looking at me and winking.

"Why didn't you say anything?" I asked, shocked.

"I did tell you. Well, part of it, that is. Lisa is a big fan of our band, and she talks about us all the time. She'd even recorded a few of our classroom concerts on her cell, and showed them to her dad. He came today to see us perform live. I didn't tell you because you were all freaking out enough already. I knew it was a done deal, though," he said, smiling broadly. "Because I know we are amazingly good. We just needed to show it today."

"GET THE F—!!" I started to shout, and Tristan clapped his hand over my mouth.

"Okay, no need to swear, now! So, a record deal, eh?" Tristan asked, uncovering my mouth and tapping Seth cheerfully on the back.

Then Tiffany began shrieking and jumping, hugging Seth, who just stood there limply and let himself be hugged and squealed at.

The rest of the band arrived at this moment and I fought with Seth to see who was going to tell them first. Seth and I kept talking over each other, while Tristan and Tiffany laughed at our overly-eager, excited faces.

When we'd finished our battle to share the big news, we looked at the boys to watch their reactions. Sam laughed so hard that he ended up on rolling on the floor, pulling Seth along with him. Josh went pale with shock, just like Seth had a few minutes ago, but then he snapped out of it and jumped on top of Seth and Sam on the floor, joining in their celebration. Harry just watched them in silence, a huge grin plastered on his face, before climbing on top of the pile of Lost Boys on the floor. I shouted "Pile-up!" and jumped on top of Harry, and Tristan and Tiffany followed my lead. It was the best pile-up of all time! We celebrated our asses off that night.

The next day would be our last at school, and it was the day we were supposed to say our goodbyes and head home before we decided what we were going to do with our lives. Josh had been accepted at Harvard, but it wasn't really what he wanted to do, more what his parents wanted. He was incredibly relieved when the news of the record deal came up. Seth and Sam both had a place at a Performing Arts school, but were putting that on hold as well. Harry hadn't considered anything for the future yet. Now he didn't need to worry about it any more. This was everything he had dreamed of happening for his future life.

All our plans were going to change completely now, because of the record deal. We needed to sign contracts with Mr. Silver as soon as possible, and then begin the recording and producing process of our first album. I couldn't believe it: we were going to make our own album! All our parents had been flabbergasted at the news, but they were very supportive and rearranged everything they could to make this happen for us.

Tiffany was supposed to travel to Europe to stay with her parents, but she postponed it to stay with us until her Christmas visit. Mr. Silver told us we had a year to produce this album, with six months to record the songs and soundtracks in a small studio he'd found for us in Esperanza, and the other six months to finalize producing, marketing the release, radio interviews and a few shows to help promote the album around the state. After all that, we had to sit and wait for the response of the public and go from there.

He also lent us a small house right next to the recording studio, as we were going to spend most of our time in there, working on our songs. We called it the Green House because it was all painted in vivid green outside. The house had all we needed to do our work; it even had three bedrooms and two sofa beds in the lounge if we wanted to crash there for the night. The recording booth was booked only for a few specific dates, and we would play there only when we had everything worked out perfectly to be recorded. Recording studio sessions were really expensive, so we couldn't waste any time in there.

Since Seth was the only one who lived out of state, and was theoretically "homeless" in Esperanza, it was decided he would stay with Tiffany in one of the many houses the Worthingtons owned in the area. But Tiffany and Seth were constantly in my house anyway. They had adopted my mom already, and vice-versa. They had a lot of sleepovers, and I was happy to share my room with Tiff whenever she wanted to, and Tristan shared his with Seth. So, when we weren't at the studio, or at the Green House next door, we hung out mostly at my home. Harry, Josh and Sam already crashed at mine too whenever they wanted. My mom was so happy with so many kids around the house all the time, she looked like she was going to explode with joy! It was like she had adopted a bunch of loud, hyper-active kids all of a sudden.

Now we were not only best friends, we were like family. We worked, ate, slept and played together. And Tristan and I didn't have to hide anything from anybody any more. We agreed to keep it low-key when we were around my house, because we hadn't told my mom about us yet, but otherwise we were free to be an official couple. He hugged and kissed me all the time at the studio, and made me sit on his lap even when there were plenty of places to sit elsewhere. I was on cloud nine with all his lovely attention.

The guys that worked at the studio teased and laughed at us constantly, saying we were the cutest couple they had ever seen, which always made Tristan grin from ear to ear. Tristan, of course, knew all the guys working there by the end of the first week – their names, the names of their families and their life stories, from the producer and sound-check guy to the janitor and security guards. And they all loved having him around, and tried to get his attention as much as they could, to talk to and even ask for advice. It was funny hearing them talk sometimes; a bunch of old guys asking advice from an eighteen-year-old kid, even if he had been around longer than any of them.

During those months working on the album, we also paid regular visits to Miss Violet. She was trying to find out more about a conjuring spell that could help us with Vigil. She kept saying she needed more time and that we couldn't do anything but wait patiently. But time was becoming increasingly valuable for Tristan.

There was a shadow looming over my heart; a weight constantly on my shoulders. The excitement of what was happening with our record deal might keep it at bay, but I felt it more keenly every time we walked out of Miss Violet's house without a plan.

I tried to cover up my anxiety the best I could, to help Tristan remain strong, but I could see that as the end of the year approached, Tristan began to falter. He didn't laugh as much, his eyes didn't shine so bright, even when we were playing. He was growing afraid we might have no way out of this.

We had all signed our contracts with Mr. Silver, except Tristan. He kept putting it off, making up excuses every time he was asked to sign the paperwork. He'd managed to stall Mr. Silver and his record company for a long time. And by the end of October, when we started to actually record our tracks, Tristan had convinced everybody to let his songs and his parts be recorded last. I started noticing he had drifted from being inside the booth playing, to staying outside, helping out with the producing part. Nobody else in the band noticed his strategic shift; everybody was busy and focused hard on playing the best they could. The boys thought he was having more fun working on the mixing desk, and they left him to it. But I understood well enough what he was up to. He was discreetly stepping back, little by little, taking care that no one noticed *what* he was doing. And *why*.

"You're trying to stay off this album!" I accused him bluntly.

Tristan sighed, knowing I would catch up with his plan sooner or later. "Joe, please."

"You are and you know it," I insisted. "Why haven't you signed your contract yet with Mr. Silver?"

"You haven't signed yet?" Seth chipped in, surprised.

"No, he hasn't!" I ratted him out.

"What's going on, man?" Josh and Seth asked together.

Tristan pursed his lips and stared at the floor. "I'm just trying to be practical here, guys. We don't know what will happen at the end of the year."

"Tris, please, don't say that!" I protested vehemently.

"No! It's true, Joey. I know every time I bring this up you get really mad, but we have to face it! I may not be here next year! And then what are you all going to do? I'm going to screw this up for you! Everything you have worked so hard to achieve!" he said, standing up in aggravation. "How are you going to explain my disappearance then? What are you going to do with the songs I'm on? I don't want that. It's best I stay behind the glass at the recording booth."

"Look, I get it," Josh said, standing up. "But you are really going at it the wrong way. Even if you are right, and something happens at New Year, that's no reason you shouldn't do this with us right now! We are in this together!"

"You are going to be on this album no matter what happens," Seth added.

"You can't bail on us now," Harry said.

Tristan stared thoughtfully at his friends.

"So, are we on the same page, here?" Seth asked, staring at him hard.

Tristan took a while to respond, but then he sighed quietly and looked Seth in the eyes. "Yeah. We are," he answered and smiled faintly. "If that's what you really want. I'm in."

"All right, then." Seth nodded happily while the boys in the back cheered. I kneeled in front of Tristan and put my hands over his legs, looking straight at him. So much sorrow passed through his eyes.

"I'll sign the contract tomorrow and I'll start recording my songs," he said, resigned, trying to appease me.

"Tristan, please. Don't be like this," I pleaded again. "You should be excited about it, not sad like this."

"I...I know. I'm sorry, Joey. It's just...I have this huge ticking clock hanging over my head all the time. It's driving me nuts," he muttered. "I try to keep the hope up, but sometimes it's hard.

"I know it is. But I promise we'll find a way." And I leaned in, giving him a small kiss.

After that day, Tristan tried to act cheerful for our sake, pretending everything was fine and that he was staying positive and holding on to hope, but he wasn't very convincing. I could sense depression setting in. He was more quiet and contemplative, and he would stare at nowhere with blank eyes whenever he thought nobody was watching him. But his gloomy moods came and went away in turns. Sometimes he did look truly hopeful.

Miss Violet finally called us for a meeting in her home. She had been contacting many of her witch friends all around the world to find a spell for us. Tristan and I were sitting on her living-room couch on the first day of December, listening to what she had discovered. We only had a month now. Tristan's hourglass of sand had almost run out. New Year was coming.

So far, things didn't look promising.

Miss Violet suggested she could try an old powerful spell that would intensify the magical protective properties of Tristan's beaded wristband, preventing Vigil from getting close to him after New Year had passed. If Vigil couldn't get close to Tristan, he could not "fix" him. It was worth a try.

However, it seemed that, for this spell to work, we needed to invoke Vigil. He needed to be present in our actual physical world in order to conclude the spell and keep him away from Tristan. The risk? Tristan needed to be there too, beaded wristband in place. Even though Vigil would be restrained in some sort of magical barrier, it was a big risk

"Okay, let's do this," Tristan agreed after we'd spent long hours debating the plan.

"Tristan! It's too dangerous! There must be another way!" I exclaimed. "You can't! I-I...forbid you!" I huffed, the same way he had done the first time we talked about my meeting with Sky.

He shot me an annoyed glance. "Don't mind her. She's just being a smart mouth," he said, turning to look at Miss Violet. "Do you really think this spell could work, Miss Violet?" he asked.

Miss Violet seemed to ponder the question for a while

and then she replied, "Yes. It is risky, but...it can be done, I think," she said.

"I'm running out of time." He put a consoling arm around me. "I'm willing to take the risk."

"B-but..."

"And I want to meet him," he added suddenly.

I reeled back in surprise. "Why do you want to meet Vigil?"

"I want to talk to him. Man to man."

"He's not a man!" I snapped, upset.

"Okay. Man to unearthly being, then."

"Why?"

"Listen, Joe, do you have any other ideas?" Tristan snapped sharply. "Because if you don't, I'm doing this. And maybe if I talk to him I can reason with him. Maybe if he sees I'm a real person, he'll change his mind. I need to try something! Anything! I can't just sit here and wait for my time to run out!" he exclaimed, and leaned back on the couch, staring hard at me. "Are you with me?"

I stared back at him, hard, but he was adamant. I sighed loudly and uncrossed my arms. "Yes. I'm with you," I muttered, resigned. I had a bad feeling about this, but Tristan was right. We should try anything that might help him and save his life.

"Good. It's settled, then," he said, and turned eagerly to Miss Violet. "When can we do this, Miss Violet? Can we do it today?"

Miss Violet snorted loudly. "Of course not!" she said, waving him away. "I need to be prepared. It's not a cheap parlor trick I'm doing here, boy!"

"When, then?" he pressed.

"I need a week or so. We can try next Saturday," she said, sniffing loudly.

"Okay. Next Saturday it is! Thank you so much, for all your help, for everything, Miss Violet," he said, making amends. "I'll be for ever in your debt."

"That's all right. Now, you two go away and let me get to work here," she said, shooing us out.

The following Friday night we had a little dinner at the Green House – me, Tristan and all the boys – before the big day. The boys insisted on being there for support as well, and Seth had the idea of making a nice meal and celebrating our friendship before we embarked on this dangerous venture. We missed Tiffany, who was finally doing her duty and visiting her parents, but we toasted her in her absence. It was a happy evening, spent with the best friends in the world. We sat on the floor in the lounge of the Green House, eating pasta and reminiscing about our good old days at school. It didn't feel like almost a year ago that I had first arrived at Sagan's front gates, all splashed in mud.

But the whole time, Tristan and I couldn't help thinking about what tomorrow would bring. Whenever the boys noticed Tristan or me getting edgy, they would try to cheer us up with jokes and positive thoughts. We were all going to be there for him tomorrow when the spell was cast. We went to bed really early but I don't think anybody got any sleep that night; the thought of what we were about to do the next day loomed eerily over all our heads.

Chapter Thirty-Seven

Lady Knight

The next day, we were all subdued. Even Harry was in his "quiet mode", and Sammy had quit all his jokes for the day. Josh and Seth kept glancing between each other and back at Tristan all the time.

Miss Violet had said she needed the whole afternoon to gather the ingredients for the spells, and she needed to be left alone to concentrate on getting everything sorted out at the cemetery. We were to arrive there at sunset. This was the best hour to perform the spell.

There were actually three spells to be cast: the invocation spell that would call Vigil to the cemetery; a containment spell that would keep him restrained and imprisoned in a magic circle; and the hinder spell that was supposed to keep Vigil away from Tristan for good. This was the spell that would save Tristan's life. It was also the hardest to perform.

Miss Violet told us she was going to cast the spells in the middle of the grass circle in the centre of the cemetery, the same place Tristan had first physically "appeared" to us.

She told us it was the strongest magical spot in the whole of Esperanza.

I wondered if any containment spell would be strong enough to hold Vigil. If he broke through, Tristan would be lost. Miss Violet said it was the most powerful containment spell she knew of. It could be used to bind any supernatural being and in ancient times had commonly been used to summon Death – so even Sky could not escape it. Miss Violet also said that she had prepared a backup plan. If something went wrong, she could break the connection by chanting a three-word incantation, and Vigil would be sent straight back to wherever he came from. It was like an emergency evacuation button. She had covered all bases and tried to make this as safe as possible for all of us.

We left the house a couple of hours before sunset to meet Miss Violet. Tristan wanted to get to the cemetery early, to get prepared. We walked through the cemetery lanes in silence, the boys a few feet ahead of us. It was the first time we had been to the cemetery with them, and I could see how worried and scared they all looked as they shuffled through the quiet lanes.

Tristan held my hand and stroked his thumb absent-mindedly over it, like he always did whenever he was deep in thought. We walked quickly to the grass circle in the old part of the cemetery to find Miss Violet kneeling there with her hand on the grass and her eyes closed. When she heard us approaching, she raised her head and snapped her eyes open.

"Don't step on the grass, *any of you*!" she ordered harshly. "And be quiet."

We stood there for a long time, staring at her and preparing ourselves for the magic hour. She kept muttering quietly under her breath, but I couldn't make out any actual words. Then she stood up and waved at us.

"You can come over now. Don't get too near the centre, though, am I clear?" she bellowed in a stern voice. Everybody nodded, too scared to say anything. All the boys positioned themselves close to Tristan, surrounding him in a protective huddle, and I stood a few feet in front of Tristan with my back to them. I had dealt with Vigil before and I saw myself as Tristan's guardian. I should be in front of them, shielding Tristan from sight. If things went wrong, I could protect him.

Miss Violet grabbed a bottle filled with a thick white liquid and turned to face us. "Everything's set now. So, are you ready? When I finish pouring this, the spells are going to be put in motion," she told us. I turned to look at Tristan. He gave me a nervous smile and a short nod. I turned again and nodded to Miss Violet too. We were ready.

"Let's do this," I said.

Miss Violet poured the liquid then, using it to draw a white circle on the grass, a few feet in front of me. We waited a few seconds, wondering if this was going to work. Miss Violet kept muttering in a low tone as she walked to the border of the grassed area. I watched her take position on my far right. When I turned my face back to the white circle, Vigil was already standing inside.

One second there was nothing, the next second he was there in the middle of the circle, looking directly at me. In my dreams, he was always somewhat shifty, a blurry image, not really defined, even when he took human form. This time he was very clear.

Long black locks of soft hair fell over his pale, angelic, androgenous face. He was wearing gray pants and a gray short-sleeved shirt. He looked about my age, if not younger; delicate and frail. You could almost mistake him for a weak boy. But I knew better. It was just a very clever disguise. He was neither weak nor fragile.

Vigil looked confused for a split second, before he resumed his blank expression. He hastily assessed his surroundings and turned his gaze back to me. Then he tried taking a step forward and stopped abruptly, puzzlement flashing across his face to be quickly replaced by blankness again. He glanced down curiously at the white line on the ground.

"Restrainment. Clever," he said, amused, and looked up at Miss Violet. She didn't say anything, just stared back at him with serious eyes. Vigil stared back for a while and then turned his face to me, watching me unblinkingly. "Is this how you treat me, Joey, after all the help I have given you?" he accused coldly.

I felt immensely guilty, but I couldn't back down now. "I'm sorry, Vigil, I really am. But this was a necessary precaution we had to take. You're a threat."

"I am a threat?"

"Yes, you want to hurt Tristan," I explained.

He frowned, deeply displeased with my last line. "I do not '*want*' anything. What I *have to do* is just put Tristan back where he belongs, nothing more. I have told you this before. Why do you insist on not understanding this?" he said, and I caught a hint of resentment in his voice.

"I understand. I just don't accept it," I told him.

Miss Violet started chanting quietly, but Vigil caught the words and glared fiercely at her. Then he waved a hand and Miss Violet appeared to choke and splutter, losing her voice.

"So this is what you wanted of me after all. Your witch is trying to cast a hinder spell to keep me away from your ghost. It is a pity you are so weak and pathetic that you need to vocalize your incantations, old woman. I can take your voice away, and there is nothing else you can do." He turned back to stare at me again. "I cannot be stopped, Joe Gray. As soon as you are no longer his guardian at the end of the year, he is mine for the taking," he promised in a cold voice.

I glanced around, trying desperately to find another way out. Vigil had stopped Miss Violet in her tracks by stealing her voice. She couldn't complete the last spell. She couldn't even chant the emergency spell to get rid of Vigil now. We were royally screwed.

"I need to talk to you, Vigil." Tristan's voice came from behind me.

"Tristan, don't!" I warned with a shout.

"He's here?" Vigil asked, surprised, and then looked sharply at the boys standing behind me. His gaze roamed across all of them, not sure which one was his real target. Tristan's magic wristband was still working, keeping him guarded from Vigil's scrutinizing eyes. But then Tristan took a step forward, revealing himself. Vigil turned his attention immediately to him, squinting his eyes in deadly focus. He made a small movement, but was stopped once again by the magic circle on the grass.

I tensed, worried that Miss Violet's restrainment spell would not hold him. But clearly he couldn't pass.

Vigil and Tristan stared at each other for a long time before Tristan broke the silence.

"I want to ask you something," I heard Tristan say, his voice steady. Vigil's gaze flicked between Tristan and me.

"There is nothing you can offer me, boy. I cannot be bought, or bribed. I will not bargain," Vigil stated. "I will do what I came here to do; that is my purpose. There are rules to be obeyed – you cannot escape the natural order of things," he intoned before Tristan could even say anything. I remembered Vigil's love of rules; I'd already tried that angle with him once.

Tristan seemed to be thinking about Vigil's speech for a second before he spoke again. "All rules have exceptions, yes?" Tristan asked calmly. "You live long enough, this is one of the things you learn eventually. I reckon you have lived for... for ever. You must know this to be true."

Vigil stared at Tristan for some time in silence, pondering his words.

"Yes," Vigil finally conceded. "All rules have exceptions."

"So why can't I be an exception this time?" Tristan asked again.

I smiled. *Clever boy.*

"This is not my decision to make. My duty is only to put things in their rightful places," Vigil answered.

"You can pretend you did. That you fixed this. And then walk away. Nobody would know." Tristan pondered. "If you don't tell, who's to say you did or didn't do your job?"

"There will be questions asked."

"You could lie," Tristan replied.

"I do not lie." Vigil sneered. "I never lie. And I will not lie; not for you, human boy. Not for anybody."

"Better a liar than a murderer," Tristan said bluntly.

"I am not..." Vigil began.

"Ah. But that is *exactly* what you are. That is exactly what you are going to do, Vigil," Tristan cut in. "You can sugar-coat it all you like, but you are going to kill me. And you don't even care. Which makes it even worse," Tristan said hotly.

Vigil's eyes still kept dancing back and forth between

Tristan and me, but he didn't reply. He seemed to be debating something, struggling with an inner fight. His face was still smooth and cool, not showing anything, but his eyes betrayed him. Anger, pride and guilt as the glint of his eyes reflected the eerie light of the setting sun around us. He looked quickly at me again, a cautious nervous sideways glance.

"Why do you keep...?" Tristan started to ask, and then he stopped and stared accusingly at Vigil. Vigil snapped his gaze back to Tristan, and for the first time since he had arrived in the circle, I could see a flash of panic and fear.

Fear? What was Vigil afraid of? The two locked eyes again. Black fathomless eyes staring deep into piercing bright gray ones. I watched them carefully, switching fast from Vigil to Tristan, but I couldn't see what they were feeling. They seemed to be having a silent conversation.

After a few tense seconds Tristan gave a tiny smirk, like he had just understood an inside joke. "That is *never* going to happen," he said quietly, without breaking eye-contact with Vigil's cold hard stare.

Vigil's jaw twitched and clenched; his fist balled up at his sides. He looked angry. Really angry. For a non-human entity, he was sure mimicking human emotions increasingly easily.

"I don't know what you're talking about," Vigil snapped, a menacing tone in his voice and loathing in his eyes.

Tristan stared for a few more seconds in complete silence. "It. Is. Never. Going. To. Happen," Tristan repeated slowly, deliberately, and with the most absolute certainty. He sounded angry too now. "Do you understand the concept of never?"

"Oh, *I do*, ghost boy." Vigil sneered in hatred. "More than you'll ever know."

And then he stepped outside the line.

A loud thunderclap crackled as soon Vigil's foot trespassed. A wave of pure intense energy hit us all, pushing us backwards. When we looked up again, Vigil was outside the circle, staring menacingly at Tristan.

Tristan searched urgently for Miss Violet at the other side of the grassed area, but her body lay crumpled in the grass, motionless.

"The old witch cannot help you any more, ghost boy."

"What did you do to her?" I shouted, running to Miss Violet in panic. Harry and Josh were already there, kneeling by her side. Fear filled my whole mind. He had broken the circle! He had killed Miss Violet!

"She's breathing, she seems all right," Josh consoled me. "The impact must have struck her the most, since she was the spellcaster," he quickly reasoned, but his voice held panic as well. He was scared too, but fiercely trying not to show it.

I turned and started walking towards Tristan at the same time as Vigil began walking towards him too. "How did you break the circle, Vigil? Miss Violet said it was ancient and powerful! Even Death cannot break it!" I said, trying to divert Vigil's attention from Tristan.

He stopped for a second. "When you gave me a name, you gave me this power, Joe Gray. I told you this once," he said, turning to look at Tristan again. "Fear is a powerful thing," he added mockingly.

"I don't understand! What your name has anything to do with this? You're not supposed to cross that line!" I shouted desperately, my mind racing madly. Now that Miss Violet was unconscious and unable to make the emergency break-the-invocation spell, I had to do something myself to stop Vigil.

"I am not *supposed* to?" Vigil said, sneering. "What do you know what I *am* and *am not* supposed to do? Not even Death can hold me against my will. You humans, so presumptuous to think you could hold me with your feeble magic," he said, and turned to face Tristan again. "So conceited... such foolish, small, weak little *things*."

I was still walking fast in Tristan's direction, but when my eyes shifted to him, my heart skipped a beat. His face was contorting in pain. Vigil was doing something to him! "Stop it!" I shouted at Vigil. "Stop hurting him!" I said, running now.

Vigil took a step forward, and Tristan kneeled down, letting out a loud grunt, one hand grabbing at the grass, the other clutching his chest. His knuckles were white with the pressure of his grasp, his face a mask of pain.

"Vigil! DON'T!" I shouted madly when I saw blood trickling out of Tristan's nose. Vigil was killing him! Right in front of my eyes! Everything was happening in slow motion and I felt like I was walking in foam, trying desperately, futilely, to go faster. Vigil was only a few inches away from Tristan now, his face marked by anger and loathing. Tristan held his head up defiantly and looked angrily at Vigil's eyes, which were now glowing an icy white. Ghastly cold enveloped the air around him.

"Decided to show your true nature, Vigil?" Tristan mocked, saying Vigil's name with such venom. I wasn't going to make it; I wasn't going to reach Tristan in time! Vigil was right there already, in front of him. "How does it feel, all this anger, all these *emotions*?" Tristan said, putting emphasis on the last word. "Aren't emotions against the *rules*? Because they sure make you act irrationally, don't you think? Aren't you supposed to be logical and cold now, *Vigil*?" he spat out, and Vigil hesitated.

And that moment of indecision was all it took for me to get between then. I launched myself in front of Tristan, at the last second stopping Vigil from touching him.

"I will *never* let you hurt him!" I growled, breathing heavily and raising an arm protectively. For a fraction of a second, I saw an invisible glassy barrier over my arm. It was wavering and luminescent, and it looked like a ghost of a shield, but somehow it made Vigil step back fast, as if he'd been forcefully pushed by something solid.

And then, with my other fist, I punched him with all the strength I had.

The shock of the impact travelled up through my arm and was so violent that when my fist connected to Vigil's chest, it felt like it would rip my arm from my body. A piercing, blinding light shone from my fists, shooting an energy blast straight to Vigil. It felt as if time were slowing down. All I was focused on was the need to save Tristan! It was the most pure, direct and fierce purpose of my life! I didn't care about the unbearable pain tearing up my arm; it was as if shards of broken freezing glass were shredding my flesh, bones, all my nerve endings. But I didn't care about anything.

I heard Vigil's voice, a loud, distorted cry of pain, and then he crackled and exploded into a million brilliant pieces, vanishing along with the blinding light. And then time rushed back to its normal pace, and I stumbled forward. I had accumulated so much speed that I was caught off balance and fell, hitting the ground fast and hard. I shut my eyes tight, because that bright light felt like it had burned through my eyelids, and when I tried to move the pain redoubled, ripping through the whole right side of my body.

What the hell had just happened? I tried opening my eyes a fraction. I saw Tristan still kneeling in the grass a little further away, looking at me with terror-filled eyes, his hand still tightly clutched tight to his chest. He was breathing in short, labored breaths and was trying to say something to me. I couldn't hear his words, because my ears kept ringing with an annoying buzzing sound. Then Harry was kneeling next to me, cradling me in his arms, checking for damage. Josh, Sam, Seth and a slightly dizzy Miss Violet came over to us too.

"What happened?" I managed to mumble. "Is Tristan okay? See if he's okay!" I shouted in panic at Harry.

And then I heard his voice.

"I'm okay now, Joey. Don't worry about me," Tristan said, and then he was beside me. "Are *you* okay?" he asked urgently, wiping the blood from his face with the back of his hand. The sun had set and the place was getting darker by the second.

"You're bleeding! You're hurt!" I cried out, and tried to reach my hand to touch his face, but I recoiled immediately as a vicious stabbing pain shot through my arm, making me wince as I stumbled back into Harry's arms. I clenched my teeth and cried out in pain again.

"Joey? Where does it hurt?" Tristan's voice reached me, filling with panic. I slowly extended my right arm, the arm I had punched Vigil with. We all watched as a thick, dark liquid ran underneath my skin as if spreading inside my veins, throughout my whole arm. That didn't look good. Everybody was clustered around me now, watching intently with scared wide eyes.

"What the hell? What's happening to my arm?" I grunted, trying to keep my voice level and not sound too frightened. Tristan carefully took my arm, trying not to move it much, and his soft touch made painful stabs pierce through my skin. The dark liquid in my veins was disappearing where Tristan's hand touched my skin. As soon as he realized this, he started moving his hand up my arm, and I cried out in severe pain. It felt like he was cutting my arm with razors wherever his hand touched my skin. He immediately let go of me, scared of hurting me more. The lines started flowing again, and we heard Miss Violet's voice for the first time, coming from behind Seth.

"You have to keep going, Tristan. You have to touch Joey where all the dark lines are in her arm."

"But it's hurting her!" he protested.

"It's for her sake. It'll hurt, but you have to keep going! You saw how they disappeared after you touched them. If they spread any further, God knows what they can do to her."

Tristan looked doubtfully at Miss Violet and then back at me. His eyes were questioning; he didn't like that it was going to hurt me. I looked around at all the scared faces staring back at me. The dark lines were resuming their slow trail up my arm, and it hurt like hell. Soon they would reach my shoulder and chest, and breathing was starting to feel strenuous. I nodded silently and Josh kneeled down by my side, taking my hand in his, to give me support. Harry put both of his hands over my shoulders to hold me still, and Tristan leaned in closer.

"I'm so sorry, Joey. I'll try to do this as quickly as I can, okay?" he whispered with sorrowful eyes.

"I'll be fine, go ahead," I said in a brave voice. Inside I was bracing myself for the pain that would come. I couldn't let him see how much it was hurting.

Tristan started touching my arm, and the stabbing cuts slashed strongly through my skin again. I squeezed Josh's hand, but I didn't cry out this time. I had to be strong and endure this, or Tristan would never keep going. He wouldn't stand seeing me in so much pain.

Gradually the dark lines disappeared beneath Tristan's touch until they were all gone and my arm looked normal again. The pain was subdued now.

"How are you feeling?" Tristan asked worriedly when he had finished.

I flexed my arm a little, testing my fingers and wrists to see if there was permanent damage. A little pain still remained, making my muscles sore and tired, but I kept it to myself. It was a feeble ache now, nothing to worry about. The important thing was that I had my arm back, functioning as normally as it could after such an ordeal, and Tristan was still here. For now at least.

"I'm okay," I said, giving everyone a weak smile. Tristan sighed in relief and took me carefully in his arms, hugging me softly.

"Are you sure?" he whispered in my ear.

"I'm okay, Tris. Are *you* really okay?" I asked, burying my face in his neck. I'd been so scared for him. I couldn't believe I had saved him! He was here! He was fine!

"I'm really okay," he said, smiling. "Thanks to you." But he looked unbelievably exhausted.

Miss Violet looked fairly normal and said she was feeling

perfectly fine, like nothing had happened. She didn't even remember fainting or waking up! Seth told me how they had all watched me throw myself between Tristan and Vigil, and there had been this intense bright light shooting from a spot in the middle, with a loud thundering sound. We had scared them to death! I think the guys had remained somewhat skeptical about this whole magic deal, even after seeing Tristan's fading away trick, but after tonight they had no more doubts.

And now we all knew how truly dangerous Vigil was.

Josh and Sam helped Tristan up and supported his arms over their shoulders, while Harry helped me, and Seth gave a hand to a resisting Miss Violet. Tristan seemed really weak and tired, barely managing to walk. I wasn't feeling in my best shape either: my legs were wobbly and shaky, and my right arm still throbbed a little, sharp stabbing needles piercing painfully through it. All I wanted now was to get back home and get some rest. Tristan and I left the graveyard with weary hearts and tired footsteps, in the arms of our friends.

Chapter Thirty-Eight

Full-Blast Christmas Spirit!

Mom freaked when she saw the state of me, and all the blood on Tristan's shirt, but we reassured her everything was fine and nobody was hurt. She had been waiting anxiously since we left the house a couple hours before sunset, holding her breath until she knew the results of Miss Violet's risky plan. She had wanted to come with us to the cemetery, but I'd pleaded for her to stay behind. I didn't want her to be at risk, too. It would have only been one more person to worry about and I was stressed out enough as it was. I wasn't even sure why I had agreed to the boys coming along. Maybe because they were determined to be there for Tristan and weren't taking no for an answer!

Eventually, Mom was persuaded to take Miss Violet and the boys to the kitchen to hear what had happened and to have a hot cup of tea to calm her nerves. Tristan took off his coat and dirty shirt, and lay down on the couch. I lay down next to him. We were so tired we could barely talk. I don't remember anything else after that. Somehow a blanket and pillow were "magically" produced for us, and we fell asleep right there on the couch for the rest of the night.

The house was dead silent when I blinked awake the next morning. Then I heard noises coming from the kitchen. I knew it was my mom, because she tended to drag her feet way too much over the floor. She shuffled her way to the living room and sat on the couch in front of me. I felt a little uncomfortable lying with Tristan like that while she was watching, so I risked a peek, opening my eyes slowly. Mom was looking at us intently. Okay. Definitely weird, having your mom stare at you while you lay with a boy wrapped around you. Definitely on my Top Ten Awkward Moments list.

I shifted slightly, trying to dislodge myself from Tristan's hold without disturbing his sleep. I thanked the gods that my arm didn't hurt when I moved. Tristan didn't move an inch after I left the couch; his body just slumped a little forward but remained in almost the same position.

"Hi, honey." My mom smiled at me, trying to keep her voice low. "How are you feeling?"

"I'm okay. We were so tired last night. I don't even remember falling asleep," I said, rubbing my eyes.

"How is he?" she asked, worried.

"I think he'll be fine," I said, watching him sleep.

"Seth told me everything that happened yesterday. You were really brave, Joe. I'm so proud of you." She squeezed my hand.

"Really? Thanks, Mom," I said, a little surprised. I'd been thinking she was going to bite my head off because of what I did last night! And she was actually congratulating me? I rested my face on my hands and watched Tristan sleeping. He looked so peaceful. So perfect. For a second I lost myself and completely forgot that my mom was by my side, but her voice snapped me back to reality.

"So, how long have you two been together?" she asked, casually.

"What?" I said, deciding to go for the act-dumb routine.

"Joey, I'm not that stupid! You practically have stars coming out of your eyes every time you look at him, and he's so gaga over you he's not even bothering to pretend to hide it any more! I know intimacy when I see it," she finished smugly. Mom and her freaking detective skills! This was definitely in the running for number one on the Awkward Moments list!

"I hope you've been using protection," she continued, taking my silence for an answer. "I'm too young to be a grandma," she muttered to herself.

Okay, I stand corrected. This was definitely number one on the list.

"Oh my *God*, Mom!" I mumbled, burying my red face in my hands. It was too early in the morning to be having *that* conversation. In fact, it would always be too damn early for that conversation!

My mom smiled at me kindly. "He's your first love," she said quietly. After a few minutes of silence she spoke again. "I'm worried about you, Joe."

"About me? Why?" I asked in surprise.

"Listen, munchkin. I know how it is, to be in love. I *also* know how it is to lose the love of your life. Some people never recover from it. I'm worried about you, because I can see how much you love him...and the end of the year is coming. Honey, please, you must still prepare yourself for the possibility..." She trailed off, unable to continue her sentence.

I knew what she was going to say next. I tried to look away, but Mom touched my face softly, making me look at her again. "I'm sorry, honey. I know it upsets you. He says he's tried talking to you a few times, but you always get angry with him for bringing it up. Thinking about it doesn't mean you're giving up. But you must start preparing yourself."

I remained in silence for a long time, staring at Tristan sleeping peacefully on the couch.

"Did he talk to you about it?" I asked quietly.

"Yes, honey. He's willing to fight with all he's got to stay with you. But if everything else fails, he said he's not afraid to die. He's afraid for you, though. He doesn't want anything bad happening to you."

I sighed deeply and stared at the floor. "Okay, Mom. I understand," I said, and she patted my hand reassuringly.

"I'm sure everything will be all right," she said, and then glanced up because Tristan started waking. He blinked at us with heavy eyelids and smiled awkwardly, a little freaked out at the two of us staring silently at him.

"Hey, you're up." My mom broke the silence. "How are you feeling, son?"

"I'm okay." I raised an eyebrow inquisitively, because I could see clearly in his eyes he was still very tired and not okay at all. "I might need a couple of long naps today, though," he added, chuckling at my silent, doubtful stare.

Mom smiled and stood up. "I'll go make some breakfast for you. The boys should be waking up soon too, and will be hungry, I'll bet. Might as well get an early start on the food," she said cheerfully, the weary frown gone from her face "And Joey, stop doing your 'truth stare' on the boy. A man needs to have his private thoughts!" She scowled at me. "Especially now, that you two . . . *you know*." She stared intently at me and then at him before heading back to the kitchen.

"Especially now that we '*you know*' what?" Tristan inquired curiously.

I went to sit by his side on the couch. "Yeah, well. The good news is that Mom already knows about us. We don't need to keep pretending in front of her any more. And apparently she's cool with it," I said, smiling.

"Really? She is?"

"Yep. She figured it out with her weird Sherlockian skills. But the bad news is that my mom really knows about us. So prepare yourself for her 'sex talk'," I said, chuckling at his pale, terrified face.

"Okay," he mumbled in a small voice. "How are you feeling?"

"My arm is still bothering me a little."

"Is it still hurting?" he asked, his tone snapping to worried in a beating second.

"It's more tender, like I've spent the day exercising, you know?" I said, flexing my hands.

"I'm so sorry, Joe." He sounded sad. "I shouldn't have insisted on this idea of meeting Vigil. I thought I was the only one that could get hurt. I never imagined you could end up in pain," he said, and passed his hand over my arm. Feeble pinpricks floated over my skin, leaving the usual tingling sensation in the wake of his fingertips.

My eyes drifted to my hand and I caught sight of a black smudge on my wrist. Was it dirt? Tristan noticed the dark spot too and reached out, touching it softly with his thumb. I brought my wrist up to have a closer look. There was a small black drawing under my skin, like a tattoo of my arteries and veins on that small patch on my wrist. Tristan stroked the black lines carefully, but it didn't disappear like last night.

"What is that?" he asked, worried.

"I don't know," I mumbled, rubbing the spot and flexing my wrist again. "Do you think it's going to stay like this for long?" I asked, staring at the black mark.

"I don't know," Tristan said. "If it does, at least you'll have a cool tattoo now without needles," he pointed out weakly, trying to cheer me up.

"Yeah. I'm in a rock band. A tattoo would be cool," I said, still staring at it. "My mom's going to freak out when she sees it, though. It'll be worse than the sex talk."

Tristan laughed at my frightened face. "It sounds as if nothing is worse than the sex talk, Joe."

I sat on the couch and touched my newly acquired wrist tattoo. "Those dark lines appeared after I punched Vigil last night," I muttered. Then I looked out of the window. "Do you think Vigil is gone for good?"

"I really don't know, Joey. It was a pretty mean punch. What do you think?"

I bit my lips, not really liking my answer. "He said nothing could ever stop him, not even Death. He's still out there, somewhere. He'll be back at New Year," I said.

"I think you're right." Tristan agreed quietly by my side.

"And all this was for nothing," I mumbled disconsolately, rubbing my wrist.

"It wasn't," Tristan said quietly, sitting down next to me. "I learned a lot of things from my talk with Vigil. Things I'll try to use at New Year."

"He does seem to be developing emotions he doesn't understand," I said, thinking of all my encounters with Vigil since I'd named him. "And what did you mean by 'It's never going to happen'? He was truly angry when you said that."

Tristan shifted uncomfortably and stared at his feet.

"Tristan?" I pressed.

He looked me in the eyes. "He likes you," he stated.

"Stop being silly, Tris."

"I'm not being silly. He fancies you. I could see it. How could you not? It was right there, every time he looked at you."

"Tris...are you *serious*?"

"Yes! I was pretty pissed off too when I realized it. He went mental when I told him you and he were never going to happen. That was what set him off and made him cross over the line," he said, aggravated.

"I...don't really know what to say to that." I was shocked by that little revelation. After all, I was a girl and Vigil was a supernatural being. *Could* he even like someone in that way?

"What I don't get is why you haven't noticed this before. It should be a piece of cake for you to read it in his eyes. Why didn't you?"

Yes. Why didn't I? Vigil had always been really hard to interpret. Especially at the beginning: I couldn't get anything from him at our first encounters. But then...he'd started changing. Every time we've met he looked a little different. He started trying to help me then, getting worried about my safety. Were those all signs he had been giving me? How could I have missed this?

"He...is hard to read. When he's not a total blank, it's like he's in fast forward mode with his emotions. Just when I think I've spotted one, he's already passed on to four new ones. I really never suspected," I muttered, astonished.

"Well, it's another thing we can use against him now, another weak spot. We'll try to work all his angles and make him crack! If all fails, I was thinking about something Seth said once..." Tris turned to look at me expectantly. "It was fairly nerdy but it may well be our best shot."

"A new plan?"

"Yes. This whole thing is about the New Year because that is when our spell ends and your protection ends with it, right? What if we renew our spell again? Exactly like we did last year? Then I would be guarded again. Like renewing a subscription that has expired. Seth got the idea from one of his comic books – he said that if the spell is what gives you the ability to protect me, even from a being as powerful as Vigil, then we need to make that 'superpower' yours again. What do you think?"

"I think...it's a fantastic idea!" I said, amazed by Seth's ingenuity. Clever geek boy!

"I thought so too!" Tristan said with a huge grin. "I think it might actually work!" He smiled, hope fully back in his eyes and in his heart.

Seth and Harry decided to come downstairs then, still looking half-asleep and with messy hair.

"Seth! You're up!" I shouted happily and ran over to him, giving him a loud smacky kiss on the lips. His sleepy eyes shot wide open in complete surprise.

"Uh...yeah, I'm up. I've never had that kind of reaction from anyone for just being awake, but I suppose it's an accomplishment of sorts," he mumbled.

Harry crossed his arms, pouting at me. "Hey, I'm awake too! Although that's not a hard feat, with Seth's loud snoring pounding in my ears all night long!" he grumbled.

I side-stepped over to Harry and gave him a light peck on the lips too, though not as smacky and excited as I had done with Seth.

"And *shut up,* I do not snore!" Seth complained to Harry, affronted.

"Yeah, you do a little," I said, giving Seth a hug now. "But I don't care! I even miss it, sometimes. It was always like a tiny chainsaw lulling me to sleep! Seth, Tristan told me your plan for New Year…It's brilliant! I don't know what we would do without you," I said happily. Having a new plan improved my mood a whole lot.

"My plan? What plan?" he asked, baffled until Tristan explained how he had come up with his idea after hearing Seth's ramblings about comic book heroes and their superpowers. "Ah, I see it now! I do have the most brilliant plans, don't I?" Seth beamed, proud of himself "So…do you really like it?"

"Yeah!" Tristan and I said at the same time.

"Like, a lot? As in, *'I would do anything to repay Seth for this idea'*?"

I raised a suspicious eyebrow at him. "Okay. What do you want, Seth?"

"If I were to ask for some Christmas spirit here, would you be inclined to say yes?" he asked, all hopeful with shining hazel eyes.

"What?" I didn't get where he was going with this nonsense.

Harry started grinning madly now, understanding dawning on his handsome face.

Josh came into the living room then, and looked curiously at our huddled assembly.

"Hey, guys! What's going on?" he asked, looking at Harry.

"Seth's asking Joey for a full blast of Christmas spirit here!" Harry exclaimed, excited at the news.

"Oh, dear God! Did she say yes?" Josh asked in a strangled voice.

Sam came downstairs at that moment. He saw Josh's face, Harry squirming and Seth jumping up and down and stopped in mid-step, looking worried. "What's up?" he asked, rubbing his eyes.

"Seth's gonna go all Xmas-maniac on us again," Josh mumbled warily.

"Oh, boy. Well, it should be fun seeing Joey dealing with Seth in Christmas mode. We all know what's *that's* like. I guess she needs to experience it too." Sam chuckled.

"Okay, I'm kind of getting a little scared now," I said, looking from one boy to another. "What is this all about? Be serious, now."

"Well...it's like this. We've all spent a little of December with Seth in the past, so we've got used to it," Josh started explaining.

"Not like we had any option," Sam mumbled.

"But...the thing about Seth preparing for Christmas that you don't know about yet, Joe, is that he goes completely bonkers during this month," Josh continued.

"Totally mental," Sam added.

"He goes total coo-coo fuckin' bananas," Harry added thoughtfully.

"Hey!" Seth shouted, not amused at all by all the adjectives coming up.

"Come on, it can't be *that* bad!" Tristan chuckled, watching Seth rubbing his hands in excitement.

"Oh. It's *bad*," Josh mused.

"Dude, you're in for it," Sam stated plainly.

"I don't care how bad it gets, he deserves it!" I said, closing the deal and hugging Seth one more time. He's given us the best plan ever for New Year! Full Christmas spirit it is!"

"Yay!" Seth shouted and whooped.

Sam and Josh slapped their faces with agonized expressions, and Harry jumped up and down, shouting "Hurraaay!" in a cartoony voice.

Seth didn't care about anybody mocking his jolly spirit, though. He was in his own private festive world now, far away at the distant snowy Christmas Land of his dreams.

At first, I thought the boys had exaggerated Seth's Christmas spirit. I mean, how festive can a boy get? But Seth truly was a Christmas maniac! He had our house filled with green and red stuff and sparkling glass balls and stars and everything related to Christmas he could get his jolly hands on. He was also making us wear Santa hats inside the house during the whole week, and he even had a little blackboard nailed on the kitchen door with a countdown in chalk until Christmas Eve. It was so much fun just watching *him* having fun!

He was surely in full-blast Christmas mode!

The week before Christmas, Tiffany came back from visiting her parents. Her folks had wanted her to stay with them for the holidays, for a big party they were throwing, but she'd told them she wasn't going to be there. She was pretty mad at them because every year they left her alone at Christmas, travelling for business or a vacation somewhere, and she was always left behind with a last-minute "Sorry, hun, we can't be there with you" telephone call. So now she'd just left *them* without much explanation, and had returned to spend Christmas with her *real* family, as she now called us.

Seth was really happy when she arrived, and I'd missed her too. So much had happened while she'd been away! Tiff could hardly believe her ears when I filled her in on our encounter with Vigil, and she was even happier to be back with us. Seth had cleared it with his own family to spend Christmas with Tristan and me this year. He wanted to share this special holiday with his best friend and brother-in-arms this year – in case it was Tristan's last...

Harry, Sam and Josh were over at my house a lot during the week as well, having fun and enjoying the festive frenzy that Seth was whipping us all into! And Mom was on cloud nine. It was like all her wishes for a big family Christmas had come true.

Christmas Day arrived and Josh, Harry and Sam went to spend the day with their families, but they were going to come back again after supper, to exchange gifts and celebrate with us. I put on my red dress for the evening; the dress Mom had given me for my birthday. She was so happy when she saw me wearing it that her beaming face alone was worth the effort.

The boys arrived a little after nine and we all spread out across the living room for the gift-exchanging part of the evening. When everything was done, there was so much giftwrap, bows and ribbons all over the room, it looked like a wrapping monster had swallowed us all!

We kept celebrating until early in the morning, and as the sun rose, the first snow of the year began to fall outside the window, ending a perfect Christmas day.

And that night, it seemed all my troubles had been forgotten, while Christmas lights kept shining on.

Chapter Thirty-Nine

A Matter of Time

After Christmas was over, Seth returned to his normal self, and the house went back to a quiet daily routine. The anticipation of New Year was making everybody a little more tense and edgy, especially me.

I checked and double-checked the spell with Miss Violet, making sure we hadn't forgotten anything in our plan to renew it, and that we were all going to be really prepared for New Year.

Just like the first time, when the spell was originally cast, we needed seven people on the grassed circle, so Sam, Harry, Josh and Seth were going to be standing on the borders in a cross formation. Tristan and I would be in the middle, and Sky would count as the last person to attend. Five elements would be included: a glass of water, a candle for fire, air by the breeze, earth under the grass, and the last element, the one that would make the spell work and close the bond again...my blood. I was bringing a pocket-knife to provide the fifth element.

All we needed to do was wait for New Year's Eve night. During the days leading up to it, I couldn't shake the uneasy feeling that these were my last with Tristan. Somehow everything we did or said felt like we were doing it for the last time. On the second night before the turn of the New Year, Tristan snuck in to my room to spend the night with me. We lay in my bed and talked quietly most of that night, and again I got that sad feeling that this could be the last time I would rest my face on Tristan's broad chest.

"You remember the first time I saw you? Back then at the cemetery?" I asked him quietly.

"Yeah. Of course," he said. "I couldn't believe it when you started talking to me. You thought I was crazy, because I just stared at you, but I was so shocked that you could see me!" He chuckled at the memory.

"Yeah, I almost ran away from you. You know why I didn't?"

"Why is that?" he asked softly.

"Because you smiled at me, after you jumped down off your tomb. It was the most beautiful smile I have ever seen. I couldn't leave after you smiled at me like that. I love your smile so much," I said. "I love it so much when you call me Buttons," I continued. "And I love to see you blushing when you curse by accident. I love the sound of your voice; it's quiet and low and sexy. And I love hearing you singing! I love how your body fits perfectly to mine, and the way we click in all the right places when we go to sleep together. I love sleeping with you. I love making love to you."

The words kept tumbling out of me like a confession. "I love your smell! I wish I could bottle it up and carry it around with me all the time. You don't know how special you are. You gave me the best first kiss I have ever had. The best first date I have ever had. And I don't take any minute with you for granted. I save them all in my heart and treasure every one of them," I finished at last.

I just wanted Tristan to know how I felt about him. I couldn't tell his reaction to my speech, though, because my head was resting on his chest. He lay there in silence for a while, taking in all I'd said. Then he spoke very quietly.

"You never cease to amaze me," he whispered, cupping my face with his hands, making me look at him. "Extraordinary," he said passionately, his eyes shining. He didn't say another word for a long time. He didn't need to. I could see it all flashing in his eyes. The intensity of his love was mind-blowing; the look in his eyes was worth a thousand words. A tear broke through and ran down my face. He smiled tenderly, the corners of his eyes crinkling, while he wiped the tear from my face with his soft fingers.

"Thank you for telling me." He spoke in a low, shaky voice, leaning in and kissing me deeply.

He embraced me and sighed, tracing his fingers slowly over my, connecting invisible dots on my skin. Whenever his fingers touched me, he left a tingling sensation in their wake.

"Joey, sweetheart...this isn't goodbye," he whispered softly.

"I know," I whispered back. "But I wanted to tell you how I feel about you," I explained.

"We'll be fine, love. I'll always be with you. No matter what," he murmured, stroking my hair before falling into silence. We held on to each other during the entire night, afraid to let go, afraid of the future and what the New Year could bring us.

On New Year's Eve, everybody gathered at my home, waiting anxiously for the night to come. Today there were no jokes, no laughter, only nervous glances and tense shoulders. Nobody was talking much; everybody was immersed in their own private thoughts. When night finally came, we all headed to the cemetery. Miss Violet, my mom and Tiffany were going to stay by the gates, waiting for us there. If anything bad happened, they would be close enough to come to our aid. We didn't want to mess up the number of people needed for the spell to work.

The cemetery was once again decorated for Esperanza's New Year's party; yellow lanterns were spread all through the gloomy lanes and people were beginning to arrive to celebrate, mostly lingering by the area near the front gates. The place looked pretty much the same as last year, the only difference being that this year was a little colder, and snow piled up in little mounds over some headstones.

My mom hugged Tristan when we passed by the cemetery iron gates. "I'll see you soon, son," she said, ruffling his hair. He nodded, smiling, and went to hug Tiffany.

"Be careful and stay safe!" Tiffany ordered him. She couldn't let go of her bossy ways, even now.

He nodded again. "I will. Thanks, Tiffany," he said before walking away.

The boys and I followed him through the lanes in silence. The lights began to dim and everything turned darker with each step we took deeper into the graveyard. I could hear our footsteps echoing on the ground and sometimes the sound of people talking and laughing drifted in the background.

As soon we arrived at the small grass circle, everybody took their place without a word. Tristan and I walked to the middle of the circle. Seth had a small glass of water in his hands, and Harry had a candle. Sam had grabbed some grass and earth, and Josh stood calmly, with empty open hands. I had my pocket-knife clutched tightly. We all stood still and counted the minutes passing eerily by, each of us glancing at our watches in turns.

I had been waiting for this moment for so long that now that it was so close at hand, I didn't know what to feel.

Tristan held my hand and squeezed, trying to reassure me. It was close to midnight now. I let go of his hands to hold my pocket-knife more firmly, to make sure the fifth element would be present when the clock struck twelve. A single firework exploded a few seconds too early. I watched as it ascended into the dark winter sky and exploded into hundreds of tiny bright sparks, but the explosion seemed to happen in slow motion.

And then everything froze completely. I glanced around and the world was standing still, as if holding its breath. Tristan was frozen in his spot, and all the boys too. My eyes darted back and forth, trying to catch a sign of movement, but the only thing moving was me. And then a stabbing pain shot through my wrist, making me wince. I grabbed my wrist and pressed my fingers hard against the dark tattoo marking it, trying to make the throbbing stop.

When I looked up, Vigil was there, standing a few feet away from me, watching me with his unblinking black eyes. So he was back; we hadn't banished him at all. I instinctively stepped in front of Tristan, trying to block Vigil's path to him, the pocket-knife still clutched tight in my hand. The pain increased in my wrist, flowing gradually up to my hand and elbow now. But Vigil didn't show any sign of wanting to approach or attack us. He just stood where he was, and looked, to my utter surprise, almost like he was...sad?

Was this a trick? I would have expected him to be angry

and vindictive, lashing out at us with his might. But he remained still, only tilting his head a little, like he used to do a long time ago, a quirk of his that always made me think of him as bird-like. It was like a nervous tick. I watched him with extreme caution; Tristan's life was on the line here.

Maybe it was time to conclude the spell, before Vigil could try anything on us. I needed some of my blood now to remake our bond. I pulled my knife slowly up and leaned the blade closer to my hand.

Vigil's eyes followed my movement and lingered on the flicker of the blade. He sighed sadly, holding his hands behind his back in a non-threatening stance. "Please, I wish you wouldn't do that, Joe," he said, his dark locks falling softly over his pale smooth face.

I squinted my eyes at him. Yeah, I'll bet you wish I wouldn't! I'll bet you wish I won't renew the spell again, and win my guardian powers back. Best of luck next time, then, pal, I thought to myself. But before I could press the blade any harder against my hand, he spoke again.

"It will not do you any good, and I would hate to see you hurt. I really would," he said. "How is your fist, by the way? I hope you weren't in too much pain after that punch you gave me."

Was he mocking me? I only saw sincerity in his eyes. He was truly worried about me. Was he trying to play the nice guy, then, to get back on my good side?

"It was a very powerful spell you cast when you threw your punch that day," he said. "It was raw and unintentional, but very powerful. You managed to disarm me and scatter the pieces everywhere. It was very...unpleasant for me," he continued, but he smiled a little, like he was somehow proud of my feat. "But you aren't ready to yield that type of force yet. A spellcaster should be objective, trained and prepared before handling that amount of magic, and you were none of those things. I imagine it cost you something. Magic always comes with a price. I hope you didn't suffer much," he said, looking worried again.

I removed the blade from my hand and glanced at my wrist. The black tattoo was still there and the pain was shooting through my entire arm now. I decided to be honest. "After I punched you, this appeared and spread all over my arm. Tristan made it go away, except for this small mark in my wrist." I twisted my wrist up, showing him the black lines on my skin. "This one won't go away. It started hurting when you showed up," I said.

He stared at my wrist. "Like I said, a spell of that amplitude leaves its mark. I do not think it will go away. It is the price you have paid. Your intentions were pure. But the consequences of casting it may never fade away. The fact that you used it against me could be the reason it hurts in my presence. May I see it closer?" he asked, but didn't move from his place, waiting for my authorization first.

I eyed him suspiciously. He seemed genuinely concerned, but how far could I trust him? He was the enemy. He noticed my hesitation and the sadness in his eyes returned.

"I will not do anything to harm you or the boy while we are in here," he vowed. "You have my word," he said.

I frowned, not understanding why he referred to us as being "in here", but nodded all the same, walking closer to him. I didn't want him anywhere near Tristan. I reached Vigil and held out my wrist. I clenched my teeth hard, trying not to give away how much pain I was in. He reached out and took my wrist in his hands, stroking the dark lines with his thumb. The pain stopped as soon his hand came in contact with mine.

I raised my eyebrows in surprise, but said nothing.

"I am sorry, Joe," he said, staring down sadly. " I cannot undo the mark."

I snatched my wrist away from him, and the pain returned. So this "thing" would stay on my wrist for ever, to always remind me of the cost of using magic. Would it also always hurt in his presence, but stop if he touched me? I took a cautious step backwards and glanced quickly around me. Everything remained frozen still.

"What is happening here? Did you stop time?" I asked, worried. For how long could he keep this up? Could he stop time for ever?

"No, this is not time holding still. We have side-stepped present time for now. Like stepping out of a flowing stream. This is where the places between dimensions are. A patch of solid ground between the water streams, you may say," he said thoughtfully. "It is a little tricky to explain." He scratched his head and I almost smiled at seeing him make such a human gesture.

"Okay, so this is like a backstage area for a gig," I said, trying not to be freaked out.

He raised his eyebrows. "You have always had a way with words," he mused. "Yes, I think you can call it that."

"Why have you done this, Vigil?" I asked.

He took a deep breath and a stone bench appeared out of nowhere and he sat on it, motioning for me to follow. I needed to keep in mind he was still a threat. A being with great power, capable of side-stepping time and realities, and making benches appear out of thin air. This wasn't a friendly little talk.

"I need to explain some things to you, Joe," he said ominously. "Would you mind sitting with me for a minute?"

"Okay. It's not like I have a choice here, is it?" I muttered quietly, still holding my blade tightly in my hands. I sat on the bench, as far away from him as possible, and glanced up at Tristan, standing still in the middle of the plaza. He looked foggy, blurred, like an old faded statue.

"Before we get back to your time, you need to know what is really happening now, Joe," he said quietly. "I will be completely honest with you. After you hear all I have to say, you can make your final decision."

"Decision about what?" I asked nervously.

"About what you want me to do."

"Are you saying I get to decide what happens next?"

"Yes. But you have to hear me out first," he pleaded.

"This isn't a trick of yours, is it?" I asked, still suspicious.

"No. I do not do tricks. I do not lie."

"You tricked me with your frail looks, trying to make me think you were weak, but you're really not. And you're not remotely human, but you've made yourself look like one. That's a lie of sorts," I pointed out.

"When I was first assigned to this task, I was late. I arrived here and you two were already gone," he said. "I had your trail, though, and tried to follow it. But the boy was guarded from me; I couldn't track him. I had no way to get to him, but I had you. At least when you were asleep, I could get to you. But then you surprised me. I could not force his location out of you. You were his guardian, and with that came a fierce protection spell. I was truly shocked the first time you struck me. I had never been hurt before," he said, looking down at his feet.

"So I tried to approach you in a more appealing way," he

continued. "I thought that maybe if you weren't scared of me, you would listen, you would understand my reasoning and capitulate. I was not trying to trick you into thinking I was weak, Joe. I was trying to make you see you could trust me. That was when I had the idea to change into this human appearance, a young male body that you could identify with and feel more comfortable around. To talk to," he said, crossing his hands, his eyes glazing at the distance. "And you kept giving me hints about human behavior, what to do, what to change. I tried to understand your species, so you could accept me more easily and help me do my job. I was sure that if you understood the importance of keeping things in order. . . . It was a different approach for me to this job, but I believed it was going to be more effective in the end, more so than forcing it out of you," he explained.

"Well, you've managed the mimicking pretty well. I almost believed you cared," I said quietly.

"Oh, the caring part wasn't pretending. That was when things started to go wrong for me," he said, still gazing into the distance. "Somehow a few emotions began to seep through. It was very subtle at first, and I didn't realize what was happening. But then I started to get these . . . *feelings*," he said, making it sound like it was a virulent disease. "It was very aggravating. I didn't know what to do, how to deal with it. It is an alien thing for us. *Emotions*. They lead to irrational chaotic behavior. You may not know that, but we frown upon chaotic behavior," he said, looking at me with serious, scared eyes.

"Yes, I've noticed that," I said trying to keep a straight face.

"And I think it all started after you gave me a name," he said, starting to get really agitated.

"I really don't understand what the fuss is all about!" I said, a tad aggravated myself now. "It's just a stupid name. Vigil. It doesn't mean anything!"

His face softened with a small smile. "Yes. I am Vigil now," he whispered gently, almost like he was scared to say it out loud but at the same time proud of it. "You gave me a name, and when you did this, you also gave me an identity. I am no longer a member of the masses. I am some*one* now. Individuality brings personality, so I have discovered.

"After I realized this, it was already too late to make it stop," he muttered with a contemplative expression. "I thought that having a name would mean more power: every time you mentioned my name, I felt it. Every time you feared me, I grew stronger. Your fear and his..." he said, pointing at Tristan, "...it was like the most powerful fuel to me. But it is not just fear but love too. Every strong emotion is a potent energy source, if you direct it to a name." He laughed but there was an edge of mania to it.

"I have discovered, though, that with the name comes the emotions. Like a virus, taking over everything. I am ruled by chaos inside now. I've become the thing I have worked against all my existence. How can I fix this? How can I fix myself? I cannot. Not without ceasing to exist. And I do not wish to die," he affirmed. "And I have discovered I am capable of emotions too. I...I really do care about you, Joe."

His voice was hard, like he was trying to fight against it with all his will. He looked down at his feet, his shoulders hunched and head down in defeat. "I think I...I love you," he said quietly. "It is very strange, and alien and new. And I don't know what to do with it. I hope I will be able to fight it. I'm sure it will pass, when I'm not around you as much," he said, smiling a little, like he was hopeful that he really would heal himself of love. "I asked around for a good remedy for viruses and people told me that chicken noodle soup is good," he said, puzzled. "It doesn't make much sense, but I am willing to try."

I smiled softly at him. He was talking about love as if it was actually a sickness, a disease.

"So, Joe, if you really ask me not to do my job now, I will accept your wish. I will do as you say," he stated plainly, cutting into my thoughts. I stiffened and looked at him, not believing in my ears.

"You will? You really will?"

"Yes. But I need to tell you something first. If I don't finish today what I came here to do, I will have to go back and report it to my colleagues. I don't work alone. As I've told you before, there are many out there like me. They will know that nothing was fixed here. They will want to know why I haven't fixed it. As soon I explain, I'm doomed. I will be chaos myself, something out of its natural order. They will '*fix*' me then."

"Fix as in . . ." I asked, dreading the answer.

"Cease to exist."

"They will kill you."

"If you prefer to put it in those terms," he said and smiled at me.

"If you ask me, I will comply. But I need to know, Joe. Now you know what will happen if I attend to your wish, would you still ask me not to do my job?"

He looked me directly in the eyes, and I stared back at him in utter shock. My mind was racing, trying to absorb everything he was saying to me. I opened my mouth but no words came out. I would do anything to save Tristan, but asking someone else to die in his place was stepping over the line, wasn't it?

Maybe I could still renew the bond spell and get my guardian powers back. Vigil could say he was unable to finish his job, then, and it wouldn't be his fault; it wouldn't be his choice.

Vigil was looking at me seriously, waiting for my answer.

"No," I answered. "I would never ask for you to die, Vigil."

He let out a long, deep breath, his eyes shining with emotion. He nodded and stood up. "Thank you for telling me that. I needed to know. I would still do it, Joe, no matter the consequences to me. I want you to know that," he said, extending his hand to me.

I took his hand and stood up, the stabbing needles in my wrist stopping momentarily because he was holding my hand now. As soon we stood up, the bench disappeared out of sight.

"But I have other reasons for having to take Tristan away from you tonight," he continued, and I pulled my hand away abruptly. He looked surprised for a second, and I saw hurt in his eyes, but then he turned and waved. Suddenly Tristan unfroze and stumbled, looking around in confusion at the same time that his wristband snapped and broke into pieces, black beads falling softly over the grass beneath his feet. Tristan frowned angrily when he spotted Vigil right by my side, and started in my direction. He was about to say something but stopped when Vigil began to speak again.

"And now this is the part that 'he' needs to know to make his decision," Vigil said, turning to look at Tristan, sadness shining in his fathomless black eyes.

Chapter Forty

Winter Song

"You gave me your word you wouldn't hurt him!" I shouted, stepping away from Vigil and walking in Tristan's direction.

"I will not do anything without both of your permission," Vigil vouched again. "But he needs to know this, before he decides."

"Know what? What is he talking about?" Tristan asked, grabbing my hand and stepping in front of me protectively.

"You two plan to renew the bond spell tonight, to reinforce your deal with Death once again," Vigil stated. "You should not try to do this. You are not aware of the consequences."

"Why shouldn't we? You are just trying to trick us, because you won't be able to stop us if we do this!" I said angrily, flipping the blade and pressing it to my hand again.

Vigil just stood still and stared unblinkingly at us. Then he shifted only his eyes to Tristan. "If the spell is renewed, my term here will be over after tonight, but then my colleagues will send another to do my job. And I must warn you: they will not handle this as badly as I have."

His expression was urgent now. "They will be insensible to your distress, destitute of affection, and unmoved by any of your appeals. As soon as they realize they cannot track you in the physical world, as happened to me, they will attack Joey with all their might in her sleep. She is responsible for the spell that brought you back; she is the one they will punish; she is the key to restoring the natural order, and they will never leave her in peace. She might be able to break the connection at first, as she did with me, but eventually she will become tired. They will break through then," he said, and now his voice had an edge of desperation.

"They will torture your location out of her. Every night, if they have to. She won't hold out longer than a week. Even though they'd be doing it in her dreams, in her mind it will be very real. They will break her. Can you bear to see her fighting and in pain every night? Can you put her in this position? Because if you go through with this spell tonight, that is what you are going to do to her," he said desperately, begging for Tristan to understand.

I looked at Tristan. I was terrified. I didn't know what to say, what to do. He stared at Vigil for a long time, his eyes as urgent and despairing as Vigil's.

"We don't have much time, you need to make your decision now," Vigil urged, and Tristan still remained quiet. "You *have to understand*. I'm trying to protect her. I don't want to see her hurt."

Tristan clenched his teeth and let out a harsh breath. Then he turned to me and glanced down at my hand still clutching my pen-knife. He took the blade carefully from me and tossed it far away from us.

"Tristan, what are you doing?" I yelled at him,

understanding too late what he had decided to do. "You can't do this to me! Please, Tris!" I pleaded.

He cupped his hands around my face and looked deep in my eyes. "Joe, do you remember what I said to you, a long time ago? That I meant you no harm when I chose this life a year ago, that I would never willingly do anything bad to you?"

"Yes, but…" I pleaded desperately.

"No, Joey. I can't go through with this spell tonight, not knowing that it will mean getting you hurt. I do want to live, but not at this cost. I won't do it," he said with determination, and then he kissed me with so much love and adoration it made my heart break. "Don't be afraid. You'll be fine," he whispered as his lips parted from mine. His eyes were hard, purposeful. He was trying to be ready for what he needed to do. He turned and started walking towards Vigil.

"No! No! Tristan, please don't do this! You can't do this!" I said, grabbing his hand. He turned his face and smiled softly, trying to reassure me everything was going to be fine, telling me with his eyes that I would be fine.

"I can't let them hurt you because of me, Joe. I can't. I won't. I have to do this now. I love you. I will always love you. You *have* to let me go," he said, pulling his hand away.

I couldn't believe what was happening! We had a plan! And he was giving up on everything! He couldn't do that! I turned to Vigil, my eyes filling with despair and pain. "Vigil! Don't do this to him!" I begged.

He didn't dare to look me in the eyes. He stared at the ground and didn't say anything.

"I'll hate you for ever if you do this," I threatened him.

"I know," he said sadly. "I hope you forgive me some

day," he said. He turned and looked at Tristan. "The others will have no mercy. I'm doing this to protect her," he said, with so much sadness in his voice.

Tristan nodded and walked towards him.

"Please, don't!" I shouted again.

Vigil made a small signal with his hand, and then I was outside the circle, looking at Tristan and Vigil still standing in the middle of it. Time returned to its natural pace then, as the clock finally struck midnight and fireworks exploded in the dark sky, loud and piercing bright.

New Year had come.

An excruciating pain ripped inside my chest, making my knees buckle, and I hit the ground hard. I looked up and saw Vigil's hand resting on Tristan's shoulder.

Our bond was breaking; I could feel it dissolving inside me. I wasn't his guardian any more. I couldn't protect him. There was nothing I could do but watch him go.

A stabbing pain exploded in my wrist, flooding up my arm, making me cry out in agonizing pain. All the boys turned their faces to look at me, surprise and shock flashing in their eyes. They didn't understand why one second I was in the middle of the circle and the next I was kneeling outside, farther away from everybody and crying in pain. Harry ran in my direction while I watched Tristan sitting in the grass, Vigil kneeling right by his side. Seth was coming over to help me too, and Josh and Sam.

Nobody was looking at the middle of the circle; nobody was paying any attention to Tristan there. They were too worried about me to realize what was happening. I cried out again, trying to warn them, but no words came out. Tristan was lying down now; I couldn't see his eyes any more, his beautiful, sad gray eyes.

Sky appeared out of thin air, and was standing still right behind him. She glanced up and her eyes locked with mine for a split second. She winked at me at the same time that Harry moved, kneeling in front of me, blocking my view for a brief second. The pain in my body was unbearable.

It felt like someone had ripped a piece out of my chest. I stood up and pushed my way clear of the boys. No one was in the circle any more. Sky and Vigil had vanished. And Tristan was gone. I buried my hands in my hair, trying to organize my jumbled thoughts. Seth wrapped an arm around my shoulder.

"Joey, w-what happened?"

"He's gone. Tristan's gone," I whispered, staring at the ground. "There was nothing I could do."

Fireworks were still exploding in the sky, loud and disrespectfully cheerful.

"I need to find him," I said, standing up, a deranged look on my face. "I need to see him. I know I still can see him. I could always see him, even as ghost! He must be in here somewhere!"

"Joe..." Seth began, but I was beyond any reasoning. I needed to see him again.

It was all that mattered to me now. I started walking through the cemetery's dark lanes. The fireworks were fewer now, the noise dying out gradually. I was thankful for that. The New Year's celebration made me feel like the world's happiness was mocking me, sneering at my pain. I walked alone, calling out for Tristan, seeking desperately for a glimpse of him between the gravestones, but I found nothing.

I don't remember how long I walked for. I bumped into a few people wandering into the graveyard, still celebrating the New Year, but after a while the celebrations ended and people went away to their homes, and there was nobody left in there but me.

I found myself again near Tristan's tomb. I had already passed by it a couple of times. Maybe this time he would be there. Maybe this time I'd get to see him. I stopped in front of it, calling out for Tristan one more time. Again there was no reply. I sat on the ground and leaned my back against the tomb, pulling my jacket closer to my body, trying to keep the warmth inside. Why wasn't he here? Why couldn't I see him any more?

Was he gone for good?

I must have drifted off to sleep soon after that. I was so tired, I didn't even remember closing my eyes. When I opened them again, the place was pitch dark and I could scarcely see anything around me. I blinked a couple of times, adjusting my eyesight to the darkness. I saw snow falling over the headstones, and over me. I tried to shake the snow off of me, but my movements were stiff and slow. I was so cold. I pushed myself up, but I wasn't strong enough and my body slumped heavily back again onto the ground. I was freezing to death. I tried to shout for help, but my voice came out as a rough whisper. I looked around, trying to figure out what to do.

I tried to hoist myself up, but had no strength left. My body was shutting down, little by little. I was feeling so cold and so very tired. I knew if I went to sleep here, I would not wake up again. I was probably hypothermic. I buried my face in my hands, but a piercing pain shot through my wrist again, making me flinch and whimper. When I unclasped my face, I saw Vigil standing right in front of me.

"What the hell are you doing here?" I growled at him.

"You need to leave this place, Joe," he said quietly, and took a step closer.

"What do you care?" I shouted, anger making my voice rise up.

"I care about you, Joe," he said sadly.

"No, you don't give a shit about me, or you wouldn't have taken him from me! Where is he?" I asked angrily.

"He is where he is supposed to be," he said and glanced around. "You need help to leave, Joe," he said quietly, and leaned in, trying to help me stand up.

I immediately flinched, screaming and thrashing against him. "No! Don't touch me!" I screamed.

"Joe, please. Let me help you," he pleaded.

"NO! This is all your fault!" I yelled, and thrashed even more when he tried to get a hold of me. "I don't want to see you ever again! It's you who should be dead, not him!" I spat out angrily. I was beyond crazy now, lost in all my pain.

He took a step away from me. "They would have come for him still," he said coldly.

"I hate you!" I shouted, losing all control. "I don't want to see you again! And I don't need your fucking help!"

Vigil stared at me sadly for a second and disappeared. The fight with him had taken away all the remaining energy I had. I lay there on the ground, trying to think. My fingers were blue and I stuffed my hands in the pockets of my coat, trying to keep them warm, and my hand nudged cold metal. My cell phone! In my frozen state I had forgotten about it. I switched it on and the first missed-call message popped on to the screen. It was Josh. I hit the call button and pressed the phone to my ear, praying for him to pick up. "Josh, pick up, pick up, pick up," I whispered.

His voice buzzed in on the second beep. "Joey? Is that you?" he asked, sounding worried.

"Josh! I need your help..." My voice came out softer than I intended.

"We've been calling you and looking for you for hours! Where are you?" he asked urgently.

I looked around. I had no idea. All I could see was snow, and darkness, and graves. "I-I don't know where I am, Josh. I'm s-so c-cold. I fell asleep and lost track of time," I said desperately.

"I'm in the centre of the cemetery, do you think you can shout?" he asked. He was searching for me. But I was too weak to shout. "Wait..." Josh said. "Okay. Got it. I know where you are. I'm coming to get you," he said, hanging up.

I stared at the phone, trying to understand what had happened. How could Josh find me here, in this dark? The place was too big and I didn't even have the energy to cry. Then I saw a dark silhouette coming over to me, a few feet away. I inhaled deeply and shouted Josh's name as loud as I could. He responded by kneeling at my side and hugging me.

"I'm so glad you're here," I whispered.

"It's all right. Everything will be all right. I've got you," he said, and carried me away in his arms. I didn't have the strength to explain anything. I just wanted out of this cold.

I don't remember much of how Josh got me home. I found out later that all The Lost Boys had been looking for me, and that my mom and everyone had been frantically worried. Back in my room, my mom put blankets and covers over me. Soon I wasn't feeling so cold any more, and was able to ask Josh how he'd been able to find me so quickly.

"That Vigil dude just zapped in front of me and told me where you were. Scared the hell out of me, I thought it was a trick, and all, but I followed his directions and you were there where he said you'd be," Josh said.

Before they all started asking about what had happened, my mom said, "Okay, guys, she needs to rest now. You all go downstairs now, and I'll make you some tea," she ordered and they all obeyed promptly.

But after they had all left, she sat on my bed with a serious look on her face. "Honey, I was so worried. Please tell me you're not going to do this again," she pleaded.

I sighed heavily and lay my head on the pillow. "I'm not going back to the cemetery any more, Mom. He's not there," I said numbly, and turned my back to her. "I just want to be alone now," I said quietly.

"Okay, Joey. Rest. Call me if you need anything," she said softly.

After she left I tossed and turned in my bed, unable to sleep. I could still smell Tristan's scent when I sunk my face in the pillow. I felt grateful for it and tortured by it at the same time. I kept replaying New Year's Eve night over and over again in my head, remembering Tristan's last words to me. I stood up and walked to my closet, opening the first drawer where I kept Tristan's photo booth shots. I needed to see his face again. I fumbled inside the drawer and pulled the photo strip out. A paper note came wrapped around it. I opened it and instantly recognized Tristan's neat handwriting on the paper. I picked up the paper and walked back to my bed, turning on my night-stand lamp. I unwrapped the note and smoothed the paper, focusing hard on the writing.

*Promise you'll remember me, and give your smile for
    the world to see*
*Promise you'll live life to its fullest and that you
    won't let sorrow take over*
*Sing, dance, shine, be the best you can be, and I'll be
    happy knowing that you did*
Be my rising star
Be the joy in my heart
*Promise that you'll try to see that your happiness
    means everything to me*
*I will always be with you, no matter what, until the
    very end and from the start*
In a soft wind stroking your face, in a sunny day
When you feel your heart go warm
When you shiver in a wavering storm
Whenever a song touches you inside
I'll be there by your side
Promise you'll dream of something new
And know that I will always, always love you
No matter what
Until the end and from the start.
Yours always
Tristan

Tristan was saying his goodbye to me in a poem; the
goodbye he didn't have a chance to say before. I felt tears
falling down my face and I couldn't stop them any more.
Tristan was gone, and he was never coming back.

Chapter Forty-One

Keep Breathing

Next day I woke up with a start and immediately reached for Tristan. Then I remembered I was never going to find him there again, and I started crying and didn't stop all day long. My mom came to talk to me, and then the boys and Tiffany, but I didn't listen to any of them, I curled up in a small ball beneath my covers, not answering any of their pleas for me to eat or to go downstairs or get out of bed.

I kept Tristan's note under my pillow. Just knowing it was there comforted me. Night came and I still couldn't sleep, but at the same all I wanted to do was lie in bed. I prayed for the blessing of unconsciousness. It was the only time I wasn't thinking about Tristan. I was heartsick, a devastating emptiness where he used to be. He had been my best friend, my room-mate, my companion, the love of my life...and now he was gone.

My mom kept telling me that the pain would fade with time, but days and nights passed and the emptiness in my chest remained. How can you forget a piece of you that is missing? I missed him all the time. I longed for his kisses, the taste of him, his face smiling at me, the warmth of his embrace, the blazing gray of his eyes. I kept replaying all those little moments of immense happiness we had together, all the times we'd shared: they flashed like a movie in my mind.

When I finally managed to drift into sleep, the night-mares came to haunt me. I dreamed that I was drowning and couldn't breathe. I woke up every time sweating and breathing fast, and started crying all over again until I was exhausted and drifted into sleep and yet another round of horrible nightmares.

My mom, Tiff and the boys came every day to try to talk me out of my depression. But the only time I talked was to tell them to go away. But they kept coming back.

I lost track of time completely. Sorrow was taking over, claiming me piece by piece until there was nothing left to fight for. Then one day I was woken by a soft knock on the door. I turned over in my bed and blinked sleepily at Harry standing there. He walked slowly inside with a tray of food, and put the tray down on my night-stand, staring at me with a deep, serious frown.

"Harry? You're still here?" I mumbled, confused. "I thought you'd all left..."

"No. I'm still here. *We* are all still here," he said, and he balled up his fists at his sides. "You need to stop this," he said angrily. I had never seen Harry so angry before. His eyes were hard and his voice was sharp and clipped. "I know you're hurting. But you need to eat. I've lost him too, but I'm not going to lose you!" he added, and I saw so much pain in his eyes it made me realize I wasn't the only one grieving for Tristan.

"I'm so sorry," I whispered. "Please forgive me," I said,

and finally left the cold comfort of my bed to hug him. He wrapped his arms around me, tears in his eyes. I had never seen Harry cry either. It was a side of him I wished I hadn't seen. I wanted him happy again. I wanted to hear his loud laughs and see his emerald eyes smiling at me.

"I'm gonna eat. I'll do whatever you want. Please stop crying," I whispered in his ear. I hugged him for a long time, until I sensed he was calmer, and then I stepped away and sat on my bed, patting a place for him to sit next to me. I grabbed the tray and put it over my lap, staring at its contents.

"So... what's lunch?" I asked, smiling weakly at him.

"It's...I don't know," he said, sitting next to me and wiping his eyes with the back of his hands. "Seth made it. I think it's soup of something," he mumbled.

"Soup of something. My favorite!" I joked feebly, grabbing the spoon. I gave him a sideways glance as he watched me eat. He looked paler and thinner than usual. I ate in silence for a while. "You look like you haven't been eating either," I pointed out between spoonfuls.

"I have been eating," he said, smiling softly at my concerned looks.

"Did you eat this soup?"

"Yeah, yeah. Soup of something is my favorite too," he muttered, then he shuffled uncomfortably. "I'm sorry, Joe. I didn't mean to shout at you..."

"That's okay. I needed it. I've been a lousy friend." I put the empty bowl back on the tray. "Do you think Seth, Tiff, Josh and Sam will forgive me? None of you guys deserved this treatment from me."

"Tiff, no doubt about it, and Seth will forgive you too if he sees you eating again. As will Sam and Josh, if you get out of your room sometimes and spend time with them again," he said hopefully.

"What about you? Do you forgive me?" I asked quietly, glancing up at his glinting green eyes.

"Only if you keep up that *'I'll do whatever you want'* deal," he said seriously.

"Okay. Deal," I said, hugging him again.

"So you can start by taking a bath now. You've outdone me with the longest-time-without-a-bath record."

I smiled and nodded. "Okay, Harry. A bath it is, then."

I took a long bath, enjoying the feeling of hot water on my skin. I washed my hair and stayed under the water for a long time, because it felt really good, like it was washing away a tiny piece of my pain. When I walked back to my room wrapped in a big towel, Harry was still there, snoozing away in my bed. I tiptoed inside and put on fresh sweat pants and a clean top before sitting back on my bed at Harry's side. He was sleeping so peacefully that I didn't have the courage to wake him up. I lay down and snuggled close to him, and the sway in the mattress made him shift and turn to his side, settling his head comfortably in my pillow, facing me. I looked down at Harry for a long time, looking at his straight nose and thin lips, the pale skin over his cheekbones. He was one of my best friends and I loved him so much. I immediately planned to go downstairs and apologize to the boys – and to mom and Tiff – but I fell asleep by Harry's side instead.

I woke up in his arms the next morning. At the first second of consciousness, I thought it was Tristan by my side, but the weight of his arms was wrong, and his scent was different, hazelnutty. I knew it was Harry even though my eyes were still closed. I had one arm wrapped over his waist, my face resting cozily against his collar-bone. I had slept through the whole night uninterrupted by my usual nightmares. Harry had guarded my dreams.

My stomach rumbled for the first time in a long time, surprising me. I shifted carefully out of Harry's arms and snuck out of the room, walking downstairs. I walked pass the living room and saw Josh sleeping on the couch with the TV on. The TV was showing an old movie from the fifties. I thought of Tristan and my heart twisted. This missing piece, this hole, would never go away. But the presence of my friends could make it more bearable, I realized for the first time. The minute I had let Harry in, I felt so much better, like he was sharing some of this heavy load I'd been carrying by myself all this time. If it wasn't for Harry yelling some sense back into me...

I walked silently into the kitchen and bumped into a sleepy Seth on his way out, making him almost spill the mug of hot tea in his hands. He looked at me, surprised that I was out of my room and a little apprehensive, but then he softened when I lunged forward and hugged him tight.

"I'm so sorry for shutting you all out, Seth," I said, burying my face in his chest. "And I really liked your soup."

He exhaled, relieved, and smiled and hugged me back.

"Harry made you eat, then," he said softly.

"Yes, he *ordered* me to. And from now on, I have to do all he says. He can be very bossy, you know," I muttered with a small smile on my lips.

"Yeah, he waits for the best moments to unleash his dictatorial side..." Seth said, chuckling lightly.

Seth looked thinner, with black rings under his eyes, his hair unkempt and messy. Tristan had been his best friend, his brother-in-arms. How could I have been so blind, so selfish, so unaware of my friends' suffering?

I hugged him again and whispered in his ear. "I know you miss him too." And he wrapped his arms around me again, and squeezed me softly.

"I'm sorry there was nothing I could do to help him," he said in a choked voice. "But I'm here for you. We all are. Anything you need, just ask," he whispered in my ear.

"I know. Thank you, Seth," I said. "I want something else to eat now. Then we can watch some TV with Josh, okay?"

He looked at me, surprised and happy. "Okay," he murmured. He sat next to me in the kitchen and watched me eat, just like Harry had done the night before, and he walked with me to the living room. Josh woke up lazily the moment Seth changed the channel. He glanced at us with surprised eyes, rubbing the sleep off his face. I sat next to Josh and snuck under his blanket, lying with him on the couch.

"I wanna watch cartoons, Seth," I said, pretending I wasn't seeing Josh's wide eyes glaring at me. I grabbed Josh's heavy arm and pulled it over me, making him hold me in his arms. He understood that I wanted a hug from him and held me tight, wrapping his arm closely around me. We watched some cartoons for a while, and then Sam woke up and stepped into the living room, also with wide eyes glaring in my direction.

"Hey, Sammy, you're up!" I greeted him, raising my head off Josh's pillow. "I was waiting for you to wake up and give me a hug." I extended my arms to him. He smiled so much it made dimples appear on both sides of his cheeks, and then he walked over to me, kneeling by the couch and hugging me tight.

"Hey, Joe," he said softly in my ears. "You're back. We've missed you."

"I missed you too, Sammy." I hugged him back.

Sam went to grab something to eat for breakfast and Harry woke up shortly after that, joining us in the living room. They were all giving me cautious sideway glances to begin with, but after a while they started to relax and soon they were all talking and making funny remarks at the TV shows, like we used to do at school. I watched them chatting casually and sometimes a shy laugh would burst through. Every time it happened, my heart felt a little lighter.

Seth told me Tiffany was sleeping at her house down-town most the nights, but she always came back near lunchtime and stayed until late at night. When she saw me sitting in the living room with all the boys, she ran over and gave me the biggest rib-crunching hug ever. We stayed together all afternoon, and when my mom arrived home from work she was also shocked to see me in the living room, huddled between Tiffany and Seth on the couch. She smiled and gave me a peck on the forehead, then hurried to the kitchen to prepare some food. But not before I'd seen her tears. She was happy to see me out of the room and with my friends again.

"Hey, what do you want to do tomorrow, Joey?" Seth asked out of the blue.

"Tomorrow? Nothing. What's happening tomorrow?" I asked, confused.

"You seriously don't know? It's your birthday, Joey."

"Oh. Really?" I said, genuinely surprised. I couldn't believe almost fifteen days had passed. It felt like it was only a couple of days since New Year. I glanced up, think-ing hard about what I wanted to do for my birthday. I never liked celebrating my birthday at the best of times, but now it felt wrong. But I should try to make up for my poor behavior to my friends. "You know, there's something I'd really like, but I know you guys can't do it," I mumbled.

"Of course we can!" they all said in unison, taking the bait as expected.

"Anything you want, name it!" said Harry. "We promise."

"Okay, I'm not quite ready to face the world yet but I'd like you all to celebrate my birthday for me. I want you all to go out and have some fun. You've been sulking around here, worrying about me. That's what I really want," I said, smiling at them.

My friends all looked surprised at my request.

"Aw, Joe. We're are not going to leave you alone on your birthday!" Sam was the first to complain.

"Hey! It's my birthday wish! And you promised me!" I frowned and crossed my arms.

They were still reluctant but eventually they all agreed to my wish, though they got me to concede a little and agree to have a birthday cake at least.

After we'd eaten dinner, we returned to the living room to watch some more TV. I ended up falling asleep on the couch and dreamed about a frozen desert, where a sun made of glittering ice floated in the cold sky; but now, strangely, snow fell on the soft warm sand, melting as soon as it touched the ground...

Chapter Forty-Two

A Birthday Wish

The morning of my birthday, Seth and Tiff were still reluctant to leave me on my own. I hugged them both tight and admonished them: "Remember you promised me you'd have some fun today, okay?" I smiled and tried to make them stop worrying about me.

Seth gave me a half-smile and nodded a little apprehensively. My mother had to go to a work event and Josh, Sam and Harry had already left, like they'd promised me, but Seth was really hard to convince.

" Are you sure?" he started to ask again, but I cut him off.

"I'm sure, Seth! I don't need babysitting any more. You need a break from here, and it's my birthday wish," I said, stretching up to give him a kiss on the cheek.

"All right, then," he said, resigned and a little sad. "Come on, Tiff. Let's go have that promised fun, then."

I closed the door behind them, letting out a big sigh. I wandered through the house thinking about Tristan and The Lost Boys. For some reason I also thought of Vigil. I felt guilty for how I had treated him at our last encounter. He hadn't deserved all the hate I had thrown at him. I twisted my wrist and touched the black mark underneath my skin. I remembered him saying he could feel every time I said his name. It was worth a shot. I closed my eyes and concentrated hard, visualizing his name over and over again in my head.

"Vigil. Vigil. Vigil. Vigil. Vigil," I repeated to myself. It took only a few seconds before a sharp stabbing pain shot up my arm, making me cower on my bed, but I was smiling. It had worked. I opened my eyes and Vigil was standing in the middle of the room, looking at me with frightened eyes. He still had his androgynous looks, a gray outfit, and his soft long black hair falling over his black eyes.

"It worked," I whispered to myself. This magic stuff always surprised me. "Thanks for coming, Vigil. I wasn't sure if you would show up after the last time we saw each other..." I muttered, feeling a little embarrassed when I remembered my last words to him.

"You were in pain. I understand," he said quietly, looking down, ashamed and guilty for being the one that had caused me pain. I stood up and walked closer to him.

"I wanted to apologize. You didn't deserve to hear all that, and I'm really sorry for everything I said to you." He looked astonished at my words. "I wanted you to know that I forgive you, Vigil. I hope you can forgive me too," I said, looking him straight in the eyes.

His eyes were wide in disbelief. "I-I'm s-sorry too," he stuttered.

I took a step closer and hugged him then, so we could be officially and mutually forgiven. He stiffened, more surprised than ever, holding his arms close to his body. The instant I had touched him the shooting pain in my arm stopped and I relaxed a little, making the hug last longer than I originally intended to be. It was nice not feeling the tearing pain in my arm. I broke away and looked up at him. He looked confused. I smiled and walked to my bed, sitting on the same spot I had been in when he'd first appeared in the room.

"Thanks, Vigil. It means a lot to me that you came when I called. I hope I didn't interrupt any work you were doing, and all…"

He walked hesitantly closer to my bed, sitting a little further away from me. He must be thinking I'm bipolar or something, one day wailing at him like a banshee and the next apologizing and being super nice.

"It is not a problem, I was not…working. I am glad you called," he said, still with a worried tone in his voice. "How are you…doing?" he risked asking.

I put my hands on the mattress and stretched my legs. "I'm not doing so good." I stared down at my feet to avoid looking at him. "I've been treating people very badly these past few days, but I finally came to my senses and thought it was time to start apologizing. Good way to spend your birthday, huh? Apologizing for all the crap I've been putting people through." I smiled weakly.

"Today is the anniversary of the day you were born?" he asked curiously.

"Yep. Nineteen years ago today. We celebrate the day every year. Stupid tradition, huh?"

He looked puzzled for a second. "What is the mode of human celebration for birth days?"

"Well, we usually have parties with friends and family, receive presents, eat cake, blow out some candles and wish a happy birthday. I guess that covers it all for humans."

"I see," he said and paused, looking at me. "Well, happy birth day, Joe."

"Thanks."

"Where are your friends and family?"

"I asked them to go out and have some fun today, as my birthday present."

He stared at the walls of my room in silence for a while. He seemed to be thinking hard about something. "I wish I had brought something for you today...a present. That is the tradition, yes?" he asked.

"I didn't call you here for that. I just wanted to apologize, that's all," I said truthfully. "Besides, the only thing I want most in the world right now you can't give me," I mumbled, staring at my feet again, trying hard not to think about Tristan and failing miserably.

Vigil glanced down to the floor as well. "I am sorry. I cannot bring him back. It is out of my reach," he said, and his voice became sad again as he looked at me with concerned eyes. "You need to move on. Dwelling on this matter will only bring you pain, Joe." he said.

"Yeah, no shit, Sherlock," I snapped at him, a little too sharply. "I'm sorry, I know that, Vigil. It's not that easy. Take you, for instance. How is it going, the 'getting over me' part of the program? You did answer pretty fast. Were you waiting for my call up there?" I jabbed at him and instantly regretted it. "I'm sorry," I said passing my hand over my hair, frustrated. "I don't want to be mean. I was just trying to explain that it's hard to forget and move on."

"I-I know. You are right. It's not easy," he said, hunching his shoulders. "I tried the soup...it didn't work."

I couldn't help but laugh out loud, making him look up at me, startled.

"Yeah, I tried the soup too. It sucks, I know." I smiled weakly. "I thought about going to talk with Sky again," I said. "One last chance to convince her, you know? But I didn't have the courage to do it…"

"You should not try to do that, Joe!" he replied with urgency in his voice. "Do not try to meet her again! You do not have your guardian protective spells any more. You would not make it back this time. Do you understand?"

"Okay! Okay. I get it," I said, raising my arms in surrender. I guessed I knew deep down another visit to Death might be my last. Maybe it was my witchy instincts flaring up. We both stared at the wall in front of us in silence for a while.

"What if you ask her to drop by, pay me a visit? Maybe tell her I need to talk to her?" I suggested.

He shifted uncomfortably. "She knows what you want to talk about. She would not come," he said plainly. "You really do not give up easily, do you?" he asked quietly, staring into the distance.

I smiled softly to myself, remembering Tristan's husky voice telling me how I was so damn stubborn, and how that always earned me a passionate kiss from him. He loved my stubbornness. "This is something worth fighting for."

"Yes. I think so," he said quietly. "I was willing to die for it. I suppose you are doing what you have to do."

"Well, she is the only one that could do something about it, isn't she?" I said.

Vigil stayed quiet for a few minutes before answering me. "I think there might be *a way*," he said after a while. He turned to look at me with serious eyes. "I think I can help you talk with 'Sky'. I can give you *that* for a present."

"Really? You would do that for me?" I asked incredulously, hope rising again.

"Yes," he said, and his eyes told me silently he would do anything for me. He explained his plan quickly and I nodded, excitement flooding inside with each word he spoke. "Did you understand everything I explained to you?" he asked seriously.

I nodded eagerly.

"Good. You need to do it now, then," he urged me.

"Okay. I'm not so sure how I did it the last times I went there, but I'm trying anyway," I said lying down on my bed.

"Just relax and slow your breathing and slow your heartbeat as much as you are able. Concentrate hard on her and her desert. I will be there with you as well, I promise," he said, putting his hand over mine. I instantly relaxed, because the stabbing pains stopped with his touch.

"Why do you do that?" he asked curiously.

"Do what?" I asked, opening my eyes to look at him.

"You let out a deep breath of relief every time I touch you, or you touch me."

"Oh. Sorry. It's just…my wrist hurts when you're around, remember?" I asked, lifting up my wrist to show him the black mark under my skin.

"Yes, I remember. I thought that would make you want me as far away from you as possible," he reasoned.

"Yeah, well, the pain stops completely when you touch me."

"It…stops?" he asked, surprised.

"Yeah. Completely."

"Curious," he said thoughtfully.

"That's all you have to say? I thought you would have an explanation."

"I do not. So I should try to always touch you whenever I am close to you, then," he vowed solemnly.

"Uh…that sounded really weird, but thanks, I guess. Just don't say that out loud to anyone, please?" I asked, blushing a little.

"Why? I do need to touch you when we are together; it is for your own good," he said like it was the most logical thing ever. "Why are your cheeks all colored? Are you unwell?"

I coughed, trying to hide my embarrassment. "I'm all right, don't worry. It's just…let me handle the touching. If the pain gets too uncomfortable, I'll tell you, okay? Now, let's go," I said, lying back again and closing my eyes. But I was too excited and anxious to relax and fall asleep. After a while I opened one eye, and Vigil was there, staring at me.

"What's wrong?" he asked, worried.

"Nothing," I grunted. "I'm too anxious. I can't fall asleep right now."

He eyed me wearily. "I can help you stop your heartbeat; it only needs to happen for a few seconds so you can get there. But it is going to be unpleasant. It would be best if you do it yourself," he explained.

" Just do it, it's all right with me," I authorized him.

"Okay, then. Lie down, please," he asked. He leaned really close to me, his eyes focused fiercely on mine, and he rested his hands on my chest, palms stretched wide open. I blushed again, because it looked like he was "copping a feel". He frowned slightly and gave me a puzzled smile, his face really close to mine.

"Why do I feel strange being this close to you?" he asked quietly, a disconcerted look on his face.

"It's normal to feel weird. It's the 'feelings' thing acting out. Don't worry about it."

"Oh. I see. Curious," he mumbled. "Close your eyes now. And concentrate," he ordered. I did as he told me. He placed his hand over my chest again and the strangest sensation spread all over my body. It was as if all the air in my lungs rushed out, and my heart felt like it was going to burst out of my chest. He wasn't kidding when he said it was going to be really unpleasant. I felt really horrible for about a second, then I opened my eyes again and I was sitting on warm glittery sand. I realized I was back at Sky's desert place, and I sat up and looked urgently around. Vigil was right next to me, like he promised he would be.

"You need to call for her quickly!" he urged me.

Our plan was set in motion; I needed to hurry now. I looked up and the night sky was already clearing in the horizon, the sun already starting to rise, and really fast. I shouted as loud as I could for Sky, and just as I was starting to panic, the blazing sun coming up fast, she appeared right next to me.

She looked as beautiful as ever, with that angelic, innocent pale face of hers.

"You're here!" I exclaimed, and looked at Vigil. He waved his hand quickly in the air and everything stopped, the light ball frozen on its path in the sky. Vigil had done it again! He had side-stepped us "backstage" in time. Now I wasn't in immediate danger from the boiling sun, I could talk freely, without worrying about time. Sky looked around curiously for a second, but she didn't seem surprised.

"Hi, Sky. Sorry about all the shouting and freezing time, and all, but I really need to talk to you!" I greeted her awkwardly.

"That's okay. We can talk here. I do love your visits, Joe.

It's nice seeing you again," she greeted me back, walking over to me.

"You don't seem surprised to see me."

"I'm not. You are very persistent. I knew I would see you again." Then she turned to look at Vigil. "Seeing him here helping you...now *that* is a surprise!" she said, raising an inquiring eyebrow at Vigil. "Breaking rules? How very unlike you, *'Vigil'*," she said, putting emphasis on his name.

"Milady." Vigil bowed lightly at her in a formal greeting and watched her with his unblinkingly stare. "I have changed my ways," he answered plainly and truthfully.

"I can see that." Sky smiled.

"I asked him to bring us here so we can talk," I said.

She smirked a little and looked at Vigil. "Taking orders from her now, Vigil?" she teased, and he looked disgruntled for a second. I sensed Sky didn't like Vigil very much.

"I didn't *order* him to do anything," I cut in. "He agreed to help me, because he's my friend. And today is my birthday, so I asked him for this as a present, and he was kind enough to agree," I defended him.

Vigil looked surprised at my description of him as a friend.

"Is that so?" Sky said. "It is very *kind* of him indeed. The Gray Hooded ones are not famous for their kindness, you know. You must have had quite the effect on him, Joe Gray. I knew it'd be very interesting watching over you. You're very good at changing people's ways," she said playfully.

And that was a good cue for the script I had been rehearsing in my head. "Oh, yes, don't you know? I'm very special and unique. And I like visiting you here. I want to be friends," I said cheerfully and watched as she beamed happily at that. "And I also happen to be very entertaining, as I'm sure you must have noticed by now. I'm part of this big dramatic love story – girl falls for ghost. It's got drama and romance and tragedy too. It's all very exciting. And I get into fights, I cast dangerous spells, and I have these amazing friends. We're in a band. Too. It's fun 24/7!" I said like a TV voice-over announcing the most amazing series ever seen. "But now, I'm afraid I must tell you, that the show is over." I dropped the excitement from my voice.

Sky's bright smile faltered as she heard this.

"Yes, I'm done. It's moping around all day long in the house for me now. No more jokes or fun and adventures for me. I'm through with it all. I'm quitting the band. I'm taking this show off air. You'd better start browsing for other channels." I walked up to Sky and wrapped an arm around her shoulder. A bold move, I must admit, but I was a desperate woman.

I continued my monologue. "But I have a proposal for you," I said, leaning in closer to her. "Let's make a deal, right here, right now, just you and me. You bring Tristan back to me, without any magic deadlines or tricks like last time – and in a way that Vigil's people have no say over, because it won't be a mistake that needs to be fixed. You bring him back and I promise you the best show yet for your personal enjoyment. It'll be a life full of possibilities that you can watch and enjoy. Plus, you can always visit, whenever you want. When you're off work, you know. That'd be cool. I'm sure no one has ever offered that to you before," I said, watching for her reaction closely. She was impossible to read, though.

"I know you said you can't meddle in these kinds of

affairs, but I know for a fact that you do it all the time!" I continued. "You do it subtly, trying not to draw too much attention to yourself, but I know there are sometimes miracles, cases where someone was dead one minute and came back to life the next... There are stories everywhere of people *cheating Death*," I said, all excited. "But they weren't really *cheating* you, were they? No one can cheat *you*! You *let* them live, because you wanted too. Right? You allowed it to happen! They probably all had interesting lives. I do know how much it sucks when there's a good show you really like and then it's cancelled!" I tightened my grip on her shoulder. I was pushing my luck now. "So I know you can do this one thing for me, if you really want to. What do you say, Sky? Do we have a deal?" I asked and held my breath, waiting for her answer.

I had given it all I had, used all my powers of persuasion. Sky wasn't going to be convinced by pleas of how much I loved Tristan and wanted him back. She needed a good reason. *For her*. I was praying with all my might that I had judged her correctly. She did always mention how entertaining I was. And being Death for millennia must be a little dull.

She looked thoughtfully at me. "You have been moping around a lot lately," she mumbled, and turned to look at Vigil. "What about you?" she asked him, and started walking towards him, untangling herself from my hold. Vigil had been watching our conversation with an indecipherable expression on his face. "I'm sure you would want to *report* this to your people," she inquired.

"There is nothing to be reported here," Vigil said with a slight bow. "As the girl said, this is a deal between you two. I have nothing to do with this."

"You are more powerful now because of the girl's naming," Sky reasoned.

"I have more power than an individual alone. But they are many. I cannot subjugate them all," he stated.

Sky looked up thoughtfully. "But you won't report anything and they won't be coming to annoy me over any of this?" she asked, a tiny smirk playing on her lips.

Vigil nodded.

"So, let's make this really interesting, shall we?" she said, grinning broadly now. *"You have yourself a deal, Joe Gray!* You can have your ghost boy back and a life full of possibilities! And you..." she said, turning back to Vigil "...should have an even bigger advantage to handle your fellow hooded colleagues now." She pressed her thumb in the middle of Vigil's forehead. His eyes widened in shock as a bright white light flashed inside his eyes. "That should be immensely entertaining to watch!" She giggled after taking her hand away from him. He stood still with shocked eyes, staring at her in awe.

"What have you done to him?" I asked, really worried. He seemed fine, a little surprised but not harmed. Sky chuckled at my concerned glare.

"Don't fret, I've just upgraded his 'abilities'. He shouldn't have any problems dealing with his buddies now, one or many. Use your new powers wisely, now, Vigil," she advised him seriously. "And you should go back to your ghost boy, Joe Gray. But I'll keep in touch and pay you a visit, when I'm 'off work', as you invited me."

I ran and hugged her tightly and a cold shiver went up my spine as I embraced her.

"Thank you, Sky," I said, trembling with emotion.

"No need to thank me. *We have a deal*. Keep your part

of it and I'll keep mine." And then she chuckled, highly amused. "You're so unexpected; nobody has ever wanted to hug me before!"

I gave her an awkward smile. I couldn't say it was a pleasant hug. Cold shivers were still running up my spine. I guess that was normal, when it came to hugging Death...

"Where is he? When can I see him?" I asked, barely able to contain myself.

She laughed at my eagerness. "I will go fetch him now. He should be there when you get back. Take care, Grays," she said, bowing slightly at me and Vigil, and then she shimmered away without waiting for a reply.

I looked at Vigil and he was smiling, his eyes glinting with admiration as he walked up to me.

"Come on, Joe Gray. Time to go home." he said, pressing the palm of his hand over my chest, and a bright piercing light burst through my eyes and my heart pounded in my chest, hard and loud. I looked around and saw the walls of my room surrounding me. Vigil's soft voice was right at my side, soothing and calm. His hand was resting over my arm.

"Try to breathe slowly and relax, the discomfort will soon pass," he instructed me. I tried to relax, while Sky's words kept bouncing in my head. *'Go back to your ghost boy,'* she had said. *'He should be there when you go back.'* I had convinced Death to send Tristan back to me!

Vigil was looking at me and smiling kindly.

"You look happy," he said.

"*I am.* Thanks to you, Vigil," I said, sitting up slowly.

"You were brilliant, there. I was really impressed."

"Ah, you know me, I'm very special, unique and entertaining," I joked.

"Yes, *you are* very special." He smiled softly. "I am proud to be your friend."

I glanced up and saw there was a smidgen of melancholy behind his eyes.

"You're a good friend. I couldn't have done this if it weren't for your help, Vigil. Thank you so much," I said, truly grateful.

"I am glad I could help. I did not like seeing you sad."

"Will you visit me some times?" I asked him out of the blue. He looked surprised for a second.

"Do you want me to?"

"Yes! Of course! You're my friend. I hope you keep in touch," I said with a smile.

"I will. You know how to find me if you need me," he said and stood up.

I looked down as my wrist started hurting again because he had stopped touching me, and then the pain ceased and I glanced up. Vigil wasn't there any more.

I bolted from my bed and ran downstairs, calling for Tristan. I looked everywhere, the living room, the kitchen, all the rooms. The house was empty. Where could he be? The cemetery popped in my head. The grass circle, that was the place he'd first appeared.

It was the strongest magic spot in Esperanza.

I ran into the cemetery as fast as I could, passing its iron gates in a blur, my boots scratching and slipping on the icy paving. I speed through the lanes, jumping over snow banks, my hair flapping wildly over my face and hot breath puffing from my mouth. I only stopped when I reached the lawn circle and looked around urgently, but there was no one there. I called out for Tristan and nobody answered. Had Sky lied to me? Maybe she needed more time . . .

I stomped my foot impatiently and stared at the ground. There were footprints in the snow! Someone had been here, and it was recent. They started in the middle of the lawn circle and headed to my left. I followed the footprints, walking fast, keeping my eyes focused on tracks. After a few minutes I recognized the path I was following. The footprints were leading to Tristan's tomb!

Now that I already knew where the footprints were headed, I started to run, and in seconds I was at Tristan's tomb. I looked up.

And then I saw him.

He was sitting on his tomb, looking at the cold horizon. So much sadness shone in his gray beautiful bright eyes.

"Tristan!" I shouted.

He snapped his head in my direction, his eyes wide in surprise, shock and joy. He leaped off his tomb, his feet stomping loudly on the snow. "Joey," he whispered, his breathing heavy with emotion. He began to run in my direction and I ran towards him too, and we both stopped a few inches apart, looking at each other in wonder. "I knew you would be able to see me, even though I'm a ghost again," he said with a mix of happiness and sadness in his voice.

I looked at him, puzzled. He thought he was dead. He must have woken up in the cemetery and thought he'd come back as a ghost.

"Of course I can see you. I will always be able to see you," I said, cupping his face in my hands and leaning in, kissing him deeply. His eyes shot wide open in utter shock and he stopped breathing for a few seconds in surprise. "And I can touch you too, so you know," I said, laughing at his shocked face.

He grabbed me by the shoulders, to make sure this

wasn't a trick. Then he kissed me so fiercely like he had never kissed me before. We were both out of breath when he stopped and he wrapped his arms around my waist and spun me round until we were both laughing like we were little kids again.

"How can this be?" he asked, amazed, after he'd got his breath back.

"I convinced Sky to bring you back. We just need to be very entertaining from now on!" I chuckled at his puzzled face. "I'll tell you all about it later. I just need to hug you right now." I squeezed him with all my might.

He laughed his sexy laugh and my heart almost burst at the sound. I looked up and locked eyes with him. He was crying. And so was I.

"Your eyes...are still...really...gray," I said, sniffing. It was the very first thing I had said to him when he'd woken up over a year ago on my living-room couch. He smiled and his gray eyes crinkled and sparkled brightly with tears.

"Yours are still black as night," he replied softly.

"How are you feeling?"

"Like the happiest boy alive," he said, and kissed me again, deeply and lovingly.

And I felt like the happiest girl alive.

I had my ghost boy to love, my band of brothers reunited, and together we were ready for anything – life was again full of possibilities.